LOVE, FOREVER MORE

"Who is it?"

. . . before Serena had time to be truly alarmed, a powerful arm was around her waist and a hand clamped over her mouth. She was picked up as easily as a baby and carried struggling and kicking toward the door. Now the hand was over her mouth and her nostrils as well.

Serena fought for breath. Dimly she heard the door being opened and closed, and felt the cooler outside air on her face. She struggled harder still to get a breath of it. The struggle fast weakened her, and finally she slumped in the grip of the man carrying her, unconscious.

When she regained consciousness, it was to an awareness of strange surroundings and the strong odor of incense. She was in a small, windowless room. She was lying on a hard pallet on the floor, not a bed.

Suddenly it crashed in on her growing awareness that she was not only completely naked, but bound as well. At the foot of the pallet were two posts set into the floor several feet apart. Her ankles were bound to the posts, leaving her most intimate parts exposed to the gaze of anyone who might come into the room.

In her panic Serena uttered a cry and struggled to rise. To one side, she saw a pile of clothing. Her new, beautiful outfit, torn from her body, completely ruined!

Then the room's one door was flung open, and a frightening figure stood in the doorway. It was a man dressed in rough clothing, but the most terrifying thing to Serena was the gold demon mask that completely covered his face. Even his eyes were hidden behind narrow slits. In his right hand he carried a short, thonged whip. He was caressing the palm of his left hand lovingly with the thongs . . .

Other Pinnacle Books by Patricia Matthews:

LOVE'S AVENGING HEART
LOVE'S WILDEST PROMISE
LOVE, FOREVER MORE

Love, Forever More

Patricia Matthews

PINNACLE BOOKS   LOS ANGELES

"For my sister, Nancy, who also loves the old times and places."

LOVE, FOREVER MORE

Chapter One

Serena Foster sat drowsing on the seat of the covered wagon. Eyes closed, she was peripherally aware of the heat of the blazing desert sun through the material of the poke bonnet, which her mother had made her wear to protect her hair.

The steady clop-clop of the mules' hooves and the rocking of the wagon—to which she had, after four long months, become adjusted—all contributed to the almost hypnotic inducement to sleep. Serena felt bone tired. Tired of the weary months of travel after tearing the roots of nineteen years from her home soil back in Illinois, tired of the heat and the dust that even now permeated her hair and clothing and stung her nostrils.

They had left Independence, Missouri, in April of this year 1863 as part of a wagon train bound for Oregon, and had stayed with the train through the terrible haul over the Rockies and across the salt flats of Utah. Once into the territory of Nevada, the Foster wagon had branched off—destination Virginia City. They were now on the last leg of their arduous journey, crossing the Forty-Mile Desert, hopefully only a few days from Virginia City.

Serena felt her mother shift beside her on the seat, and she deliberately tried to escape deeper into slumber. If she opened her eyes, Serena knew that she would only see the vast stretches of desert, to which she had become far too accustomed. These vast, empty, dry spaces frightened her and made her feel small and unprotected.

Suddenly, the wagon rocked as the mules shied, and a hoarse shout broke the near stillness. Serena's eyes flew open as she turned in the direction from which the shout had come. Toward their wagon, across the scorched earth, a figure came stumbling in their direction. It appeared to be a man.

Serena watched him stagger and fall, then unsteadily get to his feet again, waving his arms and shouting. She grabbed her mother's arm.

"Yes, child. I see him." Mercy Foster stuck her head around the side of the wagon and called to her husband, who was dozing atop his horse in the shady side of the wagon. "Hiram! Best wake up. Someone's coming!"

Hiram Foster ranged his horse alongside the wagon seat. "Yes, wife?"

"Look." Mercy Foster pointed. "There's a man out there!".

Hiram Foster followed her pointing finger. "Why, by the Lord, so there is! Mercy, pull the mules up."

Mercy Foster, a thin, pale, worried woman of fifty, sawed on the reins, halting the mules.

2

Serena leaned back into the skimpy shade of the canvas top and removed her bonnet, shaking out long, heavy hair the color of corn silk. At nineteen, just reaching the ripeness of womanhood, she was a medium-sized girl, with fine features and large, luminous gray eyes.

The four mules slumped in the harness, heads down, and the three people waited with some apprehension as the approaching figure stumbled closer.

Hiram Foster, a small, compact man of fifty-odd, with graying brown hair and a beard, watched the man through worried gray eyes. Not for the first time he wondered if he wasn't placing his family in jeopardy by not possessing a weapon of any kind. Hiram was a God-fearing man and did not believe in killing any of God's creatures, man or beast. Hiram had been warned that he was foolish to strike out through a wild, lawless country without the means to defend his family. If nothing else, they could starve without any way of killing fresh game, but Hiram had stubbornly maintained, "The Lord will provide. He will see us through." And at least so far, they had survived, although they had been on lean rations for days now.

Hiram formed several conclusions as he watched the man draw nearer. The man was young, he was in dire straits, and he, in all likelihood, needed help. The question in Hiram's mind was—what kind of man was this? A good man, down on his luck, perhaps a victim of vandals; or one of the various pieces of flotsam that littered this brutal country, preying on the helpless and unwary? His being on foot posed less danger, yet he could be armed and a predator, having lost his mount in any number of ways.

"Mercy! Serena! Get back out of sight," he said in a low voice.

Serena looked at the shambling figure and frowned at her father. "Daddy, the poor man can hardly walk. He has no weapon that I can see." She started to get down from the wagon seat.

Hiram gestured sharply. "No, daughter. Stay where you are. If he's a lost pilgrim and needs succor, I will provide it."

With a resigned sigh, Serena remained on the wagon seat. She loved her parents, but sometimes they were annoyingly overprotective. If they had their way, they'd keep her a child forever, shielded from all contact with, and knowledge of, the world. She knew they were thinking only of her welfare, but if she was always to be protected, always shielded, how could she ever taste the tang and flavor of life, the life she longed for? Their way, life might be safe, but it had a dull, flat taste, about as exciting as unsalted soup. Sometimes of late, Serena found herself wanting to do something wild, something daring. What, she was not sure, but she wanted to do *something*.

The stranger was quite close now. Serena could see her father relax, reassured by the stranger's appearance. The man was tall and broad-shouldered, twenty-two or thereabouts. He wore Wellington boots, and a black, broadcloth suit, now covered with dust, like ash fallen from a prairie fire. His hair was black and long under the broad brim of his hat, and his wide-cheeked face wore a dark stubble of beard.

Hiram Foster slapped a hand down on the saddle horn. That was it, he thought; that's why I trust him! He looks like a preaching man!

He dismounted and went to assist the stranger. He

4

caught him under the arms and helped him to the shade of the wagon.

Through cracked and bleeding lips, the man muttered, "Water . . . please, could I have some water?"

"Daughter!" Hiram called. "Fetch the canteen."

Serena sprang nimbly down from the wagon seat and came hurrying with the canteen. Hiram took it and held it to the young man's mouth. He drank greedily, but Hiram allowed him only a few swallows.

"Easy now, easy. One thing I've learned out here. A man without water for long can get almighty sick taking too much at once. How long you been out there without water, pilgrim?"

"Four, five days," the man whispered.

Serena watched the stranger with interest. Despite the coating of dust and the unshaven face, it was still clear that he was uncommonly well set up. His eyes, ice blue and thick-lashed, were in startling contrast to his dark, sunburned skin. She looked at his hands. He had a gentleman's hands—long fingered and unmarked by hard labor. Serena didn't realize that she had been moving closer to him until her mother drew her back.

"Now, Serena," her mother said, "let the poor man breathe."

Serena flushed and pulled away from her mother's grasp.

The young man's gaze came up to Serena's face, and their eyes locked. Serena felt a strange, galvanic tingle in her belly as he looked at her, seemingly unable to remove his gaze from hers, and then her father's bulk moved between them.

"You a preacher, boy?"

The young man hesitated, then said, "My pa is."

"What's your name?"

"Rory Clendenning."

Hiram nodded. "Well, we'd best get you into the wagon, Mr. Clendenning, as it appears you're in no condition to walk. We're headed for Virginia City." The last few words were a question.

Clendenning said, "I'd appreciate it if you'd take me along."

Hiram nodded again. "You'd better know who *we* are then. I'm Hiram Foster. My wife, Mercy, and this is our daughter, Serena."

Rory Clendenning glanced up long enough to acknowledge the introductions, then his head fell to his chest. Hiram gestured to Mercy, and together they lifted Clendenning to his feet.

"We have to keep moving," Hiram said. "Unless the crude map I have is wrong, we'll hit the Carson River at the end of the day's journey. I'm hoping to camp there tonight. Hardly enough water left in the barrels to keep us going, much less the mules. You'd better ride in the back of the wagon, young Clendenning."

Clendenning attempted to walk on his own, fending off their efforts to help. But when it came time to climb into the back of the wagon, where the Fosters had their sleeping blankets, it was too much for him. Together, Hiram and Mercy got him into the wagon.

Serena said, "I'll stay with him, daddy, and give him a drink of water from time to time."

Hiram mounted his horse, motioned to his wife, and the mules strained forward in the harness, the wagon on the move again.

Clendenning had already fallen into a doze. The jolting of the wagon roused him, and he stared up into the concerned gray eyes of the girl beside him.

"More water?" Serena held out the canteen.

Clendenning grabbed at it.

"Just a few sips now," she warned.

Clendenning took a few sips and put his head back. Serena took out her handkerchief, wet it, and began to wash some of the dirt from his face.

"Would you care to tell me what in heaven's name you were doing out there, no water, no horse, nothing?"

"I had a canteen of water, but it ran out." His head rolled on the blanket. "I had a horse, a fine animal, and some money, near two hundred dollars."

She wiped the dust from his forehead, which, she saw, was fine and wide. "What happened? Were you robbed?"

"Yes!" he said. Then he shook his head. "No, that's not the truth of it. I lost my gear by being a Lord God fool. Five days ago, I was camped for the night when a stranger rode up and introduced himself as Darrel Quick. I invited him to share my supper. After we ate, he suggested we play a few hands of cards to pass the time. He said it would be more sport if we wagered. In the beginning I won, and he euchred me into betting more and more. Before I knew it, he had all my money, and my horse. When I finally realized what a fool I'd been, I lost my temper and demanded it all back. He pulled a gun on me, took my horse and some food, and pointed out where the wagon trail was. He said I'd come across a wagon sooner or later." Clendenning's voice was bitter. "Jeremiah warned me not to get involved in the devil's game,

7

but I was too Lord God headstrong to heed. Now look at what condition I'm in!"

"I wouldn't fret about it. In this rough country, it's happened to more experienced men than you. Who's Jeremiah?"

"My pa."

Clendenning sank back, as if the telling of it had exhausted him. As he lay quietly, Serena studied his face. It was a strong face, and she suspected that if he survived the trials he would undoubtedly face out here, he would soon be able to hold his own.

Suddenly conscious of his nearess, she felt an odd mixture of excitement and apprehension. Due to her parents' protectiveness, Serena knew little of the opposite sex, and could not remember being so close to a man, other than her father. She felt a strong curiosity concerning everything about this young stranger.

He spoke suddenly, startling her. "And you, Serena, what are you and your folks doing out here?"

"We're going to Virginia City. Daddy received a letter from a lawyer, a man named Spencer Hurd, telling us that my Aunt Hetty had died and left my father her estate." Serena smiled slightly. "I didn't know my Aunt Hetty Foster. She came west before I was born, and we've had no word from her since. Daddy was tired of working our hard-scrabble farm in southern Illinois, and what with the war getting worse and all, he sold the farm for enough to buy the wagon and mules and to outfit us. So here we are. We don't even know what Aunt Hetty's estate is, but daddy figured it had to be better than what we were leaving behind . . ."

Serena let her voice trail off, as she realized that he was asleep. The rest of the afternoon she dozed off

8

and on, waking when Clendenning did to give him rationed sips of water and bathe his forehead. The sun was low in the west when there came a shout from her father, "There it is, there's the river!"

Serena scrambled over their meager belongings toward the front of the wagon and climbed upon the seat beside her mother. She looked off to their right about a half mile, narrowing her eyes. She had learned to mistrust what she had found were heat mirages. Many times she had seen cool, blue lakes shimmering in the distance, only to see them melt away into dry sand on approaching. But the sun was down, dropping behind the range of mountains looming up, and the cottonwood-fringed river was still there.

Hiram Foster directed his wife to park the wagon in a clearing in a grove of cottonwoods. While he unhitched the mules and led them down to the river to drink, Serena helped her mother unload the Dutch oven and other cooking utensils and their scant supply of food. Rory Clendenning offered to help, but he was still too weak to be of much use, and Serena sternly ordered him to sit back against a wagon wheel. Then she quickly collected wood for a fire.

Her father was back by the time the fire was going.

Serena said, "I'm going to have myself a bath." She flew about gathering up a bar of lye soap and two rough towels.

As she started off, Hiram Foster called after her, "Now you be careful, daughter. Don't wander too far away."

Serena made her way through high reeds along the river bank until she was well out of sight of the camp. The sand ran down to the water's edge, and the river ran shallow and clear over flat stones. Although she knew her mother would disapprove, Serena undressed down to the skin, shaking the dust out of her dress and petticoats before laying them on a nearby bush.

Back at the campfire, Clendenning began to salivate at the cooking odors. His shrunken stomach rebelled and began to cramp. Hastily he got to his feet. "Excuse me, folks, I'll be back shortly."

Mercy Foster glanced up from her cooking with a worried frown. "You suppose it's all right, Hiram, for him to go off, with Serena out there alone?"

"You concern yourself too much, Mercy." Hiram squeezed her shoulder. "After all, this young man is a preacher's son. Besides . . ." He indulged himself in a rare flash of humor. "In his condition, I very much doubt he could offer Serena any harm."

At that moment Serena had no thought of any harm to herself. She was sitting in the cold, shallow water, busily soaping and scrubbing, humming to herself. It was sheer luxury. Not since she had left home had Serena been able to indulge herself so. On the wagon trip, water had been too scarce for washing, and her mother would never let her go bathing in the rivers they camped beside.

It was fully dark when she finally emerged, clean and refreshed, from the water. She began to hurry now, drying herself briskly with the rough towels, and then getting into her clothes. Supper would soon be ready, and if she knew her folks, they would be worrying about her.

Just as she pulled her dress over her head, Serena heard the sudden thunder of hooves, and stood still to listen. It sounded like several horses, and they were heading for the wagon. She gathered up the towels and hurried toward the campfire. She had taken only a few steps, when she was frozen in her tracks by the sound of gunfire. A terrible coldness clawed with icy fingers at her stomach, and then panic sent her running, fighting through the thicket of reeds.

Now she could see the campfire and several horses milling about. Without any thought of danger to herself, Serena plunged ahead. Just before she was about to burst through the reeds into the clearing, she was seized around the waist from behind and thrown to the ground. She opened her mouth to scream, but a hand was clamped over her lips, and she choked back the sound.

A voice whispered in her ear, "Quiet now. It's Clendenning. Don't make a sound, or they'll know we're here."

Serena ceased struggling. From where she lay on the ground, she could see the wagon and the campfire clearly. But where were her parents? And she was puzzled by the activity and the appearance of the half-dozen mounted men. All wore handkerchiefs over the lower half of their faces, all except one who wore a mask over his entire face, a frightening demon mask. The man in the mask seemed to be the leader.

The men had tied ropes to the wheels of the wagon on one side, and as she watched, the ropes were tossed over the canvas top. Two men on horseback took the ends of the ropes, hooked them around their saddle horns, and sent their horses plunging forward. The ropes tightened, and the wagon slowly began to tilt as the horses strained against the ropes. Then, with a rumbling sound and a cloud of dust, the wagon fell onto its side.

The flames of the campfire flared up at the rush of air from the wagon's falling, and Serena's gaze was drawn to two still figures on the ground. Her mother and father!

Serena moaned deep in her throat and began to struggle against Clendenning's hold.

"No, Serena, no!" he whispered fiercely. "I think they're dead, and I'm Lord God sorry. But if we rush out there, those men, whoever they are, will kill us, too. We have nothing with which to defend ourselves."

The mounted men milled about for a few more minutes, then the man in the demon mask fired his pistol into the air, motioned with it, and they rode off into the night.

Clendenning waited until the sound of hoofbeats had died away, then let Serena go. She was up at once and running. When she reached the clearing, she dropped to her knees beside her parents where they lay in the dust. Hiram Foster was half across his wife, as though he had tried to throw himself between her and the gunfire. They were both dead; each had been shot several times.

At the sound of Clendenning's footsteps, Serena looked up at him with streaming eyes. "But why? Why on earth would someone do this? We have nothing to steal!"

Clendenning shook his head. "I don't know, Serena. It seems such a senseless thing."

Serena, sobbing brokenheartedly now, reached out to touch her mother's face tenderly. The whole thing had happened with such violent suddenness that her mind was numb with shock and disbelieving horror.

Clendenning stared helplessly down at her. He

12

longed to comfort her, but didn't know how to go about it. He had never witnessed a killing. The senseless violence, in addition to his own recent ordeal, had left him empty of emotion and drained of strength. At the same time he was driven by a sense of urgency, and the certain knowledge that the sooner they were away from this place, the better.

He forced himself away from the weeping Serena and began to search for the animals. They were still several days ride from Virginia City, and if they had to walk out of here, they might never make it. He finally found three of the mules. Hiram's horse and the fourth mule were not to be found.

Clendenning tied the mules to a cottonwood and examined the wagon. All the spokes in one wheel were shattered, and the wagon lay like some great beast with a broken spine. It would never roll again. Not that they could pull it anyway, Clendenning thought, not with three mules.

Turning toward Serena, he was startled to see her going through her father's pockets. Just as he reached her, she spun around on her knees and waved a man's purse at him. Her eyes glittering as if from fever, she said, "You see, here's daddy's purse. It has fifty dollars, all in the world of value he had. But they didn't take it! If not to rob him, why then?"

"I don't know, Serena. I wish I had an answer for you . . ."

"No, no, you don't understand!" In her agitation, she stood up. "Men don't just ride up in the night, with masks over their faces, killing the first family they come across for no reason. I felt it, watching them. There was a purpose about them, as if they were looking for *us!*"

13

The notion startled Clendenning into momentary silence. Then he said, "Lord God, Serena, why? You said no one knew you in Virginia City."

"No, but someone knew we were coming."

"Then why didn't they look until they found you? Why ride off with the job unfinished?"

"I don't know the answer to that. And the one with the strange mask." She shuddered. "It was horrible!"

"Serena, we haven't time for this now. We have to ride away from here. Suppose they come back? We have to bury your folks and move on as soon as possible."

"No!" For a moment Serena had forgotten her dead. "No, I'm not going to bury them out here!"

"We have to. What choice do we have? The wagon will never move again, and I could only find three mules . . ."

Serena knew that he was right, yet she fought against the knowing. "Tonight? Can't we at least wait until daylight?"

"If those men do come back, they won't wait until after daylight. We can't be here. What if you're right?" He gripped her shoulders. "What if they were after the whole Foster family? Couldn't they come back for Serena Foster? We'd be at their mercy, Serena." A thought came to him. "Did your father have a gun?"

"No." She shook her head. "He didn't believe in killing."

"It seems some people out here have no such compunctions," he said grimly. "But you see, that's only the more reason for us to leave here."

"But bury them out here? In the middle of nowhere?" Tears filled her eyes again.

14

He said gently, "Serena, it's the only sensible thing to do."

Finally, she nodded her consent.

While Clendenning delved into the broken wagon for a spade and began digging the graves in the sand, Serena leaned against a cottonwood, her face turned away, sobbing quietly. Only when the graves were finished did she turn back. As Clendenning bent to pick up her father, she ran forward, pushing him away. Falling to her knees on the ground, she touched the faces of her parents, then stood up resolutely. "You may go ahead now."

When the mortal remains of Hiram and Mercy Foster were into the earth, Clendenning stood at the head of their graves, hat held over his heart. He tried to remember the words that his father used to speak, searching among the memories of the years he had accompanied Jeremiah Clendenning on his preaching journeys up and down the Mississippi River. He began to speak, haltingly. "Our Lord Who art in Heaven, I knew Hiram and Mercy Foster only for a few short hours. But they were good people, struck down most foully in their prime. Dear Lord, we know that their souls now dwell with You in the Kingdom of Heaven. We pray that there they shall know eternal happiness . . ." He coughed, cleared his throat, and added, "Amen."

Again, he had Serena to deal with. She had turned her back while he shoveled the sand into the graves, but she faced about just in time to find him smoothing the sand in an effort to eliminate any indication of a grave.

"What are you doing?" She ran to him. "I want to

have markers left here, so I can come back and visit their graves."

"No, Serena, no."

She looked at him uncomprehendingly. "But why?"

"For the same reason as before. If the killers come back and find the bodies buried, they may strike out on our trail."

"But they'd think the same thing, finding daddy and mom gone!"

"Not exactly, Serena." His glance fell away. "The country here is full of . . . well, predators. Animals that feed on . . . I'm sorry to have to put it to you that way."

"Oh," she said in a small voice.

"Now," he said briskly, "take from the wagon those things you want, but only what we can carry on one mule. All the canteens you can find, of course, and blankets. It gets cold, I've found, out here at night, even in summer."

Glad of any activity to occupy her thoughts, Serena climbed into the wagon. Everything was a jumble from the wagon being overturned. She found two canteens and handed them out to Clendenning.

He said, "I'll go fill them at the river."

Her personal trunk had sprung open, her clothes spilled out helter-skelter. Serena picked through them, collecting what she thought she would need, and made a bundle of them. She also gathered together what remained of the small store of food. By the time Clendenning had returned, she had collected several blankets.

"Are you ready, Serena?"

"In a minute."

She stood, holding onto one of the canvas-top

hoops for support, looking around at the jumble of their belongings. They had been warned not to load the wagon down too heavily. The warning, she remembered, had been well-given. All along the trail west Serena had seen piles of furniture thrown off alongside the road, from other wagons before them. Somewhere in all this mess were albums of family pictures, a family Bible, and a diary she had kept from childhood. She had no idea where they were . . .

"Serena!" Clendenning's voice held a note of urgency.

"Coming!"

With a last, sorrowful look around, she clambered out of the wagon. It seemed that she was leaving all of her past here in this small clearing, all of her girlhood. Carefully she noted the location of the spot where her parents were buried. She was determined to return and put markers on their graves.

Clendenning helped her up onto one of the mules. Since Serena had often ridden bareback on their farm back in Illinois, she would manage well enough. As they rode out of the clearing, she turned for one last look, choking back tears. The time for weeping was past, but a cold anger filled her. Some day the killers of her parents would pay for their senseless crime!

Clendenning called back to her, and Serena turned her face forward, and they rode off into the night.

A gibbous moon cast a pale light, and they were able to follow the wagon trail well enough. It was cold, a bone-chilling cold. Serena, with a blanket wrapped around her shoulders, rode behind the pack mule, which Clendenning was leading. She was weary in mind and body, yet she wasn't in the least sleepy. Now that nothing was required of her but to sit on the mule, her thoughts kept returning to the horrible thing that had happened back at the wagon, and to memories of her parents.

Her eyes felt tender and swollen from crying as she pictured them lying there under a thin covering of soil. Why, oh why, hadn't she been kinder to them? Why had she hurt them with her willfulness and disobedience?

She had always been a little fearful of her father, with his rigid, God-fearing ways and open-handed punishment of what he referred to as her godless behavior; but she knew that he loved her, and even while she rebelled against his rules, Serena had known that he was doing what he thought best for her.

And her mother, her poor, gentle mother . . . Serena felt a deep shame, remembering the times she had looked at her mother with secret contempt at the way she had lived in the shadow of Hiram Foster, always and forever bending to his will, even though she had known that her mother had been happy in doing this.

Serena's tears began afresh as she thought of the love and care her mother lavished on her, and of the pain she, Serena, must have caused by her stubborn willfulness. Forgotten now was Serena's own feelings of anger and helplessness at being kept within the narrow confines of what her parents considered a "proper life." She felt terribly, terribly alone, and unready to cope with whatever lay ahead of her. She was all too aware of her own inexperience.

Prior to this trip, Serena had never been farther from home than the one-mile walk to the local schoolhouse, and the two-mile ride to church on Sunday. Her only knowledge of the world came from her schoolbooks, and her only real knowledge of men from her father, the Bible, and her few male schoolmates, who usually left school as soon as they were big enough to work in the fields. She was poorly prepared for the situation in which she now found herself, and at this moment only wanted her parents back again. Whatever their faults, they had been her parents, and they had loved and protected her.

Grief threatened to overwhelm her again. To stave it off, she called, "Clendenning? Are we going to ride all night? We must have been riding for hours!"

He reined in the mule and let her ride up beside him. "To tell the truth, I'm having trouble staying awake myself. I think it's safe enough now to pull off the road a ways and catch a few winks. At least until daylight."

Clendenning dismounted and helped Serena down, then led the mules out of sight of the rutted road, where he tethered the animals to the cottonwoods along the river. He took the blankets from the pack mule and unrolled them, making two beds on the soft ground close together.

Serena removed only her riding boots, tucked her skirts around her, and rolled up into two of the blankets. She heard Clendenning doing the same.

She closed her eyes, but despite her fatigue, she couldn't sleep. Scenes of her dead parents and the night riders danced across her eyes in a series of frightening pictures.

And she was cold. She lay shivering, sure she would never be warm again. After a long time, she called out, "Clendenning, are you awake?"

19

His drowsy voice answered, "Almost. What's wrong, Serena, can't you sleep?"

"I can't get out of my mind what happened back there. And I'm freezing!"

After a moment he said hesitantly, "It might help if we shared the blankets. With our body heat combined, you'd probably soon be warm."

With chattering teeth, she said, "Anything would be better than this."

Clendenning got up, helped her out of the blankets, then rearranged them into one bed. Serena got under the blankets at once. Clendenning crawled in more carefully, trying to manage it so that he would be close to her but not touching.

Despite the strangeness of the situation, Serena grew drowsy. She squirmed closer, seeking the warmth of Clendenning's body. Soon, she was pressed tightly against him.

In a choked voice he said, "Serena . . ."

"What?" she said sleepily.

He made no reply, and she began to drift into sleep. But something bothered her, something unusual, and strange. Finally, she realized what it was. There was something poking against her buttocks through her dress and petticoats, something that was increasing slowly in size and hardness.

"Clendenning?" She turned on her back. She said fuzzily, "What is . . . ?"

"Lord God!" With a smothered groan his arms went around her, drawing her close, his mouth pressing on hers.

An unfamiliar, yet far from unpleasant sensation flowed through Serena. She was dimly aware of what was happening, yet her always strong curiosity de-

20

manded that she learn more. And besides, it was so comforting to be warm, to be held close in loving arms, to be kissed, to be stroked, and to have murmured endearments poured into her ears. Kisses or expressions of love had rarely been exchanged between parents and daughter in the Foster family. Her mother hadn't held Serena, or kissed her, since she was a small girl.

Serena let all thought of her parents, of the horror that had happened to them, go out of her mind, and gave herself over to feeling. In her drowsy state it was almost dreamlike. Her blood pulsated, and warmth seeped through her, as if she were turning slowly before a fire.

Even when she felt Clendenning's hands, still stroking, up under her skirt, she made only a small murmur of protest. The feeling she was experiencing was pleasant, and she did not want it to stop. Only when Clendenning moved to place himself over her, only when she felt him part her thighs and push the hardness against the tender, secret parts of her did she protest.

"It's all right. It'll be all right, Serena, you'll see," he said in a thick voice. He silenced her with his lips, and Serena was lost in the honey-sweetness of the kiss.

The probing pressure continued. Then there was a brief, sharp pain that caused her to stiffen and cry out, as he had penetrated her completely, and began a thrusting motion that soon changed from pain to pleasure. All Serena's feelings were concentrated in her lower body. As her ecstasy spiraled, an instinct as ancient as womankind took possession of her, and she began to move her hips, adjusting the movements to the rhythm of his powerful thrustings.

Dimly, she seemed to hear an echo of her father's voice far back in her mind, "It's a sin against God, daughter, to revel in the joys of the flesh."

Then even that thought was swallowed up as she yielded herself entirely to rapture, to pure, sweet pleasure. At that moment, the man giving her such ecstasy was the only man in the universe, and then the delicious tension shattered. She could almost feel it break inside her, like the snapping of a taut wire, and she went soft and lax, and seemed to be floating. She was so content, so sleepy . . .

". . . Sorry, Serena. I couldn't help myself."

His words made no real sense, and she was asleep while he was still talking.

Serena awoke to the blaze of sun in her face. She floated up out of sleep, a smile on her face. She moved her arms out from under the blanket, stretching, and her elbow hit something beside her.

Complete memory flooded back, and she sat up with a cry.

Dear God! What had she done? Her parents only in their graves a few hours, and she had . . . Clendenning had . . . hot shame flooded over her.

What must he think of her? What kind of a girl did he think she was?

Clendenning started up, blinking, still groggy from a sleep so deep he might have been drugged.

"What is it, Serena?" He stared around. "What's wrong?"

"You! You're what's wrong! You took advantage of me!"

He gawked at her. "What do you mean, took advantage?"

Serena knew she was being unreasonable, but she

22

could not stop the flow of words. "I was dazed with grief, numb with shock, and so weary and cold. You took advantage of my condition to . . ." Her voice faltered and died.

His face turned scarlet, and his glance slid away. "I'm sorry, Serena. I tried to tell you that last night."

"Sorry! Daddy would have horsewhipped you for a cad, Rory Clendenning!"

"I didn't rape you, Serena." He was growing angry now. "You didn't fight me off. You made no effort to stop me."

"I . . . I had never been with a man before."

His gaze was level. "What does that have to do with it? You knew what was happening."

Now it was her turn to look away, and she felt a blush stain her cheeks. He was right, of course. And that thought only made her angrier.

"Serena . . ." His voice had softened. "I'm sorry it happened the way it did, and yet I'm not sorry it happened. Lord God, it was the nicest thing that ever happened to me."

He reached out a hand and laid it gently on her cheek. She slapped it away. "Don't you touch me!"

She jumped up from the blankets. She felt guilt and shame, and was furious because of it, so furious that she was shaking. "If you think I'm going to let it happen again . . ."

"I had no such thoughts. I force myself on no woman."

"You did last night!" she said harshly.

Clendenning got to his feet. "I did nothing of the sort. You know what I think? I think you enjoyed it as much as I did, and you're too ashamed to admit it,

23

even to yourself." He began folding the blankets. "It's time we were on our way."

"Yes! I want to get to Virginia City as quickly as possible. For when we get there, I want to see nothing more of you, Rory Clendenning!"

"That will suit me fine," he said grimly. "The minute we reach town, we will go our separate ways."

Chapter Two

During the three and a half days it took them to reach Virginia City, Serena and Rory Clendenning rode in constrained silence, speaking to each other only when necessary. When they made camp at night, Clendenning was careful to make their beds a good distance apart. He made no more overtures toward Serena.

Serena, perversely, found herself wishing that he would. They hadn't been on the road an hour, that first day, before she found herself regretting the harsh words she had flung at him and wishing she could take them back. She knew she had been wrong, very wrong. In her shame and guilt, she had lashed out at him. She had been unfair. If any blame should be placed, they should share it equally.

Yet, Serena was too proud to admit that she was sorry. Why didn't *he* say something? Why didn't he ask *her* forgiveness? She would gladly grant it. He must be dense indeed not to realize that! Dense, stubborn, and pigheaded! Thinking about this, she became angry all over again, but obstinately would not broach the subject herself.

In spite of all her efforts to the contrary, her thoughts kept returning to those warm, exciting moments in Clendenning's arms and the pleasure she had experienced. From earliest childhood, Serena had been taught that submission to a man, outside of marriage, was a wicked and unthinkable thing; and yet, that night it had not seemed wicked. It had seemed loving, and warm, and somehow right. It was only the next morning that it had seemed wrong. Now, she felt full of guilt, and questions, questions she dared not ask.

As they drew near to Virginia City, the land rose steadily, the jagged mountains to the west becoming clearer and clearer, until they looked so near that it seemed possible to reach out and touch them.

By the time they reached the small village of Dayton, they found themselves in the midst of considerable traffic. They passed, and were passed, by men, both afoot and on horseback. Huge, highbedded ore wagons, called wains, pulled by as many as twelve mules, rattled by in the midst of clouds of dust and profanity; the drivers cracked long whips over the heads of the mules, urging them on to greater effort. Serena drew her shawl around her shoulders and watched with nervous eyes as the huge wains came so close to their own animals that the mules reared and snorthed in fright.

Along the banks of the Carson River, Serena could

see wooden buildings and machinery; a busy area that seemed to be the destination of the ore wagons. She could hear a steady thumping sound coming from the buildings. She was later to learn that these buildings housed stamp mills for refining the ore. The mills in use at that time needed water to operate, and the Carson River was the nearest water to the mines up the canyon.

At Dayton they turned in a northerly direction, following the road up Gold Canyon, always climbing now. The traffic of ore wagons going and coming was much heavier. Before reaching Virginia City, they rode through two other roaring mining camps—Silver City and Gold Hill. Just outside of Silver City the road narrowed between solid rock rising sheer on both sides. They had to wait their chances to squeeze through. A miner on foot told Clendenning the small pass was called Devil's Gate.

Finally, they crested a rise and saw Virginia City before and below them. The town was built mostly on the side of Sun Mountain. Serena found her first sight of Virginia City disappointing. She was not certain just what she had expected, but it was not this; this dusty conglomeration of ugly, wooden buildings clinging to the slope of a barren mountain. Below the main part of the town, a motley collection of shacks and tents fought for space.

Clendenning looked over at Serena, and she thought she read sympathy in his glance, but she turned away, deliberately, and drummed the flanks of the mule with her heels, heading him toward the town.

As they came into the town, the noise became al-

27

most deafening—the sound of shouting voices, tinny piano music, and drunken laughter coming from the many saloons, and thunderous rumbling sounds from the side of the mountain. Serena started in fright at the first of these; even the earth trembled. Then she realized that it must be the sounds of blasting in the mines.

All the buildings had a raw, new look, and very few had ever been touched by paint. Up on the side of the mountain, Serena caught glimpses of what appeared to be several fine mansions.

They rode into town on C Street, which appeared to be the main business street. Certainly it was busy enough; Serena had never seen so many wagons, buggies, horses, mules, and people.

Finally, Clendenning pulled up his mule in front of a livery stable. He looked at Serena for a long moment before he spoke. She watched him hopefully. Would he now say he was sorry? He looked somehow as if he wanted to. She leaned toward him, almost ready to speak the words herself, when he said, "Well, I'll leave you now, Serena. You will be able to stable your mules here, and I'm sure the hostler will be able to direct you to your lawyer. Thank you for the loan of your mule."

He began to dismount. Serena experienced an almost painful emptiness in her belly that had nothing to do with the lack of food. She felt both frightened and angry. "You'll leave me all along then?" she asked in a not-quite-steady voice.

On the ground now, he gazed up at her. "You have made your feelings about me quite clear, Miss Foster. I wouldn't think of inflicting my company upon you any longer. I'm sure your lawyer will be able to help you find lodgings, and with your inheritance, I've no doubt you'll make out well enough." He turned to go.

"Wait!"

He stopped, looking back.

"What will you do? You have no money. At least take one of the mules. I'll have no use for them."

"I want nothing of yours, Serena. You'll forgive me if I'm unable to take your sudden concern to heart. And I will manage somehow, never fear." He doffed his hat. "Goodbye, Serena Foster."

He set the hat squarely on his head, turned his back on her again, and strode away.

Serena half-raised her hand, wanting to call him back. Then she set her lips stubbornly. Why should she apologize to him? If he could manage on his own, so could she. Still, she felt a strange, aching sense of loss as she watched him disappear in the crowd on the street.

Serena sat the mule a moment longer, looking about her. She marveled at the activity. In a way it was frightening, yet slowly she began to realize that there was an air of excitement about Virginia City. It was raw and vulgar, true, but there was something vital and alive about the people, about the town itself, and some of it seeped into Serena. She had been yearning for a different, more exciting life than the one she had known for nineteen years; certainly this appeared to be a likely place to begin. It seemed to offer her a chance at excitement and adventure.

Her spirits somewhat lightened, Serena dismounted and led the mules into the stable. When the stablehand approached, she asked him to take care of the animals until she came for them. "And the pack . . ." She indicated the pack on the one mule. "Take care of that, too, will you, please? I'll be back for it." It contained what few clothes she had taken from the wagon.

"Yes, ma'am, glad to do that for you." The stablehand, a grizzled oldtimer with a beard stained by tobacco juice, bobbed his head.

"Thank you." Serena turned her back and surreptitiously counted the money in her father's purse. About forty dollars, enough to house and feed her for a few days anyway. "And could you direct me to the offices of the lawyer, Spencer Hurd?"

"The Judge?" The stablehand grinned. "Sure thing, ma'am. The Judge has been a fixture here in Virginia since it was Washoe Diggings." He conducted her outside and pointed a dirty finger along C Street. "Two blocks down, and turn right a half block. You'll see his shingle hanging on the corner of a two-story building. There's an outside stairway going up to his office."

Serena was puzzled by his reference to Virginia, but didn't bother questioning him about it. She made her way along the street. Almost every other building seemed to be a saloon, and more than once she had to step aside as doors crashed open and drunken miners staggered out. The first time this happened, she held herself rigid. The grimy, bewhiskered miners were a frightening sight, particularly when made wild-eyed and fume-breathed by drink. But even the ones staggering drunk were unfailingly polite, muttering apologies and lurching out of her way.

30

Finally, Serena turned the corner the stablehand had indicated and walked down to an unpainted, two-story wooden building. Hanging out over the wooden, open stairway was a sign: SPENCER HURD, ATTORNEY-AT-LAW. Serena went up the steps, holding onto the single outside railing. The door at the top of the stairway opened onto a narrow hallway. There was an open door halfway down the hall, with another sign duplicating the one outside.

Serena knocked timidly on the door. She heard someone humming snatches of "Sweet Betsy from Pike." She peered around the door frame. The room was a haze of cigar smoke. "Lawyer Hurd?"

The humming stopped. "That's me," a deep voice boomed cheerfully. "Enter!"

As Serena entered hesitantly, the owner of the voice stood up from behind an ancient desk. He was tall and stooped, with a shock of iron-gray hair, and a face like a melancholy horse. Only the eyes broke up the gloomy cast of the features; they were tiny and black, and twinkled with a puckish humor.

"My apologies, ma'am. I wasn't expecting a lady." He put the cigar out in a can of sand on the desk. He came around and pulled out the one other chair in the sparsely furnished office.

Serena perched nervously on the edge of the chair.

Spencer Hurd went around his desk to resume his seat. He tilted his head to one side, his eyes bright and probing. "Now, how may I serve you, young lady?"

"I'm Serena Foster."

He looked at her blankly.

"I have a letter here . . ." From her purse she

31

took the letter her father had received and held it out.

"Hurd accepted the letter and glanced at it. His face lit up. "Oh, Hiram Foster!" He looked up. "Then you must be . . ."

She nodded. "Yes, Hiram's daughter."

Hurd smiled, showing long, yellow teeth. "Hetty didn't tell me about a daughter."

"Aunt Hetty left Illinois before I was born. That letter was the first we've heard from her since."

Frowning slightly, the lawyer looked past her at the open door. "But where is your father?"

"My father is dead," she said tightly, embarrassed by the quick tears she could feel in her eyes. She blinked them back. "As well as my mother."

"My sympathies, young lady." His thick eyebrows elevated. "You came all this way alone?"

"No, I . . ." The tears threatened to return, and she paused a moment to compose herself. When she was in control again, she told him what had happened.

Before Serena had finished her story, Spencer Hurd was up and pacing, muttering under his breath. When Serena was done with her tale, he took her hand. "Great Godalmighty, girl! What an experience for you. This lawless country!" He took another turn around the room, smashing a fist into his palm. "The law here has little bite, I'm afraid, but at least we can bring your folks here for a decent burial."

"It was senseless, the whole thing," she said in a choked voice.

He nodded grimly. "Senseless crimes out here are more common than not. I'll inform the sheriff, and he'll go out and nose around. But the odds are against his ever finding the culprits." He continued to pace, muttering to himself.

Serena cleared her throat to get his attention, and said, "Mr. Hurd, in your letter you referred to this town as Virginia City. Yet a stablehand giving me directions to your office called it Virginia."

"Oh, that." He faced her, smiling slightly, glad to be able to direct her thoughts away from her parents. "Some of us are campaigning to have the town officially renamed Virginia City. The place was originally called Washoe Diggings, and was just a mining camp for some time after gold and silver was discovered. Then, one night a drunken miner named Old Virginny Finney dropped a bottle of Virginia whiskey accidentally. So it wouldn't go to waste, he shouted, 'I christen this blankety-blank place Virginia.'" Hurd smiled again. "Now I'm from the state of Virginia, which you may know is green most of the year around. This place is as barren of greenery as hell's doormat, if you'll pardon the expression, ma'am. But Virginia City we're trying to make it, and in the end we'll succeed . . ."

Serena, sensing that he was rambling on in an effort to take her mind from the murder of her parents, coughed again to get his attention. "Mr. Hurd, about the inheritance . . ."

"Ah, yes, the inheritance. The Paradise." He sighed, assuming a sober countenance. He sat down behind his desk. "This is going to be difficult, Serena. Do you know what a bordello, a fancy house, is?"

Serena frowned. "A bordello?"

"That's what I said." Hurd heaved another sigh. "I

can see we're going to have a little problem here. Although I must say Hetty warned me. A bordello, Serena Foster, is a whorehouse. Your Aunt Hetty's inheritance was, is, plain and simple, a whorehouse." He added hastily, "Of course, there *is* a fair sum of money, too. Hetty did very well for herself."

Serena remembered her father's readings from the Bible, and she grasped, with dawning horror, what this man was trying to tell her. "You mean Aunt Hetty ran a house for . . . for harlots?"

"Harlots?" Spencer Hurd looked startled. Then he smiled slightly. "I suppose you could put it that way. Yes, Serena, Hetty Foster owned a house of harlots. But no matter her profession, your Aunt Hetty was a lady. If you'd like, I'll tell you about Hetty Foster."

Still stunned by this new concept of her Aunt Hetty, Serena managed to nod. "Please. I'd like to hear."

The attorney leaned back, his eyes dreaming. "Everybody called her plain Hetty, and she was well-liked, even by some of those who didn't approve of her . . ."

Hetty Foster had been one of the few people to call Spencer Hurd Spence. For a time the only lawyer in town, he had the status and respect accorded a judge. In fact, even when Washoe Diggings exploded overnight with new-found wealth and growth, judges were scarce for a time, so Hurd often served in that capacity, settling minor legal disputes.

"A frontier Solomon," he had once remarked wryly to Hetty. "Dispensing justice from an outhouse throne!"

"Don't badmouth yourself, Spence. The men here might all become savages but for you."

"Seems to me they're pretty much savages, anyway. Even the Biblical Solomon, resurrected, couldn't do much to save them."

"Well, you do all you can, and it's a heap more'n anybody else would do . . . considering that you usually don't get paid."

Of course, Hetty had always been his stout advocate, as he had been hers. But then Hetty had been in love with him and made no bones about it. Hurd loved her, too, but there was a wife in the way back in the state of Virginia, a staunch Catholic who would entertain no suggestion of divorce. Hurd realized, after Hetty's sudden death, that his refusing to take the final step and make things right with her would probably nag at him, like a thorn under his skin, for the rest of his life.

The couple of times he had half-heartedly mentioned divorce and marriage, Hetty had scoffed. "Marry me? Spence, you're a respected man in these diggings. What do you think would happen to that respect if you took a hoor for a wife?"

"Hetty, you're not a whore! You told me yourself that you've never . . ."

". . . laid on my back for pay. And that's true, I never have. But I keep a bunch of girls around who do, and that makes me the same in the eyes of most folks."

"But most people know how it is between us, and as far as I can tell, they don't seem to think the worst of either of us because of it."

"They come into the Paradise and pay to spend a

few minutes with one of my girls, and nobody thinks the worst of them for it, either. Maybe their wives do, but not other men. And most of their wives are down below, back in San Francisco, anyway. But what if one of them married a hoor, what then?"

"I've known men who married whores and were happy with their bargain. Whores make good wives."

"Don't give me that heart-of-gold mule manure." Hetty snorted. "Most of my girls are lazy, good-for-nothing, not much more brains than a child. Except maybe for Madeline Dubois. They can't even boil water, much less keep house and raise a family. Why else do you think they're hoors?"

And yet, in Hurd's judgment, Hetty Foster fitted the heart-of-gold image, even if not technically a "hoor." She certainly would do anything in her power for Spencer Hurd, and she mothered her girls, nursing them when they were sick, flying to their defense when a man came in drunk and abusive, taking them back into the fold after they had run away with some man to escape the degradation of whoredom and came back with tails dragging, usually beaten up and starving.

Hetty was in her late forties when she died, a small woman, with a peppery temper and a tart tongue; always charged with energy, she moved quickly, with the darting motions of a feeding bird.

Hetty died as she had lived, neatly, quickly, without a great deal of fuss. She had been totaling up the house receipts one night after closing and had keeled over, dead before she hit the floor. Jonas, the drunken sawbones who tended Hetty's girls, said she had probably died of a stroke.

Hurd wouldn't have trusted Doc Jonas with a spavined horse, but what did it matter what Hetty died of? She was dead.

Maybe she'd had a premonition of the end; maybe she hadn't. But she had come into Hurd's office a week before her death. It was the first time she had ever been there.

"This is legal business. Spence, not bed business, so I thought it best I come to your office."

"What business, Hetty? You in some kind of trouble?"

"No trouble, Spence. I want to make out a will."

"Everybody should have a will. As an attorney, that's always my advice. But why all of a sudden?"

"I may die tomorrow."

"Nonsense! You're young yet, and healthy as a horse."

"So that's what you think I am? After all these years. I finally found out."

"Hetty, I didn't mean . . ."

"All these years and you still don't know when I'm joshing you . . . Spence, you going to draw up this will or do I get somebody else to do it?"

"Of course I'll do it. Who's your beneficiary?"

"Beneficiary? That's who gets what I leave, right? I didn't have much education, Spence."

"You're educated in all the ways that count, Hetty. And yes . . . your beneficiary is who you leave it to when you die, God forbid it should ever happen!"

"You, a backsliding Papist, calling on God? My brother, Hiram Foster, that's who I leave it to. Don't know how he'll take to being left a hoorhouse, since he was as strait-laced as a corset, last time I saw him, twenty years ago. He has no idea what I've been doing all these years. I'd like to be here to see his face when he finds out. But he's the only one I've got, him and his wife."

"A bluenose inheriting a sporting house?" Hurd threw back his head and shouted laughter. He opened his cigar drawer and took out a box of long nines. "Have a stogie, Hetty, and we'll draw up your will."

"Don't mind if I do."

Hetty enjoyed a good cigar as much as a man, but she smoked them only in private. A bordello madam, she believed, should always be a model of decorum in public, even in front of her girls, never smoking, taking a drink, swearing, or wearing a wanton's clothing.

Hurd lit both their cigars, then said, "You say you haven't been in touch with your brother in . . . what? Twenty years? What if neither he nor his wife are still alive? Then who will be your heir?"

Hetty looked startled. "Never crossed my mind that he wouldn't be. Well now . . ." She puffed on the cigar. "How about you, Spence?"

He was already shaking his head. "Oh, no, not me, Hetty. It wouldn't even be legal, my drawing up a will in which I'm the legatee."

Hetty smoked for a moment, thinking. Then she waved a hand. "If Hiram and wife are no longer with us, then what difference does it make? I could leave it to Madeline. I'm fond of the girl, but somehow I've a feeling about her. If I left everything to Madeline, I have this feeling she'd go hog-wild and be broke in no time, the girls losing their happy home. If the reins are in somebody else's hands, she can manage the Paradise well enough." Hetty took a deep breath. "So, it all goes to Brad Stryker then."

Hurd reared back. "Brad Stryker! Godalmighty, why *him?*"

Hetty was laughing quietly. "Because of his daddy, Eli Stryker, may the Lord have mercy on his soul. Guess you didn't know that old Eli loaned me the money to buy my house and set it up, did you, Spence? Paid him back long before he died, of course, with heavy interest."

"Hetty, if you needed money, why didn't you come to me?"

"Come to a respectable lawyer to borrow money to open a fancy house?" She looked scandalized. "Never!" She gave him a crafty look. "So you have a choice, Spence. If Hiram and wife are dead, it's either you, or Brad Stryker. I'll write my brother a letter, see if I get an answer."

Hurd sighed. "Second beneficiary, Brad Stryker, it is then."

They finished making out Hetty's will and had it signed before witnesses. But Hetty never wrote the letter to her brother. A week later Spencer Hurd buried her in Flowery Hill Cemetery, with at least half of the town's population present, mostly male except for Hetty's girls.

Usually a whorehouse was a rented place, with girls who came and went from day to day, worth little more than one night's profits. However, Hetty had owned the two-story building which housed the Paradise, and the land on which it stood, free and clear. Most cribs and brothels in Virginia City were located on the lower end of D Street, but Hetty's place was out of town a discreet distance.

It was unique for this time and place. The furniture was expensive, collected over several years, many valuable pieces originating in the East, some coming by ship from Europe. And insofar as one person could belong to another, short of outright slavery, the girls had all *belonged* to Hetty. They had been carefully selected, trained, groomed, cuddled, spoiled, and made almost totally dependent on her. They had been desolated by her death, left helpless as babes. Hurd didn't doubt that some would literally starve to death if left to their own devices.

For that reason, and to keep the estate intact for Hetty's heirs, Hurd had kept the Paradise operating, the girls working—all under the supervision of Madeline Dubois.

The plain fact was, as long as the Paradise remained staffed as it was and continued in operation it was a profitable business. Perhaps not as get-rich-quick as silver strike on Sun Mountain, but lucrative enough. And it would never go broke, as Hetty had told Hurd once in private, as long as it was operated properly, and as long as there were men around with stiff peckers and dollars in their pockets.

Madeline Dubois, a dusky, handsome female of thirty, was somewhat the woman of mystery. Rumors had it that she was a Creole, that she was octoroon, that she was of royal blood in exile from Europe. Madeline neither confirmed nor denied the rumors. Unlike Hetty, Madeline *had* laid on her back for money, but not long enough for it to begin to show. And Madeline ran counter to Hetty's dictum that all "hoors" were brainless as children. Madeline had some education, an unusual circumstance with most frontier women, whores or otherwise. Hurd had no idea why Madeline had become a whore. She had gone to work at the Paradise a year ago and had stayed. In spite of all the time he had spent in Hetty's place, as familiar as he was with the girls, Hurd had never once asked Madeline how she'd gotten into the business.

True, Madeline was something of a martinet, making the girls toe the line, but discipline was what they needed to keep them together after the shock of Hetty's death. Hurd didn't know if Madeline was now retired from active whoredom; he didn't consider it any of his business . . .

"And that," Spencer Hurd finished, "was Hetty Foster, your Aunt Hetty."

"She sounds like quite a woman," Serena said slowly. "I wish I could have known her." In spite of never having seen her aunt in the flesh, Serena experienced a sense of loss.

"She was indeed quite a woman," Hurd said solemnly. "And now the question remains . . . what about your inheritance?"

"Oh, my . . . that!" Brought back to the present with a start, Serena sat up. "It's all so sudden. Inheriting a house of . . . a brothel . . . a . . . I just don't know . . ." without warning a giggle escaped her. "Oh, Aunt Hetty was right! I can just see daddy's face!" She sobered. "But I could never run a place like that!"

"You don't have to, you can always sell it."

"I don't know." Serena shook her head. "I just don't know."

41

"And there is a sum of money, something over five thousand, I believe. I'm sure you could use that."

"But it was earned from running the Paradise, wasn't it?"

"Of course, But see here, young lady." Hurd was frowning. "There's not all that much disgrace attached to the profession here. Prostitution *is* the oldest profession, you know."

"I know, Mr. Hurd, I know. I'm acting like a prig, just like Aunt Hetty said about daddy. But it's all so sudden! I need some time to think."

"Of course." Hurd spread his hands. "Take all the time you need."

Serena got to her feet. "Right now I need to find lodgings somewhere. I need a bath, and a change of clothing."

Hurd also stood up. "I regret that I cannot offer you hospitality, but I inhabit bachelor quarters. There is a decent boarding house down the street. Ma Taylor's. Quite respectable, and serves good meals. Do you need any money, Serena?"

"No, thank you, Mr. Hurd. I have enough to last a few days."

As she started out, Hurd said, "I'd like to take you to the Paradise, have you meet Madeline Dubois. At least there might be some mementos, Hetty's personal stuff, papers, and the like, that you'd wish to have."

"Yes, I'll probably be wanting to do that. Thank you again, Mr. Hurd. You've been very helpful."

As Serena turned to leave, she found her way blocked by a stocky man of forty, with wide, muscular shoulders, thick black hair, and a heavy moustache on his upper lip. He had the coldest black eyes Serena had ever seen.

42

Removing his hat, he stepped back. "My apologies, ma'am."

Serena nodded and moved past him without speaking. As she went down the hall, she heard Spencer Hurd saying, "Hello Brad. What can I do for you?"

Chapter Three

Brad Stryker stood staring after the pretty, blonde girl, trying to recall if he'd seen her before, and he scarcely heard Spencer Hurd's greeting.

Hurd frowned at him, fishing the cold cigar out of the can and relighting it. Although he occasionally handled legal matters for Stryker, he didn't particularly like the man. There was a coldness about him that Hurd found repellent, and he had a brutal nature. He was a powerful man physically, and being touchy of temper, he was often involved in brawls. Unlike many men in Virginia City, he seldom used a gun to settle his differences, although he usually carried one in his belt. He didn't need a pistol; his two fists were like sledgehammers, and more than once Hurd had seen him use those fists to hammer a man into insensibility. Each time his face had worn a cold, reptilian smile, and Hurd had sensed that

Stryker experienced great joy at beating another man senseless.

Brad Stryker owned one of several freight lines hauling ore from the mines down to the mills along the Carson River. He was doing very well at it and was slowly but surely forcing some of the other freight companies out of business. He was not adverse to using the most ruthless means to force a competitor to the wall.

His cigar going, Hurd said impatiently, "Well, Brad?"

Stryker started, turning. "Sorry, Judge. Pretty girl, that one." He jerked his thumb. "Don't think I know her."

"I don't imagine you would. She just arrived from Illinois. That was Serena Foster, Hetty's niece."

Stryker had schooled himself to keep all emotion out of his face, but he was hard put to conceal the shock he felt at this news. "I didn't know Hetty had a niece. I thought her only relative was a brother?"

"That's what I thought. That's what Hetty thought, too. It appears we were both wrong."

Keeping his voice casual, Stryker said, "But where's the girl's father?"

Hurd's face hardened. "Dead. Both the poor girl's parents were murdered a few nights ago on the way here. It seems a bunch of ruffians rode up to their wagon and gunned them down."

"Ah, that's too damned bad. How come they missed the girl?"

"It seems she was away from the camp, taking a bath in the river."

"That's lucky for her. Don't suppose she saw the killers then? No way of identifying them?"

46

"Oh, she saw them."

Stryker tightened up inside.

Hurd was going on, "But she can't identify them. It seems they were all wearing masks over their faces." Hurd struck the desk a blow with his fist. "Godalmighty, something has to be done about·the lawlessness around the camps, all the senseless killing. This one was more senseless than most. Hell, the Fosters weren't even robbed!"

"Yeah, I agree, Judge. We could use more law and order around these diggings." Stryker forced a laugh. "At least one good thing comes out of it . . . I won't be winding up with a whorehouse on my hands. Why on earth Hetty ever put me in her will for that place, I'll never know."

Hurd leaned back, smiling slightly through cigar smoke. "I don't think Serena's going to run it, Brad. If anything, she'll be selling it. Could be you could buy it off her."

"Now, Judge, what in the hell would I do with a whorehouse? I've got enough on my hands to keep me busy, without riding herd on a bunch of the frail sisters."

"To get back, Brad . . . what can I do for you?"

"Oh . . . yes." Stryker sat down. "Larry Jenkins is suing me again."

Hurd sighed. "What is it this time?"

"Oh, he claims one of my drivers forced one of his wains off the road and down into a ravine. Jenkins is suing me for the damages. I'd like you to try and reach some kind of a settlement with him, so it won't get to court."

"As small a settlement as possible, I suppose?" Hurd asked dryly.

47

"Of course. You're my attorney, ain't you? That's what an attorney is for, right?"

Hurd didn't like being labeled Stryker's attorney, but since he had represented him before, he couldn't very well quibble. "This makes the . . . What? Fifth time this has happened, am I correct? *Did* your driver run the wagon off the road?"

Stryker assumed a wounded look. "It was an accident, Judge."

"Just like the other times, eh?"

"Just like the other times. You think I'd order a driver of mine to do that on purpose? If Jenkins would hire decent drivers, instead of drunks tumbling out of the saloons along C Street, he wouldn't have so many accidents."

"I'm sure not." Hurd sighed again. "All right, I'll see if he'll settle. He probably will. He always has before."

"I knew I could depend on you, Judge. Thanks."

Stryker gave the man behind the desk a wave and walked out of the office, leaving Spencer Hurd scowling after him through a haze of cigar smoke.

In the hallway, out of sight of the lawyer, Stryker gave vent to the black rage boiling up inside him. Halfway to the outside stairway, he stopped, clenched his fists, and started to beat on the wall with them. At the last moment, a wind of caution blew across his fevered brain, and he leaned against the wall instead, eyes closed, until he could regain a measure of control.

Across his mind's eye danced a vision of what had happened out there in the desert—the orange spouts of gunfire, and the man and woman falling dead; then, as a triumphant gesture, the turning over of the

48

wagon. He had thought *all* the Fosters were eliminated, and now he had learned that one still existed. If only he had given an order for the men to scout around for survivors, they likely would have found the damned girl and he would be rid of her as well. Now he had to scheme some way to do it here, where it wouldn't be so simple. The death of a young woman fresh from the East couldn't be handled easily without arousing suspicion, especially since she also happened to be related to Hetty Foster. Spencer Hurd was a shrewd old codger, and he might, just might, make the connection if a third Foster met an untimely death, apparently as motiveless as the murder of her parents. If Hurd did that, he might nose around and find what Stryker didn't want him to find.

So, he was going to have to be very, very careful as to the manner in which he went about disposing of Serena Foster. It would either have to appear an accident, or some way would have to be devised so that her death could be blamed on someone. A killer with a definite motive would have to be handed to Spencer Hurd on a platter. Either way, Stryker knew, there could be no breath of suspicion directed at him.

He pushed away from the wall and took out his pocket watch. It was close to four o'clock. Li Po was due late this afternoon from San Francisco; Stryker had received a telegram from Carson City this morning to that effect. Li Po would be arriving in his personal coach, naturally. Chinamen weren't allowed passage on the regular stagecoachs. Stryker didn't have a high opinion of Chinks himself, but Li Po was a different dish of noodles. Oh, very different indeed! In the first place, he was undoubtedly the richest, and the most powerful, Chinaman on the West Coast, if not the entire United States; and Stryker had found doing business with him most profitable.

Since only Stryker and Li Po knew of their business dealings, they always met secretly in a small house in the Chinese quarter, on the flats below the town. The house was owned by Li Po and was used only for his infrequent visits to Virginia City. Li Po's arrival, with his fancy coach and entourage of *boo how doy*, or bodyguards, would not go unnoticed, but Stryker would sneak down to the house after dark. Meanwhile, he had some business to finish before the day was done.

Outside, the evening shadows were long and slanting, and the air was cooler. Stryker set off at a brisk pace toward his freight office on the south edge of town.

Rory Clendenning had not gone far after leaving Serena, before he was cursing himself for his damnable pride. He didn't have even a short bit in his pockets. How was he to pay for food and lodgings for the night? Why couldn't he have swallowed his pride enough to at least have accepted a small loan from Serena? He would find work soon, he was sure, and could have paid her back.

Walking along the busy, dusty street, he recalled something Jeremiah had told him once: "If you're ever in a strange town, son, and without money in your pockets, seek out a minister of the Gospel. Through him, the Lord will provide what sustenance you need."

The first church he came to was a weathered building, never having seen a lick of paint, with a tilted, wooden cross on top. It was down a short side street, almost hidden behind a livery stable. The stench of horse manure was strong inside the church, providing an unchurchly incense.

At first Clendenning thought the building was empty. The few windows were dirty, filtering the afternoon light. There was twin rows of hard benches, with an aisle between. At the far end of the room was a platform, with an altar on it.

Clendenning started uncertainly down the aisle, calling out, "Anybody here?"

A voice murmured something from the rear. At the same time Clendenning saw the open door directly behind the altar. He ducked his head under the low door frame. The room was little more than a closet, and the man in it seemed scaled to size.

He sat in a ladderback chair, a Bible open before him on a rickety table. He was a short, thin man of fifty, with wisps of gray hair trying vainly to conceal a pink scalp. His face had a gray, pinched look. Smeared spectacles perched on a hooked nose out of which gray hair grew like a fungus. Eyes like poached eggs swam behind the thick glasses. His black coat was shiny with age, and his shirt collar was frayed and soiled.

"Yes?" he demanded suspiciously, in a high-pitched voice.

He was one of the most unappetizing individuals Clendenning had ever seen, and he thought that might go a long way toward explaining the poor-mouth condition of the church.

Clendenning strode to the table. "Rory Clendenning, sir. I'm from back East. My pa, Jeremiah Clendenning, is a preaching man."

51

After a moment's hesitation, the man stood up. His hand had the feel of a river bottom catfish. "Reverend Elmo Parker, Brother. But I must warn you that while Virginia is a den of sinners, it supplies few souls for Christ. Do you know how many attended Sunday services last? An even dozen, only two men. They offered up four dollars and six bits for the Lord. So if it's your intention to preach here . . ."

Clendenning felt his temper spark. He had no such intention, but something in this man's manner rubbed him the wrong way. He cleared his throat and smiled with embarrassment. "It's just that I find myself in rather dire straits, Reverend Parker. To be frank, I'm without means for supper and a bed tonight."

After another moment's hesitation, Reverend Parker's clenched features relaxed briefly in what could have been a smile. "You are more than welcome to sup with us, Brother. Poor fare, but sustaining. And we have a spare bedroom. You are welcome to stay . . . for tonight." He held up his hand. "If in return, I receive a promise from you that you will not take up preaching here."

Clendenning stared. "I don't find that a very Christian attitude, sir."

"Perhaps not, but these are hard times for our brotherhood, and a man must look after his own first."

Clendenning's anger grew. Lord God, what kind of country was this, what kind of people dwelled here? Within a space of ten days, he had been fleeced by a gambling slick, seen two innocent people murdered for no reason, and now a man of God was asking a promise from him in exchange for food and a bed for one night.

For one of the few times in his life, Clendenning indulged in profanity. He said softly, "And you, *Brother*, can go straight to hell!"

The pinched face took on a look of shock. Clendenning turned on his heel, strode out of the tiny office and out of the church. But once outside, his step slowed. Why had he been so quick to lose his temper? Once again he had let his pride rule him. Since he had no intention of preaching here, or anywhere else, why couldn't he have given Reverend Parker the promise he wanted?

Now what?

No supper, no place to sleep.

As though in answer to that question, his empty belly rumbled loudly. He hadn't eaten a thing since a meager breakfast with Serena that morning.

He walked along C Street, mingling with the throng. He spent the afternoon trudging through the town. At several places he asked for work, but the only jobs he was offered were swamping saloons or washing dishes. A number of people told him that labor was badly needed in the mines, but that was of no help to him at the moment. His damnable pride wouldn't let him take menial jobs in exchange for a meal.

Finally, long after dark, shivering with the night's chill, he found himself walking back toward Reverend Parker's church. Why, he had no idea. Certainly he had no intention of falling on his knees before the man and begging his forgiveness.

Clendenning was weary to the bone, heavy with discouragement. Starting past the livery stable, he broke stride and veered toward it. The big doors swung open to his touch. The stable odor was strong, yet it was warm inside out of the wind, the body heat of the animals enveloping him like invisible steam. A horse neighed down the line and rattled a stall.

The stable was very clean, no visible horse droppings. One lantern at the far end gave off a weak light.

Clendenning went from stall to stall until he found one empty. There was a fresh pile of hay against the far end. He made a bed for himself, then sat down and removed his boots with a sigh, using them for a pillow as he arranged himself on the hay. He was hungry, badly in need of a bath, but he was also Lord God tired.

He thought he wouldn't go to sleep easily, what with everything on his mind, but he fell into sleep like a stone tumbling into a deep well.

He couldn't have been asleep more than a few minutes when a cruel rap across the bottoms of his stocking feet brought him groggily awake.

"Wha . . . ! What?"

A woman's voice said, "On your feet, you bum, and drag your drunken carcass out of here!"

Clendenning sat up, shielding his eyes from the bright glare of a lantern only a few inches before his face. "I'm not a bum, and I'm not drunk!"

"Then what are you doing sneaking in here to sleep?"

The woman stepped back a little, and Clendenning got to his feet with as much dignity as he could muster. Her face and most of her figure were still in darkness. She seemed fairly young, wore a pair of man's trousers, and had a shotgun cradled in her arms, the muzzle pointing at him.

"I'm broke, that's why, no money for a bed. I'm a preacher's son." Now why, he wondered, had he added that last?

"A preacher's son! For God's sake!" The sharpness left her voice, and she lowered the muzzle of the shotgun. "You hoping to start up preaching here?"

"I came here to . . ." He broke off, remembering his experience with Reverend Parker. "I haven't thought yet what I'm going to do."

"Well, I'm not hard-hearted enough to throw a preaching man out into the night. What's your name?"

"Rory Clendenning."

"Clendenning, is it? Well, I'm Kate Rogan. I own this hay barn. I'll make a bargain with you. My swamper quit on me yesterday. You ever clean out a livery stable? Doesn't matter, you look strong enough. You clean out the place in the morning, and you can sleep here tonight, and I'll feed you breakfast. A bargain, Clendenning?"

This time, he had sense enough to swallow his pride and humiliation. "It's a bargain, Miss Rogan."

"All right, Clendenning. Sleep tight." She added sharply, "And don't be smoking in here!"

"I don't smoke."

"That's good. One spark and this whole town could go up in flames." She started off, then swung back. "Good night, Clendenning."

"Good night," he said stiffly.

It was nearly nine o'clock when Brad Stryker, carrying a small black bag, slipped along a noxious alley-

55

way in the Chinese quarter, until he reached Li Po's house. A messenger had come to his office late that afternoon telling him of Li Po's arrival.

There was a faint glow of light from inside the small house filtering through a dirty window. What few windows the house had were filmed with dirt, so that is was impossible to see through them, and the building was unpainted and dingy looking. This was a facade, Stryker knew. The inside was luxurious. Everything was directed toward Li Po's comfort during his infrequent visits here. There was an armed man always in residence, to look after the building. The local Chinese, knowing that the house belonged to Li Po, never came near it, unless summoned by Li Po.

Stryker rapped on the back door. In a moment it opened, and a sibilant voice said, "Yes-s?"

"It's Brad Stryker," he said shortly.

"Ah, yes-s, Mistel Stlykel. Please to come in."

Stryker brushed past the stocky, powerful figure. The man was dressed in the almost uniform-like garb that a tong lord's bodyguards usually wore—a loose-fitting, black tunic and black trousers that ended just below the ankles, showing black, slipper-like shoes, and what looked like white gaiters. His queue was wound around his head, and on top of the queue sat a small, circular, pill-box hat. The man's flat, yellowish face was pleasant enough, but Stryker knew that he was as deadly as a diamondback rattlesnake coiled to strike. Stryker had little fear of any man, but he had seen these bodyguards of Li Po's in action, and he would rather not tangle with them.

The man's hands, as was the custom, rested within the sleeves of his tunic. Stryker knew that one hand surely held a pistol, and if there appeared to be any possible danger to Li Po, the man would use the gun with quickness and deadly skill.

The heavy, cloying odor of incense, mixed with the scent of opium, assailed Stryker's nostrils as he went into the house. Several heavily ornamented lanterns with painted silk screens illuminated the room with soft, golden light, and although Stryker had been in the house often enough before, he stopped to give it an appreciative appraisal. There was one thing he had to admit; the Chinks had a real eye for beauty, and Li Po had the money to indulge his tastes.

All of the interior walls of the room were masked with heavily embroidered silk hangings. The figures on the hangings were wondrous and complicated; a golden dragon, with irridescent scales; a likeness of a strange animal that looked like a cross between a dog and a demon; flowers, and the ubiquitous designs made by the characters of the Chinese writing.

There were also intricately carved sandalwood cabinets against the walls, and a low, delicate sandalwood table in front of the pile of silken pillows upon which Li Po reclined. Upon the table there were a decanter of rice wine and several platters of delicacies.

As Stryker approached, Li Po took the long, ornately carved opium pipe from his mouth and inclined his head. "Ah so, Mr. Stryker."

Before meeting Li Po, Stryker's experience with Chinese had been limited. He had never known one who spoke anything but pidgin English, and certainly never one who didn't bow to him, hissing apologies, "So solly, Mistel Stlykel!"

Li Po had better command of the English language than Stryker himself, and never bowed, never uttered an apology. This lack of respect in a Chinaman for a white man still aroused Stryker's ire, but he swallowed it. Not only was his association with Li Po too lucrative to put into jeopardy, but Stryker knew that if he ever displeased this man, he would be found in an alley with his throat slit. So, he would put up with the man until his association was no longer profitable, but Stryker had vowed to himself that some day he would see Li Po hung by his queue for his insolence.

He sat on a cushion opposite Li Po. There were no chairs in the house. He said, "How goes it, Li Po?"

"Excellent, my Occidental friend, excellent."

Li Po was tall, thin, with a jet-black queue hanging down his back. His almond-shaped eyes were also black, and the black moustache had ends drooping below his chin. The long, sallow face had never, in Stryker's presence, revealed much expression, neither anger nor humor. On occasion, the thin lips would stretch in what could be a smile. Li Po's age was impossible to determine. He could be sixty; he could be forty.

His clothing, while similar to that of his bodyguards in style, was nevertheless very different in quality. His tunic, which flared slightly, was made of the finest red silk and was embroidered with a thread of pure gold, as well as several colors of silk thread. His trousers were black, but were also of fine silk, and his black slippers were as heavily embroidered as his tunic. He wore several rings upon his long, talon-like fingers, and Stryker turned his gaze away from the long, womanish nails, which he found revolting, particularly the nails of the little fingers, which must have been several inches in length.

Li Po drew on the opium pipe and expelled a thin

stream of smoke. Stryker had been in some of the joss houses on the downside of Virginia City and seen others on the opium pipe. Most of them were in a stuporous state after a couple of pipes. Stryker had watched Li Po smoke pipe after pipe with little visible effect.

Li Po said, "Did the last two cargoes of my people arrive?"

"Yes, and I found them all jobs."

Among many other things, Li Po was an exploiter of his own people. The mining camps of the West, the railroads being built, the telegraph lines now stretching across the country—all were clamoring for cheap coolie labor. The nation of China, with its teeming millions, was poor, and Chinese families were delighted to emigrate to this new land of opportunity, if someone would pay their passage and provide them with jobs. Li Po was that someone. He paid their passage and then sold them into virtual slavery throughout the West. In cahoots with other agents such as Stryker, he got his people jobs, for which privilege they paid Li Po and his agents a stiff monthly stipend out of their wages, for as long as the job lasted. Stryker had found this to be a very profitable sideline.

Stryker opened the black bag and took out a bundle of banknotes. "Here's your split for the last six months, Li Po."

Li Po accepted the banknotes and gave them to one of his hovering men without bothering to count them. His black eyes contemplated Stryker. "Have you encountered any problems?"

"Problems?"

"Of discipline?"

59

Stryker nodded reluctantly. "A few stubborn ones. I've had them whipped, a fine levied on their wages. Even with that, there have been a few still giving trouble."

Li Po nodded gravely. "I hear much the same from other areas. It has even occurred with some of my own in San Francisco. These rebellious ones must be dealt with severely, Mr. Stryker."

"That's easy enough to say," Stryker shrugged. "But what do you do after you've beaten them and fined them? If you beat them too much, they can't work."

"You make an example of some, Mr. Stryker." Li Po smiled one of his rare smiles, a smile of pure evil. "I will tell you of such. I paid passage from my native land for a young man and his mother. The young man was of extraordinary size, by Chinese standards. I visioned a goodly sum for his services. But he was indeed a rebellious individual, so much so that he went about speaking against me, telling my people that I, their sponsor, was exploiting them."

"So what did you do?"

"I had his tongue torn out by the roots. He speaks no more against me."

Even Stryker's hardened nature was shocked by this revelation. He stared at the man in fascination. "What happened to him after that?"

Li Po raised and lowered narrow shoulders. "I know not. I had no further use for him. I simply made of him an example, and that example had quieted many an incautious tongue."

"I can well believe it," Stryker said.

"You must be firm with them, Mr. Stryker," Li Po said primly. "They are much like children and must be treated as such."

Li Po drew on the opium pipe. He closed his eyes, his narrow face taking on a dreamy expression.

Stryker waited, squirming inwardly. Finally, his patience expired. He coughed loudly.

Li Po opened his eyes. "Ah so, Mr. Stryker? You are still present? Perhaps this will be of interest to you. With me I brought four young Chinese girls, for the joss house brothels here. One is very young, very pretty, and is a virgin. The others I have placed, but the young one is still here, in the usual bedroom. I thought, as a favor to a friend and business associate, you might like the honor of deflowering her?"

"A virgin, you say?" Stryker licked suddenly dry lips. "And a beauty?"

"As beautiful, and fresh, as a new blossom."

Stryker delved into the black bag, taking out a short, tasseled rawhide whip and a gold Chinese mask. He slipped the mask on and stood up, striking his left palm gently with the tassels.

"A word of caution, Mr. Stryker. She is small, fragile as our most delicate China. Do not harm her unduly." Li Po smiled again. "She is merchandise, after all, and we, as businessmen, understand the necessity for not harming the merchandise, do we not?"

"I understand," Stryker said hoarsely. "Now, Li Po?"

Li Po merely nodded, motioning lanquidly to the bodyguard beside him. The man in the black tunic beckoned for Stryker to follow him. In a state of excitation, Stryker followed the man, striking his palm repeatedly with the whip.

Chapter Four

From the outside, the Paradise could easily have been mistaken for the residence of a wealthy mine owner—which was exactly the impression Hetty Foster had tried for. The house was located well away from any other residence, on the south end of D. Street. It was white, with a green trim and yellow shutters on the windows, and was painted at least once a year, something rare in Virginia City. There was a wide front porch with a rocking chair, but only the frequent "Washoe zephyrs" moaning out of the canyons had ever moved the rocker. No one in Virginia City had ever seen anyone sitting in the chair.

In the daytime, only two things hinted at the business of the house. A small, discreet sign hung over the porch steps: "THE PARADISE." And there was a neat row of six privies out back, far more than was necessary for the needs of one family. At night, other elements were added—the muted sounds of gaiety, faint laughter, sometimes voices raised in snatches of song, and the tinny sound of a piano, but the latter was so muted it could strike the unknowing as the sound of a ghost piano carried on the wind. Also, there were usually horses and buggies tied up at the long hitching rail, the animals nodding as they waited for their masters to finish their business inside.

There were no red lights, large or small. This had been another dictum laid down by Hetty: "I don't want just any miner with a dollar in his pants tromping in here, knocking mud from his boots. If I can't make the place pay with a better class of customer, I'll go into some other line of business."

Madeline Dubois had continued Hetty's policy of no overt advertising of the purpose of the establishment, even to the "By Invitation Only" policy originated by Hetty. Hetty had kept a supply of business cards on hand, not printed but with just the words, "The Paradise," written in her fine Spencerian script, with her initials, H. F., inscribed in the lower right-hand corner. These cards were handed out to choice customers, and admission to the Paradise was open to cardholders only, with possibly a friend included. Also, the cardholders were given an extra card from time to time to pass out to friends. But if they were unwise in their choice and the new cardholder caused any sort of ruckus in the Paradise, both men were barred forever from the place.

When Hetty had initiated this policy, other sporting house and crib operators in Virginia City had scoffed. She would soon go broke.

They were proven wrong. Men drove up from Gold Hill, Silver City, even from as far away as Carson City to Hetty's establishment. Of course her prices were steeper, and her girls fewer in number, but chosen carefully. "Quality is better than quantity, in my opinion," Hetty often said.

Madeline Dubois had changed none of Hetty's policies.

Madeline sat now, near midnight, in the small room off the downstairs hall, totaling up the night's receipts. She was a tall girl, with long brown hair to her shoulders, a heart-shaped face with clear complexion, and dark, sultry eyes. There was, Hetty had once remarked, a little of the Madonna about her, a look that would drive men wild at the thought of bedding her.

Madeline had a voluptuous figure, full-breasted and strong-thighed—all well hidden at the moment in a full balmoral skirt all the way to the floor, the waist with black buttons, the bow between her breasts like a yellow rose.

For a weeknight business had been brisk. It had tapered off now, only three customers upstairs with the girls, and there wouldn't be any more visitors this late. To come calling at this hour, a man would have to be drunk and troublesome, and any cardholder knew better than to come staggering into the Paradise in such a condition. Madeline had sent Chuck Gentry, the piano player on home. Foxy, the combination barkeep and bounce, was still cleaning the barroom. He always locked up the house when he left, and the door was never opened to a visitor after that—unless Madeline had a personal caller of her own. The only time that happened nowadays was when she admitted a lover, and at the moment she had no lover.

Madeline had been in the barroom a few minutes ago, and there had been two girls drinking sarsaparilla, waiting in the unlikely event a late customer did show up. None of Hetty's girls ever drank hard liquor in public. Madeline had sent the other girls off to bed.

Finished with her counting, Madeline locked the night's receipts away in the cashbox and lit a small cigar, a habit she had picked up from Hetty.

God, how she missed Hetty!

Madeline's mother had run off with a whisky drummer when the girl was twelve, and she had never known her father. Hetty was the closest thing to a real mother she'd ever known. And she had known Hetty for less than a year. In the beginning Madeline had taken her turn on her back with the other girls, but somehow Hetty had developed a liking for her and things changed. Not that Madeline had stopped whoring altogether, but Hetty had said, "Let's make you into something special, girl. We'll dress you like a schoolmarm, you'll wander around looking demure and virginal, although that last will be a little hard with that figure of yours. Anyway, the boys will be pawing the ground to get at you. And we'll make 'em pay for the privilege, indeed we will!"

It had worked just as Hetty had foreseen. Madeline became something special, and the customers who could afford it had to pay a goodly bounty for the privilege of getting her out of all those clothes.

Well, at least that was over. Now she devoted all her time to running the establishment. As long as she was in her present position her whoring days were finished.

How long that would last would naturally depend on Hetty's brother. As though aware of her impending death, Hetty had told Madeline, just a few days

66

before it happened, that she could remain here as long as she liked. "Of course, it all depends on that Bible-thumping brother of mine. He's my only blood kin left alive, and he's entitled to my property when I pass on. But if he don't cotton to it, and I think it likely that he won't, he'll probably sell it. I'd like to leave it to you, Madeline, but I have other obligations. All I can do is state that I wish you kept on to run the place. I'll say that in the will I'm having Spence make out. Of course, the Paradise'll be worthless when the silver runs out on the mountain. So make it while you can and squirrel it away. The winters out here get hard, girl."

Well, the silver hadn't run out as yet, and wasn't likely to for some years to come, but according to Spencer Hurd, Hetty's brother had been notified and was on his way here. Naturally, Madeline wished that Hetty had left the house to her, but she understood Hetty's position. She only hoped that the brother would be willing to sell, and that he would not ask an excessive price.

And in that moment, as though her thinking of Hurd had somehow conjured him up, Madeline heard his booming laughter. She opened the door and lounged against the jamb, watching his tall figure stride down the hall toward her. He had a glass of whiskey in one hand, a cigar smoldering in the other.

"Madeline, Hetty's heir is here, just got in today."

"I thought he was about due." She put out the Argand lamp on her desk. "Let's go into the parlor, Judge."

In the parlor she crossed to the cellarette, got out a decanter of whiskey and splashed some in a glass.

"Why didn't you wait until you got back here for some of the prime stuff, Judge?"

He laughed, small black eyes twinkling, and waited for her to be seated before sitting beside her. "I'm not that particular what I drink, my dear. Save the prime stuff for special company."

"Hetty and I used to have a glass apiece at the end of the evening. Since she died, nobody has been at this decanter but me." She looked at him challengingly. "Whether you believe that or not."

He stared at her intently, long face melancholy. "Now why wouldn't I believe it, Madeline? I've never had any reason to doubt anything you tell me."

"I'm sorry, Judge. It's just . . ." She made a brushing gesture across her face. "Since Hetty died, I get touchy so easily. I guess I believe everybody's thinking the worst of me. Hetty always said that many people believe that a sporting house madam will do anything her girls do, or worse . . . God, Judge, I miss her!"

"And I too, Madeline. I do indeed miss Hetty Foster."

In the brief silence that followed, they both took a drink and drew on their respective cigars, as though in an unvoiced toast to the departed Hetty. Then Madeline cleared her throat and said briskly, "Well, how did Hiram Foster take to it when he learned the truth about his inheritance?"

Spencer Hurd began to laugh. He laughed so hard that tears came to his eyes.

Madeline glared at him. "What's the joke, Judge?"

He finally choked off the laughter. "The joke is that the heir is Serena Foster, not Hiram."

Madeline's brows elevated. "Who is Serena?"

"Hiram's daughter, Hetty's niece." He sobered. "And it isn't actually all that funny."

He told her then what had happened to Hiram and Mercy Foster, and Serena.

"The poor girl! How horrible for her!" Madeline said. "So, what happens now, Judge?"

"To be frank, I'm not sure. She was shocked pink at the idea of inheriting this place." Spencer Hurd studied the glowing end of his cigar. "You go on as before, Madeline, for the time being. I'm going to try and get her to come out to meet you. Meanwhile, you continue, deduct your usual salary, and hang onto the rest, until it's all decided."

"I don't mind doing that, I'm happy doing it, but I won't be too happy if she comes in here, takes over, and kicks me out."

Hurd said dryly, "From what I've seen of the young lady, Madeline, the chances of that are small. People do surprise you, of course. So we'll just have to wait and see. My opinion is, she'll either sell it, or pull up her skirts and run. Either way, you'll come out ahead. Since she *is* the legal heir, Brad Stryker will have no say in the matter."

"I meant to ask you, Judge. How about Hetty's cards? I'm running out. Do we stop that altogether, or make new ones?"

"Make new ones. Put your initials on them."

"*My* initials?" she said in astonishment.

"Why not?" He shrugged. "Might as well break the customers into it, so they won't be surprised when you finally take over." He tossed off the rest of his drink and got to his feet. "I guess I'll amble along and let you get to bed."

"Judge . . ." Madeline gestured toward the

whiskey decanter. "Why don't you stay for a little? Keep me company and have some of the prime stuff?"

"Well . . ." He hesitated, his glance lingering on the decanter. Then he looked at her appraisingly, that mischievous twinkle lurking far back in his eyes. He hummed a few bars of "Sweet Betsy from Pike." He said soberly, "Just so long as nothing else is expected of me."

Just as soberly, Madeline said, "Nothing else is expected of you, Judge."

***

Rory Clendenning awoke with a start, the sound of blasting echoing in his consciousness. For a moment he was disoriented, mystified as to where he was. Then, in the early light of morning, memory flooded in on him, and he recognized the stable and the empty stall where he'd spent the night. His bones ached abominably, wisps of straw stuck to his clothes like leeches, and his gut rumbled emptily, reminding him that he had eaten almost nothing yesterday.

He sat up, pulling the boots onto his swollen feet with an effort. At his stirring, horses snorted in stalls down the line. One kicked at a stall door.

Clendenning stepped outside just as the sun burst over the eastern horizon. He rubbed the sleep from his eyes and looked around. He could see part of C Street from where he stood, and already loaded ore wagons were rumbling along it, heading down the canyon for the stamp mills.

Clendenning shivered, rubbing his arms. The morning was chilly, although he knew it would be scorching as soon as the sun climbed higher. Virginia

70

City, what he could see of it, was coming to life, the pulse of the town quickening.

Then a horse neighed inside the stable, another ore wagon turned onto C Street, wheels creaking rustily, a door slammed to his right, and his reverie was broken.

"Good morning, preaching man," said a voice from his right.

Clendenning turned. From the voice he knew it was the woman who'd held the shotgun on him last night. She stood in the side door of a building a few yards removed from the stable. It was hardly more than a shack, a weathered gray, but an attempt had been made to pretty it up a little. Bright curtains hung in the windows, and a few flowers struggled toward the sun in a planting border alongside the house.

Kate Rogan was a good-sized woman, with red hair that reflected coppery glints from the rising sun. She had on a man's shirt and trousers, and stood barefoot on the small side porch.

At least she wasn't carrying the shotgun this morning. He started toward her.

"Sleep well, Clendenning?"

Up close, her eyes were green. He said, "Well enough. Much obliged for letting me sleep in your livery stable."

"Oh, you'll pay for that. You agreed to clean my hay barn this morning in exchange for a bed and breakfast. Speaking of breakfast, it'll soon be ready." Those green eyes took on a mocking glint. "Unless you ain't hungry?"

At the mention of food, Clendenning's belly

71

growled again, so loud he was sure she could hear it. He said gruffly, "I'm hungry, ma'am."

"Kate's the name, Clendenning. If you want to wash up, over there's a dishpan of water, and a clean towel. And a razor."

She jerked her head toward the side of the house. There was a wooden bench holding a dishpan, and a towel hung on a nail above it. Clendenning saw a triangular slice of mirror on another nail.

As Clendenning approached the bench, he was surprised to see steam rising like swamp fog from the water. He had expected cold water, but Kate must have heated a kettle for him. He took off his shirt, splashed his upper body and face with water. There was several days growth of beard on his face. He picked up the straight razor and shaved quickly, cutting himself a couple of times in the process.

The nicks had stopped bleeding by the time he'd finished washing and had dried himself. He put on his shirt and coat, slicked his hair down with water, and ran a comb through it. The comb was about the only thing he owned after the poker game with the man who called himself Darrel Quick.

The side door stood open. He knocked on the jamb and went in. The room was a small kitchen, filled with the tantalizing odors of ham and baking powder biscuits. Lord God, he was hungry!

Kate Rogan was at the wood-burning stove frying eggs. "Pour yourself a cup of coffee and sit, Clendenning." She motioned up the blackened coffee pot on the stove. "Eggs will be done in a minute."

He took a heavy mug from the table, already set for two, and poured the mug full of black coffee. strong and pungent. At the table he added cream from the pitcher and a spoonful of sugar. He drank the hot coffee in quick gulps. By the time Kate came to the table with a platter of steaming ham, a half-dozen eggs and a pan of golden biscuits, Clendenning was feeling somewhat better.

At least he felt better enough to be civil. "I want to thank you, both for the bed and the breakfast."

"Just eat, Clendenning." She gestured. "Not that your thanks ain't appreciated."

They began to eat. The coffee and the cooking odors had made him even more ravenous, and he had to force himself to eat slowly. After a few bites he said, "I find it a little strange, a woman running a livery stable in a town like Virginia City."

"Would you think it less strange if I worked in one of the cribs along D Street?"

Clendenning felt his face burn, and he looked down at his plate. "Certainly not."

"Then don't ask stupid questions!"

They ate for a few moments in silence, then Kate resumed the conversation as though there had been no interruption. "There ain't much choice for a woman in this country. She can get married to some miner. She can become a hurdy-gurdy girl, or work as a waitress in a restaurant. Or as a seamstress, except it so happens I can't sew a straight line. So that's it. Not much choice, wouldn't you say?"

"No, I guess not," he mumbled, not looking up.

"But, for your information, I inherited this hay barn. It belonged to my father, Amos Rogan. He started this hay barn before the boom hit Virginia He was a stubborn man. He starved through the lean years, endured through the death of my mother. Then, the boom hit, and he was beginning to make

73

money when he was killed. Even his death was an indication of his stubbornness. A drunken miner wanted to sleep in the stable, just like you. Pa barred him away. The miner used foul language in front of me. I told pa it didn't matter, but he started for the miner to thrash him. The man had a gun. He shot pa down. The miner was hanged two days later from a cottonwood at the edge of town. Justice is quick here, and people liked Amos Rogan. I didn't have my shotgun then, or I'd have killed that miner myself." Kate paused to draw a breath. "Anyway, there I was, without kin, with only the hay barn left to me. I could have sold it, sure, but I guess I'm as stubborn as pa. I decided to run it myself. I could have used the money from the sale to go back East, but that didn't appeal to me. I like the West, I like Virginia. Its rowdiness, its rawness, doesn't bother me. And it didn't take me long to prove to people here that I can hold my own running a man's business.

"Besides, if I *had* gone back East, I would have had to wear a dress, stays, corsets. All the damned, confining garments expected of a respectable woman. Here, I can wear men's clothes and get away with it." She looked across the table at him. "And I'm doing all right, thank you. Just so long as that shotgun ain't too far out of my reach!"

Clendenning could think of nothing to say. He avoided her gaze while he finished the food on his plate. Then Kate got up and brought the coffee pot to the table. She poured their mugs full again.

Sitting down, she said, "And you, Clendenning, what are you going to do?"

"I don't know yet."

"Going back East?"

74

He hesitated. Then something made him say, "No, I'm staying around."

"Not much money in being a preaching man out here."

"I'm not a preacher. That's my pa. I don't feel the calling, like pa did."

"Then what?"

"I'll find a job."

"There're plenty of jobs . . . in the mines. But it's a rough life, Clendenning. Especially for a man not used to hard labor."

"I'll manage. I'm not afraid of hard work." He pushed his chair back and got to his feet. "I'll clean your stable now, ma'am."

She let him get all the way to the door before saying, "Those soft hands of yours, Clendenning, will grow blisters handling a pick and shovel."

He glowered at her, his temper sparking. Then he spun on his heel and stomped out, her laughter trailing him halfway across the yard. He was so angry that for a moment he considered going right on up the street. Let her clean out her own blasted stable!

But a bargain was a bargain. He found a rake and shovel in one corner of the stable and began cleaning.

At least this wasn't something new to him. Many was the time when he and Jeremiah had had to do menial work around a farm between preaching stints.

As he worked, Clendenning thought of Kate Rogan's question about his going back home. Why had he answered as he had? There seemed to be nothing here for him; he was out of his element. Yet he knew that his answer, given out of some gut instinct, had been the right one. He was going to stay. If not in Virginia City, then somewhere in the West. He knew

75

now that he had never intended to become a preacher, and if he returned to Jeremiah, that was what he'd probably end up being, and a sorry one he would make.

There was a challenge here, and somehow, some way, he was going to meet it.

Finished cleaning the stalls, he returned the rake and shovel to the corner. He noticed that one boot was smeared with horse manure. Muttering to himself, he used a handful of straw and old rag to clean the boot.

"Get a little something on you, Clendenning?" said an amused voice behind him.

He straightened and turned. Kate leaned against a stall door, grinning at him. She was still wearing the men's clothing.

Clendenning, out of his need to strike back, said sourly, "Don't you ever wear a dress?"

"Hardly ever," she retorted. "I told you that. Wouldn't I be something in here shoveling horse droppings in a dress?"

"Ladies shouldn't go around in men's clothes."

"I've never laid claim to being a lady." Those green eyes were amused again. "Don't any females back where you come from ever wear pants?"

"None that I ever saw. It's not considered proper." He shrugged into his coat. "I'll be going now. I'm finished."

Her critical gaze swept the stable. "You did a fair job, Clendenning . . . for a preaching man."

"I told you I'm not a preacher!"

"If you find you can't make it preaching, or as a miner, I can always use a good man here."

"I doubt it'll ever come to that. Goodbye, Miss Rogan. Thanks again for everything."

As seemed to be her habit, she let him get as far as the stable door before saying, "Clendenning?"

Bracing himself for another barbed comment, he faced around and stood without speaking.

"I can tell you where you can find females wearing dresses, real purty dresses, with pink underdrawers. In the cribs, and Virginia has plenty of them!"

Once again, her laughter pursued him as he stamped off.

It was nearing noon now, and activity in Virginia City had reached a frenzied peak. Men, a few women, and some children thronged the wooden sidewalks along C Street, going in and out of emporiums and other places of business. The street itself was a surging river of ore wagons. At the cross streets buggies and smaller wagons waited patiently for an opportunity to cross C Street.

Clendenning hesitated briefly, uncertain of just where he was headed, or what he wanted to do. Then he saw the offices of a mining company across the street. Now was as good a time as any to look for a job in the mines.

His purpose firm now, he started across the street, dodging in and out between ore wagons. A few feet short of the opposite side of the street, he saw a team of twelve mules towing a wain bearing down on him. Without looking, he leaped up onto the sidewalk to avoid being run down.

In so doing, he collided with a man ambling along the walk, sending him reeling back against a building.

77

Clendenning turned, an apology forming on his lips.

He met a murderous glare from red-veined eyes. "Whyn't the goddamn hell don't yu watch where yu're going, yu goddamn pissant!"

Even at the distance separating them, Clendenning got a strong whiff of whiskey-rank breath. The man was big and burly, with a heavy black beard, a miner's broad, sloping shoulders, and hands like dangling hams.

"I'm sorry," Clendenning said tightly.

"Sorry! Yu come booming up here and knock me ass over tea kettle and say yu're sorry! Say . . ." The man's small eyes almost disappeared in folds of grimy flesh. "Yu did that a-purpose! I'll show yu . . . !"

He charged, balled hands already swinging. Clendenning ducked the man's charge easily, but one fist clubbed him a glancing blow on the shoulder. It didn't really hurt, but it was, in effect, the last straw.

All of a sudden Clendenning had had enough hard luck, disappointments, and just plain abuse to do him for a long, long time. Lord God, he'd had enough!

He loosed a bellow of pure rage and charged at the other man. Although Clendenning was slightly the taller, the miner was heavier by some twenty pounds, and was clearly experienced at mining camp brawling, while Clendenning had very little fisticuff experience. Yet his sense of outrage more than made up for the factors against him.

The two men stood toe to toe, slugging it out, blows missing more often than not. Clendenning took brutal punishment about the chest and shoulders, and one hard whack on the cheek, just missing his eye. It set his head to ringing.

He got in one glancing blow alongside the other's head and felt the skin split across his knuckles. The miner's head felt as hard as iron. But the blow did tip his antagonist slightly off-balance. Clendenning set himself and swung his other fist up from his knees, putting all his weight into it. His fist sank to the wrist in the man's belly. Air whooshed from the miner's mouth, and he gagged, half-bending over.

Clendenning stepped back a little and hit the man across the face with all his strength. He felt the other's nose collapse under his fist. Blood spurted scarlet.

The miner went staggering back. He struck the wall with a mighty thump and began to sag, his whiskery face slack with astonishment. His eyes rolled up, and he flowed down the wall like water. He ended up slumped sideways against the wall. Breathing hard, Clendenning stood waiting for him to get up, feet planted solidly, fists cocked.

But the miner was finished. Fierce, atavistic joy spurted through Clendenning, and he felt good for the first time since he had set foot in Virginia City.

Hands clapped softly behind him, and a familiar voice said. "Bravo, Clendenning! But I must say that I'm surprised, and shocked, to see a preacher's son brawling in the street."

Startled, Clendenning glanced around, expecting to see an audience. But the only person watching was Serena Foster, who stood smiling wickedly at him.

Despite her recent travails, Serena had slept well. It was the first time she had been in a real bed in months, and her sleep had been deep and restful, untroubled by dreams. The boarding house recommended by Spencer Hurd, Ma Taylor's, was clean, comfortable, and not overly expensive. Serena was to learn that it was one of the few boarding houses in Virginia City that accepted women boarders.

"Decent women," Ma Taylor had told her. "Not those strumpets that come flocking in here, nor the hurdy-gurdy girls from the saloons. Only ladies. But you look the part of a lady, and if the Judge sent you, you must indeed be one."

Ma Taylor was a large, plump woman of fifty, a widow, her husband having been killed in a mine cave-in. She had a merry disposition, unless her temper was aroused, and then she could be fierce. Serena took to her at once. After a good meal and a bath, Serena had climbed into the soft, comfortable bed and slept until the sounds of the town awoke her. She had then put on her one clean dress, eaten a hearty breakfast, and left for a stroll.

"You'll be safe enough, dear," Ma Taylor had warned her, "so long as you stay out of the crib section along D Street and don't venture into the saloons and dancehalls."

This had necessitated an explanation of what the "crib section" was. On the street outside, her cheeks still pinked by Ma Taylor's explanation, Serena was amazed and dazzled anew by the noise and the bustle of the town. Even being a stranger as she was, the excitement all about imbued her with a sense of adventure. She could make a new, and exciting, life for herself here, she knew she could! Her spirits thus buoyed, Serena momentarily forgot about the death of her parents and walked along, drinking it all in.

Soon she found herself on D Street. Remembering Ma Taylor's admonition to avoid the crib district,

Serena was about to continue along the cross street, when she noticed a line of people standing in front of a large new building. As she came closer, she could clearly see the sign on the front of the building: MAGUIRE'S OPERA HOUSE, and a large banner declaring; *Grand Opening!*

The smell of fresh-cut lumber filled the air, and the excitement of the crowd was contagious. Serena rather timidly moved closer. There were small knots of people on the walk, chatting among themselves, and children ran back and forth, getting in everyone's way. There was a festive air about the gathering.

Serena managed to push close enough to see one of the handbills which was tacked to the wall: "Maguire's Opera House is pleased to present to the public, upon the occasion of their Grand Opening, on July 2, 1863—MONEY!; or THE POOR SCHOLAR—starring Walter Leman and Julia Dean Hayne! Seating for 1,600!"

The title of the play meant nothing to Serena, nor did the names of the players, but the very idea of it all captivated her imagination. She had never seen a play, had never been inside a theater, but she had often longed to do both. It had long been a secret desire, never, of course, expressed in front of her parents. Now, in this strange new town, she was presented with her opportunity.

Eagerly she looked for a list of ticket prices, but when she found it, her spirits fell. The lowest-price tickets, those in the parquette, were marked "sold out." Seats in the dress circle and orchestra were $1.50, and private boxes were $5.00 and $10.00. Back in Illinois that was a great deal of money. Serena knew that she dared not be so wasteful of the few precious dollars she had left.

Regretfully, she continued on. Reaching C Street, she was once again struck by the heavy flow of vehicles and animals along the street. Men cursed at their animals and at each other. Dust boiled up. The direction of the traffic was mostly south, and was almost frightening in its relentless, inexorable flow.

Serena walked along, peering into the dirty windows of the emporiums. The display of items for sale took her breath away. She had never seen such a wealth of goods. There were many things she needed. For just a moment she thought of the sum of money Spencer Hurd had told her was waiting in the bank, only a part of Aunt Hetty's estate—all hers just for the claiming. With that money she could buy a new wardrobe; she could even purchase a ticket for the opening of Maguire's Opera House!

With a sharp shake of her head, Serena forced all such sinful thoughts out of her mind. Seeing a sudden break in the C Street traffic, she darted across to the other side.

She hadn't proceeded a half block before she came upon two men brawling, having at each other like savages. She supposed it was a common sight here; certainly the fight was attracting little attention. The stream of foot traffic was simply detouring around the two combatants.

Serena started to do the same, when she recognized one of the men, and stopped in her tracks. It was Rory Clendenning!

Even as she watched, he struck his opponent a great blow, sending him back against the wall. The other man, a miner from the looks of him, slowly slid down to a sitting position, his chin falling onto his chest, He was unconscious. Clendenning stood over him, fists clenched, chest heaving.

Serena clapped her hands together and said, "Bravo, Clendenning! But I must say that I'm surprised, and shocked, to see a preacher's son brawling in the street!"

Clendenning turned slowly. His face was bloody and cut. Serena took an involuntary step toward him, her hand going out toward his face. Then she made herself stop.

"I'm Lord God tired of being made fun of, being sneered at and taken advantage of," he said harshly. "I decided it was about time I gave punishment in return."

She could only stare at him. There was something a little different about him, a pride in his bearing, an air of self-confidence. He stooped to pick up his hat from where it had fallen to the wooden sidewalk.

He nodded stiffly. "Good day, ma'am. I hope you are faring better in Virginia City than I am."

Turning, he strode away. She started to call him back, then clamped a hand over her mouth. She stared after him until he had vanished in the press of people before she went on up the street.

In the next block Serena came upon another altercation. This was of a different kind. Three men in rough clothing were herding a tall, hulking Chinese youth before them. His hands were lashed together behind his back. Serena saw that he was quite young, around her own age. Now she noticed that one of the men held a gun against the Chinaman's spine. Every time he broke step, the gun was rammed cruelly into the small of his back, sending him stumbling forward.

As Serena watched, the three men turned the Chinese youth into the doors of the Silver Dollar Saloon. As they disappeared inside, Serena stood in an agony of indecision. What were they going to do to the poor boy? She looked around for help, but this episode was being ignored in the same way as the fight had been. She even looked in the direction Clendenning had gone, thinking of asking his help, but he had long since vanished, and Serena knew she could never find him in time.

She faced the saloon doors again, debating with herself. From inside came the sound of tinny piano music and the sounds of raucous laughter. Maybe they weren't going to really harm the boy. It was really none of her business. She recalled Ma Taylor's warning about entering the saloons and started to turn away. At that moment she heard the noises of scuffling: a dull thud that sounded like a body hitting the floor, and a strange, choked cry. She *knew* it was the Chinese youth. They were hurting him!

Serena, without further thought, pushed open the doors of the Silver Dollar Saloon. Just inside, she halted, shocked by what she saw. The saloon stank of spilled liquor and the rank odor of many men. The place was packed—men at all the gaming tables and standing at the long bar. Play had stopped at the tables, and the men at the bar had faced about. All were watching, and laughing, at the tableau taking place in the center of the long room.

There, face down on the filthy floor, was the young Chinese. The man with the pistol stood over him, the weapon held at the back of his head. The other two men were balanced on his legs, holding him pinned to the floor, and dancing on his back was what Serena took to be a hurdy-gurdy girl. The girl had on a pink dress with a low-cut bodice, and was dancing wildly to the piano music, skirts flying high, exposing limbs sheathed in red-net stockings. And what was worse, on her feet she wore tiny dancing slippers with high heels. The pain must be terrible for the young man on the floor. He was opening and closing his mouth, but no sounds came forth, except strange, animal-like grunts.

Serena took a few steps into the room. She felt some of the same anger she had experienced after her parents' death. "Stop that!" she cried. "Stop it at once!"

No one paid the slightest heed.

She raised her voice to a shout. "Stop it, I say!"

The piano halted in mid-chord, the laughter died, and everyone turned to gape at her. The man with the pistol also turned, and Serena saw that it was the man she had seen just outside Spencer Hurd's office yesterday afternoon, the man with the cold black eyes.

He scowled at her. "What are you doing in here, ma'am?"

"You must stop this awful thing at once! Why are you torturing this poor man?"

"Why?" He laughed. "Because the Chink here bumped into me on the sidewalk and then refused to apologize."

"But that's no reason to treat a person in such a cruel, humiliating manner!"

"Person?" His laughter was cruel now. "He's not a person, he's a Chink. He must be taught a lesson, made an example of." He turned back, motioning with the pistol. "Start the music, piano player."

Serena sent a frantic glance around. "Somebody do something! Make him stop this!"

The man with the cold black eyes sent a glance back over his shoulder. "It's best you leave, ma'am, if you don't care to watch. No one dares to interfere in my business."

"You are in error there, suh," said a voice in a soft, Southern drawl. "I suggest you do as the lady suggests and cease torturing that poor wretch."

Everybody in the saloon, including Serena, whirled to stare in the direction of the voice.

Standing to one side of a card table, his back to the wall, was a tall, slender man of about thirty. He was dressed in black; black frock coat and trousers, a white shirt with lace-ruffled front, black string tie, and highly polished black boots. He wore a planter's hat, but even under its wide brim, Serena could see a thin but handsome face, brown eyes, and a full, sensual mouth that wore a slight, sardonic smile. His skin was pale, as though untouched by sun. His hands were delicate, with long, supple fingers, and one of those hands held a long-barreled revolver, pointed casually in the direction of the man with the cold black eyes.

"And who might you be, stranger, butting into my business?"

"Who I might be is of small importance at the moment, Mr. Stryker. I do know who *you* are, you see."

Brad Stryker started, almost imperceptibly, to turn, swinging his pistol up, and the man in black said softly, "I wouldn't advise it, suh. I can drill you through the heart before you can face about enough to draw a bead on me. If I may be forgiven a touch of immodesty, I am rather handy with Samuel Colt's product."

Stryker froze, his face flushing darkly.

The man in black gestured with the revolver. "Flossie, if you will be so kind as to step off the poor man."

The girl said huffily, "My name's not Flossie!"

"I'm sure you have many names," he said dryly, "but Flossie will do as well as any." When the dance-hall girl had stepped off the prone Chinese, the man in black said, "Now, you other two ruffians help the man up and undo his hands."

Sullenly, Stryker's cohorts obeyed, one of them cutting the bonds with a knife. When the youth was on his feet and freed, he approached Serena humbly, bowing at the waist, his eyes filled with gratitude. He opened and closed his mouth, and Serena saw with horror that he had no tongue.

"It's monstrous, what you've done!" she cried. "The poor man has no tongue, that's the reason he didn't offer an apology!"

Stryker ignored her, his baleful gaze fixed on the man in black, who was coming toward Serena, the Colt still leveled in Stryker. He said, "If you will kindly step outside, ma'am, with your friend, I will follow you."

"You'll be sorry for this, damn you!" Stryker said in a choked voice. "You'll pay with your life!"

"The name is Darrel Quick, Mr. Stryker, and I am at your service at any time."

As the man in black gave his name, it sounded familiar to Serena, but there was no time to ponder the matter. Quickly, she took the hand of the Chinese youth and led him outside. In a moment Darrel Quick came backing out of the saloon. He holstered his revolver, but kept a wary eye on the saloon door.

The Chinese youth was motioning with his hands, and Serena understood that he was trying to express his gratitude.

"It's all right," she said gently, patting his hand. "Is there some way you can tell me your name?"

He shook his head violently, and his face took on a look of terror. Abruptly, he turned and hurried off, vanishing into the crowd. Serena started after him, puzzled.

At her side Darrel Quick said amusedly, "There's an old Chinese saying, you know, to the effect that once you save the life of a person, he forever after belongs to you. I'm glad he sees you as his savior, not me."

"Why do you suppose he took off like that?"

"Poor fellow is probably frightened to death. I can't blame him after what happened in there."

Serena faced around. "I'm Serena Foster, and I want to thank you for what you did in there, Mr. Quick."

"It was a pleasure, ma'am." He smiled crookedly, then snapped his fingers. "In return, perhaps you could do me a favor." He dug into his coat pocket and took out two pieces of pasteboard. "I have two tickets to the opening of Maguire's Opera House to-morrow evening. Would you do me the honor, Miss Foster, of attending with me? They are choice seats, in the dress circle."

Serena's eyes went wide, her breath quickening. "But how did you come by those? I passed the opera house on my way, and a sign said that all tickets but the cheaper ones had been sold."

His full mouth quirked. "I won them a short time ago in a game of poker."

"You're a gambling man, Mr. Quick?"

"I am." He inclined his head. "That is my profession. Would you care to attend with me?"

Serena opened her mouth to say, "no," with her mother's words of warning echoing in her ears. One simply did not accept invitations from strange men. This man had done a kind thing, but she did not know him, and he was an admitted gambler. Then, her mother's words faded, as a sense of excitement grew in Serena.

"I would be delighted, Mr. Quick," she heard herself saying.

He leaned down, picked up her right hand, and pressed it to his lips. Serena, blushing and embarrassed, hurriedly looked around to see if they were being observed, but the passing throng seemed intent upon their own business, and no one gave them a second glance.

Darrel Quick raised his head, smiling at Serena's apparent discomfiture. "And where shall I pick you up, Miss Foster? Where are you staying?"

"Ma Taylor's boarding house, just down the street and up a few blocks."

He bowed slightly from the waist. "I shall pick you up at six o'clock tomorrow evening. Until then, Miss Foster."

Serena nodded, then echoed his last words. "Until then."

As she watched, in some astonishment, he turned and reentered the Silver Dollar Saloon. She stood nervously, for some minutes watching the door. She did hope that he didn't go and get himself shot before tomorrow night. Then, feeling as tightly wound as a

89

watch spring, she turned and continued on down the street.

As she looked into the shop windows full of merchandise, a dismaying thought made her stop short. She had absolutely nothing to wear! She couldn't possibly go tomorrow night, unless she had a new dress.

The she remembered the money Spencer Hurd had said was waiting in the bank for her. Quickly, she about-faced, and started up the street toward the lawyer's office.

Chapter Five

Serena walked in silence beside Spencer Hurd as they went along D Street. Hurd was spruced up, cigar pluming smoke behind them as they strolled along. Serena was also wearing her least-worn dress for the occasion.

When she had rushed into his office, breathlessly saying that she would accept the money Hetty had left to her, the lawyer had promised to transfer the money to a bank account in her name in the morning. In return, he had asked for one favor; Serena had to make at least a token visit to the Paradise and meet Madeline Dubois.

"You'll like Madeline, Serena. When you see her, talk to her, you must make a decision about what to do with the Paradise. Either sell it or turn it over to her, one or the other. It's not fair to her otherwise. She'll have us to supper this evening, and you'll dine sumptuously, as though you were in Paris. Madeline sets a table you wouldn't believe."

So here she was, visiting a house of harlots! How horrified her father would have been!

There was nothing particularly shocking about the outside appearance of the Paradise, and Serena would have thought they had come to the wrong place except for the sign. The sun had just gone down behind the mountain, and the house was in shadow.

As they climbed the steps, Hurd said unnecessarily, "This is it." He glanced sidelong at Serena, grinning faintly. "Feel any pride of proprietorship, Serena?"

Growing familiar with Hurd's rather strange sense of humor, Serena refused to rise to the bait. She followed the lawyer up onto the porch. Hurd, in passing, tipped the rocking chair and set it to rocking. There was a hand-lettered sign on the door: "Closed for the evening."

"You see, you have nothing to fear, Serena. We'll be the only visitors here tonight." Hurd rapped lightly on the door.

In a moment the door opened a crack, and a plump face peered out at them, slanted eyes dark as shoe buttons.

"Miss Madeline is expecting us, Chu Chin."

"Yes-s, Judge. Please to come in."

Inside, there was nothing in sight that hinted at the house's purpose. The front door opened directly into a long hall. Doorways, all closed, lined the left side, and there was a narrow stairway at the far end. On the right was a wide doorway, with a beaded glass curtain instead of a door. Through the curtain, Serena glimpsed a short bar, with bottles behind it, and several divans, upholstered in plush, red velvet.

There were two ornate wrought-iron light fixtures overhead in the hall, each holding several rows of candles.

As they followed Chu Chin down the hall, Serena watched her in fascination. She had never seen a Chinese until recently, and her meeting with the young mute had been so full of violence, she hadn't had time to study him. This was her first opportunity to view one of the women close up. Serena was amazed by the young woman's smooth, seemingly poreless, yellow-brown skin, and her heavy black hair, which was wound around her head, but it was Chu Chin's eyes which intrigued Serena the most; those dark, almond-shaped eyes, with no hollows to define them.

The Chinese woman opened a door on the left and stood back for them to enter. "Missie Madeline say help selves to dlinks. She be in soon."

"We'll do that, Chu Chin. Thank you," Hurd said.

Chu Chin closed the door behind them. The room they were in was clearly a parlor. Serena was astonished at the quiet taste of the obviously expensive furniture. Each piece could have belonged in a rich man's home. Through a high archway, she saw a dining alcove, the table already set for supper, glittering crystalware and china resting atop snow-white linen. Three-pronged candlesticks decorated each end of the table, and a beautiful crystal chandelier hung directly over the table. Serena was almost breathless with delight and awe. She had never seen anything so grand or beautiful. It was outside her experience.

Hurd crossed directly to a cellarette across the room, and opened it. "A drink, Serena? Hetty kept nothing but the best whiskey around for her special guests."

Serena hesitated. "I have never had a drink, Judge. Is there something besides whiskey?"

"Brandy, a French brandy. Goes down smooth as silk."

"I'll have that then."

Hurd poured whiskey for himself and brandy for Serena. He brought it to where she was sitting on a divan. He hoisted his glass. "Shall we drink a toast to Hetty Foster?"

"I think I'd like that."

He looked down at her with approval, smiling. "I do believe there's hope for you yet, Serena Foster. To Hetty then, may her soul rest in peace." He knocked back most of the glass of whiskey in one swallow.

Serena took a cautious sip of the brandy. It was smooth, as he said. It was only after it was down that she felt the fire in her stomach. She took another sip while Hurd went to the cellarette to refill his glass.

"Judge . . . are there many Chinese people in Virginia City?"

"Quite a number." He came back toward her. "They're needed for cheap labor. They live on what's known as the downside of the city. Live in squalor that's unbelievable, and they're treated like dirt by most of our so-called 'Christian' citizens."

"I know. I saw something today . . ." She told him about the episode in the Silver Dollar Saloon.

"That Brad Stryker." Hurd shook his head. "He's a mean coot. I'd stay out of his way, were I you. Not that I think he'd offer harm to a woman, but he has a temper like dynamite exploding. Still, he's really no different toward the Chinese than others around.

94

Dirty Chinks, they're called. You can even kill them and the law won't bother with you. I've seen it happen many times. They're not considered human."

"How can people be so cruel?"

He shrugged. "Different color, different culture. The whites don't understand their ways, and what they don't understand, they're afraid of. Look at how we've abused the black man. That's what the Civil War is about, isn't it? Although people in the South attribute it to nobler reasons . . ." His mouth took on a bitter twist. "I should know, being from Virginia. That's one of the reasons, one of many, that I got out of there. And, of course, I find it no better here . . ."

A throaty voice broke in, "You expounding again, Judge?"

Spencer Hurd turned, beginning to smile.

Serena also turned toward the woman who had just come into the room and could only stare. All she knew of whores came from pictures she'd seen once in a religious tract—painted harpies, with hard, depraved faces, wearing the clothes of wantons. Expecting a painted, bedizened hussy, Serena found herself gaping.

Dark hair framed a heart-shaped face that bore a marked resemblance to a Madonna Serena had seen in a painting once. The woman's eyes were green, innocent as a young girl's, and the faint smile on her face was demure. Her attire was in quiet good taste, nothing at all bold, no brazen display of flesh.

This woman *couldn't* be a harlot, Serena thought.

And yet Spencer Hurd was striding forward to take her hand, bowing slightly over it. "My dear Madeline, you are as radiant as ever."

"Why, thank you, Judge." Her voice was low and pleasing.

Hurd turned, still holding her hand. "Madeline, this is Hetty's niece, Serena Foster. And this, Serena, is Madeline Dubois, Hetty's good friend and mine."

Serena was at a loss what to do. Should she get up and shake the woman's hand? What was expected of her?

Madeline solved the problem. She came toward the divan, holding out her hand, and Serena got hastily to her feet to take it.

"I'm delighted to meet you, Serena. My condolences on the awful death of your parents. And I could never put into words what I thought of Hetty. She was the mother I never really had."

"I never knew her."

Madeline nodded. "I know, the Judge told me. Hetty told me that she often regretted never going back to Illinois, not even for a visit, but she could never make it."

Serena said, "I think that I'm beginning to regret that I never knew her."

"What a nice thing to say," Madeline said warmly. "Hetty would have been pleased."

Serena was again at a loss for words. This was a warm, charming person, and quite beautiful. Serena had the feeling that she was going to like her . . . but that was impossible! Madeline Dubois, no matter what a nice appearance she made, was a harlot!

An amused smile flickered about Madeline's mouth, as if she were reading Serena's mind, and she half-turned away to say, "Supper is ready to be served, if you are ready. Forgive my tardiness. I have been supervising the cooking."

Hurd rubbed his hands together. "I start salivating like a bear just out of winter hibernation when I come near your cooking, Madeline." He turned away to tip his cigar into a bowl on the cellarette.

Madeline's laughter tinkled. "You're a flatterer, Judge. Serena, shall we go in?"

The smallness of the dining area, the candles on the table, Madeline Dubois directly across the table—it was a combination that lent an air of intimacy to the scene, and acceptance of Madeline, that unsettled Serena.

As though on signal, Chu Chin arrived the moment they were seated, carrying a platter on which rested a roast duckling. On the table were numerous side dishes, consisting of fruits and vegetables, conserves and relishes.

"Would you carve the duckling for us, Judge?" Madeline asked.

"I would be delighted."

Hurd stood up, Chu Chin handed him a carving knife, and the lawyer carved the fowl with the delicacy of a surgeon, humming his usual ditty under his breath as he did so. He broke off to say, "Why the fatted bird, Madeline? It's a long while until Christmas."

"Perhaps I can find another before then." Madeline glanced across at Serena. She was all innocence. "The duckling is in honor of the occasion. Hetty's niece must be considered an honored guest, wouldn't you say, Judge?"

"Oh, yes! Yes, indeed!"

Serena felt her face flushing. She had to wonder if Madeline, perhaps the Judge as well, was making sport of her. Meanwhile, Chu Chin had brought a bottle of wine, filling the goblets at each place. To cover her confusion, Serena drank some of the wine. It certainly was an occasion for her—a visit to a house of harlots, a glass of brandy, and now a glass of wine, all in one evening. She refused to even consider what Hiram Foster would have said.

The food—there were several courses after the duckling—was marvelous, the best Serena had ever tasted, and her embarrassment receded as she ate. Also, the conversation astonished her. Nothing was said about the Paradise, very little about the town of Virginia City, except for a few amusing anecdotes from Spencer Hurd about some of his cases. Instead, Madeline directed most of the talk to the subject of Illinois, questioning Serena about the life there, and about her experiences on the wagon train. Madeline was a surprisingly articulate woman, well-spoken, and showed signs of having some education. Serena found herself relaxing and talking freely. It was the most she could remember ever talking about herself.

Throughout the meal, Serena covertly studied the woman across the table, finding it harder and harder to think of her as a harlot. On the surface at least Madeline Dubois seemed as much a lady as any woman Serena had ever known.

Then something happened that almost spoiled it all. After they were done eating, Chu Chin came with a bottle of brandy. Serena, already aglow with wine, accepted the liquor readily enough. Now Spencer Hurd took out his cigar case and offered it to Madeline. Madeline accepted a cigar and calmly drew on it while Hurd held a lighted match to the end.

Serena stared, appalled. She had never seen a woman smoke! This must be a true measure of Madeline Dubois, drinking liquor and smoking cigars. The things she would probably do to a man in the privacy of one of the rooms was unimaginable!

Madeline caught her glance and returned it serenely. She took the cigar from her mouth, smiling slightly. "I imagine you've never seen a woman smoke?"

"No-o, I never have," Serena stammered. Then she felt a rise of shame. What right did she have to judge this woman? "But Mr. Hurd told me that Aunt Hetty smoked, in private, so why shouldn't you?"

Hurd applauded softly. "Serena Foster, I'm liking you more every minute!"

"I, too," Madeline said. "I like her, too, Judge."

"And I . . ." Serena broke off abruptly. She simply could not bring herself to tell this woman that she liked her. Not yet. Things were moving too quickly for her. All of a sudden, she was taken by a huge yawn. Too late, she tried to cover her mouth with her hand.

She felt flustered. "I *am* sorry. But I'm unaccustomed to wine, and all this lovely food." She gestured. "I'm suddenly so sleepy . . ."

"And exhausted, I imagine," Madeline said. "After the ordeal you've just been through, you must be wrung out."

Hurd got to his feet. "I'll escort you back to Ma Taylor's, Serena."

As she rose, Serena said, "It was a marvelous supper, Madeline. Thank you for inviting me."

"It was my pleasure." Madeline also stood up. Her

face took on an anxious expression. "But we will have a chance to talk again soon?"

"Of course . . . oh! Judge Hurd told me that I should . . ." Serena fell silent for a moment, thinking as fast as her tired brain would function. "Madeline, I'm not going to sell the Paradise out from under you, I promise that. Yet I'm not ready to make a final decision. Why don't we do this? For the time being, run it as if it's yours. All . . ." She coughed behind her hand. "All the profits will be yours, and I will certainly not interfere. Is that satisfactory?"

Madeline managed to conceal her disappointment. From what the Judge had told her, she had been expecting Serena Foster to allow her to buy the Paradise for a nominal sum. Evidently that was too much to expect. "Whatever you say, Serena. The Paradise is yours, after all. Your aunt had a small strongbox, with her private papers. It's locked and I've never opened it. But I do have a key. When you have the time, I think you should open it. I don't know if there's anything of value in it, but I would think it likely, since Hetty treated it like a treasured possession. She even had her initials burned in the lid. You should take time to go through it soon."

"I will, Madeline, but not tonight. I'm too tired."

After they had said their good nights and Chu Chin had escorted them out the front door, Serena and Spencer Hurd walked along. Hurd was unusually quiet for him, thoughtfully smoking his cigar.

After a little Serena burst out, "Why don't you say it? You expected me to give the place to her, didn't you? Or let her have it for almost nothing?"

"It was in my mind. You made it clear, Serena, that you wanted no part of it."

100

"And I still don't. But I keep remembering what you told me Aunt Hetty said; 'Thank you, Judge, and good night.' She was afraid Madeline wasn't capable of managing the place on her own."

"But why should that concern you?" Hurd said in some astonishment.

"Because it was Aunt Hetty's wish, that's why! This way, you can keep overseeing Madeline, keep a rein on her."

Hurd looked at Serena speculatively. "You have a keen mind in that pretty head of yours, my dear." He nodded to himself. "There is the other alternative. As I told you, Brad Stryker is next in line to inherit. You can take the money, and sell Stryker the Paradise . . ."

"No!" she said vehemently. "That horrible man will get nothing of Aunt Hetty's. I will see to that. I'm sure that if she had known the kind of man he is, she wouldn't have put him in her will."

"I doubt that would have affected her decision. Hetty had a strong sense of obligation, and she felt she owed Brad's father a debt."

"Well, I owe him nothing, and I'm determined he'll get nothing that belonged to Aunt Hetty!"

"You're a woman of strong mind and spirit, Serena," Hurd said. "I admire that, and it'll stand you in good stead out here."

By the time they reached Ma Taylor's boarding house, Serena felt she could go to sleep standing up.

Hurd said, "I'll bid you good night, Serena. You come to my office in the morning at your convenience, and I'll arrange to change the bank account into your name."

101

Serena, feeling fragile and ladylike in her new pink silk gown, held her head carefully so that she would not displace the curls that Ma Taylor had so carefully arranged. It was the first time Serena had worn her hair up, and she thought it made her look very adult and sophisticated.

Another first was the full crinoline that buoyed the skirt of her gown so that it flared like the petals of a flower beneath her waist. The crinoline felt different than the petticoats she was accustomed to, and she moved with caution.

Crowds of people were standing on the walk; the women dressed in their summer best and being careful that they were seen; the men smoking cigars and eyeing the ladies.

Serena kept a firm grip on Darrel's arm, suddenly afraid that she would be swept away in this human tide and would lose both Mr. Quick and his precious tickets.

Many people were still lined up at the ticket window, fighting for the few remaining seats. Serena felt very privileged and a trifle smug at her good fortune.

Just then Serena's glance came to rest on a man dressed in a broadcloth coat and a starched white shirt standing a few feet away. He had a thick moustache and was smoking a cigar. Several men were gathered around him. Apparently the man with the cigar was regaling them with a funny story, since the men suddenly burst into laughter.

"That's Samuel Clemens," Darrel said into her ear. "I met him on the Mississippi. He was a pilot on the riverboats for a number of years. Now he's a writer, I hear, working on the ENTERPRISE here, using the name Mark Twain."

Darrel smiled down at her. "Half the town must be here," he said. "At least the respectable half."

As he spoke these words, Serena saw Madeline Dubois approaching the entrance doors. Her first instinctive feeling was to call to the woman, but then she realized how such a thing would look. Hastily, she lowered her gaze. When she looked up again, she saw that Madeline was turning away from the door, her ticket still in her hand. The woman's dusky cheeks burned bright with color, and from the way Madeline held her body, Serena could see that she was blazing with anger and humiliation.

Both Serena and Darrel watched as Madeline, head held high, walked quickly away from the opera house. Serena overheard whispers from the people around them, and she saw the sly, triumphant looks that the women gave each other behind their fans.

All at once, Serena felt angry at their smug attitudes, as well as shame at herself for not stepping up to lend Madeline support. How dare they be so righteous? Did they think Madeline would somehow dirty their precious new opera house? Wasn't she a human being, just as they were?

Darrel noticed her agitation. "Our good friends seem to have forgotten the virtue of tolerance," he said. "They also seem to have forgotten the times Madeline Dubois has helped them. I understand that several men here tonight might not be alive if Madeline hadn't nursed them through the epidemic last winter."

Serena was tempted to ask Darrel how he, having only been here a few days, knew so much about Madeline Dubois, but just then there was a forward surge of the crowd, and she could see the front doors opening. For the moment, Madeline was forgotten in the rush of excitement that warmed her. Serena and Darrel were pressed forward into the building, pausing only the moment necessary for Darrel to hand over their tickets.

Serena listened avidly to the snatches of conversation she overheard in the crowd: "It cost over thirty thousand dollars, my dear." "Just look at that chandelier, and see, he's put gas fixtures in too!" "Yes, all the latest conveniences." "Oh, look at the private boxes, aren't they elegant?"

And it was elegant, the entire theater. Serena had never seen anything to equal it. It was a fairy tale come true, and she felt just like Sleeping Beauty, now awake for the first time.

"I understand that Julia Dean Hayne played for thirty continuous nights at the Metropolitan Theatre in San Francisco." The woman next to Serena, a plump woman in an ornate silk dress, was speaking in a carrying voice to her escort, an elderly gentleman with a pink, clean-shaven face.

He nodded ponderously. "I believe that her stage heroine is the most acceptable of our time. I saw her in New York, when she was just a girl of fifteen, in *The Hunchback*. She was marvelous even then."

The woman with him looked impressed, and Serena tightened her grip on Darrel's arm. This was what cultured people talked about. They talked about the theater, plays; they talked about beautiful, interesting things; not about farms and pigs and cows, and going-to-church-on-Sunday. This was what life was all about!

Because of the huge crowd, it took a while to find their seats, but at last Serena and Darrel were seated, near the front, with an excellent view of the stage, of the four, luxurious private boxes with their privileged occupants, and the magnificent but unfinished, hand-painted curtain with its picture of a lake at sunset. One of the boxes in particular caught Serena's eye. There was a screen set up in it, hiding the occupants from view.

As Serena waited for the curtain to rise, she fidgeted impatiently. The muffled roar of more than a thousand murmuring voices made her suddenly conscious of the huge crowd she was a part of, and the idea both excited and frightened her. Then, as she was about to question Darrel about a beautifully gowned woman in one of the boxes, Serena heard a hoarse shout. Looking up, she saw a tall man in a broadcloth evening coat stand up in one of the boxes. She was close enough to easily see the large revolver he withdrew from under his coat tails; and she watched in horror as he pointed the gun at the box directly across from his and pulled the trigger.

The roar of the gun was thunderous in the enclosed space. Women screamed as the gun roared again, and yet again. Serena could hear the sound of shattering glass and glanced up in alarm to see a splendid crystal wall fixture falling in shards to the floor.

Most of the people remained in their seats, but a number of gentlemen came running in from the bar, billiard room, and roulette parlor, with an assortment of weapons, champagne bottles, and billiard cues. By this time the shooting had stopped. The man in evening coat was glaring at his gun in disgust. It was apparently empty. Across the theater, the object of the fusillade of shots was, unbelievably, unharmed.

In a surprisingly short time, everything had calmed

down, and the members of the audience were back in their seats. Serena marveled that an incident such as she had just witnessed could be smoothed over so quickly, yet she had already learned that this strange town functioned according to other rules than she was used to.

"I hope you enjoy it," Darrel said, as a sudden hush fell over the audience.

A slender, attractive woman had come onto the stage, and a round of applause rolled through the theater. The woman—Serena's playbill said that it was Mrs. Hayne—smiled and began to read a poem. She had scarcely begun when a terrible racket filled the theater. It sounded as if heavy hailstones were pounding down upon the roof and walls. Serena cried out and reached for Darrel's hand.

"Good heavens!" Serena exclaimed. "What is it?"

Darrel smiled reassuringly. "Just a lovely Washoe zepher, Serena, arriving at a most inappropriate time."

"Not hailstones?"

"No. Just stones scooped up by the wind and blown against the building. A not unusual occurrence, I understand."

For the remainder of the poem reading, the audience had to strain to hear the famous actress' voice above the hail of stones clattering against the building. By the time the tinkle of a small hand bell signaled the rising of the curtain and the stage came into view, the wind had died somewhat and the rest of the production could be enjoyed.

Li Po was a great lover of opera. For that reason, he had timed his visit to Virginia City to coincide with the opening of Maguire's Opera House. Chinese, of course, weren't allowed in the place, but Li Po had long since learned the power of money. The opera house had only four boxes, one of which belonged to Sandy Bowers, probably the richest mining magnate on the Comstock. Fortunately, Bowers and his wife were presently in Europe, and for a large sum of money, Li Po had convinced the manager to let him use the Bowers box, slipping Li Po and two of his bodyguards in a side entrance and into the box before the house filled. A screen was put up, making it difficult for anyone to see into the box, but Li Po could see out easily enough.

His coach was waiting a few blocks away on a side street. He would be leaving for San Francisco at the conclusion of the performance. He never remained in Virginia City more than a day or two. Li Po detested the town. It was raw, vulgar, and the Chinese were treated like ordure. San Francisco was still a frontier city, true, but it had at least some sophistication. The prejudice against Chinese didn't bother Li Po in San Francisco. There, he had his own empire, and he ruled it like a lord, having very little contact with Occidentals—with one notable exception.

He had not inquired in advance as to what was being performed, assuming that an opera house would naturally produce an *opera*. Consequently, he was disgusted when a woman began reciting a poem from the stage. And the play that followed was a silly, frothy nothing.

He was about to get up and quietly slip out, when his gaze came to rest on a young woman seated in the "dress circle." Her hair was the color of ripe wheat in the sun, and she was wearing a pink silk gown that exposed tender shoulders, almost luminescent in their whiteness. At that moment, as though she felt his glance on her, she turned and looked directly at the screen in front of him. Her face was exquisite, with large eyes and delicate features. Li Po felt a warmth in his loins.

Instead of leaving, he lingered, never taking his gaze from the young woman, imprinting her every feature in his mind, so he would never forget her.

Very few people, even among his own, knew of Li Po's interest in beautiful white women, especially those with pale skin. He delighted in dallying with them, brutalizing them until they were eager to bend to his will. He knew himself well enough to realize that part of his delight came from humiliating them, paying back the Occidental race for their treatment of Orientals. When he was done toying with the women, it was no problem to dispose of them, since one of his profitable sidelines was white slavery.

Li Po sat on, watching the young woman, not listening to the inane lines of the banal play being performed on the stage. Just before the final curtain fell, he gestured to the two men who had stood behind him all the while, and they slipped like shadows out of the opera house.

When the play was over, to much applause and acclaim, Darrel took Serena to a late champagne supper at a restaurant on C Street. It was Serena's first taste of champagne, and she found it delicious, although it gave her a tendency to giggle. The food was excellent, and Serena could not help but think how different things were from what she had imagined they were going to be for her here. Last night she had dined sumptuously with Spencer Hurd and Madeline Dubois. Tonight, dressed in garments so costly and exquisite they would have scandalized her parents, she had attended a glittering theater event with a charming, handsome man, and now was having champagne for the first time.

They discussed the entertainment they had seen. Darrel was a witty conversationalist. He compared what they had seen tonight with plays he had seen in other theaters and with the musicial entertainments he had seen on Mississippi showboats.

"You seem very familiar with the Mississippi," Serena said.

"I should be," he said dryly. "I was born on the Mississippi, in Louisiana, and worked on the riverboats long before I reached my majority."

"As a gambler?"

"Yes, Serena. I was a Mississippi riverboat gambler."

"Why did you leave and come out here?"

"The war, what else?" He shrugged. "It has destroyed a way of life, my way of life, at least for the duration. Most of the riverboats are now being used to carry soldiers and military supplies. There was nothing left there for me." The memory seemed to depress him. He said abruptly, "Shall we go, Serena? It is growing late."

It *was* very late when they left the restaurant, and Serena was giddy from the champagne, the excitement of the evening, and sheer happiness. In all her nineteen years she had never dreamed she would experience such a marvelous evening.

Darrel offered to find a carriage for them.

"No, let's walk," said Serena. "It's not all that far, and I'm dizzy-headed. Maybe the walk will clear my head a little."

"I'm delighted you had a good time, Serena," he said in that soft drawl.

"I had an absolutely magnificent time," she said, and squeezed his hand.

They walked along in a companionable silence for a time. The cool night air did clear Serena's head somewhat, and she remembered something. "I've been puzzling about something since I met you yesterday."

"And what might that be?"

"Your name. It seemed familiar to me."

"I don't know how it could be. I've been here less than a week."

"No, I heard it before that, and just before going to sleep last night I remembered. Rory Clendenning mentioned it to me. He stumbled upon our wagon out in the desert. He told me that a man had come upon his camp, shared his supper, then got him into a card game, and won all his money, his horse, and left him out there to die. The man's name was Darrel Quick!"

"But he didn't die, did he?" Darrel said quietly.

"No, but that's no fault of yours! Don't you feel any shame at all, a professional gambler doing that to a preacher's son?"

"He said nothing to me about being a preacher's son."

"Would it have made any difference if he had?"

"Touché." He laughed softly. "No, it would have made no difference, Serena. As I told you at supper, I

110

have known nothing but gambling since the age of sixteen. I suppose when I die and confront St. Peter at the Pearly Gates and he shows some hesitation about admitting me, I'll offer to roll the dice to decide the fate of my soul."

In spite of herself, Serena had to laugh. "But don't you feel any shame at all? That was the first time Clendenning had ever played cards, and you took him for everything."

"I didn't *take* him for anything," Darrel said sharply. "I do not cheat, never have. I've never found it necessary." Then he laughed again. "So he was a pilgrim and I plucked him. I'd not hesitate to do it again. Look at it this way, Serena . . . consider that he simply learned a lesson, perhaps an expensive one, but a lesson that could be of value to him in the future. Out here, you grow up fast, or you don't survive long."

"I never thought of it that way," she said thoughtfully.

"What is this Rory Clendenning to you, anyway?"

"Nothing, absolutely nothing at all," she said instantly.

"Then why in heaven's name are we wasting all this time talking about him?"

He took her hand and turned her to face him. She could feel his breath warm on her cheek. There was an attraction, a strong magnetism, about this man that both stirred and disturbed her. She sensed that he was about to kiss her.

She stepped back, saying brightly, "Here's the boarding house. I want to thank you for a lovely evening, Darrel. I had a grand time."

He frowned slightly. Then, after a moment, his

111

mouth took on a teasing smile. "You're more than welcome, Miss Foster. And this is the end of it?"

"Isn't it?" she said in pretended innocence.

"It's customary for the lady to give the gentleman a kiss at the end of a grand evening."

"Even on such a short acquaintance?" To her amazement, Serena realized that she was flirting.

"Life moves at a swifter pace out here, Serena," he said gravely.

She stepped close, but not close enough for her body to come into contact with his, and kissed him on the lips. Before he could put his arms around her, she stepped back.

"There! The lady's obligation is fulfilled," she said, laughing. "Good night, Darrel Quick."

She started toward the porch, pausing as he said, "Serena, wait!" There was no anger in his voice. "May I have the pleasure of your company at supper tomorrow night?"

"You may, sir. Now I must go in."

She went quickly up the walk and onto the porch. She had to admit to herself that even that brief a kiss had stirred her deeply. Her thoughts went back to that night on the desert with Rory Clendenning, and guiltily she felt the glow of heat in her lower body.

It was long after midnight, and she let herself in quietly, so as not to wake anyone. Ma Taylor always left a bracket lamp burning at the far end of the hallway, by the stairway going up. To Serena's dismay, the lamp was out, and the hall was black as the inside of a cave, once the outside door was closed. She didn't have a match with which to light it. She thought of arousing Ma Taylor, but the woman was no longer young and needed her rest.

112

Serena's room was on the second floor. She felt her way along the wall toward the stairs. Halfway there, she heard a faint sound and felt a stir of air as though someone was moving toward her. She froze.

"Who is it? Is someone there?"

Before she had time to be truly alarmed, a powerful arm was around her waist and a hand clamped over her mouth. She was picked up as easily as a baby and carried struggling and kicking toward the back door. Now the thumb and forefinger of the hand over her mouth closed over her nostrils as well.

Serena fought for breath. Dots of light danced before her eyes, and her lungs were on fire. Dimly she heard the back door being opened and closed, and felt the cooler outside air on her face. She struggled harder still to get a breath of it. The struggle fast weakened her, and finally she slumped in the grip of the man carrying her, unconscious.

When she regained consciousness, it was to an awareness of strange surroundings and the strong odor of incense. Her eyes fluttered open. She was in a small, windowless room. In one corner was a small, sandalwood table on which burned two oil lamps and an incense burner. She was lying on a hard pallet, on the floor, not on a bed.

Without moving, fearful that she wasn't alone, Serena let her gaze roam around the room. It was strange, unlike anything she had ever seen. The walls were covered with silken hangings, embroidered with strange figures. One in particular caught her eye; the figure was an animal such as she had never seen—a combination of a dog with a demon's head. Along the

113

edges of the hangings were vertical rows of characters that she dimly recognized as Chinese writing . . .

Suddenly it crashed in on her growing awareness that she was not only completely naked, but bound as well. Her hands were tied tightly behind her, and her feet . . .

She raised her head with difficulty. At the foot of the pallet were two posts set into the floor several feet apart. Her ankles were bound to the posts, leaving her most intimate parts exposed to the gaze of anyone who might come into the room.

In her panic Serena uttered a cry and struggled to rise. She finally managed a sitting position, but with her hands bound cruelly behind her, there was no way she could reach the post and untie her ankles.

To one side, she saw a pile of clothing. Her new, beautiful outfit, torn from her body, completely ruined!

Then the room's one door crashed open, and a frightening figure stood in the doorway. It was a man dressed in rough clothing, but the most terrifying thing to Serena was the mask on his face. It was a gold demon mask, and it completely covered his face. Even his eyes were hidden from her behind narrow slits in the mask. In his right hand he carried a short, thonged whip. He was caressing the palm of his left hand lovingly with the thongs . . .

Serena gasped. The mask! It was the same mask the leader of the gang who had murdered her parents had been wearing! Could this possibly be the same man?

He took two steps toward her, and Serena cowered back, a scream bursting from her throat, which was tight with fear. In short, quick steps, he reached the pallet and slashed her across the breasts with the whip. It stung like streaks of fire. Glancing down, Serena saw blood welling up from the lash marks. Again, she screamed, and again he struck her, this time across the belly. Again and again, he flailed at her with the thonged whip, until she was almost fainting from the pain. All the while Serena could hear her own voice screaming hoarsely. Surely someone must hear!

Through a haze of pain, she saw the man unbuttoning his trousers. He unsheathed himself, his manhood erect and thrusting. Holding his organ like a weapon, and without removing a stitch of clothing, he came down on his knees between her spread thighs.

Serena reared up and tried to butt him with her head. Almost casually, he hit her across the face with the back of his hand, knocking her flat again. He pinioned her on the pallet with both hands gripping her shoulders, and Serena felt herself being penetrated.

He drove into her brutally, but Serena was in so much agony already, she scarcely noticed. The most frightening aspect of it, aside from the demon mask, was that he had not spoken a single word since entering the room; he had not uttered a sound. Except for her screams, it had all been conducted in complete silence.

Now, for the first time, her attacker did make a sound, as he grunted out his lust.

Past the point of fear, as he started to get up, she said, "You're a pig, whoever you are! You sound like a pig, you act like a pig, and you killed my mother and father!"

The whip slashed her across the thighs. The pain was excruciating. Mercifully, Serena fainted.

When she awoke, she was alone in the room, but still in the same position. Her body was a mass of pain, and blood had soaked into the pallet from the many cuts on her flesh. Her throat was sore and hoarse, and her mouth was dry. She realized that some time had passed, but she had no way of judging how much.

Then, to her horror, the door opened, framing the man in the mask. He strode toward the pallet, the thonged whip swishing, swishing, against his palm. Reaching the pallet, he trailed the rawhide thongs between her thighs. With his other hand, he began unbuttoning his trousers . . .

Chapter Six

Serena lay as the masked man had left her, shamed, humiliated, wounded and bruised in body and soul. And she lay in numb dread, expecting him to return any moment. When he did not, she allowed herself to relax a little. Perhaps he had gone for good, but even if he had, her circumstances were still bad enough so that she could hardly bear to think about them. What if no one came? Would she lie here and die of starvation and thirst? And almost worse, what if someone *did* come, and saw her like this? She turned her head frantically from side to side. Oh, God! How could this be happening?

She felt soiled, and she hurt in a hundred places. Without a window, she had no way of knowing if it was night or day. It seemed she had been here forever.

Nonetheless, she must have dozed off, for she awoke with her heart pounding, startled at the sounds of commotion in some part of the house. Then there was the noise of splintering furniture, followed by a howl of pain.

The howling shut off abruptly, and utter silence followed. Serena held her breath, listening. She heard a slithering sound outside the bedroom door. It began to open, not with a crash this time, but slowly, inch by inch.

Then it stood wide, and a figure again loomed in the doorway. But not the man in the mask, thank God! This was a much larger man, and he was Chinese, and he . . .

A choked cry escaped her as she recognized the voiceless Chinese youth she had helped rescue from humiliating treatment in the Silver Dollar Saloon. Face averted from her nakedness, he approached the pallet. He looked around, then stepped to the wall, ripped away one of the tapestries, and gently placed it over her. He untied her ankles from the posts, then her hands. As the blood began to circulate again, Serena's feet and hands pained her, but the pain was so much less then what she had recently suffered that she made no outcry.

He wrapped her in the tapestry and carried her out of the small room into another, larger room, which was beautifully furnished and decorated. It was illuminated by subdued light coming from shaded Chinese lanterns. Serena's gaze was drawn to a still figure in black lying in the middle of the floor, where a sandalwood table had been turned over and splintered. The neck of the man on the floor lolled at an odd angle.

The Chinese youth carried her outside, then paused, gazing back at the building, seemingly trying to reach some sort of a decision. He made a low sound in his throat, then placed Serena on the ground. Standing up, he made fluttering motions with his hands, and she understood that he would be back. He reentered the building and came back a few minutes later dragging the man she'd seen on the floor inside. It was clear to Serena that the man was dead. To her surprise, her rescuer went back inside the house once more.

He was gone longer this time, and when he did come back, he didn't pick her up at once, but stood staring at the house. Suddenly, there was an explosion of flame from inside the house, and Serena realized that he had set it on fire.

She looked at him and saw that he was laughing without a sound, clapping his hands together softly. Now, he turned, scooped her up in his arms, and began to run away from the burning house, carrying her effortlessly.

Serena glanced back and saw that the house was burning fiercely now, the flames hot and bright against the black night sky.

From Brad Stryker's hotel room, he could see down onto the flats. Although it was very late, not too long before dawn, he sat at the window, staring in that direction. He could almost imagine that he could pick out Li Po's house among the others.

He was troubled, wondering if he had made a mistake in not killing Serena Foster tonight, instead of waiting until the next day. But he had so enjoyed having her that he couldn't resist the prospect of taking her at least one more time.

Stryker thought that he had hit upon the perfect scheme for ridding himself of Serena, with no suspicion attached to him. She would be found dead in Li Po's house, strangled, the marks of the whippings on her body. Since Li Po had left Virginia City this night, everyone would figure that Li Po, or one of his *boo how doy*, had committed the crime and then fled back to San Francisco. It was common knowledge that Li Po was involved in white slavery. If Li Po was ever caught and convicted for the murder, well and good. Stryker figured that he could do without Li Po's business now. His freight line was doing well, and with Serena Foster dead, he stood a better then even chance of becoming the wealthiest man on the Comstock.

There had been no trouble using Li Po's house tonight. Li Po had let him use the house before, and the guard knew this. All he'd had to do was grease the man's palm, and it had gone easy as pie. The Chink would have to die, of course, but what was another Chink more or less? Nobody would give him any thought. Almost every night a Chink was found down below with his throat slit.

Just thinking about those two times with Serena Foster tonight excited Stryker all over again. Late as it was, he was strongly tempted to return for another go-round with her . . .

He blinked suddenly, squinting. Did he just see the flicker of flames down there, or was his imagination playing tricks on him? No, there it was again! And it was near Li Po's house, certainly in the vicinity. If by some chance the Foster woman was found down there, still alive . . .

120

Then he heard the fire bell clanging, and he saw the fire wagon racing along the street below, behind the straining horses. The citizens of Virgina City were deathly afraid of fire, and were not cheap when it came to providing the best fire-fighting equipment available. With almost every building wooden and dry as tinder, a mere spark could set the whole town ablaze.

Quickly, Stryker stepped into his boots and clattered down the stairs and outside the hotel. He set off at a brisk trot in the direction of the flames, which were leaping high now. It was not far, but when he reached it, Li Po's house was little more than ashes and glowing embers. The volunteer firemen could do nothing but watch it, careful to keep it from spreading.

Stryker saw the Chink guard on the ground. He walked over and gazed down at him. He was dead, his neck broken. But where was Serena Foster? Casually, Stryker inquired of one of the firemen if anyone had been rescued from the house, and received a negative answer.

Had she burned up in the house? Stryker wasn't afraid of her being able to identify him if she was still alive, but if she had been burned to a crisp, it would be the ideal solution to his problem.

He lingered with the firemen until dawn, until the ashes had cooled enough for them to poke around. They discovered no body.

Stryker quietly slipped away, a sorely puzzled man. What had happened to the damned woman?

The Chinese youth carried Serena to a small, one-room shack farther down the slope. Inside, on a small box, a lamp burned, revealing the sparse furnishings. There was a small brazier on which a pot of tea simmered, two pallets spread on the dirt floor, and another, large box in the corner.

A tiny, incredibly delicate Chinese woman rose from one pallet and came toward them. Hands tucked into the sleeves of her jacket, she bowed, then motioned for the youth to put Serena down on the pallet. The youth made signs with his hands. The woman watched intently, then nodded, motioning again. The youth went back outside.

The Chinese woman kneeled beside Serena and gently drew the tapestry from her body. She sucked in her breath and made a hissing sound at the sight of the bloody welts.

Serena said, "Who are you?"

"Name Tang P'ing."

Serena looked up into the pale, smooth-skinned face above her. The woman appeared to be not much older than Serena herself, and she was very lovely in an exotic way. Was she the youth's sister, or perhaps his wife?

"I'm Serena Foster. Where did the young man go? I want to thank him. He saved my life."

"You save *him*. He watched you since."

"Who is he?"

"My son."

Serena stared at the woman in astonishment. "Your son?"

"Yes. Son. Name Tang Teh." The woman's black eyes showed a flicker of amusement. "Call him Shu-toe. In Chinese, mean stone."

"You mean, because he can't speak?"

"Yes-s."

Tang P'ing got to her feet, went to the corner of the shack, and opened the large box. She came back with a washcloth, a pan of water, and two small jars.

She began to wash the blood from the lash marks. Serena winced, and Tang P'ing said, "Sorry. Must wash."

"I know, it's all right. Your son . . . how did he lose his tongue?"

"Li Po, evil man! Have Tang Teh tongue tore out."

Serena shuddered. "How awful! Who is this Li Po?"

"Man own house Shu-toe found you in. Shu-toe hate Li Po."

"You mean this Li Po was the man in the mask?"

Tang P'ing shook her head. "No. Li Po leave early tonight."

"Then who was the man who . . . the man who beat me? Do you know?" she asked urgently.

"Not know man. Shu-toe not know. Man bad, do this to you."

"How did your son know I was there?"

"Heard you scream. No other man dare go to Li Po house."

Serena lay back, silent for a little. Now Tang P'ing was gently rubbing some kind of ointment on the wounds. It stung briefly, but the pain was almost immediately eased.

Serena asked, "Why did your son do this for me?"

"You save him from shame in saloon," the woman said simply. "He always watch after you, rest of life."

Serena stared, wanting to laugh, but afraid of offending the woman. "You can't be serious!"

123

"Is Chinese way."

Serena remembered what Darrel had told her about saving the life of a Chinese. At the time she thought he had been joking, but apparently it was true! It could become awkward, embarrassing, yet at the same time she was deeply touched and grateful.

Tang P'ing was finished now. She tucked a worn blanket around Serena and said, "Serve tea now?"

"Yes, thank you."

The woman called through the door in Chinese, and in a moment Shu-toe came in. He looked at Serena shyly.

She said, "Does he understand English?"

"Shu-toe know English language. Can understand."

"Shu-toe, thank you for what you did. I will be eternally grateful." Her voice grew hard. "If you ever learn the identity of the man in the mask, tell me! He killed my parents! I will see him suffer for their death, and," she paused and swallowed, "the unspeakable things he did to me!"

Shu-toe placed a hand over his heart, looked at her with soulful eyes, then wrung his hands together. He was expressing sorrow, sorrow for her, Serena realized, and was greatly pleased with herself for understanding him.

His mother brought three tiny cups and poured the tea, then offered Serena a plate of cakes. The tea was steaming hot and had an exotic, spicy flavor that Serena had never tasted before. The cakes were delicious.

After the cakes and tea, Serena became drowsy. The ointment, or whatever Tang P'ing had used, had completely stopped the pain. Her eyes closed, then flew open again. "Tang P'ing, would I be imposing on you if I stayed with you, stayed here, for a few days? At the moment, I must confess that I'm frightened and confused. I don't know what awaits me out there. I will pay you, I have money, not with me, of course."

"You stay, Selena . . . Se-rena. Stay. But no pay." The woman shook her head. "This humble house honored you stay."

Shu-toe was smiling, bobbing his head in agreement.

With a sigh, Serena lay her head back and was soon asleep. It was a troubled sleep, filled with nightmares of masked men firing guns at her, whipping her, and always, in the background, that horrible, leering mask. She awoke twice, screaming, and each time Tang P'ing was at her side almost at once, soothing her, murmuring to her.

Finally, Serena slept dreamlessly. When she awoke, it was daylight. Raising her head, she saw Tang P'ing stirring something in a pan on the brazier.

The movement caused Serena pain, and she cried out. She seemed to be a mass of soreness from head to foot.

At the sound of her outcry, Tang P'ing came hurrying. "You hurt, Se-rena?"

Serena managed a smile. "No, I'm fine, Tang P'ing. Just sore all over." She looked around. "Where's Shu-toe?"

"Shu-toe work job. Wash dishes." Tang P'ing averted her gaze, as though in shame, and scurried back to the brazier.

Serena was wondering how Shu-toe could work at a job all day and keep watch on her at night. Of course, he didn't watch her all the time, or he probably would have stepped in and saved her when she was taken from the boarding house.

She said, "How long has Shu-toe been . . . like he is?"

"Two years. Not long after we came from own country."

"It's a pity. Why did this Li Po do such a terrible thing to him?"

"Li Po evil man. Shu-toe tell this to own people. Li Po do thing to silence him."

Serena said nothing for a moment. What *could* she say? She changed the subject. "For someone who has only been here two years, Tang P'ing, you speak good English."

Tang P'ing glanced around. "Have to learn to speak for two." When she smiled, a tiny dimple appeared in her left cheek. "Shu-toe not speak English, so Tang P'ing have to learn."

"Well, I think it's admirable."

Tang P'ing was bringing a bowl of rice toward her. "Have only rice to eat. You know chopsticks, Serena?"

"Chopsticks?" Serena frowned, staring at the two thin sticks. "No . . .oh, you mean to eat with. I've never even seen one." She could not imagine how one might use them to bring food to the mouth.

"Must learn."

Tang P'ing gave her the bowl of rice and a pair of the chopsticks. As Serena clumsily tried to use them, Tang P'ing attempted to instruct her. It was difficult for Serena, and exasperating when she saw how expertly the Chinese woman used them, but soon, they were laughing together about it, and in the end Serena was able to handle the chopsticks well enough to get the rice into her stomach.

After their breakfast, Tang P'ing inspected the lash marks again and applied fresh ointment. "Heal good. Well soon."

As the woman busied herself tidying up the small room, Serena lay deep in thought, wondering about what to do. She couldn't hide here forever. For one thing, it made things difficult for Shu-toe and Tang P'ing. Just an extra bowl of rice must be a strain on their meager food budget. That, of course, she could, and would, reimburse them for. But she knew that Shu-toe had slept outside last night, so as not to impose his male presence in the shack.

Beyond all that, she simply couldn't hide away forever. Now that the first shock and fear had worn off, Serena was growing angry. Why should she cower here like a frightened mouse, while the killer of her parents and the violator of her body walked about somewhere in Virginia City? The next time she would be prepared for him.

By the third day she had healed well enough and could move around freely without too much pain, wearing an old robe of Tang P'ing's. The garment was much too small for her, and they both laughed about it. She had discovered that the Chinese woman had a marvelous sense of humor. After listening to all the hardships she and her son had suffered, both in China and here in America, Serena marveled that the woman had any laughter left in her.

That evening, after they had eaten their meal, Serena made up her mind. "Shu-toe looked at her intently. "Tomorrow, I want you to do something for me. You remember the man who helped us in the saloon, the man in black?" He bobbed his head. "His name is Darrel Quick. Tomorrow, I want you to seek him out and tell him . . ." She broke off, remembering. "I'll write you a note to give him."

Tang P'ing brought a scrap of paper, a bamboo pen, and ink.

Serena wrote her note:

"Dear Mr. Quick:
The bearer of this note is called Shu-toe. He will lead you to me. I am in great trouble, and need your help. Be discreet. Shu-toe and his mother might suffer great harm if it's learned they've been hiding me. I will tell you what happened when I see you. I need clothes, a complete outfit. Will you pick them up for me at Ma Taylor's? Show her this note, and let her make the selection. Caution her not to breathe a word to anyone.

Sincerely, Serena Foster."

She folded the note and gave it to Shu-toe.

Darrel Quick and Shu-toe slipped into the shack not long after dark the next evening. Darrel was carrying a bundle of clothing. He went to Serena at once, taking both her hands in his.

"My God, girl, what happened to you? When I found you hadn't slept in your bed, and Ma Taylor knew nothing of your whereabouts, I looked everywhere for you. It was as though you'd disappeared off the face of the earth!"

128

"I almost did." She hesitated. "I might as well tell you now and get it over with."

Darrel listened intently until he had heard it all.

"That's almost beyond belief, Serena. Damn this man!" He stroked the hand he held. "You poor girl! To go through all that. You say he's the man who killed your folks?"

"I think so. At least he was wearing the same mask."

"But why? And why do those things to you?"

"I have no idea," she said.

"No hint at all as to his identity?"

"Not the slightest, Darrel."

Darrel looked at the two Chinese. "And they know nothing, except that the house belonged to this Li Po?"

"That's all they know, Darrel. Shu-toe rescued me. I'm sure the man in the mask intended to kill me, even though he didn't speak a single word."

Darrel clasped Shu-toe's hand. He said sincerely, "My gratitude, Shu-toe. And to your lovely mother . . ." He bowed in Tang P'ing's direction. Both mother and son were obviously embarrassed to be so singled out. Darrel reached into his pocket. "I'd like to reimburse you for . . ."

"No, Darrel!" Serena interrupted quickly. "They would only be offended. They consider it an honor, my sharing their house." She smiled at them. "As I too consider it an honor, and I will be forever grateful. And now, Darrel, if you would step outside for a minute or two, I will get dressed."

Darrel nodded, motioning to Shu-toe, and the two men went outside.

129

With Tang P'ing assistance, Serena got dressed. There was still some soreness, but she was pretty well healed. Dressed, Serena turned to Tang P'ing and impulsively embraced her. "You are a dear, dear person, Tang P'ing, and I will be back to see you."

Brushing a tear from her eye, Serena went outside, and took Darrel's arm. "Would you escort me to my lodgings, sir?"

"Well, we are perky, aren't we?" Smiling, he bowed slightly. "It shall be my pleasure, ma'am."

Looking back, Serena said, "Goodbye, Shu-toe."

With a grave face, Shu-toe motioned with his hands, expressing his sorrow at her leavetaking. Serena wondered if he now felt his obligation to her was discharged. Or would he continue to watch over her? Although Serena knew that would be expecting a great deal, she took comfort from the possibility that he might continue to keep her under surveillance.

They were nearing Ma Taylor's now, and Serena's step slowed. She could not help but think what had happened the last time she had entered that house.

Darrel glanced down at her. "What is it, Serena?"

She hesitated. "Darrel, I don't want to go in there. Not tonight. I'm sure it's safe enough, but I can't help remembering . . . tomorrow, in the daylight, I'm sure I can face it, but not tonight!"

"But there is nowhere else for you to stay. The town is bursting at the seams."

She looked up at him. "Couldn't I stay with you, just for tonight? I could sleep on the floor, on a blanket. I'm used to camping out."

Darrel smiled, and shook his head. "Serena, Serena, what an innocent you are."

130

Serena turned her head away. "Don't say that! You know I'm not. Not any more!"

Her words were a cry, and Darrel pulled her head to his chest, holding her close. "Serena, don't castigate yourself. This thing that happened to you has nothing to do with the real you. It was forced upon you, from the outside. The real you is as innocent as you ever were. It's what happens to the mind that matters, not the body."

"Then I can stay with you?"

Gripping her shoulders in his hands, he held her away from him and looked deeply into her eyes. "Serena, I am going to speak plainly to you. The fact of the matter is you are a beautiful and very desirable woman, and well . . . let's just say that I have a feeling for you. If you were to share my room, there is absolutely no way I could promise you that I would not try to make love to you. I am your friend, Serena, but I am also a man, not a saint."

For a long moment, Serena held his gaze, trying to understand what he was saying. Her request to spend the night in his room had been an instinctive one. She had been hurt and shamed, and she was frightened. With Darrel she felt safe, cherished, and protected. She had only wanted to shelter herself in that protection a little longer. That was all she wanted. Wasn't it?

Suddenly, she was aware of the strong male magnetism flowing from him, and she knew that she wanted to be near him. To have him hold her, to comfort her, to have him . . .

Memory of the night with Clendenning flashed quickly in and out of her mind. Was *that* what she wanted? Serena tried to tell herself no, yet her own honesty compelled her to examine the question again, trying to be candid with herself. Yes, it *was* what she wanted. Something good, a loving experience to wash away the horror and degradation of her violation. Somehow Serena knew that she must reaffirm the idea of the beauty of love's physical expression, or possibly lose forever the capacity to give herself wholly to any man.

Still looking into his eyes, she said, "It's all right, Darrel. I don't want you to be a saint."

He stared at her wonderingly. "Are you sure? Do you know what you're saying?"

She nodded. "I need . . . I need to forget the other. I . . ."

He hugged her quickly, then released her. "Sh-h, Serena. It's all right, I understand."

When they reached Darrel's hotel, he didn't take her in through the main entrance, but led her around to the side of the building, to a small door under a dusty lantern. Darrel said, "This hotel has a gentleman's entrance. We can go upstairs without being seen."

They reached Darrel's room without incident, and he unlocked the door. The interior of the room was surprisingly opulent and well-furnished. It was clear that Darrel Quick was a man of some means. Serena looked around self-consciously. "I didn't realize that hotels here had such splendid accommodations."

Darrel turned up the lamp. "This is one of the more expensive hotels. Most of the men staying here are wealthy men; mining magnates; businessmen from San Francisco; and a lucky gambler or two." He smiled, and Serena realized that he was trying to put her at ease. "Yes, the place is full of 'Washoe widowers,' men who come here to do business and leave their families down below."

"Down below?"

"Yes, in San Francisco. But if you're thinking of trying to throw me over for one of these rich gentlemen, I had better warn you that it is very hard to tell them from the common herd. They all dress in the same rough clothing, and it's difficult to tell the mine owner from the miner!"

Serena answered his smile, and tried to match his banter. "I shouldn't think of it, sir. After all, a wealthy mine owner can hardly compete with a knight in shining armor, who has just rescued a lady in distress."

Darrel looked at her intently, sensing her nervousness. "Would you care for a brandy, Serena?"

"That would be nice, thank you."

Serena accepted the brandy and drank quickly, welcoming the warmth and immediate easing of tension.

Darrel removed his frock coat and hung it up. He draped his gunbelt over a chair within easy reach of the bed, then removed the string tie. He unbuttoned the buttons of his ruffled shirt and took a good swallow of the brandy.

Finally, he came toward her, his brown eyes glowing. "Serena . . ." He stroked her cheek with the back of his hand. "Don't be afraid. It's all over now."

"I'm still frightened." She shivered.

"You had reason to be."

"And how do I know that it won't happen again? That man, whoever he is, is still out there."

"We'll see that it doesn't!" His face was grim. "For

one thing, I'll take you to a gunsmith in the morning, and you can arm yourself."

"I know nothing of guns, Darrel. I've never fired one in my life."

"Then it's time you learned. Don't worry." He grinned. "It'll be nothing like the one I carry on my hip. They make derringers for women to carry on their person; in a purse is the best place. They're only effective at short range, but that's all you'll need. I'll show you how to handle it. I'm familiar with them," he said wryly. "A sleeve derringer is a handy weapon for a gambling man to carry."

Without warning, he cupped her face between his hands and kissed her full on the mouth. His lips were warm, his breath sweet with brandy.

With a sigh, Serena surrendered to his kiss. In a moment she was returning it with ardor.

Gently, he moved her away a few inches and began to undress her. His fingers seemed to have a mind of their own, and knew exactly what button, what fastener, to undo. When her breasts and stomach were exposed to his view, Darrel paused. His face turned hard and cold. "That rotten scum! Serena, what cruel treatment! If I ever find him in my sights, whoever he is, he'll not live to harm you again!"

He bent to tenderly kiss the welts. And soon, his lips were at her breasts. The touch of his tongue to her nipples sent a shudder racing through Serena. Instinctively, she tangled her fingers in his hair and forced his face closer. Sensations such as she had never experienced raced along her nerve-ends.

Before she fully realized it, she was stretched across the bed, fully exposed to his gaze. He stood back and stared down at her. His breath came quickly. "God,

134

Serena, you are a lovely woman! A marvel of God's creation!"

Serena knew, without vanity, that she possessed beauty, but no man had ever told her so, and hearing it from this worldly man made her glow with pleasure.

Darrel undressed hurriedly. His body was slender, but fully masculine, with narrow hips and broad shoulders. He had very little body hair, and his skin was smooth and unblemished. He could have been a male statue Serena had once seen pictured in a forbidden book, but for the muscles that rippled under his skin as he moved. There was another difference, of course . . .

She stared curiously, without embarrassment, at his erect manhood. She had never seen a man naked before. Naturally, she had felt Clendenning in the darkness out there in the desert, but she had not *seen* him. She had refused to look at the man in the mask . . .

When Darrel got onto the bed with her, her thoughts flew back to that brutal entry into her body a few nights ago, and she could not control her tensing, could not keep herself from cringing away.

To her surprise, he began to caress her, adroit, tender strokings with his fingers and tongue. He explored every inch of her body with the expertise of an experienced lover.

Soon, Serena's fears fled, and as the heat of her body grew, she began to return his caresses, timidly at first and then with a growing boldness.

When he finally made to enter her, it was done with gentleness. She felt no pain and no need to flinch away. As he filled her, Serena experienced a

135

feeling of closeness and a pleasure so great that she rose to meet him with a cry of joy.

Joined, they moved together, their movements rising to a frenzy, until Serena felt an explosion of passion within her like a sunburst. Her head arched back in a soundless cry of ecstasy. At the same time Darrel shuddered, moaned, and then was still.

Serena lay for a little in the aftermath of passion, at peace, nothing in her mind but the timeless moment.

She stirred, her hand coming up to stroke Darrel's damp head, which lay on her shoulder.

He murmured something, and moved to stretch out beside her. He placed an arm under her head and cradled it on his shoulder.

Serena ran the tip of her tongue along his neck. It tasted faintly of salt.

"Thank you, Darrel," she murmured. "After what happened to me, I didn't know . . . I wasn't sure . . ."

"I know, sweet," he said softly. "I know how fearful you were. But hush now. Let it all go out of your mind, and sleep. In the morning the world will seem a brighter place. And we'll make it a safer one for you. My promise on it."

Chapter Seven

When Serena and Darrel left the hotel the next morning, Serena was flushed and bemused. On awakening, with the sun just coming in the window, Darrel had made love to her again. This time it had been slow and leisurely, with none of last night's urgency; and Serena had been left content. She was amazed and preoccupied with her response to his lovemaking. Had all this feeling been inside her all along? She felt as if she had discovered a new world of the senses. The fact that it was supposedly a forbidden world only seemed to make it more exciting.

The world, and Virginia City, did indeed seem a brighter place this morning. There was no way of forgetting what had happened to her, but perhaps she was only imagining a connection between the man in the demon mask and the death of her parents. After all, there was a large Chinese settlement in the town;

137

there must be many such masks, belonging to many people. It might have been coincidence that the man who had abused her had worn such a mask. It could be possible that he had taken her by chance, as he would have taken any woman he came across, to satisfy his sadistic cravings. If this was so, he probably wouldn't bother her again, but would pick a new victim the next time his depraved feelings overcame him.

Serena pushed the hastily constructed rationalization to the back of her mind and let her thoughts return to the close, warm intimacy of the night before. Enveloped in this warmth, she felt safe and able to face whatever this new day might bring.

After they had consumed a leisurely breakfast, Darrel took her along C Street until they came to a gunsmith's shop. He ushered her inside. The shop smelled of oil and gunpowder. Rifles and shotguns hung on racks along the walls, and there was a long, glass-enclosed counter with handguns of all kinds on display.

The gunsmith, a small, stooped man, wearing a soiled apron, came through a curtained doorway from the back as the bell over the door signaled their entrance.

Darrel said, "The lady seeks a gun, suh, a derringer, one she can conceal on her person, yet one with enough fire power to defend herself, should the occasion arise."

"I have just the thing," said the gunsmith. He opened a door in the glass case and took out a small derringer. "It's the latest model on the market, a breech-loading cartridge derringer, Moore's Derringer, .38 caliber."

138

"Yes, I have heard of them. Much easier to load than the cap-and-ball." Darrel picked it up, examining it closely. "This is a fine weapon." He grinned at Serena and held it out to her. "Just right for a woman, you see. You can carry it in your muff, in your purse, even snugged in the top of your stocking, if you've a mind to."

She took it with a *moue* of distaste and examined it gingerly. She scarcely listened as Darrel and the gunsmith haggled over the price. Could she use a gun in case of need? She remembered those hours in Li Po's shack and the treatment she had undergone, and she suddenly knew that she *could* use it, should she again be attacked.

Darrel and the gunsmith had agreed on a price to their mutual satisfaction. Darrel paid for the derringer and also bought a number of cartridges.

It wasn't until they were outside that Serena thought to say, "How much did it cost, Darrel? I'll pay you back as soon as . . ."

"It's no matter, sweet. I've paid for it."

Serena stiffened. "And I will pay you back, sir! I will not be a kept woman!"

"I didn't think you were." He stared into her flashing eyes. "By God, you're touchy, and have a temper, too." He softened his tone and took her arm. "If it pleases you, Serena, you may pay me back. Now, let's stroll out of town a ways and I'll give you a few lessons. But first, get your temper under control. Never fire a gun in anger, or when in the grip of fear. It's always a mistake. The one who emerges alive in a gun battle is the one who remains cool, cold as ice. No matter what rage, or fear, you may

139

feel underneath, it must always be kept under control . . ."

Brad Stryker had been across the street and had seen Serena Foster and the gambler enter the gun shop. Somehow he wasn't surprised. He had known deep in his mind that the damned woman was still alive, and he wasn't too surprised to see Darrel Quick in her company. Evidently *he* had rescued her. How he had managed that, Stryker had no idea, but that didn't matter. Plainly neither had any inkling of his connection with the affair, or Darrel Quick would have come looking for him.

Some of Stryker's fury at Darrel Quick had cooled, yet he still intended to see the gambler dead for the humiliation Quick had caused him before his friends in the Silver Dollar. But it would be *his* way, not Quick's. Stryker had never been very handy with guns; his hands were too big and clumsy. On the other hand, he knew Quick was deadly with a gun, and to face him openly in a gunfight would be suicide. Some night, he would waylay the gambler in a dark alley and finish him off without the use of a gun. Meanwhile, he would bide his time.

Now, he waited, partially hidden in a doorway, until Quick and the woman came out of the shop. Then he waited until they were out of sight up the street.

Stryker crossed the street and went into the gun shop. The proprietor grinned in greeting. "Brad! What can I do for you? You looking for a gun?"

"No gun for me, Jenkins." Stryker leaned on the counter on his arms. "I have a question . . . the woman and the man who just left here, what did they want?"

Jenkins hesitated. Stryker reached across and seized the gunsmith's wrist, applying pressure. "Answer the question, Jenkins! Don't get me riled. You know how I am when I get my dander up."

"They were buying a gun for the woman," Jenkins said hastily. "A derringer. A pretty little piece. Small, but deadly as a rattler at close range."

"So that's the way the wind blows, eh?" Stryker released the gunsmith's wrist and stood for a moment sunk in thought, wondering how this bit of information would be of value to him. The thought that Serena Foster had bought herself a weapon to defend herself against him only amused Stryker. Then he began, dimly, to grasp an idea. It would be an implementation of a scheme he was about to put into effect anyway. He might possibly make use of this little bit of news to eliminate Serena Foster without further dirtying his hands with her.

From his pocket he took some money and dropped it onto the counter. "Buy yourself a drink or two on me, Jenkins. But in return, another favor . . ." He leaned across the counter, tapping it with a forefinger. "Remember this sale, and the exact model you sold her. This is a dangerous woman, this Serena Foster. Could be that she bought that derringer to kill someone. In case that happens, be sure your memory ain't clouded!"

Ma Taylor, when Serena came into the boarding house that afternoon, gave a heartfelt sigh of relief, and clasped Serena to her bosom. "Heavens, child,

I've been worried about you! I didn't know what in the world had happened to you! Had you been any of these other flighty girls, I would've thought you'd run off with some man."

That made it necessary for Serena to tell her the whole story, omitting the fact that she had spent the night in Darrel Quick's room. During the telling of it, Ma Taylor hustled Serena into her kitchen and sat her down with a hot cup of coffee.

The woman was profuse with sympathy. "You poor girl! What a terrible, terrible ordeal! Men!" she added darkly. "They're no good, not a darned one of them. Even my late husband, rest his soul, was a lout when the drink got the best of him."

Yesterday, Serena might have shared her opinion, but the night spent with Darrel had restored her faith in men, at least *some* men. She said, "Well, it's over and done. I doubt it'll happen again."

"And right here in my own house, too!" Ma Taylor looked outraged. "Ain't you going to the sheriff?"

"What good would it do? He might not even believe my story." That reminded Serena of her parents and Hurd's promise to inform the sheriff of their death. She got up quickly. "If you'll excuse me, I must see Spencer Hurd. And promise me . . ." She placed her hand on Ma Taylor's. "Don't breathe a word of this to anyone."

Ma Taylor gave the promise, muttering darkly under her breath as Serena left.

On the way to Spencer Hurd's office, Serena pondered on how much she should tell the lawyer. She decided that the fewer people who knew about her ordeal, her humiliation, especially *that*, the better.

She found Hurd in his office, cigar going, humming

142

to himself. He put the cigar out and greeted her warmly. Apparently he hadn't been looking for her, and therefore hadn't missed her. So she told him nothing of what had happened.

Serena said, "You told me you'd get in touch with the sheriff about my parents, and have their bodies brought back here for proper burial."

"I did, Serena." Hurd sighed. "But the damn . . . the sheriff was out of town until late yesterday, chasing some bandit across the mountain. I finally caught him. He promised to go out there with a wagon this morning. He should be back tomorrow late. I'll send word to you the moment he returns. Would it be all right to bury your folks next to Hetty in Flowery Hill Cementery?"

"I think that would be proper."

"Well, there's one thing . . ." He squirmed. "There's another cemetery, for the more proper folks. Where Hetty is buried . . . well, you know."

"You mean, she's buried along with the other . . . uh, ladies of the evening?" He nodded miserably. Serena considered for a moment, then said, "I'd still like them buried there." She smiled slightly. "This may sound fanciful, but maybe they'll get to know each other better that way."

He brightened immediately. "Not fanciful at all, my dear. You're learning tolerance, Serena, a trait that I consider a fine one to cultivate." He sobered. "Have you decided yet, Serena, about the Paradise, and Madeline?"

She was surprised. "I haven't given it much thought. Why can't it go on as I said at supper that night. Is something wrong?"

He looked away and spoke evasively, "No, no,

nothing wrong. It's just that . . . well, we'll talk about it later."

Two days later, Serena found out for herself why Spencer Hurd was being evasive.

The sheriff had brought her parents' bodies in. Due to the passage of time since their death, immediate burial was imperative, so the funeral was arranged for that afternoon. There were only a few in attendance. Besides Serena, there were Darrel Quick, Spencer Hurd, and Ma Taylor. Serena had tried to find Clendenning, but no one seem to know his whereabouts.

The minister Hurd had rounded up to perform the burial rites was about to begin when there was a commotion at the cemetery gates. Everyone turned to look.

Drawing up before the gates was a handsome new coach, the doors of which bore an unusual emblem: four aces, surmounted by a lion couchant, with the initials M.D. beneath it. The crest and the intials were embossed in gold, which reflected the sunlight in considerable grandeur. The coach was drawn by four matched horses; beautiful animals, which must have cost nearly as much as the coach.

Watching the driver climb down from his seat, Serena whispered to Hurd, "Who is *that*?"

"It's Madeline," Hurd whispered back, sighing. "I didn't want to tell you about it yesterday, but she's gone hog-wild, spending money lavishly. Just as Hetty predicted she might."

"What's the crest on the door?"

"God only knows, I don't. The initials . . . well,

144

they're hers, of course. Already they're making jokes about that, saying that M.D. stands for doctor, but that the remedies she provides are not anything like that of a regular doctor. I'm sorry to have you see this, Serena, especially today."

Even under the sad circumstances, Serena was more amused than anything, and a little touched that Madeline had seen fit to attend the burial of her parents. Even when the driver helped from the coach a woman dressed all in black, even to a black veil draped over her face, Serena's amusement did not abate.

Hurd muttered, "I thought Madeline had more taste than that, driving up here in that flashy coach!"

"Oh, come on, Judge!" Serena whispered. "What does taste have to do with it? I feel honored that Madeline saw fit to come. Looking around, I don't see all that many mourners. One more is one more."

"But it's *your* money she's spending!"

"Now there you're wrong!" she said sharply. Realizing that her voice had risen, she glanced around, and lowered it. "Nothing the Paradise earns belongs to me. Let Madeline use the money as she wishes. I have no objection. Now hush, the services are about to begin."

Madeline had taken up a position by the graveside, without acknowledging the presence of anyone else. Serena noticed that Ma Taylor was glaring fiercely at Madeline. Hurd motioned to the preacher, and that individual began the services.

As the preacher droned on, Serena realized that it had been a mistake. Her parents should have been left out there. Too much time had passed, too many things had happened. What was happening here didn't seem real; it seemed in the past.

She suffered through to the end. Then, as the preacher finished and stepped back, Serena hurriedly placed the wreath of flowers she had brought along at the head of the graves and turned away. She had no desire to watch them put into the ground.

She said to Darrel and Spencer Hurd, who were standing close together. "I'll be ready to leave as soon as I have a word with Madeline."

Darrel had rented a buckboard, to accommodate the four of them.

Serena walked over to Madeline. "I'm delighted that you could come, Madeline. It was a thoughtful gesture. Thank you."

"Hetty would have wanted it," Madeline said. She took Serena's hand in her black-gloved ones. "My sympathy, Serena, for your loss." She pressed the hand between hers.

"Thank you." Suddenly, for the first time, Serena's eyes misted with tears. She turned her face aside, murmuring, "I have to go now."

Darrel, Ma Taylor, and the lawyer were waiting at the buckboard. Darrel helped her up into the buckboard, then got in beside her and flicked the reins. The buckboard started back toward town.

In the back seat, Ma Taylor sniffed. "The nerve of that hussy! She should be run out of town!"

Serena hid a smile behind her hand. She said, "Judge, did the sheriff find anything out there, any evidence pointing to the killers?"

"Not a thing, Serena. I'm sorry. But I warned you to expect nothing. Those men will likely never be found."

Darrel gave her a questioning glance. Serena had told Darrel that she had not mentioned the events of the past few days to Spencer Hurd, and he had agreed with her that it would probably be of little use to tell either the Judge *or* the sheriff.

On the short ride back to the boarding house, Serena's thoughts were melancholy. But at least today had ended a period of her life. It would never be the same again. Now was the time to start looking toward the future. What was she going to do with her life?

For as long as she could remember, Serena had never known idleness. Work on the farm had been hard, and it had been equally hard on the long trek west. Accustomed as she was to being kept busy, what would she do now? She had money enough so that she wouldn't have to worry for some time to come. Yet, a part of that money should be invested in some endeavor so she could earn a living. Serena decided to discuss it with Spencer Hurd. Perhaps he could advise her what kind of shop, or business, she should venture into. But tomorrow, or the day after, or the day after that, would be soon enough. For a time at least, she was determined to enjoy herself . . .

Her thoughts were interrupted as the buckboard pulled up before the boarding house. As Hurd helped Ma Taylor down, Darrel leaned over to say in a low voice, "Will you have supper with me tonight, Serena?"

She smiled at him. "That would be nice."

He nodded. "I'll pick you up around seven."

Madeline Dubois had had divided feelings about driving up to the cementery in the new coach, not knowing how Serena Foster would take to it. At first she had thought of going in a plain buggy, but at the last moment she had changed her mind and used the new coach. If Serena didn't already know about it, now was as good a time as any.

Madeline's intentions in attending the services were of the best; she felt that she owed it to Hetty to attend the funeral of her brother and sister-in-law.

Now, driving away from the cemetery, Madeline was smiling. She removed the veil and lit a small cigar, drawing the side curtains. It was clear now that Serena had meant it when she said that the Paradise was Madeline's to run, the proceeds hers to spend as she wished. She'd had a stormy session with the Judge over it; Hurd had finally stomped out in a rage, warning her that he was going to inform Serena of her extravagance.

Madeline knew that she was by nature inclined toward being a sensualist and a sybarite. She had never had the opportunity to indulge herself before. Now she did, and she fully intended to take advantage of it. Hetty's warning echoed faintly in her mind: "Squirrel it away, girl. The winters are hard out here."

But Hetty had been old and tended to worry about the future. Madeline was young, and she wanted to enjoy her youth.

She had something else to be happy about, as well. Just this week, she had taken a new lover. He was rough, crude in many ways. He could be, she suspected, quite cruel if so inclined. Despite her sophistication, her wide knowledge of men, Madeline delighted in lovers of rough quality. She liked to be treated with a certain amount of brutality in bed, and also

148

gloried in the fact that, with her body, she could, at least for a brief time, control even the roughest of men. In time, she had them groveling for her favors. Given enough time, she would do the same with this one.

No one knew about her secret lover, not even the people at the Paradise. He never came until after the house closed down, and then Madeline let him in through the side door. He wanted it that way. The secrecy was fine with Madeline. The less people knew about her private life, the better. The ill-fame of a sporting house madam was bad enough without adding to it.

That brought to mind the fact that she had been refused admittance to the opening performance at Maguire's Opera House. That still rankled, a humiliation that she would never forget. Madeline had made up her mind that she would find a way to attend a performance. She imagined herself sailing in on the arm of a fine gentleman, some man who didn't care a fig for that people thought. She had even considered asking the Judge to take her, but they weren't on that good terms, since she had spent all that money to buy the coach.

Madeline tossed her head, blowing a thin stream of smoke. To the devil with all of them! She was content enough, with plenty of money to spend on the things she wanted, and with her new lover. She smiled sensuously, looking forward with anticipation to the evening. She stretched like a contented cat.

Serena, to her surprise, found that she enjoyed being a woman of leisure. Several days had passed since the burial of her parents and, except for a few pangs of guilt over her idleness, she was happy. She had yet to consult with Spencer Hurd about investing her money. She had bought a new wardrobe to replace the one destroyed by her abductor. She had supper with Darrel several times and usually slipped into his hotel with him afterward. What guilt she felt was quieted by the pleasure and comfort she found in his arms.

There had been no mention of love between them, and Serena was just as content. She liked Darrel Quick, liked him very much, but becoming the wife of a professional gambler had little appeal for her.

At supper one evening she had asked him directly, "Have you ever been married, Darrel?"

"No." He gazed across the table at her with that sardonic smile. "The life of a gambling man is not suitable for a wife. I've known several gamblers who have tried it. It seldom lasted. And those few wives who did follow their men along the river, or elsewhere, were mostly miserable. Many people think gamblers lead a glamorous life, but that is far from the truth."

"Then why do you continue?"

"Because it's all I know," he said simply. He took a sip of wine. "No, that's not the whole truth. It's a life I'm fitted for. I love the thrill of it, matching wits with men across a poker table, and winning."

"But what if you lose?"

"I seldom lose, Serena. I'm good at what I do. If I may be immodest, I consider myself the best poker player in the country. The few times I *have* lost, it didn't take me long to recoup my losses. I have a feel for the cards, I have a memory that never fails me, and I never bet recklessly when the cards are running against me. Many gamblers, even old hands, get panicky when the cards aren't coming their way and bet wildly, unwisely, trying to recoup. And I never drink when I'm in a game. Unfortunately, liquor has ruined many a gambling man."

"It doesn't sound like you have much time for women in your life," Serena said saucily.

He grinned lazily. "Oh, I've found time for the ladies. It's just that I've never tried to inflict marriage on them. Of course . . ." His gaze became intent. "It could well be that I've never found one yet that I would want to marry."

Serena felt herself flushing. "I suppose I asked for that."

He threw back his head and laughed. "Don't fret, my sweet, I'm not proposing to you."

Perversely, Serena was a little piqued. Railing at herself for being silly, she kept her glance down, applying herself to the food. But a little later, she stole a look across the table at Darrel. He seemed deep in thought and didn't notice her look. He *was* a handsome man, no doubt of that, and the most charming man she had ever known. His clothes were expensive and beautifully tailored, and he would be perfectly at home in any social circle, no matter how high.

How different Darrel Quick was from Rory Clendenning, Serena thought, two days later when she accidentally encountered Clendenning on C Street in early evening.

Clendenning was in miner's clothing, his clothes, face, and hands smeared with dust and mud. At first glance Serena didn't recognize him and started on past. Belatedly, she realized who it was and swung

151

back to seize his arm before he could escape into the crowd.

"Why didn't you speak to me?" she demanded. "You must have seen me! Surely you're not still angry with me, Rory!"

Clendenning smiled wanly. "No, Serena, I'm no longer angry."

"Where have you been? I thought maybe you had left town."

"I should think it plain where I've been." He indicated his clothing. "I'm working in the mines."

"Come on." She tugged at his arm. "Let's get out of the crowd, some place where we can talk. You can buy me a sarsaparilla, or something."

He hung back. "Not looking like this, Serena."

"Why should you be concerned if I'm not? Besides, you look little different than most others I see."

Clendenning capitulated. "All right, Serena." He allowed her to lead him into a small restaurant. He *was* glad to see her, and he had felt his heart jump when he recognized her on the street. Serena had been in his thoughts often of late. However, he was so filthy, and she looked so clean and sweet in a new dress, he had intended to pass her by.

Once they were seated he commented on her appearance. "You look grand, Serena. Those new clothes become you." He smiled. "Much better than the bonnet and dress you wore when we came into Virginia City. I suppose you've claimed your inheritance?"

"My inheritance? You know what it is?" She began to laugh. "My Aunt Hetty left my father a whore-house, Rory! Can you believe that?"

He looked shocked at her use of the word, and Serena realized it was the first time she had spoken it aloud.

"Your Aunt Hetty was a . . . uh." He cleared his throat. "She was a madam?"

Still laughing, Serena said, "She was."

"But surely you're not taking her place, Serena!"

"Oh, no! I could never do that. I suppose I'll sell it in the end. Another woman is running it now." She noticed him eyeing her new clothes and added hastily, "There was some money. Aunt Hetty left some money, and I've taken that."

Their sarsaparillas came, and Clendenning took a thirsty gulp of his. He said sincerely, "I'm glad that you're doing well, Serena. I really am."

"And you, Rory? You say you're working in the mines?"

"It was the only job I could get." He sighed. "Lord God, it's hard work! Hard, dirty, and dangerous. I understand that hardly a day goes by that some miner isn't killed in one of the mines. The pay is not the best, either, but I had to do something."

Serena reached out to touch his hand. "I'm sure you'll find something else eventually. Or . . ." She smiled. "You'll become a superintendent, or something like that. You're a bright, enterprising young man."

Clendenning laughed curtly. "That will never happen. I'm lost among the other miners, and I have no skills to help me. Only these hands . . ." He held up his hands. "To handle a pick and shovel."

Serena was touched by his plight and wished to offer sympathy, but remembering his stiff-necked pride, she refrained.

As though reading her thoughts, he said, "I suppose

153

I sound full of self-pity, thinking back over what I've been saying. But I'm not asking for sympathy. I will manage well enough. It's just that I know no one here, except you, and you're the first person I've really talked to about it."

"It's all right, Rory. I know you're not begging for sympathy."

He drained his sarsaparilla and stood up abruptly. "I *am* glad to have seen you again, Serena, but I must be going now."

"But we've hardly had a chance to talk!" she said in dismay.

"I feel too self-conscious, dirty as I am, sitting here with you so . . ." He swallowed. "So clean and pretty." Then he smiled. "Another time perhaps. When I'm more presentable, we'll have a nice long talk. Goodbye for now."

He strode to the counter and paid for their drinks, then left the restaurant. Serena sat on for a while, dawdling over her drink. Darrel had been gone for two days, down to Carson City on some mysterious business, and had sent a message to the boarding house that he was back and would like to take her to supper. She had been on her way to meet him when she had bumped into Clendenning.

Now she found herself thinking of Clendenning, instead of Darrel Quick. It was very annoying that her thoughts should dwell on Clendenning at unexpected times. Why that should be was a puzzle she could not solve. Why should she think of Rory Clendenning, even when in the presence of Darrel, certainly one of the most handsome men in Virginia City? She should consider herself very fortunate indeed, and not be thinking of another man while in Darrel's arms.

With a start Serena realized that she was going to be late. She left the restaurant and hurried along C Street. Darrel was waiting for her before their favorite restaurant.

"Sorry I'm late," she said breathlessly. "But I came across Rory Clendenning. You know, I told you about him. It's the first time I've seen him in days, and we talked for a little."

Darrel gave her his arm. "And how is our preacher's son?"

"Not doing too well, it seems. He's working in the mines and having a hard time of it."

"That I can well imagine. It's a rough life, even for an experienced miner." He flashed a beguiling grin at her. "I suppose you think I should hunt him up and give him back his money?"

"I don't think anything of the sort!" she retorted. "I've come around to your way of thinking. Losing that money taught him a badly needed lesson." Yet, in her heart, Serena didn't believe what she was saying. With the two hundred dollars he had lost to Darrel, Rory would be able to stop working in the mines and live until he found something more suitable.

"And I don't believe you, my sweet," Darrel said, escorting her into the restaurant. "Not the Serena I've come to know, who has a soft heart for stray cats and dogs, as well as mute Chinese."

Serena refused to respond. As they took a table, she noticed that he was wearing a new suit. She commented on it admiringly.

"I bought it in Carson City."

"Surely you didn't go all that distance just to buy a suit! Not with all the shops here."

"Of course not," he said laughingly. He leaned

155

across the table, lowering his voice. "Confidentially, I'll tell you why I went. I sent a bank draft from the Wells-Fargo office there, opening an account in a San Francisco bank. I didn't want to do it here. Word might get bruited about as to how well my luck has been running. I'm going to San Francisco eventually. This town is fine, but what use is money if there's little of the finer things of life to spend it on?"

At her look of dismay, he laughed and covered her hand with his. "Oh, not soon. You won't be rid of me that easily, my love. And that reminds me . . . two days away from you is a long time, and my hunger for you is strong. Will you come to my room tonight?"

Suddenly breathless, heart beating wildly, Serena could only nod.

"I hoped you would be so kind. But . . ." He took out his pocket watch, frowning down at it. "I was going to escort you there after supper and leave for a short time. I have an appointment with a man, to collect a gambling debt. However, your being late . . . could you go on ahead to my hotel and wait for me?"

"Certainly." She gave him the saucy smile that she knew he expected from her and delighted in. "I *do* know the way."

"You do indeed. I'll give you the key to the side door and to my room."

An hour later, Serena was strolling along C Street toward Darrel's hotel. Since there was no rush, she tarried here and there, peering into shop windows dimmed by night. The street still thronged with people, but only the saloons were open for business.

Finally, she reached his hotel, went past the entrance, and started down the side of the building. Head down, she was fumbling in her purse for the keys Darrel had given her. It wasn't until she had them in her hand, and looked up, that she saw that the light over the side door was out, the narrow alley dark. A sense of déjà vu seized her, as her thoughts flew back to the memory of the night in the boarding house.

Just then she heard a rush of footsteps behind her. Before she could turn, she was struck from behind and knocked to the ground.

Serena tried to roll over, and a knee came down with painful force in the small of her back, pinning her to the ground. Hands were fumbling for her purse. Over her agitation Serena heard the sound of other footsteps pounding into the alley from the street. A muttered curse came from her attacker. Now her purse was ripped from her hands, and the knee was gone from her back. She rolled over and sat up, trying to peer into the darkness. All she could see was the bulky figure of a man running down the alley. Then he rounded a corner and was gone.

Serena looked around as the second figure stopped beside her and offered her a hand up. She looked up into his face and recognized Shu-toe. "Oh, Shu-toe! Thank you. My faithful Shu-toe!"

In pantomime he inquired if she was all right.

"Yes, I'm fine, Shu-toe. My pride may be wounded a little."

Shu-toe nodded vigorously, turned to stare down the length of the alley, and made as if to start in pursuit.

She caught at his arm. "No, no, Shu-toe. Let him

157

go. It was only a purse snatcher, and he's long gone anyway." She patted his hand. "I'm safe now. I'm going into the hotel."

He stood watching her as she went to the side door. Thank goodness, she'd had the keys out of the purse and clutched in her hand. There were only a few dollars in the purse anyway. She unlocked the door, turned to wave at Shu-toe, and went in, locking the door securely behind her.

It wasn't until Serena was safe in the hotel room that she remembered—the derringer Darrel had got for her was in the purse! She laughed to herself. A fat lot of good it had done her! She hadn't even thought of trying to use it.

Serena decided that she had better keep quiet and not tell Darrel about the purse snatcher. He would undoubtedly scold her. She would buy one to replace it later, and he would never need know. She should have had better sense that to venture down the unlighted alley anyway!

Chapter Eight

In the days following the funeral Serena's parents and Madeline's unexpected appearance at the funeral in the ornate coach, Ma Taylor had gone around muttering darkly that "something must be done about that brazen hussy and her ilk!"

Smiling to herself, Serena had ignored the remarks, certain that Ma Taylor was just letting off steam, and that nothing would come of it.

Serena hadn't seen Madeline since the funeral and had been postponing her final decision about the Paradise. For the same reason, she had not been in to talk to Spencer Hurd, afraid that he would pressure her, and she was just not ready to think about it yet. She was enjoying herself far too much to take time to concern herself with matters of business.

Almost every evening, Darrel Quick took her to supper or to an entertainment. In the mornings she slept very late; sometimes not rising before noon, and she spent most of the afternoon getting ready for the evening. Serena thought it was a lovely way to live, and only wished that it might go on forever.

Then, one afternoon, while she and Darrel were strolling toward their favorite restaurant, she learned that Ma Taylor's muttered threats had not been empty.

Behind them, over the usual street noises, she heard shouts of laughter and the sound of angry, hooting voices. She turned to look, but her view was blocked by the people on the street.

"What is it, Darrel?" she asked, craning to see.

"I don't know. Whatever it is, it seems to be heading this way. Let's wait and see." Taking her arm, he steered her toward the edge of the walk, where they waited.

In a few minutes, a parade of women, about fifty all told, came marching down the center of the street. Serena was puzzled to see that all wore almost identical yellow dresses and had yellow bows in their hair. Serena blinked in astonishment as she recognized Madeline Dubois in the lead, striding along with her head held high, arms swinging at her sides. She seemed oblivious to the jibes of the crowd, but as she drew abreast of Serena, Serena saw a slight, satisfied smile on her face.

As the parade went on past, Serena turned to Darrel, and found him laughing quietly.

"What's it all about, Darrel? I don't understand."

He looked at her. "You haven't heard? I thought since Madeline was . . . no, I can see you haven't heard. Come on into the restaurant and I'll explain."

Serena could hardly contain her impatience until they were seated at a table. Then she demanded, "Now tell me! What was that all about?"

160

"I have a feeling you're not going to find this so amusing," he said thoughtfully. "But here goes . . . it seems that a number of proper ladies, including your Ma Taylor, decided that something should be done about the, uh, ladies of the evening. And it appears they had their way." He grinned. "Except now it seems that Madeline Dubois has just thumbed her nose at the ladies, metaphorically speaking."

"Darrel," she said in exasperation, "do *what* about the ladies of the evening? And what does Madeline have to do with it?"

"The way I understand it, the ladies demanded that all prostitutes wear a yellow bow in their hair to identify themselves, so 'decent women' wouldn't be accosted by mistake." Darrel began to laugh. "Can you imagine any miner, drunk or not, accosting Ma Taylor?"

Serena, recalling Ma Taylor's starched propriety, had to laugh also.

Darrel continued, "At any rate, the women kept at the men until they agreed."

"You mean they passed a *law* to that effect?"

"Oh, no, they wouldn't dare go that far. I gather it was more a matter of a request."

Serena smiled and shook her head. "But where does Madeline come into it?"

"The way I hear it, she decided to go them one better. She went around to all the houses, all the cribs, and convinced the girls to put on not only yellow dresses as well, and march boldly down C Street, the demonstration of which you just witnessed."

Serena started to laugh, then stopped. Viewed in that light, it was funny. Yet, *she* still owned the Paradise, and viewed that way, it wasn't funny at all. She could just imagine people laughing at her all over Virginia City. "Madeline was behind this?" she asked, beginning to grow angry.

"Yes, my love. And I know you own the Paradise, but few other people realize that fact, and I doubt they'll connect you in any way . . ."

"Madeline had no right to do this!"

"Calm down, Serena. Don't lose your sense of perspective. Besides, it'll all die down and be forgotten. Life moves at too fast a pace out here."

"That's easy enough for you to say, but it's not you they'll be laughing at."

"Serena, you're taking this much too seriously. What do you believe most people think of a gambling man? In many circles, I'm considered beyond the pale."

"It's not the same thing at all. How do you think my folks would have looked upon my owning a whorehouse?"

"Then I'd advise you to get rid of it, for God's sake!" For the first time since she'd known him, Darrel seemed annoyed with her.

Serena remained unappeased, and the more she thought about it, the angrier at Madeline she became. "I don't care, I'm going to do something about it!"

"Do what you like, although I must say there doesn't seem much you *can* do about it, not after the fact." He shrugged, turning away as a waiter approached to take their order.

Serena was still unhappy about Madeline's antics the next day, and she was preoccupied at the noon meal, wondering what, if anything, she should do.

162

Dawdling over a cup of coffee, she became aware that the dining room was unusually quiet. She looked up, and saw that the other boarders had hurriedly eaten and gone. She saw Ma Taylor, plump face stern and forbidding, approaching, with a copy of the *Enterprise* clutched in her hand. Normally, Ma Taylor bustled about, joshing with the boarders as she served their food. Belatedly, Serena realized that the room had been unusually quiet during the meal, and she could dimly recall Ma Taylor moving about in grim silence, slapping plates down, rebuffing all jocular remarks.

"Mrs. Taylor, is something wrong?"

"This, this is what's wrong, missy." The woman slapped the paper down on the table, as though swatting a pesky fly, and jabbed a finger at the paper. "As if you didn't know!"

Somewhat intimidated, and completely mystified, Serena began to read the newspaper article Ma Taylor had indicated in growing dismay.

The article was headlined:

"MARCH ON C STREET!

"Yesterday afternoon C Street was witness to an exhibition the likes of which it has never before seen. A group of the 'frail sisters' . . . some fifty in number, marched along the street, flaunting their profession!

"It has always been this reporter's understanding that their profession has been identified with the color red, since the days of Nathaniel Hawthorne, and the Scarlet Letter A. Either this is in error, or the times have changed. But then Virginia forever delights in being different.

163

"It all came about when the proper ladies of our fair city demanded of their men that something be done to label our ladies of the evening as such, so that people will have a ready means of differentiating between the 'proper' and 'improper' ladies. The men, reluctantly you may be sure, bowed to their collective will. They requested that the ladies in question wear a yellow bow in their hair, so they might be distinugished from our *other* ladies. This has been done in other mining camps, and some of our good ladies learned of it. They claim that many times 'decent' women have been mistaken for members of the 'fair but frail' persuasion. The yellow ribbon, supposedly, will erase any doubt.

"Going a step further, the ladies of D Street dressed themselves *all* in yellow, including the yellow bows in their hair, and marched en masse down C Street. Hilarity reigned supreme, as well as much indignation, among the citizens of Virginia!

"Your reporter, through some discreet inquiries, learned that the instigator of this human comedy was one Madeline Dubois, a name familiar among 'Washoe widowers,' who runs the Paradise, once owned by the late Hetty Foster. Your reporter knew Miss Hetty well, a refined lady for all her profession, and one wonders how Miss Hetty would have looked upon such shenanigans. But the rumors have it, as yet to be verified, that this particular Paradise of pleasure is now owned by a young lady recently arrived in our fair city from the East, a relative of Miss Hetty's. Since the Paradise has garnered a reputa-

164

tion for decorum in all things. your reporter is given to wonder if the grand parade yesterday did not perhaps originate with our new arrival.

"When, and if, your reporter can manage an interview with the aforementioned young lady, the story will be made available to the faithful readers of the Enterprise."

The article had the byline, Mark Twain.

Sick at heart, Serena finally looked up to find Ma Taylor, arms crossed over her ample bosom, glowering down at her.

"Here I thought you were a nice girl, a lady, and you turn out to be . . ." She stopped, apparently at a loss for the proper word.

"I'm sorry, Mrs. Taylor, if I have caused you any embarrassment . . ."

"Embarrassment! Hah! The shame, that's it, the shame of having a woman of your stripe in my house!"

"But I had nothing to do with yesterday's demonstration!" Serena made a helpless gesture. "And as for the Paradise, I knew nothing of it until I came here. Neither my father nor I knew what our inheritance was. And I have refused to accept it."

Ma Taylor snorted. "A likely story!"

"It's true, I swear. You can ask Judge Hurd, he'll tell you!"

"I don't trust his word, either. *He* sent you here. He always hung around that place, but it's expected of a man out here. It don't matter, anyway. You're related to Hetty Foster, and that's enough. I should have connected up the name, but you seemed the proper lady."

165

"Don't cast aspersions on Aunt Hetty," Serena said heatedly. "She was a good woman!"

"Good woman, was she? Then what was she doing running a house of ill-repute?"

Serena was having difficulty holding back tears. "She was earning a living, just as you are!"

Ma Taylor gasped explosively, and her face turned a dark and unbecoming red. "Why, how dare you! How dare you talk to me like that?"

Serena, wildly angry now, went on, "And what about the men? There wouldn't be such places if men didn't want them, but nobody says that the men are terrible, and nobody shuns the men who go to such places. So why should a woman who runs such a place be thought any worse than the men who frequent these houses? Anyway, Aunt Hetty was *not* Madeline Dubois."

"That's what you say, but who was at the funeral of your parents? Madeline Dubois, the brazen hussy! Why else would she be there if you hadn't asked her?" Ma Taylor paused to take a deep breath. "I want you out of this house today!"

Serena snapped, "I have paid rent until the end of the week, and I'll stay until the end of the week! The only way you'll get me out before is to have me thrown out!"

Serena had shot to her feet, and they stood glaring at each other.

Such was the pop-eyed fury in the woman's red face that for a moment or two Serena thought that Ma Taylor was indeed going to throw her out. Certainly she had the strength and size for it. Serena was determined she would be dragged out fighting and scratching.

166

Then Ma Taylor heaved a massive sigh. "The end of the week it is, but no longer. I want that clearly understood. You can move in with your own kind!"

She turned and marched away, and Serena hurried up to her room, crying openly now. It seemed to her that the new life she was fashioning for herself here had suddenly been ripped apart, falling like shards of glass around her feet.

There was no choice left for her now—she had to have it out with Madeline. But she would wait until late that night. She simply didn't have the courage to be seen walking up to that house in broad daylight. Serena stretched out on the bed. She would remain in her room, skipping supper, until it was time to go.

Serena waited until late that evening, until she was sure all the customers had come and gone before she ventured out to the Paradise. She had to knock long and hard on the door before it was finally opened.

Before she recognized Serena, Chu Chin started to say, "House not open now . . ."

"Chu Chin," Serena broke in, "I'm not a customer, for heaven's sake! I want to see Madeline."

"Chu Chin not supposed to . . ."

With her foot Serena gave the door a shove, pushing it wide, sending Chu Chin tottering back. "I'm sorry, Chu Chin." She stepped inside. "Where is Madeline?"

Chu Chin motioned down the hall. "In sitting loom."

Serena strode down the hall and rapped on the door. Madeline's voice called out for her to come in.

167

Serena entered, leaving the door wide open behind her.

At the sight of Serena, Madeline got to her feet, face lighting up. "Serena! I'm glad to see you. I was thinking you'd never come!"

"I don't think you're going to be happy about my coming now," Serena said, her anger surfacing.

"Oh?" Madeline said warily. She sat back on the divan, picking up a smoldering cigar from a saucer and drawing on it. "Why not?"

"It's about that ridiculous demonstration yesterday!"

"Oh, that!" Madeline laughed full-throatedly. "I thought it was great fun, and we all had a fine time."

"I'll just bet you did! Why didn't you consult me about it beforehand?"

Madeline's face grew still, her eyes cold. "Why should I have? You told me to run the Paradise as I saw fit."

"The Paradise, yes. But what you did yesterday had nothing to do with the Paradise, unless you call making it an object of ridicule. What do you think Aunt Hetty would have thought of it?"

"I didn't consult with Hetty Foster. What would you have me do, conjure up her ghost?"

"I would expect you to respect her wishes! From what Spencer Hurd has told me, she was always a perfect lady in public. She would never have allowed such a disgraceful exhibition. And riding around Virginia City in that flashy coach . . . she would not have stood for that, either."

"I think I'm beginning to see." Madeline's eyes narrowed. "That's what disturbs you, the money I spent on the coach."

Serena gestured. "I couldn't care less about the money spent on the coach. It's only another example of the way you're carrying on."

"In my opinion, it's all good advertising, even the parade," Madeline said. "Last night and tonight were the busiest nights we've had in months. I was very fond of Hetty, but in my opinion she was too conservative. In this business, you have to make your presence known."

"I suppose you'll be wanting to advertise openly in the *Enterprise* next!"

Madeline said calmly, "I have given it some thought."

"You already have, *free* advertising." From her purse, Serena took that days copy of the *Enterprise,* folded to the article, and tossed it onto the table before the divan. "Did you read that?"

"Of course, that's why tonight's trade was so heavy . . . oh, I see." Madeline smiled. "You're upset about the mention of your name, aren't you?"

"Not upset, furious! You've forgotten that the Paradise doesn't belong to you yet." Serena was angry past all caution now, her voice rising. "*I* own it . . ."

"According to the Judge, you wouldn't dirty your hands with it," Madeline retorted with a curl of her lip.

"Before today, no. But now that it's public knowledge that I'm the proprietor, I've made up my mind. I know what I'm going to do. Tonight is the last night this house will operate as a whorehouse. I'm closing it . . ."

Madeline sat up, staring. "You can't do that!"

"I can and I will! Tomorrow, I'll see the Judge

169

and tell him I want to sell it as a place for a decent family to live in, not as *a* house!"

"Hetty said I could stay here as long as I liked. She stated that in her will!"

"Only as her hope, nothing else. Legally, it means absolutely nothing."

"Serena, come to your senses!" Madeline was pleading now.

"I have, just now."

"No, no, you don't understand. This place brings in a fortune. You'd be foolish to throw all that away. If you won't sell it to me, allow me to run it. I promise to behave. I'll sell the coach. I'll do anything you say!"

Serena shook her head, unmoved. "My mind is made up. I want you, and everyone else in this house, out by tomorrow evening. If you're not, I'll have the sheriff throw you out!"

Madeline sprang to her feet, her own anger blazing now. "You can't do that. You can't throw us out into the street, like used dishwater! This is the only home these girls have. It's the only home *I* have!"

"I'm sure the cribs along D Street will accommodate you," Serena said.

Madeline's eyes flashed. She took two steps and slapped Serena across the face. The slap stung enough to bring tears to Serena's eyes. For a furious moment, she was tempted to tangle her fingers in Madeline's brown hair and tear out a handful. Restraining herself with an effort, she said, "Your true colors show at last. I wouldn't be surprised to see you brawling on the streets next."

"I'm sorry," Madeline said wretchedly.

"All of you out tomorrow, Madeline," Serena

turned and started for the door. In the doorway she glanced back. "I mean every word I said. If you're not out of this place by tomorrow night, you will be sorry!"

She went out into the hall. As she started to turn toward the front door, Serena was suddenly aware of being watched. She glanced up. On the narrow stairway, from midway up to the top, were a number of women, in various stages of undress. They were all staring openly at her, and Serena remembered what she had been shouting in there. They must have overheard her. She tried frantically to think of some words of apology to tender them. Then she clamped her lips shut. Why should she apologize to them? She had meant every word of it!

Then it was too late anyway. Under her gaze, they all whirled and scampered back up the stairs out of sight.

Serena turned determinedly and marched down the hall. As she let herself out, she thought of something. This was the first time she had seen the girls in the house. The time she'd been here for supper, they might not have existed at all, for all she had seen, or heard, of them. Undoubtedly most, if not all, had marched in the demonstration yesterday, but they had been lost among so many others.

Passing through the door, she slammed it hard behind her.

After Serena's stormy departure, Madeline gave way to tears of despair. She sank down onto the divan, her head in her hands, sobbing. Her tears sprang

171

from a cold fury at Serena Foster, that pious bitch, and despondency over her own plight. What was she going to do, if Serena held to her threat and threw them out?

The sound of the front door slamming brought her head up. After a moment she dashed the tears from her eyes and got to her feet. She noticed how quiet the house was. Not a peep from upstairs. The sound of their quarreling voices had been loud, and the girls must have overheard enough to know that their fate was in jeopardy as well. Madeline was surprised that they weren't gathered around, begging her to tell them it wasn't true, clamoring for her to protect them.

They don't have that much faith in *me*, she thought bitterly; if Hetty was in my place, they would be flocking around her for reassurance.

She went to the parlor door and closed it. She poured a glass of whiskey and took a long swallow.

The thought of Hetty Foster brought to mind a remark the woman had made once: "Girl, the life of a hoor is a hard one. You've only got so many years to work at it. You know where most of the girls will end up, once the bloom is gone from their cheeks? In the cribs along D Street. Or some place like that. And after that? Who knows? Dead in a gutter somewhere, probably, of starvation, disease, or the drink!"

Was that her next step down the line—the cribs? The very thought of it made Madeline go cold with dread.

Maybe if she talked to the Judge, he would intervene with Serena in her behalf.

No, no! Madeline shook her head. The Judge was displeased with her already, and God only knew what he thought now, following yesterday's demonstration.

Madeline splashed more whiskey into the glass and paced, drinking, her thoughts chaotic. She realized that she was getting a little tipsy, but she didn't care.

When the idea of organizing the strumpets to flaunt themselves in public, in effect spitting in the eyes of the proper bitches, came to Madeline, it had tickled her sense of humor. She still thought it had been grand fun and marvelous advertising, but it had been premature. She saw that now. She should have waited until the Paradise was hers.

It had never occurred to her that the *Enterprise* would make such a big thing of it, thus arousing Serena's anger. Even in her own rage, Madeline could sympathize with Serena's embarrassment. She liked Serena, she really did. She even admired the spirit the girl had shown tonight. She just knew that, under different circumstances, they could become good friends.

Perhaps, when Serena's anger cooled . . .

No, the girl was determined. Nothing was going to change her mind.

Madeline drank again, pacing.

She stopped suddenly at a familiar knock on the side door. Two raps, a pause, then another rap. She had forgotten that her new lover was coming tonight!

Maybe he could advise her! Crude though he might be in bed, he was a shrewd man and had much power and influence in Virginia City.

She hurried to open the door and let him slip in. She began talking before he was inside the door, everything coming out in a rush. "Serena Foster was just here, in a great rage! She's going to close the Paradise down, and sell it as a residence! She gave us all until tomorrow afternoon to get out . . ."

Serena was awakened by a heavy knocking on her bedroom door. It took her a moment to realize what it was. Finally she sat up. "Just a minute!"

Tumbling out of bed, she shrugged into a dressing gown and hurried to the door. She opened it to Ma Taylor's angrily red face. "You're wanted downstairs! A Chink of all things! It wasn't bad enough before, now you're hobnobbing with the Chinks. Lord in Heaven, will I ever be glad to rid my house of you!"

"Who is it?"

"How should I know? All Chinks look alike to me!"

Shaking her head to clear it, Serena said, "All right, Mrs. Taylor. I'll be down as soon as I get dressed."

She started to close the door, but Ma Taylor got in the last word. "He's waiting out on the porch for you. I won't let a Chink in my house, and don't you be letting him in either. Conduct your business with him on the outside!"

Firmly, Serena closed the door. As she flew about getting dressed, she was wondering who it could be. *He*? Could it be Shu-toe? He was the only male Chinese she knew. She felt a sudden chill of dread.

Serena left the room and hurried downstairs. It was indeed Shu-toe, she found, who was waiting for her. There was a note in his hand. She saw in a fleeting glance that it had her name printed on it in block letters, which explained how Shu-toe had made his wishes known to Ma Taylor.

"What is it, Shu-toe?" she asked breathlessly. "What's wrong?"

He indicated that she was to accompany him and

started off at once. Serena hastened after him. There was a sense of urgency about him that only increased her apprehensions. It was soon apparent that he was heading toward the downside of the town, but the circuitous route he took, avoiding all the main streets, did nothing to allay her fears.

When they entered the shack of Tang P'ing, Serena saw that the Chinese woman wore a troubled frown. Before she could speak, Serena saw another woman in the dimness.

She took a step toward the second woman. "Chu Chin! What are you doing here?"

Chu Chin would only shake her head, wringing her hands.

"Chu Chin my friend," Tang P'ing said. "Live near. She work at Paradise . . ."

"I know that, Tang P'ing, but what does that have to do with me?"

"Chu Chin go work, early, to clean house from night before. Always go before others in house get up. This morning, she go, same time. Find woman of house dead."

"Madeline?" Serena gasped. "You don't mean Madeline Dubois?"

"That one, yes. On divan in sitting room. Shot by . . . what you call?" Tang P'ing indicated the size of the gun by her hands. "Small gun?"

"You mean a derringer?"

"Yes!" Tang P'ing nodded vigorously. "Small gun by dead woman."

With a feeling of icy fear, Serena knew somehow that the derringer was hers, the one Darrel had bought for her, the one stolen from her purse.

Tang P'ing was going on, "Last night, you and woman of house quarrel. Everyone in house hear, hear you make threat against her. Chu Chin also hear."

Her mind reeling, Serena sank down onto one of the pallets. Tang P'ing squatted beside her. "Chu Chin know you friend Tang P'ing. She find dead woman, she not tell anyone, but come to me." At Serena's blank look, Tang P'ing spoke with some urgency. "When dead woman found, will think you, Se-rena, kill her. Will think you murder."

"But why on earth would anyone think . . ." Serena's voice died away, for she knew with dismay that, in all likelihood, Tang P'ing was correct. With the bitter quarrel, and her threats, fresh in the minds of the girls in the Paradise, and the derringer, *her* derringer, easily enough identified, used as the murder weaopn—it would all add up to her being the culprit.

Could that have been the reason her purse had been stolen? To be used to kill Madeline so the blame would fall on her?

Serena fought back a rising panic and tried to think.

Tang P'ing was speaking again. "Must leave at once. Stay here, Se-rena hang."

"Hang?" Serena stared at her incredulously. "You can't be serious, Tang P'ing!"

"Oh, yes. Hang quick here. You being woman, make no difference. Hang women before."

"But where will I go?"

"Go San Francisco, Se-rena. Go with Tang P'ing and son."

Behind her, Shu-toe was bobbing his head.

"Darken skin. Tie hair back, slant eyes." The tiny dimple appeared as she smiled. "You be Tang Wu, Tang P'ing's daughter."

"Wait, wait! You're going too fast for me. And why should you do this for me? Not that I don't appreciate it." Serena took Tang P'ing's hand. "But you can't just leave your home and everything, because of me!"

"Home!" Tang P'ing said a few angry words in Chinese, then turned her head aside to make a spitting motion. "Never true home. Know other Chinese in San Francisco. You like. Leave here soon anyway. You, Se-rena . . ." Tang P'ing put a hand out, timidly, to touch Serena's cheek. "Friend. Only true friend, not Chinese."

Serena looked intently at the Chinese woman, then at Shu-toe, who was nodding again. She was deeply touched by the love of these two, strangers to her only days ago. But also their fears for her now suddenly became hers, and the danger to herself more real. Instinctively, she knew that they were right—it was not wise for her to remain here.

And with that, her decision was made. Her mind began to function again. "If we are to do this, we need a way to travel, am I right?"

"Shu-toe, me." Tang P'ing exchanged glances with her son. "We walk."

"From San Francisco? All that distance?" Serena knew it was a stupid question before the words were out of her mouth. To cover up, she said quickly, "What time is it?"

Tang P'ing said, "Near to Occidental noon hour."

"Then the bank will be open. I have to withdraw my money. Chu Chin . . ." She swiveled around to look

177

at Chu Chin. "When will you report Madeline's death?"

Chu Chin was shaking her head from side to side.

Tang P'ing said, "Chu Chin not do this. She not go back. Let other girls in house find dead woman."

"And they probably don't get up much before noon. I'll have time." Serena got to her feet. "I'll withdraw the money from my account and be back as quickly as I can. Then you, Tang P'ing, will go with Shu-toe and buy a buckboard and a team of horses. I won't risk going to the boarding house for my clothes. Can you buy me some clothes to go with this Chinese look you're giving me, Tang P'ing?"

Tang P'ing nodded, smiling.

Two hours later, a buckboard was in the turgid stream of wagon and buggy traffic along C Street, proceeding south out of Virginia City. The buckboard had a top and canvas side curtains. The curtains had been rolled down. The two women in the back seat could not be seen from the outside, and if anyone thought it curious that a Chinese should be driving a buckboard, they would naturally assume that his passengers were white.

Serena, looking in a mirror before they left, had been amazed at the transformation Tang P'ing had wrought.

Her own hair had been rolled into a knot and pulled back tightly on both sides of her forehead, giving her eyes a slight slant. It was uncomfortable, but Tang P'ing had assured Serena that she would get used to it. Over her blonde hair now rested a black wig. Tang P'ing had concocted a paste-like substance, with which she had smeared Serena's face and hands, darkening them considerably. A long black tunic and trousers completed the transformation.

"Nothing Tang P'ing can do about gray eyes, Serena. Must always have eyes looking down." Tang P'ing had smiled impishly. "People not think strange. People expect Chinese women go round with eyes on ground. Even Chinese men."

It was a stunning transformation, and Serena very much doubted that even Darrel Quick would recognize her easily. She longed to raise the side curtain and take a last look at this city she had, almost, come to think of as her home. Yet she dared not take the risk. Even if she wasn't recognized, people would think it strange that two Chinese women should be riding in a new buckboard, with a Chinese male driving.

Serena was sorry she hadn't left a note for Darrel, explaining what had happened, and where she was going, but to do that would only risk involving him in the whole mess. Besides, the angry way she had acted during their last conversation, he might even believe that she *had* killed Madeline.

She would have liked to tell Rory Clendenning goodbye as well, but of course he was at work down in some mine during the day.

She clutched her purse to her. In it was a little over three thousand dollars, what was left after buying the buckboard and a pair of horses, and all the new clothes. The clothes! She was heartsick at having to leave them behind; she hadn't dared go to the boarding house for them.

There was one other thing in the purse—a derringer exactly like the one Darrel had picked out for her. On her way back from the bank to Tang P'ing's shack, Serena had stopped in a gun shop—not the one where Darrel had taken her—and bought the derringer. Neither Tang P'ing nor Shu-toe were armed. It was a long way to San Francisco, and the little gun might be useful.

Thinking of the derringer made her think of Madeline, and she felt a wave of shame and remorse. She had been too hard on Madeline; she knew that now. It would have been cruel to close the house and put the girls out on the street, cruel and thoughtless, and done mostly because of Serena's pride and vanity. Madeline's last thoughts must have been full of despair and anger. And who had ended those thoughts? Who had used the gun, Serena's derringer, to quench that vital life? It all seemed a part of the frightening puzzle that had begun with the death of Serena's parents.

Serena looked around and saw Tang P'ing studying her with a worried frown.

Serena knew that she had at least one thing to be grateful for. In Tang P'ing and Shu-toe she had two loyal and faithful friends and companions.

Thinking this, she took Tang P'ing's hand and squeezed it. In return, she received that dimpled smile.

Chapter Nine

More than a week passed before Rory Clendenning learned of Serena's disappearance. He had overheard some gossip about a whorehouse madam being murdered, but the name Madeline Dubois meant nothing to him, and he hadn't read a local newspaper in days.

It seemed to Clendenning that all his hours now were filled with backbreaking labor, and he was so Lord God tired at night that as soon as he had finished his evening meal in the lodging house where he had a room, he fell onto his cot and was asleep as soon as his head touched the hard pillow.

Except on Sunday, his one day off, he never saw the sun. He and the other miners were down in the bowels of the earth before dawn and did not emerge again until full dark. If Clendenning had been told about the dreary life of a miner before he experienced it for himself, he would not have believed it.

Going down into the mine in the wooden cage

raised and lowered by ropes and a windlass was like descending into Hell. The miners carried candle-lanterns and picks and shovels. The lower the cage descended, the hotter it became. By the time the miners arrived at the working level at the bottom of the main shaft, the temperature was well above a hundred degrees.

The air was barely breathable, and the stench of decaying vegetable matter; hot, foul water; and human excretions, was beyond belief. The miners removed most of their clothing, wearing only a light breech-cloth to cover their loins, and thick-soled shoes to protect their feet from the scorching rocks and trickling streams of steaming-hot water. Even then, they could only work in the earthen cubicles for an hour or so at a time before they had to come up to fill their lungs with fresh air from the surface, brought down by the blower tubes; and to cool themselves under watershowers from conduit pipes.

Each miner worked in a small cubicle, which was so tiny that a man could hardly stand upright inside it. The cubicles were formed by using four heavy timbers as corner pieces, with lighter wood as crosspieces. Since Clendenning had gone to work in the mine, four cubicles had caved in and two miners had died before they could be dug out.

At the entrance to each cubicle was a hand-car. Each miner would work with a pick and shovel, breaking loose the ore-veined rock and shoveling it into the hand-car until it was full. Then the hand-car had to be pushed along the earth made mushy by seepage of water, to the cage, and transfer the contents of the car into buckets inside the cage, which was then drawn up to the surface.

182

Due to his unusual height, Clendenning found that working in the cubicles was more difficult for him than for the average miner. He always had to work partially stooped over and had developed what seemed to be a permanently stiff, sore neck. The first week had been pure hell. At the end of that time, he had hardened to it somewhat, but he still found the work backbreaking and demeaning. At the end of each shift, he was totally exhausted and disgustingly filthy.

For all this, he earned four dollars a day. This would have been considered good wages anywhere else but in a mining town, with its grossly inflated prices.

The shift bosses were brutal, unfeeling men, who constantly prowled the horizontal shafts, peering into the cubicles, goading the miners on to greater effort. If they thought a man wasn't filling enough hand-cars in a day's time, they threatened to discharge him.

The miners, Clendenning thought, were little better than slaves.

Of course, most of them had known little else all their adult lives and were content to labor for the few dollars a week, spending what they didn't need for necessities on whores, liquor, and gambling.

The labor was demeaning enough, but what galled Clendenning most of all was the fact that the mine owners and their stockholders, were growing enormously wealthy riding the bent backs of the miners. What newspapers Clendenning did find time to read were usually San Francisco papers, and he had learned from them that most of the mine owners, and all the stockholders in their companies, resided in that city on the bay. Aside from the fortunes the

183

mine owners were making, the stockholders were receiving as much as twenty percent return a year from their investments, and they had never even seen a mine!

Most of the miners weren't aware of these inequities, and Clendenning realized they wouldn't care, or even listen, if he tried to enlighten them.

As for himself, Clendenning knew that he was going to quit as soon as he had accumulated a few dollars, and find some other way to earn his living. If not in Virginia City, then somewhere else.

However, it wasn't all that easy to save money. Food and lodging alone cost him ten dollars a week—a room ten by twelve feet in size, and three meals a day, which included breakfast, a packed lunch pail to take into the mine, and supper. The food was plain fare, but ample and nourishing. The trouble was, work in the mine destroyed his appetite, at least for the first two weeks, and he ate little, losing weight. His first week's salary had gone toward buying miner's clothing, especially the boots that were badly needed. Clothes were very expensive. To buy clothing of quality would have cost him a month's wages.

So, at the end of his third week in the mine, Clendenning had saved the magnificent sum of twenty dollars.

It was at the end of that week, a Saturday evening, that he learned of Serena's disappearance, and that she was under suspicion of murder.

When he came trudging up the walk to the boarding house at dark, he found two men waiting for him. One was a man in his late fifties; he wore a broadcloth suit, smoked a cigar, and had the look of a professional man. The other man was younger, with a hard face and cold eyes, and wore a gunbelt with a pearl-handled Colt.

The older man said, "Are you Rory Clendenning?"

Somewhat at a loss, Clendenning said, "Yes, I am."

"I'm Spencer Hurd. Serena must have mentioned my name to you." Hurd held out his hand.

Accepting the man's hand, Clendenning searched his memory. Then it came to him. "Of course! You're the lawyer who sent her father the letter about the death of Hetty Foster and his . . ." Remembering, Clendenning cleared his throat. "Serena's inheritance."

Hurd smiled slightly. "I see you know about her inheritance?"

Clendenning started to reply, but the other man cut in, "When was the last time you saw Serena Foster?"

Spencer Hurd said, "This is Jake Burns, Mr. Clendenning. A deputy with the sheriff's office here in Virginia City."

Clendenning was frowning. "The last time I saw Serena was . . . oh, about ten days ago. I ran into her on the street, and we had a sarsaparilla together. I was just coming from the mine, filthy and unwashed, and we didn't talk long. What is this all about, gentlemen?"

Hurd sighed. "Suppose we all sit down?" He gestured to empty chairs on the porch. Clendenning noticed that the deputy was careful to sit beside him.

Before he could speak, Hurd said, "The thing is, Clendenning, Serena has disappeared."

"Disappeared! Lord God! When? What happened?"

Deputy Burns said, "You didn't know this?"

"Of course I didn't know!" His voice roughened.

185

"Now what is this all about? I think I'm due an explanation."

"She's been gone about a week, Serena has," Hurd said. "As to where, no one has the least idea."

"But there must be some reason! Maybe something has happened to her."

"She killed someone, that's what happened to her," Jake Burns said harshly. "That's why she cut and run, she didn't want to hang!"

"Now you don't know that for a fact, Jake," Hurd said reprovingly. "The law says a person is innocent until proven guilty."

Clendenning was stunned. "Serena is supposed to have killed someone? Lord God! I don't believe it for a minute! She wouldn't harm a fly!"

Hurd blew smoke from his cigar. "I'm somewhat of the same mind, young Clendenning. But Jake here doesn't agree."

"If her running away ain't proof enough," the deputy said, "how about the quarrel she had with Madeline? The girls in the house heard her threatening Madeline. And the derringer used to kill Madeline had been bought by this Foster woman only days before."

"All purely circumstantial, Jake. What was her motive?"

"How the hell do I know? When whores fall out, they're liable to kill each other out of hand. Don't know how many times it's happened!"

Clendenning leaned forward in anger. He gripped the deputy's shoulder and shook him. "Serena Foster is no whore! I'll thank you to remember that!"

Jake Burns knocked the hand away, then placed his own hand on his gun. "You keep your hands off me,

Clendenning. I'm an officer of the law, and I could shoot you for assaulting an officer." His thin lips drew back in a sneer. "And if she ain't a whore, why was she running a whorehouse? Answer me that, will you?"

"I've already explained that, Jake," Hurd said. "She wasn't running a whorehouse. The Paradise came to her by way of inheritance, and she wanted no part of it."

Clendenning said, "Who's this Madeline? It seems I've heard some gossip, but I didn't pay much heed to it."

"She was a protegé of Hetty's, Clendenning," Hurd said. "And she's been running the Paradise since Hetty's death . . ."

"Protegé! All them fancy words don't change the fact she was a whore, Judge," Burns said. "And I don't know why the town is so all-fired het up about her being killed, anyway!"

"Madeline might have been a whore, Jake, technically speaking," Hurd said quietly. "But she wasn't a bad person, if a little flighty, and her death was a brutal, shocking thing. Naturally, people want to see justice done."

"Find this Foster woman and you'll have an end to it!"

"Yes, Jake," Hurd said wearily. He got to his feet. "I think we should let this young man wash up and have his supper."

Jake Burns bent a fierce scowl on Clendenning. "You sure you know nothing of her whereabouts?"

"Nothing." Wits still dulled by the shock of it, Clendenning could only shake his head.

He was dimly aware of the deputy stalking away

and Hurd saying, "Thank you for your time, young Clendenning. I know this must be a shock to you. Come see me if you can find the time, and we'll talk more. It seems we're about the only ones left in Virginia City who have faith in Serena. On the basis of that, if there's anything I can do for you, don't hesitate to come see me."

Clendenning was aroused enough to mumble his thanks, and Hurd left. Clendenning sat on, sat on past the supper bell. He ignored the miners trooping into the house, merely nodding at their greetings. They considered him an odd one, anyway, so it mattered little if they thought him odder still.

He had thought of Serena often and of that night out in the desert. Knowing long ago that he had been wrong, that he had, in effect, forced himself upon her, he was sorry now that he hadn't spoken more kindly to her. One reason for his stiff-necked pride in *not* being more friendly was something that Serena didn't know, something that he could never bring himself to tell her. Clendenning had himself been a virgin, or so close to it that it didn't matter. The only experience he'd had with girls before had been fumbling, adolescent episodes that had come to nothing in the end. But how could he have told Serena that he, a twenty-two-year-old man, had never had a complete sexual experience until that night?

His feeling for her was strong, he well knew that. Having no experience with love, Clendenning didn't know if he loved her or not. One thing he did know—Lord God, he was going to miss her!

As for killing another person, he dismissed that out of hand. The Serena he knew was incapable of killing

188

anyone, even in anger. She couldn't have changed that much, not in a brief period of three weeks.

Where was she now? How was she faring? No matter where she had fled to, she was among strange people. How could a girl as young as Serena fend for herself in this rough country? She needed a man. He might be a poor excuse for a man, but if he knew where she was, he would go to her and offer his help . . . if she would accept it after the way he had acted toward her.

Clendenning stirred, sitting up. Somehow this news about Serena had made up his mind. This was his last day in the mines. It was Saturday, payday, and he vowed to himself that he would never go down into a mine again.

If he continued at the job, he would become like the others in the end—permanently stooped, health bad, a dullard content to spend his hard-earned money whoring and drinking. He hadn't the slightest idea what he was going to do. There had to be *something* better!

Clendenning got up and went inside to take a bath, to wash away the filth from the mine for the last time.

Spencer Hurd believed in Serena's innocence with all his heart. During his long career as a lawyer, he had encountered a great many killers, and he liked to think that he had developed an extra sense that told him whether a person was innocent or not. And Serena was innocent!

Leaving the boarding house, he hurried to catch up with Jake Burns. They matched stride for stride while

Hurd lit a fresh cigar. Then he said, "You were a little rough on the young man, Jake."

"People in this town are rough on *us*, Judge," Burns retorted. "Every day some muckety-muck drops by the sheriff's office and demands to know when we're going to find this whore's killer! Then the sheriff, who does little but sit on his ass all day, turns on us and says he's going to fire some asses if we don't come up with results soon!"

"Well, you took the job. You should be used to a little pressure."

"But all over the killing of a whore!" Burns said defensively. "And I'm good at my job. That's why I'm convinced this Serena Foster is the one."

Hurd blew smoke. "I never said you're not a good deputy, Jake. But this time you happen to be wrong."

"Why did she run then?"

"I'm not a mind reader, and she didn't see fit to confide in me, but I would guess it's because of the way you're thinking. She was afraid people would think she had killed Madeline."

"And she did."

They walked along in silence for a few moments. Hurd began humming under his breath, his thoughts busy with Serena and her situation.

"Tell me, Judge, what's your stake in all this?" Burns asked.

"Why, because Serena Foster is my client," Hurd said.

"How do you figure that? She never hired you to defend her against a murder charge. She hasn't even been arrested. How can she be your client until she's arrested?"

"I consider it my job to look after her interests,

190

while she isn't present to do so herself. And I will continue to do so until she *is* arrested, if she ever is. If she goes to court, I will defend her. Meanwhile, I'll do my damnedest to find out who *did* kill Madeline Dubois."

"All this trouble you'd go to without a fee?" Burns said in amazement.

Spencer Hurd smiled. "Contrary to popular opinion, Jake, not all lawyers are out for what they can get. Some of us are concerned about justice, and their client's welfare."

Darrel Quick was not overly concerned about Serena's guilt or innocence. He knew that people who under normal circumstances would never think of killing a human being could be driven to it by anger or fear; all the scruples of a lifetime could be swept away in a moment of desperation.

During the course of his life, Darrel had killed, more than once. In each instance the killing had been done coolly, no matter how much fury seethed underneath. However, he sincerely believed that each time he had killed it had been done in self-defense, or the other man deserved to die.

So how then could he blame Serena if she had killed? He knew she had a quick temper and had been cruelly mistreated here, and he had seen her ablaze with anger at Madeline Dubois only the night before the woman was killed. This knowledge, of course, was a secret he had no intention of sharing with the law.

He was however, deeply concerned about Serena. Evidently she had fled in fear of arrest. Which brought to mind the fact that he had lied to her. He had left the Mississippi under the shadow of imminent arrest for killing a man, so he was in somewhat the same situation.

If Serena was innocent, she must have had good reason to believe that others would think her guilty. But why hadn't she come to him for help? There was one answer to that, one he didn't like to think about. Instead of fleeing, Serena could have been done away with, maybe by the masked man, and was now lying dead in one of the many canyons around Virginia City.

By nature Darrel was a fatalist. He believed that man had *some* control over his own destiny, yet he was also convinced that there were events over which an individual had no control.

He loved Serena. At least, it was the only explanation that he had for the way he felt about her. Certainly she meant more to him than any other woman he'd ever known, and he'd never lacked for female companionship.

Still, he doubted that anything would ever have come of it. As he had told her, Darrel didn't believe the life of a gambling man fit for a woman, any woman. On the other hand, why had he exchanged bantering comments on the subject of marriage with Serena, if it wasn't somewhere in the back of his mind.

Perhaps it was not in the cards for them. Perhaps fate had taken a hand in the game and forced her out of his life, forever more. If that was the case, so be it. Darrel just hoped that fate hadn't come to Serena in the guise of death.

But for all his rationalizations, Darrel knew that he

was going to feel the loss of Serena Foster for a long, long time, perhaps for the rest of his life.

On Sunday morning, Clendenning was still firm in his decision to quit the mine. He knew he wouldn't be missed. The mine bosses were accustomed to miners being absent for a few days following payday. If a miner didn't come back to work, they could easily find another man to take his place.

It was midafternoon when Clendenning finally left the boarding house. Even though it was Sunday, all the saloons were open and doing a rushing business. In fact, only a few of the shops were closed. The vehicular traffic was lighter than on a weekday, but he noticed a number of loaded ore wagons heading down the canyon to the mills. To keep up with the tremendous outpouring of ore from the mines, the freighting companies worked seven days a week, and even then they were usually behind.

Clendenning was wearing the clothes he had come to Virginia City in. He couldn't spare the money for a new suit. But at least he'd had the suit cleaned; even his broad-brimmed hat had been cleaned and blocked, and he'd bought a can of polish and the Wellington boots wore a glittering shine.

Careful to keep out of the dust on the street, he strolled along, his thoughts occupied with plans for the future, plans that didn't include working in a mine. Each and every plan he thought of he had to discard. Any business he went into needed some financing, and that he didn't have. He knew it would be of little use to go to a bank for the money, since he had no character references nor collateral for a loan.

For no particular reason he could think of, Clendenning found himself heading in the direction of the livery stable Kate Rogan owned. When he became aware of the direction in which he was headed, he decided to continue on. With Serena gone, Kate Rogan was the only person in Virginia City he knew to speak to, and she was the only one who had in any way been kind to him.

As he came to the cross street on which the livery stable was located, Clendenning started to swing down it, then stopped and turned back. A laden ore wagon, pulled by twelve laboring mules, was creaking along C Street.

The idea came to him then, not in a flash, but as though it had been gestating in his brain since he'd turned up Gold Canyon with Serena and had seen the incredible number of wains on the road. Now, just now, the idea began to take definite shape. It was a little far-fetched, considering his financial position, and would depend on a great many factors before it could become a reality. The first factor was Kate Rogan. Without her cooperation and whole-hearted support, Clendenning knew he hadn't a prayer of succeeding.

His step quickened as he walked down to the small, flower-bordered house. He was surprised to see that the sun had set. Without realizing it, he had walked the streets of Virginia City most of the afternoon.

He started for the front door, but some instinct prompted him to go down to the side door instead. His boots resounded on the small porch. He knocked, and in a moment the door was flung open. Kate, in the usual man's shirt and trousers, looked out at him. Her arms cradled the shotgun. There was one difference from the last time he had seen her—her face and hands were dusted with flour, and her face was flushed. It was then that Clendenning noticed the waves of heat coming out of the small kitchen. No wonder, the wood stove was roaring.

Recognizing him, Kate leaned the shotgun against the wall and said, "Well, Clendenning! The preaching man! I never thought I'd see you . . . come in, for God's sake, come in!"

Clendenning hesitated. "If you're expecting company . . ."

"Of course I'm expecting company. You!"

"Me?" Clendenning was puzzled. "But how could you know I was coming?"

"I didn't." The green eyes glinted with mischief. "But since I wasn't expecting anyone at all, you're it. Perhaps I'd better explain." As he came in, she brushed a strand of hair out of her eyes. He caught the odor of whiskey on her breath. "I'll tell you what the crazy hay barn lady does every Sunday of the week. Pa always like a big, fancy supper on Sunday. Since his death, I . . . well." She looked him straight in the eye. "I always cook a fancy supper on Sunday. What I can't eat, or save, I throw away. Crazy, huh?"

"Well, no," he said gravely. "Not if you don't think it's crazy."

She squinted at him suspiciously. Then, slowly, she smiled, her face coming alive. "You know, there's hope for you, after all. Pa also liked his liquor before supper, so I've had a couple in his memory. How about it, Clendenning? Have you fallen that far yet? It's good sipping whiskey."

Clendenning had never taken a drink of whiskey in

195

his life. But suddenly, just being with this lively woman buoyed his spirits. He said, "Yes, I'll have a drink." He added hastily, "Just a small one."

She splashed whiskey liberally into a jelly glass and gave it to him. "It's too damned hot in here. Why don't you sit out on the porch, Clendenning? Sit in pa's rocker. I'll leave the door open and we can talk back and forth."

Clendenning obeyed, lowering his bulk into the ancient rocker. He sipped at the whiskey cautiously at first, but before he knew it, the glass was empty, and he was more relaxed than he had been in a long time. All the while he was studying the large stable, the corral behind it, sloping down the hill. Kate was chattering away inside, mostly nonsense. He made a response now and then.

She finally came out on the proch, fanning herself with the apron. "It's hotter than the hinges of hell in there. Why do I do such stupid things? Hey, your glass is empty! Time for a refill."

He murmured only a token protest, too contented and comfortable to object strenuously.

When Kate came back with a full glass, he said. "How far down does your property go?"

"All the way down to the next street. This is a large lot, nearly an acre." Her gaze was curious. "Why do you ask? I sense something cooking in that head."

He squirmed. "Let me think on it a little, Kate. I'll tell you about it before long."

"Speaking of which . . . you haven't told me yet what you've been doing all these weeks."

"I've been working in the mines. It was all I could find," he said sourly.

"Rough, huh?" she said sympathetically. "Tell me about it, while I return to that hotbox and finish up. We'll be eating soon."

Clendenning sipped at the whiskey and told her at length about his experience in the mine.

Before he was finished, she came out again, her apron gone, her face and hands clean of flour. "Supper's ready, but it needs to cool for a bit." She sat down on the top step with her jelly glass of whiskey. "Go ahead."

"So I quit, having saved up the grand sum of twenty dollars," he finished up.

"What now?"

"Thas . . . that's why I came to shee you." Dimly Clendenning realized that he was a little drunk.

"Don't tell me you've come for that stablehand's job I offered?"

"No, no." His tongue felt swollen, and he had to force the right words out. "I'm going to start a freight line, hauling ore down to the mills."

"With twenty dollars? You're going to do that with twenty dollars? Wait . . ." She leaned toward him, eyes intent. "You came to me because I own a stable, right?"

"That's right."

"Of all the damned gall!" she said angrily. Then she laughed, a bray of laughter. "But then I like a man with gall, always did. Go ahead, Clendenning. Convince me why I should even *listen* to such a crazy scheme."

"I seem to remember you calling yourself crazy a bit ago."

"True, I did," she said solemnly. "But that's dif

. . ." She hiccuped. "That's different. That was *me* saying it about *me*." She rested her chin on the jelly glass and stared off into the night.

Clendenning realized that Kate was also more than a little drunk. Suppressing an impulse to grin, he said, "Do you make a good living with your stable . . . 'scuse me, hay barn?"

"I make enough to get by, Clendenning. Maybe I don't live as good as the swells up on the mountain, but I'm not complaining."

"But suppose you could make enough to move up there with them? Then what?"

"Hah!" Kate drained the jelly glass. "Why should I live among them? They don't like my kind, and I sure as hell don't like them!"

"Kate . . . you must have some ambitions. Do you realize that another freight line is badly needed in this town?"

"Possibly." Abruptly, she spun around. She appeared sober all at once. "What do *you* have to contribute to this partnership I assume you're proposing?" That bawdy laugh again. "Twenty whole dollars?"

"For one thing I have strong hands and a strong back. I have some knowledge of horses and mules. Now wait, before you explode." He held up a hand. "I know that's not enough. We'll have to buy animals and ore wagons, at least two wagons to start. The only thing I can do is borrow the money we need for that. That will be my contribution."

"Borrow?" Who will lend an out-of-work miner money?"

"I'll find somebody," he said stubbornly. "There is a lot of money here. A lawyer named Spencer Hurd

198

told me to come see him if I ever needed anything. I'll ask his advice. Maybe he can tell me where I can borrow the money."

Kate was nodding. "The judge is a good man. About as honest as they come in Virginia." She cocked her head to one side. "Do you know about Brad Stryker?"

"I never heard of him."

"He's also in the freighting business, and he's one reason there ain't more freight lines in business here. He's a mean booger, not above using fair means or foul to stamp out any competition he can."

"I can handle myself. I've learned that much out here."

"I believe you can." She studied him for a moment in silence. Then she jumped to her feet. "All right, Clendenning. It's a bargain. You do what you've promised, and we're partners." She held out a hand for him to shake. "The Clendenning-Rogan Freight line. How does that sound?"

"It sounds fine to me."

"Then let's go eat supper, before we both get falling down drunk."

Kate was an excellent cook, as Clendenning already knew from the breakfast she had cooked for him. For supper tonight, she had cornbread, a baked chicken, fresh vegetables from the farms in the Carson Valley, and milk in quantity. For dessert, she had baked a peach pie.

For the first time in weeks Clendenning's appetite revived, and he was almost ashamed of the way he ate. Kate also had a good appetite, and there was little left on the table when they were done.

Clendenning finished his slab of pie and leaned

back with a contented sigh. "Lord God, I guess I ate like a pig!"

Kate said, "A woman considers that a compliment to her cooking."

"Can I help you with the dishes?"

"Nope. I'll clean up in the morning." She wore a rather strange look now. In the soft lamplight her eyelids seemed unduly heavy, and her lips fuller than he remembered.

He yawned suddenly. "I'm sorry. With the hours I've been keeping, I'm usually in bed long before this." He hauled out his watch. "It *is* late, and I'd better get an early start in the morning if I'm to accomplish anything." He smiled across the table. "It was a fine meal, Kate. Thank you again for having me."

Kate said nothing, just looked at him. Finally, slightly discomfited, he got to his feet and said lamely, "Well, good night, Kate."

Still, she said nothing. He was halfway to the door before she spoke, softly. "Clendenning? You don't have to go."

He faced about, blinking confusedly. "What?"

"You heard me very well. You don't have to go."

His pulsebeat accelerated. "Lord God!" He took a step toward her. "Kate . . ."

She was on her feet and around the table. "Come." She took his hand and led him from the room, down a narrow hall, and toward an open door, out of which yellow light spilled. Clendenning followed, stumbling over his own feet, not quite sure how to take this unexpected turn the evening had taken.

Just inside the bedroom, Kate let go of his hand and stood back a little. "One thing I wish to make

200

clear, Clendenning." Her voice was strong, almost harsh. "I am not a tramp. I do not take every man that comes along into my bed. I'm not a virgin, not by any means, but neither am I a whore. Is that understood?"

Clendenning could only nod dumbly.

Then, in one of those quick changes of mood, she was laughing, laughing that bawdy laugh. "But I thought, since we're becoming partners . . ."

She turned from him then and began undressing. Clendenning turned his back and attempted to remove his clothes. His hands were all thumbs, and it seemed to take forever. Before he was finished, the lamp was blown out, the room plunged into darkness.

Finally undressed, he faced about, trying to locate the bed. Her low laughter sounded. "Over here, Clendenning."

Following the sound of her voice, he fetched up against the bed, tripped and came down on it with a thump.

He was still floundering when she seemed to flow into his arms.

"Ah, Clendenning!"

She found his mouth. Her kiss was fierce, demanding, and her lips had the taste of heated honey. As his hands moved tentatively over her body, Clendenning discovered that a marvelous figure had been hidden under the shirt and trousers. She was rounded and curving. Her breasts were not big, yet they were large enough to fill his hands.

Their mutual need was so great that most of the preliminaries were dispensed with. Almost before he was aware of it, she opened to him, and they locked together as he went inside her.

201

Now that she had committed herself, Kate held nothing back, displaying a laughing, wanton passion that both delighted and shocked Clendenning.

As their passion peaked simultaneously, Kate uttered a choked cry and arched to him, her nails digging into his naked back.

Finally, with a soft sigh, she relaxed and fell away. Clendenning, his senses still a riot of sensation, moved to stretched out beside her.

Kate searched for his face in the dark. Finding it, she lightly traced his features with her fingertips, one finger finally coming to rest on his lips.

"Clendenning, tell me something." Her other hand found his.

"Yes, Kate?"

"If I hadn't asked you to stay, would you have made the first move?"

It took him a moment to find his voice. "Now can I answer a question like that? Lord God!"

"I can answer it," she said in a voice soft with amusement. "You wouldn't have."

Clendenning could think of no rejoinder to that. This was, without a doubt, the strangest, most unpredictable woman he had ever known. Of course, he thought ruefully, that didn't cover a very large field.

He said, "Kate . . . do you want me to go? Or should I sleep here?"

"No! You stay right there!" Her hand tightened on his. "It's been a while since I woke up in the morning and found a man beside me. Anyway . . ." That bawdy laugh. "Who says I'll *let* you get any sleep?"

But even as she spoke, her voice took on a drowsy quality, and her hand fell away from his.

"Clendenning?"

He started. "Yes?"

"If you can't get your loan, don't worry about it. We can always use this property as collateral for a bank loan."

"No!" He raised up. "I would never allow you to do that!"

There was no response. Kate was asleep. Or pretending to be.

Chapter Ten

By the time they reached Carson City, Serena thought it was safe enough to stop for supplies. They had left Virginia City in such haste that they had not taken much with them, and Tang P'ing had told Serena that the trip would be long, and the towns where decent foodstuffs would be available few and far between. There were waystations on the stage route they were to travel, but such stations refused to serve Chinese, except at the back door, and Tang P'ing said that the food served in such a manner was slop, fit only for animals.

Serena, knowing that it was best she stay out of sight as much as possible, remained in the buckboard while Tang P'ing and Shu-toe did the shopping. They were only gone for a short time, but during those minutes Serena felt very alone. Dressed in her exotic clothing, face stained dark, she *felt* like a Chinese; she experienced something of the fear and apprehension she sensed *they* must feel in dealing with a society which considered them less than horses and mules, which were considered valuable property. She felt greatly relieved when they returned to the buckboard—Shu-toe with a large bag of rice on his shoulder and carrying a wicker cage with two hens inside.

Tang P'ing dropped her bundles on the buckboard floor and smiled. "Got many good things. Fresh, dried, vegetables, and meat. Sauce, too, and tea. We will eat well on trip, Se-rena. We go now?"

Serena shook her head. "There's one thing I'm going to have to buy myself. That is, if I can."

Tang P'ing looked troubled.

Serena patted her hand. "Don't worry. I won't be gone long.

Tucking her purse into her sleeve, Serena slipped out of the buckboard and headed down the street toward a gunshop she'd sighted through the buckboard curtains.

The gunshop owner was reluctant to sell a shotgun to a Chinese, and Serena, conducting the transaction in monosyllables, finally had to pay double what the weapon was worth. When she returned to the buckboard, she tried to give the shotgun to Shu-toe.

He shook his head firmly, waving his hands.

Tang P'ing said, "Shu-toe not like guns. Never use one, Se-rena."

"I don't like them, either, and I hope we never have to use the shotgun. But there is no way of knowing what we're going to encounter out here. I'm hoping that the sight of it will give second thoughts to anyone thinking to do us harm." She propped the shotgun on the floorboards, the barrel leaning against the seat alongside Shu-toe, where it could easily be seen by anyone riding up. "There, you don't have to use it, Shu-toe. Just leave it there where it will be noticed."

Several miles out of the little town of Genoa, they turned west onto the Kingsbury Grade Road, which, according to Serena's crude map, would eventually join the Placerville Route at Johnson Pass. They began to climb almost immediately. The road was narrow, steep, and very dangerous, in many places only wide enough for one vehicle. They had to pull off to one side time after time to let huge, lumbering wagons and stagecoaches pass.

The Concord stagecoaches frightened her the most. They were splashed with gaudy, brilliant colors, and some of them had scenes painted on the doors. Pulled by teams of six horses, and carrying up to twelve passengers, with a number sitting on top, the stagecoaches sped recklessly down the narrow mountain road, heedless of danger to other vehicles. Even on the downgrade, the drivers slackened their speed very little. On some twisting mountain curves, Serena watched in awe as the huge coaches sped past. Some of the curves were so sharp that the six horses and the coach made the form of an S on the roadway.

Serena was later to learn that the stagecoach drivers, at this particular time along the Placerville Route, were considered the elite of the West. Absolutely fearless, arrogant in their skills, very well paid, many of them were legends in their own time. It was indeed an awesome sight to see one plunging down the mountain grade as they, in the buckboard, labored toward the top.

The traffic was far heavier going east—wagons hauling material to the mining camps, the stage-

207

coaches, family wagons creeping along, men on horseback and mules, and a great many on foot.

The scenery was spectacular. Timbered peaks soared on every side, and even in this month of August many of the peaks were capped with snow. The road clung to the mountainside like the track of some giant worm, the cliffs steep on one side, and dizzying chasms dropping thousands of feet on the other. The Rockies had been awesome in their grandeur, but Serena thought that the Sierras were even more beautiful.

They made camp at night whenever they could find a mountain meadow large enough to accommodate them. It became a little easier for a time when they finally reached the top of the pass, the road leveling out for a long stretch.

Serena spotted a small grassy meadow, with a stream running through it. She leaned forward. "Shu-toe, let's camp here. Maybe stay for a couple of nights. The horses are tired, and God knows we all are."

Shu-toe nodded and swung the buckboard off the road. There had been times during the long haul up the grade when they had to keep moving all night, with Shu-toe going ahead on foot carrying a lantern and leading the horses. There had simply been no place for them to pull off and make camp.

Shu-toe halted the buckboard by the small stream, under a huge pine. Serena and Tang P'ing got out and stretched. Serena had been sitting so long that her legs and feet were numb.

"God, it's good to move around!"

"Yes, Se-rena, is good," Tang P'ing said, with her dimpled smile.

208

Shu-toe unhitched the horses, let them drink in the stream, then staked them out to graze. Much of the meadow was brown, but the grass grew lush along the stream.

It was only the middle of the afternoon, yet Serena was weary. "I'm going to nap for a little." She took blankets from the buckboard. Since Tang P'ing had been over this route before, on foot, she had known how cold the nights were and had advised bringing a large number of blankets.

Serena made a bed under the pine tree, removed only her shoes, and crawled under the blankets, making sure that her purse was with her. She always made sure she wasn't far from her purse. Not only did it contain the derringer, but all the money she had left. If the money was somehow lost, she would be destitute.

The air was clear and pure up here, smelling pungently of pine. She snuggled down to a more comfortable position and dozed off.

She awoke to the odor of cooking. Opening her eyes, Serena was amazed to find that it was dark. She had slept the afternoon away. She saw the flicker of firelight and turned her head to see Tang P'ing squatting over a small fire.

"Why didn't you wake me, Tang P'ing?"

"No need." Tang P'ing looked over at her, smiling. "You sleep good."

"Didn't you get any sleep?"

"Oh, yes, sleep, too."

"Where's Shu-toe?"

"Gather more wood for fire."

Serena was so comfortable she hated to move. She decided to remain in the blankets awhile longer. She closed her eyes and was almost asleep again when a small sound of fright from Tang P'ing startled her awake.

She sat up, glancing toward the fire. Across the flames from Tang P'ing stood two men. They were dirty, unshaven, carrying heavy packs on their backs. They were about as disreputable a pair as Serena had ever seen. Both were middle-aged, big men, and were carrying pistols in gunbelts.

Now one smiled, lewdly, exposing splintered teeth. "Now what do we have here, Robbie lad? Two Chink gals, and right purty ones, too!"

"Right tasty looking, Newt. That they are."

"And out here all alone. Now who'd thunk we'd have such luck as this, hiking acrost these double-damned mountains?" Newt leered. "Ain't you got a word of greeting for strangers, gals? Or maybe you don't speak the English so good, heh? For what Robbie and me have in mind you have no need to speak."

With sinking heart Serena thought of the shotgun leaning against the seat of the buckboard. It was too far away; they would catch her before she could get halfway there.

Stealthily, her hand crept into her purse and extracted the little derringer. Closing her hand around it, Serena glanced about the clearing. Where was Shu-toe? If he came back unawares, they would probably kill him.

The man called Newt spoke, "You take this'un here, Robbie. The one over there is for me. Got a bed already all warmed up for old Newt." He started around the fire toward the blankets.

Gathering herself, Serena came to her feet in one supple motion, the derringer centered on the advancing man. "Stop right there! Come any closer and I'll kill you!"

Newt skidded to a stop, mouth agape in astonishment. "Aw now, little gal, you wouldn't shoot old Newt . . . Hey! You ain't a Chink! You look like one but you ain't. Imagine the luck, finding a white woman out here." He took a step.

"I warn you." Serena brought the derringer up. Her heart was thudding with fear. She recalled Darrel's instructions to never let fear rule in a moment of danger. She forced herself to remain calm.

She motioned with the derringer. "Step back to the fire beside your friend." Out of the corner of her eye, she saw the other man's hand creeping toward his holstered pistol. Serena raised her voice. "You by the fire! You might be able to pull your gun and shoot me, but before you do, your friend here will be dead. Think about that!"

"For God's sake, Robbie," Newt cried hoarsely. "Don't do nothing hasty!" His face took on a sickly, ingratiating grin, and he said in a wheedling voice, "I wouldn't harm you, little gal. Not now that I know you're a white woman. I thought you two Chinese, and who cares about a pair of Chinks? Now why don't you put that popgun away and we'uns will have a little talk?"

"This popgun, as you call it, can be deadly at close range, and I'm sure you know it." Steel in her voice, Serena said, "Now I suggest you do as I say and go back beside your friend."

"All right, all right!" Newt raised his hands shoulder high and made patting motions at her. "Don't get skittery now."

He began backing up, and Serena followed step by

211

step, maintaining the same distance between them. Finally the two men were again side by side, and Serena and Tang P'ing, who had gotten to her feet, stood across the fire from them.

The man called Newt had regained some of his courage. Grinning, he said, "Now what, little gal? We all gonna stand here like this all night?"

He had a point, Serena conceded to herself. They couldn't stand here like this forever. She could force them to leave, of course, but as soon as they got out of the firelight, they could sneak back and shoot both her and Tang P'ing. Serena suspected that the man Newt was just angry enough, and mean enough, to do it.

Her glance went past the two men, and she said, "Now, Shu-toe!"

Newt laughed raucously. "That's the oldest trick in the book, little gal! There's nobody behind . . ."

His words were choked off as Shu-toe, creeping up behind the two men on cat feet, seized them by the necks and cracked their heads together. They slumped in his grip. Shu-toe let Robbie fall and fastened both hands around the throat of the other man.

"No, Shu-toe!" Serena said sharply. "There's no need to kill them. Let him go!"

Shu-toe looked at her dazedly. Then he nodded reluctantly and loosened his grip. Newt sprawled unconscious on the ground beside his friend. Serena hastened to the buckboard and returned with the shotgun.

A few minutes later, the men stirred, groaning. When Newt opened his eyes, he found himself staring into the muzzle of the shotgun an inch from his nose.

"Now you're going to leave here, both of you," Serena said. She stood back a little. "Get to your feet."

Helping each other, the two men got up.

"Take their guns, Shu-toe."

"Don't do that, miss, please!" Newt pleaded. "We can't be left without our irons. A man's life ain't worth nothing without a gun out here."

"You should have thought of that before you came to our fire, intent on attacking us. Take their guns, Shu-toe."

The two men stared in fear and awe at the bulk of the giant Shu-toe and offered no resistance as he disarmed them.

Serena said, "I'll make a bargain with you. Go back the way you came, well away from us. In the morning, I'll leave your guns by the fire here. But don't even think of sneaking back during the night. Shu-toe . . ." She nodded to the big man. "He will be on guard all night. He wanted to kill you before. If you come back, I'll let him. Now go!"

Without another word, the pair turned and hastened off into the night. The moment they were out of sight, Serena breathed a sigh of relief. Her limbs suddenly without strength, she sank to the ground.

Shu-toe and Tang P'ing hovered over her. Tang P'ing asked anxiously, "You not feel good, Se-rena?"

Serena raised her drooping head. "I'm fine, Tang P'ing. Or I will be as soon as I get over being frightened to death!" She smiled and began to laugh shakily. "I didn't think I had it in me! Did you see what I did? I don't believe it!"

Tang P'ing flashed her dimpled smile. "Brave woman, Se-rena. Did fine."

Shu-toe was grinning broadly. He clapped his hands together softly, bobbing his head.

"It wouldn't have been so fine if you hadn't shown up when you did, Shu-toe. Any minute I was about to drop to the ground in a dead faint."

Tang P'ing said, "Food ready now. You eat, Serena, feel better."

"I think we'd better move on in the morning, instead of spending an extra day here, like I told that pair. They might keep skulking around, hoping for a chance to jump us."

They left early the next morning. True to her promise, Serena left the guns by the ashes of the fire. She didn't see the men anywhere as they drove away, but she felt certain they were lurking about somewhere, watching them leave. One tiny fear nagged at her. If the two men were headed for Virginia City, would they tell everyone they saw that they had come across a white woman masquerading as Chinese? She shrugged the worry away. There was nothing to be done about it now. As soon as they reached San Francisco and disappeared into the underground labyrinth in Chinatown there, she would be safe enough. Tang P'ing had been telling her about this city beneath a city; and Serena found it hard to believe, yet she knew that Tang P'ing would not lie to her.

Their journey was mostly downhill now, and the going was somewhat easier. At least there wasn't so much danger from the careening stagecoaches. As they were going up the mountain now, the coaches had to creep along.

The lower Serena and her party descended toward

the Sacramento Valley, the more signs of civilization they saw. They passed through several small mining towns. Many of them had been worked out, and the towns were little more than ghost towns now.

The nearer they approached Placerville, formerly called Hangtown, the more signs Serena saw of the devastation wreaked on the land by the frantic search for precious metals. Whole hillsides had been denuded of timber and left covered with mine tailings; the openings of the mine shafts gaped like empty mouths on the mountainside. The streams showed signs of much panning, with debris left behind. In places, the earth had been piled high, like beaver dams, diverting the streams from their natural beds. Now, at the height of summer, the streams were little more than trickles. With a shudder Serena could imagine how it would be here in the spring, when the streams were swollen with melted snow, the denuded hillsides pouring mud across the road.

Placerville, while not the roaring mining camp it had been just a few years ago, was still busy. The buildings were graying, the untenanted ones crumbling into decay, and Serena wondered if Virginia City would come to look like this in time.

But there were stores open, and Serena was able to replenish their dwindling supplies. The prices were outrageous. In one store a single watermelon was displayed for sale. The price—twelve dollars!

Serena shopped judiciously. There were several days journey from San Francisco yet, Tang P'ing had told her. Serena bought enough food to last them, and also feed for the horses. She knew that when they got down onto the valley floor most of the grass would be burned brown by the summer's heat.

She was tense and nervous during the short time they remained in Placerville, afraid her disguise would be penetrated. If she was wanted for murder in Virginia City, the word would be out by this time. Surely the authorities in Placerville had received a wireless to that effect. If someone recognized her as Occidental, suspicion would be immediately aroused.

Nothing untoward happened. There were quite a few Chinese in Placerville, and the town was undoubtedly accustomed to them. Within two hours of their arrival in Placerville, they were on their way again.

In a few days they were out of the mountains and down into the valley. Although traffic was heavier on the road, travel was easier on level ground, and there were many places to camp. They never made camp near a town, and although Shu-toe kept a vigilant watch at night, they were not accosted by ruffians again.

The heat in the Sacramento Valley was intense both day and night. Serena was grateful for the tunic and trousers she was wearing. She would have suffered much from the heat had she been wearing a dress, with the confining undergarments underneath.

Early one afternoon, as the buckboard labored up a slight grade, Serena noticed the air here was much cooler, and she could smell a strange, exotic odor, one totally unfamiliar to her.

Tang P'ing, noticing Serena sniffing, smiled, and said, "Is sea you smell, Se-rena."

"The sea? I've never seen the sea!"

Suddenly excited, Serena leaned forward, as the buckboard crested the rise. And there, spread out before her, was a panorama that took her breath away.

216

She touched Shu-toe's shoulder. "Pull up, pull off the road! I want to look!"

Shu-toe found a place to stop the buckboard off the road. In her excitement Serena leaped down from the buckboard, and stood, drinking it all in.

The first thing that caught her attention was the sight of the mighty clipper ships, spars rising to the sky like fingers pointing to heaven. They were anchored side by side across the bay, stretching as far as she could see. "There must be thousands of them!" she breathed.

The second thing that astonished her was the city itself, the city across the bay. It was a city of hills, golden, gentle hills, covered with houses. Dimly, Serena could perceive steep streets, some seemingly going almost straight up.

After the heat of the valley, it was almost chilly here. To her right, as the bay curved west and out toward the open sea, Serena saw a gray blanket of fog rolling in. Even as she watched, it moved in over the hills, obscuring them.

She gazed in dismay at the stretch of water between them and San Francisco. She turned to Tang P'ing beside her. "How on earth do we get across all that water?"

"Take ferry, Se-rena." Tang P'ing pointed down to the bottom of the slope at a dock where even now vehicles were being loaded onto a giant ferry. "Take ferry across. Then soon be in Chinatown."

Tang P'ing smiled, and Serena realized that the Chinese woman felt that she was coming home.

Chapter Eleven

Li Po sat in his palatial suite on the third floor of the building he owned at the intersection of Clay and Dupont. As befitted his position as the wealthiest, most powerful mandarin in San Francisco, the suite was richly decorated and furnished, even the smaller room where he now reclined on plush cushions, the room he used as an office.

He began reading Brad Stryker's letter, which he had received that morning.

"Dear Li Po:

I'm sure by now you know that your house here burnt to the ground. As of this date, the culprit who set it to the torch has not been uncovered. As you know very well, the law here bothers little with what happens on the downside. If you wish it rebuilt, so inform me, and I will see to it.

219

"I have an urgent matter to bring to your attention. I would very much appreciate your help in this matter. There is a woman, Serena Foster by name, who recently fled Virginia. She is wanted by the law for the killing of a whorehouse madam. I doubt that the law will go to any great effort to apprehend the woman. But if she is found and brought back to Virginia, she will hang for her crime.

"I have more than a passing interest in Serena Foster. Since it is personal, I will not herein go into my reasons. Her being found and brought back would please me. May I hasten to add that I doubt much grief would be felt should it not be possible to apprehend her alive. The reason I am writing to you about this matter is that I have some reason to believe that she has fled to your city.

"I know, Li Po, that little escapes your notice in San Francisco. Serena Foster is a young woman of about twenty. She is of medium height, with yellow hair, large gray eyes, and an uncommonly fair, fine complexion. Those who know about such things, say she is comely.

"As business acquaintances of long standing, I would very much appreciate any help you might give me in this matter. If you could bring this about, I might, if Lady Luck is with me, be able to reward you well in time."

Finished with the letter, Li Po sat sunk in thought, still as a stone idol. The replacement of the house interested him not at all; he *had* already learned of its

220

destruction, and would use that as an excuse not to return to that barbaric town again.

A slight smile curved his lips. Knowing this man Brad Stryker as he did, Li Po could read between the lines of the letter. For reasons of his own, Stryker wanted this woman dead.

Yet there was something else about the letter that nudged at Li Po's mind. He closed his eyes, ruminating.

Suddenly, he uttered a soft exclamation.

The woman he had seen in Maguire's Opera House in Virginia City! The woman with the yellow hair and so white skin! This Serena Foster was the same woman Stryker sought. Li Po was sure of it; he felt the rightness of it in his bones!

For one of the rare times in his life, Li Po laughed aloud. This woman he had seen and so desired and thought he would never see again—she was being delivered into his hands. The gods were good to him.

It was possible, of course, that the man Stryker was mistaken, that this Serena Foster was not in San Francisco. But if she was, Li Po was confident that he could find her. Stryker was correct in that respect. Sooner or later, Li Po knew everything that transpired in his city. If she was here, he would find her in time.

Then he made a steeple of his long fingers, frowning in thought. There was one thing that might interfere. These were difficult times in Chinatown. A tong war was presently raging, a fierce feud between the Sum Yop and the Sue Yops tongs. As the high chieftain in the Sum Yop, it was not safe for Li Po to venture into the narrow alleyways. He was a member of the Sum Yop family, but he had assumed the name

221

Li Po, especially with the white race, so he would not be identified directly with any tong.

Li Po had not left his quarters for days, directing the continuing battle from his suite. He was convinced that it would soon be over, the Sum Yop emerging victorious. Li Po was supremely confident of his ability as a war chieftain. He believed that in another time and another place—his homeland—he would have been a great war lord.

But at this particular time, it was unsafe for him to leave the house, which was as secure as a fort, and venture out into the streets. Even a heavy consort of his *boo how doy* would not completely insure him from an assassin's bullet. The best he could do for the time being would be to give a description of Serena Foster to his minions and have them search for her.

If she was here, he was certain he would find her eventually. His blood coursed warm in his veins as he dreamed of what he would do with Serena Foster once he had her in his suite. He would indulge his appetites until he was weary of her, then dispose of her as he saw fit. Brad Stryker's wishes mattered little to Li Po, but he supposed he would inform Stryker of the woman's fate. It would do no harm to have Stryker in his debt.

San Francisco overwhelmed Serena. The spacious streets, the horse cars, the fine clothes the men and ladies wore on the street, the grand houses dimly glimpsed on what Tang P'ing told her was Nob Hill—it was too much to take in all at once.

Actually, she didn't see a great deal of the city itself. As soon as they left the ferry, Shu-toe drove the

222

buckboard to Chinatown. He let Serena and his mother off, then drove away.

"He will sell horses and buckboard," Tang P'ing said. "Then come to us, bring you money, Se-rena."

Tang P'ing hurried them along the narrow streets of the Chinese quarter. Serena dallied, staring in wonder at the colorful costumes, the exotically decorated houses, the extraordinary carvings on the doors and walls, the balconies overhanging the streets. Strange smells wafted out of the shops and restaurants they passed. Tang P'ing kept urging her along, casting apprehensive glances behind her.

Finally Tang P'ing darted into a dark doorway, pulling Serena along with her. Inside was only a narrow stairway leading down into unseen depths. Serena hesitated, but Tang P'ing gestured for her to follow. They started down. To Serena's amazement, they did not stop after one floor down, but continued on. One floor, two, and yet another.

On the third landing Serena stopped Tang P'ing. "Where are we going?" she asked breathlessly. "How deep does this go?"

"This last, Se-rena." Tang P'ing smiled. Now that she was inside, she seemed less nervous. "Big Chinese city underground. Go down . . . what you call? Four stairs?"

"Four floors underground? I know you told me, but . . . how far? I mean . . ." She made inadequate measuring motions with her hands. "How far does it extend?"

"All way under Chinese quarter."

Serena shook her head in awe, then nodded to Tang P'ing to indicate that she was ready to continue.

Tang P'ing opened the landing door, and they were in a corridor, dimly lit by Chinese lanterns at regular intervals suspended from the ceiling. Many people moved along the corridor, all Chinese. And many doors opened off the corridor. Most were closed, and Serena assumed that the rooms behind them were living quarters. But there were some open doors, displaying shops with food and clothing for sale, and in some she saw people eating.

They proceeded down the corridor for some distance, turning several corners. Finally, Tang P'ing stopped before one door. It had a fire-breathing dragon depicted in red on the panel.

Tang P'ing knocked on the door. To Serena, she said, "Is Ling family. Good friends of Tang P'ing and son."

The door opened, and a Chinese woman, tiny as Tang P'ing and with the same delicate features, but somewhat older, stood in the doorway.

Serena expected cries of delighted greetings and perhaps embraces. Instead, the woman inside bowed formally, hands tucked into the sleeves of her tunic. Tang P'ing also bowed in much the manner. The two women exchanged rapid words in Chinese.

Then Tang P'ing turned, drew Serena inside, and closed the door. "Is Ling Wu, best friend in San Francisco. She invite us stay. Does not speak English." She spoke again in Chinese to Ling Wu, and Serena heard her name mentioned. Ling Wu faced her, bowing formally, speaking a few words.

"Ling Wu proud welcome you to humble abode," said Tang P'ing. "Tell her you not Chinese. She keep secret. But do not tell others, Se-rena, not even other

Chinese. You may go along floors below ground. But do not go above ground. Bad for you. Understand?"

Serena nodded her understanding, but she wondered in dismay how long she was expected to remain down here. For now, it was new and strange, and would be exciting to explore, yet she knew it would eventually become confining.

Noting her expression, Tang P'ing said severely, "Many Chinese live here, never go above top floor. Ling Wu been San Francisco five years. Very few times been outside."

"Yes, Tang P'ing, I understand," Serena said. "You think it would be dangerous for me to be seen on the streets."

Tang P'ing nodded vigorously.

Ling Wu had a husband, who owned a laundry above ground, and two children. They were a quiet, very polite family, and despite the language barrier Serena was able to communicate with them without too much difficulty. Their quarters were small, but adequately furnished. There were only two rooms, the large room Serena first entered, which was used as a parlor, family room, and dining room. The family, and Shu-toe, also slept on pallets in the main room. Serena and Tang P'ing were given the smaller room for their own, which Serena understood was the bedroom of the man and wife.

Serena felt guilty about this and told Tang P'ing of her feelings.

"Not to worry, Se-rena. Family not mind. Used to doing this. Many times friends stay here."

"But who knows long we will have to remain down here? Can't we find quarters of our own? You know I have money."

225

"Tang P'ing try, but not easy. All rooms full this time. Perhaps soon we find own place."

Serena's first supper with the Lings consisted of the usual rice, with spicy pork cooked in it. And Serena was introduced to her first rice wine. Ling Wu and her husband, as well as Tang P'ing and Shu-toe, drank it like water, with little effect. Or so it seemed to Serena. The first cup of the hot liquor made Serena tipsy. She was reminded of the champagne suppers with Darrel. A shadow of melancholy passed over Serena at the memory of Darrel. She pushed all thoughts of him from her mind and accepted another cup of rice wine. By the time they had their meal, she was in a state of euphoria.

Afterward, she was very tired and sleepy, and retired early. It was wonderful to be able to sleep with a roof over her head for the first time in weeks. Despite the crowded conditions, she felt safe and secure for the first time since she had left Virginia City.

During the days and weeks that followed, Serena cautiously explored the underground city. Tang P'ing had given her a slip of paper, bearing the Ling's name and address, so that she might request help if she became lost. Although Chinese was a difficult language to learn, Tang P'ing had taught Serena a few words and phrases, enough to make a small request understood. Now and again, she would forget about her gray eyes, and find some Chinese staring at her with curiosity.

A time or two, Serena thought she was being followed, but it was difficult to be sure, what with so many Chinese moving to and fro along the corridors. She dismissed it as a figment of her imagination.

The enforced idleness bothered her more than any-

226

thing. Tang P'ing had gone to work in the Ling laundry; so had Shu-toe, driving a delivery wagon. Many times Serena offered to help clean the rooms, but each time Ling Wu shook her head in the negative, smiling politely.

Within two weeks, Tang P'ing had found a place of their own they could move into, two small rooms, complete with furnishings. This at least was something to keep Serena occupied. She insisted on paying the rent and buying the furnishings needed. It didn't cost a great deal, yet it did make a dent in her remaining funds. Serena refused to think about what would happen when her money ran out. Already she had made up her mind that she wasn't going to remain down here forever, like a mole hiding in a hole. Another month, two at the most, and she figured it would be safe enough to venture out into the city and become an Occidental again; surely they would have given up looking for her by that time. She would find employment somewhere under an assumed name.

It took Serena only a short time each day to clean after Tang P'ing and Shu-toe left for work. One thing that Serena hadn't counted on now concerned her. While living with the Lings, crowded as they were, Shu-toe had been lost in the crowd. But here, with just his mother and Serena, his presence made itself felt. And one evening it came to Serena with a shock that Shu-toe was in love with her. She had happened to glance up, and caught his gaze on her. His dark eyes were luminous with adoration. He immediately looked away, but not before Serena realized the truth. His adoration made her uncomfortable. She realized that she had not really thought of Shu-toe as a man before. Yet he *was* a man, with a man's body and a man's feelings, mute though he might be.

It was not that she had any fears for herself. She knew instinctively that Shu-toe would die before he would harm her. It troubled her deeply, however. If he had feelings of passion toward her, it was not fair for him to have to spend the evenings in such close proximity. Yet there was little she could do about it.

The feeling of confinement was beginning to press in on her, and she asked Tang P'ing if she might not venture aboveground, just for a few hours.

Tang P'ing shook her head. "You safe underground, Se-rena. Chinese people here not bother you. But tong war in streets above. Much danger above ground."

"Tong war?"

"Tongs large Chinese families. Rich, much power. All bad people. Sell opium, sell girls, what called white slavery. That how they get money. Many times two families do battle. Tong war now going on. Many people killed."

Serena shivered. "That's terrible! Why don't the police do something to stop it?"

"Police seldom come Chinatown," Tang P'ing said simply. "Tongs fight among selves, only kill other Chinese. So police San Francisco not bother."

"Sounds as bad as Virginia City," Serena muttered.

She heeded Tang P'ing's warning, for the time being at least, and confined her strolls through the seemingly endless corridors. To Serena, this huge underground city had an aura of fantasy about it. She had the strange feeling that it existed independent of the city above ground. She knew that many of the Chinese who had living quarters down here worked above ground, yet it was as if the city above ceased to exist for them too when they returned at night.

Yet, a few nights later, something happened that made her realize that there was not only an intermingling of the two worlds, but a mixing of the races as well.

Serena had learned from Tang P'ing that behind many of the closed doors she passed were the so-called opium dens, where the Chinese so inclined could spend the evening smoking the narcotic of the poppy. It was Serena's impression that the opium smokers were all Chinese, and she had no inclination to visit one of the dens.

One evening, quite late, she was making her way back to her own quarters when she turned a corner and saw four white people, two men and two women. They were obviously of the upper classes, probably high society from Nob Hill. The men wore evening clothes, with the typical silk top hats, and the women were attired in the long, elaborate dresses of high fashion. They were being escorted by a lone Chinese male.

Serenae kept her head down as they passed by her. Then she turned, looking after them, much mystified as to the reason why four Occidentals should be down here. After a moment's indecision, she tagged along behind them. Soon, their Chinese guide stopped at a door, opening it. Serena caught a glimpse of a smoke-filleed room, packed with Chinese males. When the door closed, Serena impulsively pushed at it. To her surprise, it opened to her touch. She slipped inside just in time to hear one of the ladies titter behind her hand, and say to her companion in a carrying voice,

"This place *does* look really wicked, Lilly. You're sure we'll be safe?"

"Safe as in church, dear," said the one called Lilly. "I'm well known here. They wouldn't dare offer harm to me. Wait'll you have a puff or two of the poppy, dear. Your fears will fly away like a bird."

To Serena, the room looked more sordid than wicked. The walls were lined with tiers of bunks, each bunk with a thin pallet. On each bunk a man reclined. Some were drawing on strange-looking, long pipes. Each pipe had a round object attached near the bottom end, with a small hole in the center, from which rose thin streams of smoke. Other men had fallen into a drugged stupor. None of the occupants of the room paid the slightest heed to the newcomers, who were now being escorted to thick cushions on the floor in the center of the room. The two ladies and the men arranged themselves on the cushions, and accepted four pipes from their guide.

At that moment the guide noticed Serena, and he came toward her, chattering in harsh Chinese and making shooing motions. Serena fled. Behind her, as she ran down the corridor, the guide leaned out the door and shouted after her angrily.

Back in their rooms, Serena found Tang P'ing still up. Shu-toe had retired. Tang P'ing was making tea. Serena accepted a cup and sat down beside her. She debated for a moment about telling the woman about venturing into the opium den. Her curiosity was too strong, so she related what she had seen to Tang P'ing.

"Foolish, foolish woman, Se-rena!" Tang P'ing looked angrier than Serena had ever seen her. "Could have come to great harm!"

"I know, I don't blame you for scolding me. But I'm as curious as a cat. It'll probably be the death of me." She smiled cheerfully, not at all contrite.

"Chinese guide, he know you Occidental woman?"

"I'm not sure. He spoke to me only in Chinese, and I heard him talking to the white people in English. I should think that he would have used English, had he realized I was not Chinese. But tell me, Tang P'ing . . . do many white people come to these opium dens?"

Tang P'ing made a face of disgust. "Many, yes. Some just come to look. Others come to smoke the poppy. Foolish, foolish people. Own people foolish, too. Some charge money to Occidentals to show them through opium dens."

"But these were society people. Important, and rich, I should think. I heard one call the other Lilly."

"Woman named Lilly Hitchcock Coit." Tang P'ing made a face again. "Much scandal about woman. Have much money, live Nob Hill. Always do something foolish. Much talk of her in San Francisco. Wear men clothes, masquerade as man, smoke cigars. Do what your people call, 'See the elephant.' "

"What does that mean?"

"Mean go in saloons and gambling places, stay all night, see everything to see. Come home drunk in morning."

"One thing I don't understand, Tang P'ing . . . you keep saying it's dangerous for me to go outside, yet here these people come in, bold as brass. Why isn't there danger for them?"

"Tong men not harm Occidentals. Do so would cause San Francisco police come in, arrest them. You,

231

Se-rena, supposed to be Chinese. You caught in tong battle, they kill any Chinese in way, man, woman."

Serena sipped her tea and remained silent. Yet her mind seethed with rebellious thoughts. She knew that she was going to sneak outside. She couldn't believe that the risk was as great as Tang P'ing claimed. More and more, she was feeling confined down here. She might as well be in prison.

As Serena put down her cup, the low table moved beneath her hand and the floor trembled. Dust fell from the ceiling, and Serena experienced a feeling of vertigo. The phenomenon was accompanied by a low rumbling sound and the clatter of rattling dishes and pans.

Serena cried out and looked at Tang P'ing. The other woman seemed calm, but her face was white. She hushed Serena, as she would a child. "It's all right, Se-rena. Just a small one. Will be all right."

The trembling stopped, and Serena let out her breath. "My God! What was that? What do you mean, 'a small one'?"

"Earthquake. Earth shake and move."

Serena swallowed. "Is it dangerous?"

Tang P'ing nodded. "Big one come, very dangerous. Whole cities fall down. In China, I have seen this. This," she gestured to indicate the underground city, "all be . . ." She made another gesture, bringing her two palms together. "San Francisco have many earthquakes. Some day will be big one. This, no more."

The following day, Serena went ahead with her resolve. She picked the daylight hours, when both

Tang P'ing and Shu-toe were at work. Surely she wouldn't be in any peril in the daytime. She intended to slip outside and wander through the streets of Chinatown for a time. Tang P'ing need never know.

She went up the flights of narrow stairs and opened the door through which Tang P'ing had brought her into the labyrinth. Once outside, Serena mingled with the throngs of Chinese on the streets. She remembered to keep her eyes cast down, risking only darting glances now and then.

The district was fascinating. Most of the streets were very narrow, little more than alleyways, lined with shops of every description. She saw a large number of other whites, mostly women, going in and out of the shops.

Gay streamers hung from many balconies, with the vertical Chinese lettering. On others were suspended ornate, elaborately decorated paper globes.

Shops windows exhibited an exotic array of goods. One shop had a window full of glass jars, which contained colored liquids, and odd, floating things that Serena did not care to look at too closely. Bunches of roots and dried leaves hung from the ceiling, and a row of silver needles lay on a piece of black velvet, in front of a colored drawing of a human body, showing strange dots along the head, torso, and limbs.

Serena walked along, enjoying it all, reveling in the feeling of freedom. Most of all, she enjoyed the fresh air, tangy with the smell of the sea. Down below, the air was always a little stale, musty, despite the ventilator shafts that brought air from the surface. She longed to walk out of the area, and down to the waterfront—to see the clipper ships, to view the ocean firsthand. She knew she dared not take that much of a chance today. Perhaps another time.

She turned down another street and was startled by what sounded like gunfire. Tang P'ing's warning echoed in her mind, and Serena almost turned and fled back the way she had come. Then she realized she was hearing firecrackers, not gunfire. The street she was on now was more gayly decorated, and the balconies were all thick with people. Many of them were igniting firecrackers and tossing them into the air, where they exploded, some with beautiful explosions of colored fire, others erupting with confetti of many colors. The confetti drifted down like a snowfall.

Serena remembered then something that Tang P'ing had told her. The Chinese people loved to celebrate and would seize upon any occasion—birthdays of important personages, weddings, the least excuse for merrymaking.

She stood back against the wall, letting the crowd surge around her, and watched. It was very colorful, like watching a drama performed on a vast stage. She watched for a long while, forgetting about the time. As the noise and confusion began to ebb, Serena realized with a start that she had been away longer than she intended. If she didn't hurry, Tang P'ing would have come home from work.

Hurrying along, head down, she made a wrong turn and found herself on an unfamiliar street. It was very narrow; tall buildings rising on each side seemed to lean toward each other, forming a sort of tunnel, shutting out the sun. The street was shadowy and almost deserted. Confused, Serena hesitated, at a loss whether she should continue on, or turn back. Finally, she decided to continue on to the end of the street. Maybe she would emerge on a street she recognized.

All of a sudden, halfway along the alley, doors flew open on both sides, and more than a dozen men burst outside. Before Serena could collect her wits, she was in the middle of a violent melee. All the men wore black tunics, black trousers, and black hats. They looked sinister and threatening.

As the men closed with one another, hatchets flashed in the dimness. To Serena's horror, she saw one man within arm's length of her fall to the ground, a hatchet buried in his skull. It was all done in utter silence, no words spoken, only the sounds of grunting breaths and the soft scuffling of feet.

Serena fought to free herself from the group of combatants. Every direction she turned her way was blocked. Then a body collided violently with her. She was knocked to the ground. Instead of picking herself up, Serena crawled on her hands and knees, fighting her way between the dancing legs of the men. Finally she was out of it.

She got to her feet and went back the way she had come at a dead run. At the entrance to the alley, she risked a glance back. The men were scattering, the brief battle apparently over. There were three lying still on the ground, and Serena was sure they were dead.

To her great relief, the alley opened out onto a wide street crowded with people. Heart still thudding with fear, breath coming hard, Serena slowed to a fast walk and mixed in with the Chinese on the street. After a block she looked behind her. She caught a fleeting glimpse of a man several yards behind, a man all in black, wearing a black hat.

Serena recognized where she was now—only a few blocks from the door opening to the underground city, and safety. Tang P'ing, as usual, had been right. It had been foolhardy of her to come aboveground. At the door she looked behind her again, and was sure she saw a man in black in the crowd. Was it the same man? Was she being followed?

Quickly, she opened the door and ran pell-mell down the first flight of stairs. At the first landing she paused, listening. She thought she heard the door open, and the shuffle of soft slippers.

Serena hurried on, not pausing again until she was in the corridor going past her rooms. Head down, she walked briskly, weaving in and out of the people in the corridor, and ducked inside their quarters. She didn't look behind her again. As a precaution, she locked the door.

Tang P'ing came home a half hour later, giving Serena enough time to compose herself. However, she must have still looked flustered, for Tang P'ing gave her a sharp glance, but did not question her.

Serena kept quiet about what had happened. She knew she would receive a severe scolding should she tell Tang P'ing. Anyway, it was all over now, and she resolved not to be so foolish again.

Two days later, Serena learned that it wasn't all over by any means.

During her walks along the underground passages, she kept catching glimpses of a man in black behind her. The man never approached close enough for her to get a good look at his face.

Serena finally dismissed it, again, as nothing more

236

than her imagination, conjured up by the awful scare she had received aboveground.

On the afternoon of the second day, she had been shopping for food in one of the small Chinese grocery stores. Arms laden with packages, she managed to push the door to their rooms open, not too surprised to find it unlocked, since she often forgot to lock it.

Backing into the room with her packages, Serena closed the door and turned. She uttered a choked scream. Arms suddenly nerveless, she dropped the packages, food spilling all over the floor.

Standing across the room from her was a squat Chinese male, all in black. He was dressed like the men she had seen fighting on the street. It flashed through her mind that she hadn't been imagining it, after all. She *had* been followed!

She opened her mouth to ask who he was, what he was doing here, but she closed it just in time, remembering that she wasn't supposed to speak English. Then it occurred to her that he must have already seen her gray eyes.

One hand in his tunic pocket, the man took a step toward her. His dark eyes glittered menacingly. In a harsh, hissing voice, he said, "You Selena Fostel?"

Serena shook her head violently from side to side.

Before she could move, he was beside her. Tangling his fingers in the black wig, he wrenched it from her head, letting the blonde hair spill free.

He grinned, nodding. "Yes-s, Selena Fostel." He took his hand from the tunic pocket. There was a gun in it. He motioned with the gun. "You come with me."

237

Chapter Twelve

Serena stood unmoving, her mind paralyzed by panic and fear. The only thing she could think of was that he had come to arrest her for the murder of Madeline, yet she knew that it was extremely unlikely that the forces of law and order would employ a Chinese. It had to be something else. She felt as if her mind was an empty room with nothing but the sound of questions echoing from the walls. What? Why?

Her throat was tight and dry, but she managed to choke out a few words. "What do you want with me?"

He shook his head angrily. "You come." He gestured with the gun.

His angry face somehow reminded Serena of the gold Chinese mask of her ravisher, and she felt as if a strong hand was squeezing her vitals. She heard herself whisper, "No!" And then suddenly her mind, released from its stasis, began to function. What could she do, what could she offer him to let her go? The answer came almost as soon as the question. Money!

Serena willed herself to speak calmly. "You are being paid to do this." The man's lips tightened, and he motioned again with the gun, this time taking a threatening step toward her. Serena stood her ground, although she felt her insides flinch.

"I will pay you to leave me alone. You understand? I will pay you more than you are being paid to take me with you." She prayed that what money she had would be enough. "Do you understand?"

The lines in the man's face had smoothed out somewhat, and the glittering look of greed in his eyes told Serena that he did indeed understand and that her question had reached him.

"I will give you," she hesitated, "five hundred dollars!"

The man's mouth twisted in contempt, and he again raised the hand holding the gun.

"A thousand then! A thousand dollars!" Serena almost shrieked the words. His eyes flickered, but he did not change expression.

"Fifteen hundred. One thousand, five hundred."

This time, he hesitated, and Serena knew that she was getting close to the amount that it would take. She felt a pang as she realized that it was going to be almost all she had. Left in her possession was only twenty-five hundred of the money Aunt Hetty had willed her.

"Two thousand," she whispered. "That's all I have. If you'll let me go, say you couldn't find me, I'll give it all to you."

His thin lips curved slightly in what might have been a smile, and he nodded, almost imperceptibly.

"All right. I'll get the money."

As Serena turned toward the bedroom door, her mind was moving faster than she had realized it could. She opened the door to the other room, hoping, but not really expecting, that the Chinese would let her enter alone. As she went through the doorway, she could feel him close behind her, and this hope was dashed. As she approached the corner of the room where her funds were hidden beneath a loose wall board, she turned to him.

"Please step back," she said firmly.

Although his black eyes watched her closely, he came no closer. Serena was able to turn to the wall and partially screen her movements with her body. With shaking hands, she took out the small tin and removed the money before he reached around her to snatch the tin from her hands.

As she faced around, Serena managed to slip the top notes from the wad of bills and conceal them quickly in the top of her jacket. She was aided in this by the fact that man was occupied with searching the small tin, then throwing it aside. He reached for the money Serena held toward him. She leaned against the wall, trembling, as he greedily counted the notes. Now was the crucial moment. Would he accept what he had and leave her alone?

Cramming the money into his tunic pocket, the man held her gaze with his. Looking into those shiny, black depths, which were so dark they showed neither pupil nor iris, was like looking into a soul devoid of pity or love, and Serena's spirits plummeted, but then, with his cold, almost-smile, he nodded curtly to her and turned away. Within seconds he was out of the room, his soft-slippered feet making very little sound, and Serena was finally alone.

When the front door closed behind him, Serena hurried to lock it. Weak all over in the sudden rush of relief, she sank down onto a pillow on the floor.

It wasn't over, of course. She couldn't stay here now. To trust the man in black to keep quiet about her living here would be foolish. But what Serena dreaded the most was the fact that she would now have to tell Tang P'ing that her identity had been uncovered. Tang P'ing seldom revealed much anger, but Serena knew that the woman was going to be displeased with her.

She forced herself to start preparing supper, making a pot of the strong Chinese tea. She drank a cup. It quieted her fears and allowed her to think more clearly.

Fortunately, Tang P'ing and Shu-toe came home at the same time, So Serena could tell them together while they ate their meal.

Somewhat to Serena's surprise, Tang P'ing did not scold her. Instead she sighed, and gave a fatalistic shrug, as though she had expected something like this to happen sooner or later.

Shu-toe *was* angry, but not at Serena. He stood up, smacking a fist into his palms. He talked swiftly on his fingers to his mother. Tang P'ing shook her head, speaking sharply in Chinese. Shu-toe's face set in stubborn lines, and again his fingers danced.

With another sigh, Tang P'ing faced Serena. "Shu-toe want you describe this man here. Describe closely, so Shu-toe can recognize him."

Divining Shu-toe's intent, Serena said firmly, "No, Shu-toe! You will *not* go looking for this man. I won't

242

have you taking such a risk because of something brought about by my own foolishness. Besides, what good would it do to kill him? It's too late now." She looked at Tang P'ing. "The thing that bothers me the most is that he knew my name. He knew who I was. How is that possible? And why would anyone but the police be looking for me?"

Tang P'ing shrugged. "Not know."

Serena got up and began to pace. "Maybe it has some connection with the masked man who killed my folks and was going to kill me. But I still don't know why anyone would want to kill us. It doesn't make any kind of sense!" She shook her head in baffled frustration. She stopped and faced them determinedly. "But there is no doubt of one thing. We have to get out of here. Just because this man accepted my money is no assurance that he will not tell whoever hired him where I am. In that case, they'd come directly here. So we have to leave here tonight. At once!"

Tang P'ing looked resigned. "But where, Se-rena?"

"I've thought it all out. I'll become a white . . . an Occidental again. We'll leave here and I'll take a room in a hotel, using an assumed name. Thank God, I kept *some* money back. You two will come with me." She hesitated, searching for the right words. "You will pose as my servants. If you don't mind doing that?"

Tang P'ing said simply, "Where you go, Se-rena, we go." And Shu-toe nodded eagerly, his gaze never leaving Serena's face. That dogged devotion was in his eyes again.

Serena looked away in confusion, wondering suddenly if it was wise to take Shu-toe. But these were the only people she knew, and trusted, and most certainly if someone came here looking for Serena Foster and didn't find her, Tang P'ing and Shu-toe would suffer for it.

She said briskly, "Let's pack what few things we have and leave here tonight."

"Where we go, Se-rena?"

"A hotel, I suppose." She paused, groping for a name. "In a newspaper, I read something about the Cosmopolitan Hotel on Bush Street. Tonight, we'll go there."

"That bad place."

"What do you mean, bad? It's a hotel, isn't it?"

Tang P'ing started to speak, then stopped, giving that fatalistic shrug again. She got to her feet and started to move off.

Serena stopped her with a touch on the arm. "Tang P'ing, I've behaved very foolishly. I expected a scolding. Instead, you seem . . . well, certainly not surprised."

Tang P'ing said gravely, "Already learn, Se-rena. You . . . what you call? Unpre . . . ?"

"Unpredictable?"

Tang P'ing nodded, smiling now. "So why scold? What purpose?"

Serena stared at her, then began to laugh, laughter that approached hysteria, but for a moment washed away the fear.

Li Po was probably as angry as he had ever been in his life. He was unaccustomed to betrayal by any of his *boo how doy,* and now that an incidence of it had been uncovered, he could scarcely control his rage.

244

Ranged before him were three of his minions. Two of them held the third man firmly in their grasp.

In an icy voice, Li Po said, "You have betrayed my trust, Fong Jin."

Fong Jin bowed his head humbly. "I would have come to you with the information, lord. But I was waiting for an audience."

"You lie!" Li Po spat the words. He gestured. "The money."

One of the men holding Fong Jin delved into his tunic pocket and handed a sheaf of bills to Li Po. At the sight of the money, Fong Jin paled and slumped in resignation. Li Po quickly counted the money.

"Two thousand American dollars. It was found hidden in your quarters. How did you come by it, betrayer of your master?"

"I . . . I stole the money, master. From a rich white man."

"Again you lie. You found the woman, Serena Foster, and she gave you the money as a bribe. The truth, or you will die a slow and painful death!"

Fong Jin cringed. "It is true, lord. I found her." His head hung low.

"Where?"

Fong Jin told of where and how he had located Serena Foster.

Li Po stared at him hard for a moment. Then he motioned indifferently. "Kill him. At once. Then go to this place and look for the white woman with the yellow hair."

Fong Jin went with the two men without protest. It would have done no good; he must have known he was under the sentence of a swift death from the moment his treachery was found out.

Li Po knew it would be of little use to search for Serena Foster in the place where Fong Jin had discovered her. Unless she was thoroughly stupid, she would be gone by this time. Yet there was a small chance that the Chinese woman she had been living with had been left behind. If such were the case, Li Po's men, highly skilled at torture, would wring any information she might have from her.

His fury was cooling, yet Li Po was still upset. He went into his bedroom and prepared a pipe of opium. Soon, he was soothed and at peace.

There was at least one thing he was pleased about. The tong war was over, and his men had emerged victorious. The brief skirmish a few days ago had ended it. They had decimated the other warring tong, and there would be no trouble from that quarter again. Peace would reign—until another tong family decided to challenge Li Po's power and authority.

Now he was free to devote more time and effort to finding the woman with the yellow hair. If she had not fled San Francisco, he would find her in time.

After a night in the Cosmopolitam Hotel, Serena found out why Tang P'ing had had reservations about staying there. It was little more than a bordello! True, the hotel's main business was renting rooms, and the desk clerk had been glad to accept Serena Foster and her entourage as guests, but there was much coming and going during the night, and Serena recognized most of the women she saw in the halls as females of easy virtue. She later learned that the "Washoe Club" held regular monthly meetings there. This happened to be their meeting night, and revelry continued throughout the night.

By morning it had quieted down, and Serena intended to stay until she found some kind of employment; then she would look for cheaper quarters for them. There was an ironic, amusing side to it. In Virginia City, she had been offered the opportunity to run a whorehouse and had spurned it righteously. And here she had spent the night surrounded by whores!

At least the Cosmopolitan provided excellent service for its guests. They offered room service, and Serena had breakfast sent up to their rooms. Tang P'ing and Shu-toe stubbornly remained with their rice diet. Serena had her first American breakfast in quite some time. She ate with relish.

Finished, she said to Tang P'ing, "You know my measurements. I want you to shop for clothes for me. Something neat and practical. I can't go in search of a job wearing a Chinese tunic and trousers!"

Tang P'ing looked distressed. "You think wise, Serena, go about San Francisco as self?"

"What else can I do? Besides, it might be the best disguise. Whoever is after me evidently knows that I've been disguised as one of your people. Hopefully, he will think I will continue to do so. Anyway, maybe he has never seen me in person. Maybe all he has is a description sent along from Virginia City. There must be hundreds of women in San Francisco with blonde hair. I think I will be safe, so long as I don't bruit my name about."

Tang P'ing acquiesced, departing shortly on her shopping chore. Ruefully, Serena counted what money she had left. A little over three hundred dollars. She would have to find some way of earning money, and quickly.

Tang P'ing returned with a simple gray dress with long sleeves and a modest neckline; a gray bonnet; a black shawl; high-top walking shoes; and undergarments.

Tang P'ing fingered the shawl. "Grows cold now, Se-rena."

When Serena, dressed in her new clothes, left the hotel that afternoon, she ventured out alone, even though Tang P'ing had insisted that Shu-toe accompany her, to protect her.

Serena stood firm against all pleas. "No, I go alone! No one would employ me if Shu-toe was along. And you, Shu-toe . . ." She wheeled on him, stealing herself against the hurt look in his eyes. "I know from past experience about your habit of following me. I'll be watching, and I'll send you back if I see you!"

Serena had no concrete idea as to what sort of job she was looking for, or even what she was fitted for, since she'd never held a job in her life.

For much of the afternoon, it didn't really matter, since she wandered here and there, dazzled by this wondrous city. She had never seen anything to approach it. She had read that San Francisco's population was close to sixty thousand, and it was considered the most cosmopolitan city in the West. Gawking in wonder, Serena could well believe it.

Shortly after leaving the hotel, she found herself in Portsmouth Square, with the notorious Bella Union house of joy on one side and many saloons and gaming houses on another. Then she was on Montgomery Street, the main business thoroughfare. It was paved

248

with planks and lined with shops. Many tradesmen displayed their wares right on the sidewalk. People of every description thronged the street. Long, horse-drawn street cars clanked along, crowded with passengers.

As the afternoon waned, Serena began to think again of her purpose. She entered shop after shop, at first mostly ladies' clothing stores, and inquired about employment. She was turned down as soon as she admitted she had no experience.

In one small shop, the male proprietor gave her a sweeping, insolent glance, and said, "Lady, I couldn't afford the wages you'd need to keep yourself all prettied up."

Serena looked down at herself. "What's wrong with the way I look?"

"Nothing, not a thing, miss. You're just too tony for my place." As Serena started to turn away in discouragement, he added, somewhat slyly, "I have an idea where you'd be welcomed with open arms."

Eagerly, Serena said, "Where is that?"

"Some of the places on Pacific Street." He hid a grin behind his hand. "They like to hire pretty women such as yourself as 'waiter girls.'"

"Waiter girls?" Serena said dubiously. Then she squared her shoulders. It should not be beneath her to wait on tables. She was having no luck elsewhere. "Could you give me directions?"

A short time later Serena was walking down Pacific Street. It seemed strangely quiet, almost deserted at this time of the day. There were many places lined up side by side, with strange names—the Bull Run, Occidental, Billy Goat, et cetera.

Intrigued by the name, Serena stopped before the

249

doors to the Occidental. Taking a deep breath, she pushed open the doors and went in. It was very dim inside, and she stood blinking for a moment until her vision adjusted. At this hour there were very few people present, and most of them were women. A long bar ran along one wall, and many round tables crowded the floor, with a cleared space in the center that Serena assumed was for dancing.

With a sinking heart, she realized that she was in a saloon, or a dancehall, and that the "waiter girls" must be employed to serve drinks. She almost turned and left, but a plump man, with dark, oily features, was coming toward her, a smirk on his face.

"What can I do for you, girlie?"

"I . . ." Serena swallowed. "Are you the proprietor?"

His smirk widened into a grin. "I'm the owner, if that's what you're getting at. So, what can I do for you?"

In as steady a voice as she could manage, Serena said, "I'm looking for employment. I understand you hire waiter girls?"

"If you want to call them that." He laughed. "You have any experience?"

"No, I haven't." With a feeling of relief, she turned to go.

But as she turned, the man somehow maneuvered himself between her and the door.

"What's the rush, girlie? I didn't say you *needed* experience. Sometimes it's better you're new at it." He winked. "Especially a young and juicy dollie like you. What you need to know I can teach you. Picking pockets, rolling the lushes, it ain't all that hard to learn. And laying on your back, that just comes natural."

Shocked, Serena stared at him. Panic swept over her. "I'm sorry to have taken up your time. I'm going now." She tried to move around him.

He seized her arm in a cruel grip. "Not yet, you ain't. You'd make out good here. Many of the dollies pull in two hundred a week."

Serena realized that she had again foolishly rushed into a dangerous situation. She looked around for help. But the few men at the tables were grinning in obvious enjoyment at her predicament. Now that her vision had adjusted, Serena noticed that all the women wore face-paint. Most had bosoms bursting over low bodices, and all wore short dresses, coming to just below their knees, showing boots, and stockings of many colors on their legs. There was only one man standing at the bar, wearing a bowler hat. He was short, pudgy, and from the back looked quite old. She could expect no help from him.

The proprietor was saying, "That long dress will have to go, o'course. Need to show a little leg. Let's see how yours stand up." Still holding her arm in his grip, he bent down and hoisted her skirt.

"Let me go!" Serena cried. She hit him on the top of the head with her purse. He merely laughed. Not ever dreaming that she would need it, Serena had left the hotel without her derringer.

Then a deep voice spoke up. "It would be best, sir, that you do indeed let the young lady go free."

Looking around, Serena could see the reason for his amusement. Confronting them was the man in the bowler hat. He was indeed short, not even as tall as Serena, and was at least sixty years old. He was dressed in what once had been fine clothes, but they showed signs of much wear, and he had a rumpled, untidy appearance. He also had a large paunch, across which stretched a watch chain. His face was round, plump-cheeked, with a short, rather bulbous nose veined with red. His eyes were blue, and merry even now. The one thing unusual about him, Serena noted, were his hands—small, but well-cared for, with long, supple fingers. Both hands were crossed over the pearl handle of a cane on which he leaned his weight.

Serena's dim hope for help sank. This was as unlikely a rescuer as she could imagine.

The proprietor guffawed. "Well now, little man, who might you be?"

The strange little man removed one hand from the cane to doff his bowler with a flourish, exposing a shock of snow-white hair. "Professor Phineas Trapp, sir. At your service."

"Phineas Trapp, is it?" the proprietor growled. "Well, Phineas Trapp, for what are you sticking your nose into my affairs?"

"It struck me, sir, that the young lady was in dire need of assistance." The blue eyes twinkled.

"Suppose she does? What do you aim to do about it?"

"For one thing, sir, this!"

Phineas Trapp stood erect, pointing the cane. There was a snicking sound, and a glittering, six-inch blade suddenly projected from the end of the cane.

"With this, sir, I can do considerable damage to your person. So I do suggest that you let go of the young lady's arm."

"Hey, careful with that thing!" The proprietor

dropped Serena's arm and stepped back with alacrity. "I didn't mean any harm, just having a little fun."

"Your concept of fun, sir, is far from humorous." Phineas Trapp made a sweeping bow to Serena. "After you, my dear."

Serena hurried out of the Occidental. A moment later, Professor Trapp joined her, backing out of the doors. He pressed something on the cane, and the blade disappeared. He turned to her, flourishing the cane, eyes twinkling.

Slightly breathless, Serena said, "My thanks, Mr. Trapp, for coming to my rescue."

"It was my pleasure, young lady. And please call me Professor. I detest being mistered."

Serena laughed. "All right, Professor."

"And now, may I escort you to your home, or wherever?"

"You may. I would be most grateful."

Professor Trapp offered his arm, and they started back up Pacific Street, after Serena had told him where she was staying.

"Tell me, please, what was a lady such as yourself doing in such a den of iniquity?"

Serena felt like asking him what *he* was doing there, but a whiff of his strong breath told her the reason. Professor Trapp was a toper. She said, "I was looking for employment."

"In there?" he exclaimed. "My dear young lady, don't you know where you are?"

"Well, I know now that I was foolish, that these places are all saloons and brothels."

He was shaking his head. "That is not the worst of it. This, my dear, all this area is the ill-famed Barbary Coast. Fortunately for you, it was not after dark that you ventured here. Your life, not to mention your virtue, would not have been safe!"

Serena was truly shocked. "I've heard of the Barbary Coast. I hadn't realized." She shivered.

He pressed her hand reassuringly. "Well, you are safe now." He looked at her appraisingly. "What sort of employment are you looking for? Surely nothing that is offered here?"

"Well, I was told about the 'waiter girls' I know better now about that, too." She drew a breath. "I'll be honest, Professor. I'm not qualified for much. I've never held a job."

"You are pretty and well-spoken. I might have something for you, if you should be interested."

"You?" She stopped to look at him. "What employment could you offer?"

He drew himself up. "I, dear lady, am an illusionist, a prestidigitator *extraordinaire!*" He flourished the cane.

"I'm not sure I understand . . ."

"I perform illusions on the stage, my dear," he said. "I have a troupe of traveling entertainers, and recently two of my troupe left my employ: two young people, who eloped."

Serena was puzzled. "But why didn't they stay on? I mean, they didn't have to leave just to get married, did they?"

The Professor put a finger to his pursed lips. His blue eyes twinkled. "Well, you see, both of them were already married, to someone else!"

"Oh!" Serena flushed.

"At any rate, I need someone to take their places. You would do nicely in Ruby's spot. I used her in my Invisible Lady illusion and in the act where I saw a lady in half . . ." At her look of apprehension he laughed. "Do not fear, it is all illusion. No harm will come to you."

Serena was thinking hard. Would it be wise for her to be seen in so public a place as a stage? She asked, "You perform these acts in San Francisco?"

"Oh, no, not entirely. In the summer, I tour the mining camps, and in the winter the towns in the San Joaquin Valley, sometimes venturing as far south as Los Angeles. I usually end my tour here, that is true. I just closed a few weeks ago at Maguire's Opera House on Washington Street. Alas, my assistants often desert me here, seeking greener pastures," he said sadly.

The mention of the name Maguire sent Serena's thoughts winging back to Virginia City. "Virginia City?" she asked, trying to appear casual. "Do you travel that far?"

"Oh, dear, no. That is much too far, too much time between appearances, too expensive. I tour only in California."

For the first time in two days, Serena felt hopeful. "It sounds like something I might like. There is one thing . . ." She was hesitant. "I have two more people who would have to accompany me. A Chinese woman and her son."

"The woman . . . is she young, pretty?"

"She looks younger than she is, and she is quite pretty."

"Then we can fit her in. And the young man, is he strong?"

Serena nodded. "Shu-toe is very large for a Chinese, very strong."

The Professor beamed. "Capital! The young man

255

who left me was our strongman, a mainstay of our troupe."

"Then both of our problems are solved, Professor. I and my friends have employment . . ."

"And the addition of the three of you fills out my troupe," he said, twinkling. He rapped the sidewalk with his cane. "Capital! Be prepared, my dear, to leave Monday of next week!" He bowed. "Welcome to Professor Trapp's Traveling Show and Circus of Illusion!"

Chapter Thirteen

Professor Trapp's Traveling Show and Circus of Illusion consisted of three wagons and eight persons, including himself.

The wagons bore the name of his show in large, swirling letters, ornamented with suitable decorations, and were sturdy and well-cared for. One wagon carried the equipment, food, and props; the other two wagons were fitted out as sleeping wagons, and carried the performers.

Serena and Tang P'ing shared the women's wagons with Dolly and Nora Peacock—"The Peacock Sisters, Singers and Dancers *Extraordinaire*!" They were friendly, plump women of indeterminate age, who looked nothing at all alike. Serena learned that their real names were Dolly Smith and Nora Morris, the "Peacock" name being an inspiration of the Professor, who had suggested they wear bright, showy attire to give a lift to the spirits of the lonely miners for whom they would perform later in the season.

The male members of the troupe shared the other sleeping wagon. In addition to the Professor and Shu-toe, there was an older man, Roscoe Downs, who tended the horses and wagons, and assembled the sets and equipment; and a juggler, Todd Rutelege, a tall, fair man of around thirty years of age. Todd would have been handsome except for his sullen countenance. He kept pretty much to himself and rarely spoke to anyone unless necessary. Todd also acted as the Professor's assistant during the more difficult illusions.

"It was his wife who ran away with the strongman, dear," Nora Peacock told Serena. "She's the one you're replacing. I must say he took it hard. He was always a quiet man, but now he hardly speaks at all. It's quite gloomy to be around him."

"And it's not as if Nora hasn't tried to comfort him," Dolly said from her bunk against the wall. She looked archly at her "sister."

Coloring, Nora shook her head. "I was just trying to be friendly to the poor man," she said.

"He turned her down flat, is what happened," said Dolly with a laugh. "Me too, in fact. It's a pity, too. He's quite a good-looking gent."

Serena felt rather embarrassed at this casual discussion, but did not wish to appear naive, and so she shook her head, as if she couldn't understand a man who would not wish to be "comforted" by the Peacock sisters.

The troupe played to good audiences everywhere they went, for the people were starved for entertainment. They performed in theaters, when there was one; at other times, they performed in churches, schoolhouses, and any building large enough to seat an audience.

Since it was well into winter now, it was Professor Trapp's practice to play the towns in the San Joaquin Valley, traveling as far south as Los Angeles. In the last spring and summer, they played the mining camps up the canyons.

Between performances, between towns, Professor Trapp might imbibe himself senseless, but the moment he stepped onto the stage, he was transformed. Wearing a black suit and a long black cape with a scarlet lining, he was in complete command, holding the audience literally in the palm of his hand. At the beginning of every performance, he started off with easy tricks, his supple hands causing cards, balls, handkerchiefs, and other objects to appear and disappear, while he kept up an amusing, running patter.

Tang P'ing, looking amazingly young and pretty in a gold, fancily embroidered dress slit up the sides, was his assistant during these small feats of magic.

Serena found that she enjoyed fooling the audience. Two of the illusions, both completely mystifying to the crowd, were her favorites. The first was called the Invisible Girl, and Serena never appeared before the audience. A glass casket was suspended from ceiling beams. The bottom and ends of the casket were solid, but its top, front and back were made of glass, so people could see through. From the top of the casket extended a hornlike object, flaring out into a speaking tube at the end. People were invited from the audience to inspect the casket and assure the other spectators that it was indeed empty. Then they were instructed by the Professor to ask questions of the speaking tube, which, from all appearances, went directly into the casket. To the amazement of the spectators, the questions were answered by a girl's voice coming from the speaker tube. Much speculation was voiced by the audience as to the solution of the mystery. All the guesses were wrong.

The real explanation amused Serena. There was a small room behind the casket, in which Serena sat. If there wasn't already a room there, Professor Trapp provided one by hanging a curtain behind the casket, the curtain resembling a real wall. There was always a small space between the casket and the wall, or curtain, so people could see behind the casket, but the space was not large enough for a body to pass through. The speaking tube ran along the top of the casket and into the wall, and could not be seen unless someone knew it was there. There was also a picture on the wall, or curtain—the portrait of a woman. One eye of the woman was a peephole through which Serena could see objects held up in front of casket, thus allowing her to describe them perfectly. Her voice coming through the speaking tube had a muffled quality, which only added to the illusion, making it appear that her voice came from within the glass-enclosed casket.

But the most spectacular illusion was the last one of the evening, the climax of their performance. An oblong box was exhibited on stage on a raised platform. Doors were opened in the front, back, and top, Serena was placed inside the box, and the openings were closed. Then she extended her head and hands through holes at one end of the box, and her feet through openings at the bottom end. The Professor then picked two spectators at random from the audience and invited them upon the stage to hold Serena's hands and feet.

Shortly, Professor Trapp began sawing the box in half with a huge saw. He sawed straight down through the center of the box. It was nothing unusual for spectators to start to scream and faint when the saw apparently reached Serena's body. Professor Trapp, looking solemn, shaking his head sorrowfully, continued to saw until he reached the platform. Then he pushed two square, wooden slabs down into grooves between the severed halves of the box, and one section of the box was pushed away from the other, separating them a few inches. Yet Serena's head and hands still were visible at one end, and her feet at the other.

Professor Trapp now moved sideways back and forth between the two sections to prove there was no possible connection between them. Finally he pushed the sections of the box together again, the slabs were taken out, and the top of the box was removed. Serena popped out, smiling and waving, uninjured by her harrowing experience.

The explanation again was simple. The platform itself was hollow. The box was actually considerably shorter than Serena. The doors were always closed before she extended her hands, head, and feet from the ends of the box, so that the audience could not see that she was lying with her knees drawn up. The box was bottomless, and the center portion of the platform was divided lengthwise into two sections, hinged front and back, so that the sections swung downward and inward when Serena rested her full weight on them. As the platform sagged in the middle, Serena stretched her body, so there was no visible change in her position to be seen from the outside.

There was another hinged board set upright against the back of the box. This was manipulated by Todd Rutelege, dropping forward until it formed a center strip on the platform, across the middle of Serena's body, acting as a protective measure against the saw.

The box was sawed down to the platform, the wooden slabs then inserted into the grooves so that the sections of the box could be separated without revealing their being empty. During the brief separation period, Serena stretched herself still farther, allowing enough space for Professor Trapp to edge his way between the sections.

Now the process was reversed. The halves of the bottomless box were pushed together, and the slabs removed from their slots. The center strip was raised by Todd while the doors were being opened, and Serena popped out of the box, whole again!

Professor Trapp's "Catching the Cannon Ball" illusion was also spectacular. It was for this illusion that he needed Shu-toe.

Shu-toe took up a position ten yards in front of a nine-pounder cannon. Professor Trapp then held a torch to the fuse. The cannon roared, a cloud of smoke momentarily obscuring the stage. When the smoke cleared, Shu-toe stood beaming proudly, the cannon ball cradled against his chest.

Serena learned that the secret of this illusion lay in the loading of the cannon, which was done by Todd before it was wheeled onto the stage. Although a full charge of powder was used, only a small part of the powder was placed in back of the ball. As Professor

Trapp explained it, the usual way to load a "muzzle loader" was to pour all the powder in first, pushing it down with wadding with the aid of a ramrod. Then the ball was inserted.

For the illusion, however, only a small part of the powder preceded the cannon ball. Then the wadding was rammed in, followed by the ball. Next, the remainder of the powder was poured in, along with extra wadding. Therefore, when the cannon was fired, no trace of leftover powder could be found.

The wadding was soft so it would scatter. When the fuse was lit, the full charge of powder exploded with the usual noise and smoke, but only the powder behind the ball actually propelled it. The ball's velocity was by no means slight, but a large, powerful man, heavily padded, could catch it without harm.

"Some people say that a successful illusion depends on sleight of hand. The hand quicker than the eye, et cetera," Professor Trapp expounded to Serena. "Not so. Misdirection is the key to a successful illusion, Serena. Direct the audience's attention away from the key to the illusion. Your beauty, my dear, does that very well when you are being dismembered. And Shu-toe . . . capital!" The Professor thumped the stage with his cane. "He is the best cannon ball catcher I have ever used. The audience has never seen a Chinese of such proportions and seldom take their eyes from him."

Shu-toe was completely happy with his job with the show. In addition to catching the cannon ball, he performed a strongman act between illusions. Stripped to the waist, he would display his broad shoulders and tensed biceps. Then with a great show of muscle, he would lift great weights—not as heavy as they looked,

263

and bend the iron bars. Thus, he was able to use his great strength to a useful purpose, and it pleasured him to amuse people.

Tang P'ing adapted to life with the circus with her usual equanimity. She evinced neither pleasure nor displeasure. So long as Serena and her son were content, so was she. She had soon started acting as cook for the troupe, a fact for which they were all grateful. The cooking, prior to her arrival, had been done by Roscoe Downs, and the food had been one of the unsavory aspects of the tours.

As the props were changed between each illusion, a curtain was lowered between the spectators and two-thirds of the stage, and Shu-toe and the others performed before this curtain. The Peacock sisters sang and danced. They were good dancers and fair singers, Dolly having the better voice. When the audience was all male, the sisters favored the men with a few tantalizing glimpses of stockinged leg.

Todd Rutelege was the other performer between illusions, doing his juggling act, wearing only a pair of tights. Serena soon began stationing herself in the wings to watch Todd perform. He was very supple and muscular, and his coordination as he juggled balls, Indian clubs, even lighted torches, was marvelous to behold. He was as light and graceful on his feet as a dancer, and as he became absorbed in his performance, the sullen cast to his countenance lightened. Often, he ran off the stage smiling to himself as applause sounded behind him like a rain of hailstones.

Despite herself, Serena was drawn to him, and wondered what it would be like to see him smile at her. During the long hours of travel between towns, she tried to engage him in conversation, receiving only monosyllabic responses for her efforts.

It didn't take Serena long to discover the reason why Professor Trapp had looked seedy at the first meeting in San Francisco. He made quite a lot of money on the tours, but he squandered it on two things—his thirst for strong drink and providing everything he could for the convenience of his troupe. Not only did he pay good wages, he bought the best food while traveling, and often took them all to fine restaurants in the various towns. He also had two riding horses along with the caravan for those who wished to ride, to escape even for a short time the monotony of riding in the wagons.

"He's a soft-hearted man, is the Professor," Dolly Peacock told Serena. "He showers money and gifts on us, and by the time we finish the season in San Francisco, the Professor is on his uppers. Nora and I have been with him for years. We couldn't have it any better anywhere else."

"But he's not young any more," Serena said. "Why doesn't he give some thought to the future?"

"I know, Serena, I know." Dolly sighed. "We've all tried to tell him that. But he just laughs, saying that he has one magic secret he has yet to reveal to anyone . . . the secret of eternal life. I happen to think that when the time comes that the Professor can't perform his illusions any more, he'll just curl up and die. It's a pity; he's such a nice man."

Serena silently agreed. She had come to have a great affection for Professor Trapp. But if the others had tried to talk him into saving a little of his money and failed, what could she hope to accomplish?

On the farm back in Illinois, the Fosters had owned no riding horses, and all Serena had learned to ride was a mule. She noticed that Todd Rutelege rode almost every day while they were on the road. He cut a handsome figure on the big, black stallion. His tight, Western-cut trousers showed off his long, muscular legs, and his wide-brim hat, and the gun holster at his belt, gave him a dashing, dangerous air. Shu-toe the Professor, and Roscoe Downs did most of the driving, with Todd spelling them. The rest of the time, Todd was astride the black stallion. Often he ranged far ahead, out of sight of the caravan, for hours at a time.

Serena made up her mind that she was going to ride. In her heart she knew that it was mainly a ploy to establish some kind of contact with Todd. But to the Professor, she said, "I'm sick of bouncing along in these wagons all day. I want to ride one of the horses."

"Are you a good horsewoman, my dear?"

Serena shrugged. "I've ridden mules. It can't be too different."

Professor Trapp shook his head. "The gait is quite different, Serena. I think you should practice a bit before going off on your own. Todd now is an excellent horseman and could instruct you, but in his present state of mind . . . well, no matter. At least the chestnut mare is a gentle creature, not like that black monster Todd rides. Do you have a riding habit, my dear?"

"A riding habit? What's that?"

"A split skirt, Serena. It would be . . ." He coughed behind his hand. "Even out here, it would be unseemly for you to ride a horse in a dress."

"I have just the thing!"

Serena hurried to their wagon, and dressed in the tunic and trousers she had worn in the Chinese underground city. Returning to Professor Trapp, she spun around for his inspection. "Will this do?"

"Capital, my dear!" He thumped the ground with cane. "Capital!"

The next day the chestnut mare was saddled for her, and Shu-toe hoisted her on board. He stood back, watching with concern, as she immediately grabbed the saddle horn in both hands and hung on. Todd Rutelege, astride the black stallion a distance off, snorted, drummed his heels against the animal's flanks, and rode off at a gallop.

Serena determinedly kept at it, riding an hour or so a day. For the first few days, her buttocks were sore, and the insides of her thigh were chafed raw, but she was getting the hang of it. Shu-toe always kept a close watch on her. One afternoon at the end of the week, Serena was confident enough for her horsemanship that she waved airily at the wagons and sent the mare at a trot up a rise over which Todd had disappeared only a short time before.

Winter was over now, and they were gradually moving north, soon to be performing in the mining camps on the east slope of the Sierras. It was already quite warm down in the lowlands.

Topping the rise, Serena could see Todd and the stallion some distance ahead. She urged the mare into a faster pace.

Soon, Todd must have heard the hoofbeats behind him, for he halted the stallion and watched her approach.

Serena straightened up, sitting erect and easy in the

saddle, as she had seen others do. The little mare was moving quite fast now. Suddenly, the mare lurched, stumbling. Serena, trying to grab for the saddle horn, lost her balance and went tumbling off the animal. She landed on her back on the ground. Fortunately, it was soft, mostly sand, and she was only stunned.

Hearing the thunder of hoofbeats, she sat up dazedly as Todd wheeled the stallion up and vaulted from the saddle. Handsome face concerned, he dropped to one knee beside her.

"Are you all right, Serena?"

She laughed shakily. "I'm fine, I think. Just shaken up a little." Remembering, she glanced around. "The mare, is she all right?"

"She's in good shape." Todd moved aside so she could see the mare standing a few feet away. "She just stumbled. But you're both lucky," he added with a scowl. "She could have broken a leg, and you . . . well, you could have been killed!"

"A lot you would have cared!" she snapped.

With a look of astonishment, he reared back on his haunches. "Why would you say a thing like that, Serena? What reason have I given you to think I wouldn't care?"

"You haven't spoken a half-dozen words to me."

"If you've noticed, I haven't spoken much to anyone." He smiled suddenly, and Serena had a glimpse of how he could look without the constant glower. Then he sobered again. "In the mood I've been in lately, I wouldn't make good company for anyone."

"I know, Todd. I heard what happened, and I'm sorry." She touched his hand.

"I'd rather not discuss it," he said sharply. He got to his feet, and helped her up.

He began brushing the dust from her clothes. In the doing Serena stood very close to him. He smelled of leather and horse, but it was an honest, male smell. Although he was careful not to touch her body more than necessary, Serena still felt the stroke of his hands as he brushed her off, and a warmth flooded her.

Todd laughed suddenly. "You know, in that outfit, you look Chinese, except for the hair and eyes."

She smiled. "I know."

"We'd better get you mounted up again," he said gruffly, the constrained mood on him again.

However, when they were both mounted, Todd waited for her, and they rode on together, at a slower pace.

"So you've heard about Ruby, have you?" he said abruptly.

"Ruby? That's your wife?"

"Was," he said in a cold voice. "She's my wife no longer!"

"I heard that she ran off with the strongman whose place Shu-toe has taken."

"Otto Grunther. Strong as an ox, and about as stupid as one. That's what I can't understand! Why him?" He struck his leg with his fist. "Not only is he stupid, he's ugly as well. At least he seems so to me."

"There's no accounting for what happens between a man and a woman." Serena was astonished, and not a little amused, at herself for making such a wise-sounding remark. But should she be surprised? She had matured and gained much experience since those days on the farm back in Illinois. She said, "It would seem to me that your wife must be somewhat empty-headed herself if she chose this Otto over you, Todd ... if he's like you say he is."

269

He gave her a surprised, half-angry look, as though outraged at her casting aspersions on his wife.

Then, all of a sudden, he roared with laughter. "You know, Serena, you're right! I don't think I ever realized it until just now. The bitch always was light on brains!"

It was as if some poison long bottled up in him had suddenly broken loose, a draining away of bitterness that was the beginning of a healing process.

He began to talk more easily of himself, telling Serena of his ambitions to become a great entertainer like Professor Trapp, but he had no talent as an illusionist, only as a juggler or an acrobat, perhaps as an aerialist.

"But there's no place in this country for that kind of talent. The people only want to be fooled by magic trickery, listen to some women warble, or watch dancing girls showing a lot of naked limbs. The circus is the place where I'd like to perform. That's the life for me, but the circuses in this country, especially now with the war on, are nothing more than gypsy caravans. Europe, that's the place for grand circuses."

"Then you must go to Europe," Serena said. "If it's your life dream."

"That's easier said than done. It takes money to sail to Europe, and with the money I earn it takes a long time to save up enough. And dear Ruby . . ." He laughed shortly. "She not only ran off with Otto, but she took my life savings as well, money I'd worked years to save."

"You're a young man yet, Todd. You have time to do all the things you want. Just try to forget your wife . . ."

"I'm already forgetting Ruby, Serena." He looked at her, his eyes suddenly disconcertingly bold. "I've you to thank for that."

Serena felt her color rise. "Thank you, kind sir."

They rode every day now when they were traveling. They were in the mountains by this time, in the mining camps. While the distance between towns was shorter, it took longer, since they were usually climbing, the roads paralleled a mountain stream, running full from the spring thaw in the mountains. The water foamed white over the boulders in the stream bed.

Much better time could be made on horseback, and Serena and Todd could ride well ahead of the caravan and find a nice spot along the stream to laze away a couple of hours.

Serena noticed that Shu-toe was aware of her growing intimacy with Todd; he watched with wounded eyes whenever they rode off together. She felt sorry for Shu-toe and hated to hurt him. At the same time, she couldn't allow Shu-toe's wounded feelings to rule her actions. She had her own life to lead.

One warm afternoon, Serena and Todd found a narrow strip of sand, in effect a small beach created by a long-ago shift in the stream bed. It was very isolated, well away from the road, and screened off by a thick growth of trees and shrubbery. They sat together on a blanket Todd had brought along. Serena sat with her knees drawn up, chin resting on them. She stared dreamily at the rushing water.

"It would be nice to take a swim," she said, "if the water wasn't so swift."

"Not only swift, but like ice, since most of the

271

water was melting snow from the high country only a short time ago."

"I know," Serena said absently. Her thoughts were far away, on that long-ago night on the Carson River and the brutal murder of her parents. Counting back, she was astounded to discover that it had been almost a year since that tragic night.

That was also the night she'd had her first intimate knowledge of a man. Rory Clendenning . . . how was he faring? she wondered. Did he miss her? More importantly, did he believe her a murderess? She sighed pensively.

"Serena?"

She looked around to find Todd's face close to hers, so close that she could see the twin images of her own face mirrored in his eyes.

"Yes ,Todd?"

"You sighed. Are you unhappy?"

"Not particularly. At least no more than usual." She smiled. "I was just thinking of something in the past . . ."

"Don't think of the past, Serena. That's what I was doing for too long. Life is in the present, the here and now. You taught me that."

"Did I, Todd?"

His breathing was rapid, his breath warm on her cheek. Then he was kissing her. His arms went around her, and he pressed her down onto the blanket.

Serena felt a momentary fear. Then she sighed again. It was what she had been wanting, wasn't it? To be close to him? She let her mind go blank, her body soft and heavy in his arms. He was rough, demanding, his hands urgent on her. She knew that, in

272

a way, she was seeking forgetfulness, as she had on that night a year ago with Rory Clendenning.

Todd's hand on her body roused her own passions, and soon she was so caught up in sensation that she was scarcely aware of Todd's removing the tunic and trousers and the cool air brushing her skin. For comfort's sake, she had been wearing little in the way of undergarments underneath the Chinese clothing.

Todd rolled away briefly to remove his own clothes. Serena lay still, eyes closed, breath coming fast. Then she felt him over her, hovering, and she opened to him, welcoming him into her with a small groan of pleasure.

Todd was moving rapidly, his body pounding at her. It took Serena a few frantic moments to adjust to his frenzied rhythm.

Then they were moving in rhythmic counterpoint, and for just an instant Serena's mind separated from the act, and for a heartbeat, she wondered what she was doing with this man, a stranger. Then, the instant was drowned by feeling, and as Todd's passion broke, Serena arched to him for a timeless moment, her body a bridge bearing his greater weight.

Finally, a last shudder of ecstasy convulsed him, and he fell away, releasing her. Her eyes still closed, Serena lay supine, perspiration drying on her flesh. Her own sexual tension had not broken. But as she lay there, it ebbed slowly, leaving her feeling vaguely unsatisfied. Now the air did feel cool, and she reached for a corner of the blanket to pull over her naked body.

She felt a touch on her shoulder. Opening her eyes, she found Todd raised on one elbow, looking down at her.

Somewhat hesitantly, he said, "Serena, I hope I wasn't too rough. Forgive me if I was. It has been six months since Ruby left me, and I've known no other woman since."

She kissed the tip of her finger, and touched the end of his nose with it. "It's all right, Todd. I'm not that fragile."

They were dressed and back on the main road by the time the wagons labored up the grade. Serena knew she was flushed and somewhat disheveled, and from Shu toe's sharp yet sorrowing look, she realized that the Chinese youth suspected what had taken place.

During the days and weeks that followed, Serena and Todd shared an hour or so a week of stolen pleasure, all the more thrilling to Serena because it *was* stolen. For, although she was sure that Shu-toe and Tang P'ing knew, Serena was equally convinced that no one else had any inkling of the affair. Todd was a strong lover, if less skillful than Serena thought a man his age should be, and a married man at that. Although their encounters did not always bring her complete physical release she enjoyed the closeness, the touching—the *being* with someone she was fond of.

It did occur to her that his ineptitude at love could be one reason why his wife had run away with another man. She soon discovered another, more understandable reason—Todd was possessive, almost obsessive in his jealousy.

It was well into summer now, and Professor Trapp's Circus of Illusion was completing its swing through the mining camps, gradually working back down into the lowlands and toward San Francisco.

One afternoon, following a bout of love-making that had left Serena unsatisfied again, she had just finished dressing when she heard a rustling sound in the underbrush nearby. She froze. "What's that?"

"I don't know, but I'll soon find out," Todd said.

Standing up, he jerked his pistol from his belt, and advanced toward the bushes.

In a flash of intuition, Serena knew who it was. "Wait, Todd!" Raising her voice, she said, "Shu-toe, come out here!"

The rustling of the underbrush grew louder, and in a moment Shu-toe, looking sheepish, emerged from the bushes.

"I should have known who it was," Todd said in disgust. "I've seen him giving us the eye lately. There's one way of putting a stop to that once and for all!" He leveled his pistol at Shu-toe.

Shu-toe, ignoring the gun, advanced on Todd. His face was set in the same chilling expression Serena had seen that night when he put the torch to Li Po's house.

She grabbed Todd's arm. "Don't be ridiculous. Put that thing away." As Shu-toe continued to move forward, Serena said sternly, "And you, Shu-toe, you just stop it now! You should be ashamed of yourself, spying on me like this."

Shu-toe stopped, looking confusedly at her.

"Go back now, Shu-toe. Go back to the wagons. I'm perfectly all right, I don't need your protection."

"You sure as hell don't!" Todd snapped. "But it's not all right with me. He's gone on you, Serena. If you don't know that, I do. I don't trust the Chink son-

275

ofabitch! Some night he'll sneak up behind me and slip a knife into my back. A bullet will stop that here and now." He raised the pistol again.

Serena moved so that she stood in front of Todd. She felt her anger rising. The whole affair was so silly, so unreasonable. How could a man want to shoot another man, over something so trivial?

"I won't allow you to shoot him. He meant no harm. He was only thinking of my welfare."

"There's nothing you can do to stop me, Serena. The only Chink you can trust is a dead Chink. And I don't want him sneaking around, spying on us. You're my woman, Serena, and no double-damned Chink is going to trail around after you!"

"Damn you, Todd Rutelege, I'm *not* your woman! I belong to no man. And I don't like the word, Chink. Shu-toe is a person, and as such is entitled to respect. Chink is a slur on his race."

"To me, he's a Chink." He was sneering openly. "Now you just stay out of it, Serena. I'll handle it as I see fit."

His words infuriated Serena, but she forced herself to think calmly. Moving away from Todd, she took the small derringer from her purse. As Shu-toe looked from one to the other, she stepped quickly up behind Todd, cocked the derringer, and rammed it into the small of his back.

"Drop the pistol onto the ground, Todd."

Todd stiffened. "What are you doing, Serena?"

"This is a derringer against your back. If you don't do as I say, I'll shoot you!"

"You wouldn't do that to me!"

"There, you're wrong!" Again, she jammed the derringer into his back. "I've put this derringer to good

276

use before. If you don't drop the pistol at once, Todd, I'll kill you." Not sure if she could really shoot him, Serena put all the firmness she could manage into her voice.

Evidently she sounded convincing, for Todd's hand loosened around the pistol, and it hit the ground with a thud.

"Shu-toe, go now. Go back to the wagons. Everything is fine. I'll be along shortly." More gently, she added, "I understand what you were doing, and I'm grateful."

Shu-toe hesitated, his dark eyes holding a silent plea.

Again, Serena said, "Go on, Shu-toe."

With apparent reluctance, the big man turned away and plodded off into the underbrush. When he had time to get far enough away, Serena removed the derringer from Todd's back and stepped back.

"You can pick up your gun now," she said.

He stooped, picked up the pistol, and jammed it into his belt. He turned a sullen, angry countenance on her. "I can still kill him, when you're not around to stop me."

"You do, and I'll see you charged with murder!"

His lips drew back in a snarl. "No white man is ever charged with murder for killing a Chink!"

"I told you I don't care for that word. I'll kill you myself, if you harm Shu-toe!" In a softer voice, she said, "You don't understand, Todd. I owe Shu-toe my life."

"Is that all you owe him?"

"What do you mean?"

"How many times has he had you?"

"That doesn't even deserve an answer," she said

steadily. "You have a filthy mind, Todd. I can readily understand now why your wife left you for another man. You're rough, crude, prejudiced, jealous, and possessive."

His face reddened, and he took a threatening step toward her. "And you're a bitch, just like Ruby was!"

She stood her ground without flinching. "I never knew her, but I probably should accept that as a compliment." She turned away and started for the chestnut mare, tethered a few yards away.

"Serena," he called after her. "I'm sorry. I spoke in haste and anger."

She faced around. "A fine man I once knew said something should never be done in haste and anger. Now I see what he meant. The true man underneath shows through." He took another step, and she opened her purse to seize the derringer. "Don't come near me! I still have the derringer. Don't ever come near me again, Todd Rutelege!"

Serena mounted up and rode away at a gallop, reaching the wagons long before he did. She rode directly to the wagon Shu-toe was driving. Tang P'ing was on the seat beside him.

Reining her mount in close, Serena rode alongside the wagon. "Forgive me, Shu-toe. I understand now why you've been watching me so closely. You helped reveal to me Todd Rutelege's true nature."

Shu-toe smiled shyly, ducking his head. Tang P'ing said, "Shu-toe tell me you save his life again, Se-rena. Like you did in saloon when bad men torment him."

In dismay, Serena remembered Darrel's warning. Now she had saved the life of a Chinese for a second time. Wryly, she had to wonder what that augured for the future. Would Shu-toe believe that he was now bound to her for life? It wouldn't be so bad if he wasn't in love with her.

Serena sent her horse into a trot, on ahead of the wagons. Shortly, Todd came riding down the narrow road. He passed her without a word. Serena was angry at herself for being taken in by such a clod. All the while, she had thought that she had matured to the point where she could judge a man better than that. It appeared she was wrong.

Serena went to bed that night dreading the next day, but in the morning she found that the problem of Todd Rutelege had been solved overnight. He had packed his belongings and was gone. The black stallion was gone also.

Professor Trapp took it philosophically enough. "Oh, well, it's happened before. Luckily the season is drawing to a close. We can manage without Master Rutelege." He added dryly, "Of course, he did steal a valuable animal, worth far more than the wages he had coming to him."

Serena was just as happy that Todd had sneaked away and would bother her no more. At the same time she was indignant about the theft. "But he stole a horse, Professor! I understand that horse stealing is as bad a crime out here as murder, a hanging offense. You should report him to the law."

Professor Trapp looked distressed. "Oh, I would never do that, Serena. Oh, dear, no! Just the thought of a person I've known for so long being hanged through my doing . . ." He shuddered. Then he turned to Shu-toe. "Of course, this means you'll have to fill in for him, Shu-toe. You'll have to act as my assistant during the more difficult illusions, and we'll have to figure out something to add to your strong-man act."

For the first time in a long while, Serena saw Shu-toe smile broadly. Beaming with delight, he clapped his hands together softly.

Chapter Fourteen

It was early November when Professor Trapp's Traveling Show and Circus of Illusion returned to San Francisco. They had toured most of the mining camps, venturing as far east as Placerville, and as far north as Oroville. It had been a most successful tour, and Professor Trapp was gratified. Their next engagement was a two-week performance at Maguire's Opera House, and then they would close for the season.

"The people of San Francisco are blasé, my dear," the Professor explained to Serena. "They have a surfeit of every imaginable form of entertainment, and I will be fortunate to make expenses. But it's become traditional with me to close the season here. When I put together my Circus of Illusion back in '58, I closed my first season in this city, and it's a tradition I will continue to maintain."

Professor Trapp's prediction was proven true. They

played to a half-empty house every evening, and the Professor often shortened the performance by eliminating one or more illusions when the crowd was sparse.

Serena was glad it was coming to an end. It had been a long tour, and she was weary. She was also occupied with thoughts concerning the future. Of course, the Professor had already told her that he definitely wanted her with the troupe next season, but Serena wasn't sure she wanted to tour with the circus again. Despite the hardships of wagon travel, it had been an exciting time, certainly different from anything Serena had ever known. However, she didn't think she would care to be an illusionist's assistant for the rest of her life.

Fortunately she and her companions had been able to save most of the wages the Professor paid them for their services, and would be able to support themselves for a time. Thinking about it, Serena doubted the wisdom of remaining long in San Francisco. The frightening experience with the Chinese in black was never far from her thoughts, and she had no assurance that she was not still being sought by someone in the city. Besides, there was always the possibility that the law was still looking for her.

The first thing she had done on returning to San Francisco was to search out several recent issues of the Virginia City *Enterprise*. There had not been any mention of the murder of Madeline Dubois, or of herself. That by no means meant that the case was closed.

Serena enjoyed playing in the elegant opera house, particularly since it offered one comfort not afforded her on the tour. There were several small dressing

282

rooms backstage, and she could use one to remove the scanty costume she wore during the performance and dress in street clothes at her leisure.

One evening, three nights before their final performance, Serena was in the dressing room, Tang P'ing was helping her change from her stage costume, when there was a rap on the dressing room door.

Thinking it was Professor Trapp, Serena called out, "Come in!"

Her back to it, she heard the door open. A soft voice drawled, "Could I invite the lady of illusion to share a champagne supper with me?"

Serena spun around, heart in her throat. "Darrel!"

Darrel Quick, smiling gently, made a small bow, doffing a white top hat. "It is indeed I, Serena."

Without further thought, she ran to him. Darrel embraced her, and Serena welcomed the comfort and warmth of his encircling arms. Her heart was pounding so hard she could hear the blood rushing in her ears.

"Dear Serena, I have missed you." He kissed the top of her head.

"And I you." A horrible thought came to her. She stepped back from him. "You haven't come to take me back to Virginia City?"

"Now, would I do a thing like that, my love?"

"But I *am* still wanted for murder?"

His face became grave. "That, I fear, is true. They have not stopped looking for you."

She looked at him fully for the first time. He wore a black silk frock coat with cloth buttons, a checked waistcoat, with a watch secured by a heavy gold Albert chain, a boiled shirt, stock collar, and a satin bow tie. As he moved slightly under her scrutiny, Serena caught a glimpse of the pearl-handled revolver in a holster in his hip. On one finger a large diamond ring glittered like fire. He looked very prosperous, and even more handsome and charming than she remembered him.

His full mouth quirked with amusement. "Do I pass inspection, love?"

"Yes! And I'm ever so glad to see you. But how did you find me?"

"Pure chance, Serena." He was smiling. "Having never seen Professor Trapp's Circus of Illusion, I bought a ticket. When I first spied you on that stage, I thought *you* an illusion. My head roared as though a Washoe zephyr blew through it."

Serena laughed. "I can't feature you being dumfounded."

"It was like seeing a ghost. It's been well over a year now, and I thought I'd never see you again, Serena. Now . . . how about that champagne supper?"

"I'd love it!" She looked around. Tang P'ing had discreetly disappeared. "But I don't have any fancy clothes." She gestured at herself. "Where I've been these past months, there was no need for fancy clothes."

"You look fine. With beauty such as yours, love, you'd look fine in any garment."

"You should have seen me when I first came here." She laughed. "In Chinese clothing, a tunic and trousers." In a rush, she said, "Oh, I have so much to tell you, Darrel! And so many questions to ask!"

"We will have all the time in the world. You think I'm going to let you get away from me again?" He held out his arm, and Serena took it.

As they left the dressing room, Serena came to a stop. "Wait! You haven't asked me if I'm guilty, if I killed Madeline."

"It matters not a whit to me, one way or the other."

"But it does to me. I didn't kill her, Darrel," she said passionately. "I swear I didn't!"

"I believe you, Serena." he said. He patted her arm. "Now shall we go?"

Darrel took her to supper at Winn's Fountain Head, a restaurant so elegant it took Serena's breath away. The floors had rich Turkey carpets, and there were expensive draperies, rosewood chairs with crimson velvet cushions many sofas, and Italian marble tables. The menu offered French champagne and Sazerac brandy, along with other liquors Serena had never heard of. They had a wide choice of food—venison steaks, oysters, duck, geese, partridge, snipe, and veal.

"So many things! I don't know what to ask for!" she said in dismay.

"I'll order for us, don't fret about it. First, let's have champagne."

When the waiter had filled their glasses, Darrel raised his, and said, "A toast to old friends."

They clinked glasses and drank.

Then Serena leaned forward to say eagerly, "Now tell me why and how you came to be here."

"Well, love, the life of a gambler has its compensations," he drawled. "I told you that I planned to come to San Francisco eventually and had been saving money toward the end. Due to a tremendous

285

stroke of luck, that eventuality was realized sooner than I had dared hope. One evening, a short time after your abrupt departure from Virginia City, I got into a poker game with one of the richest men on the Comstock. I played with greater skill than ever before in my life, and the cards were running my way. It was an all-night poker session. In the beginning there were five men in the game. By dawn's early light, I was playing head on head with the mining magnate. He was somewhat in his cups by that time, and betting wildly, trying to recoup his losses. To shorten my story, I won from him over a hundred and fifty thousand dollars. It made me a reasonably wealthy man. I will say this for him . . . he was a gentleman all the way and paid his gambling debt to me the next day. I quit Virginia City shortly thereafter. I won't tell you the name of the gentleman in question, since I believe he is somewhat ashamed of himself. However," Darrel added in a dry voice, "I do understand that it's pretty well known around Virginia City. It was a rather unusual poker game, and will undoubtedly become a legend in time."

He took the champagne from the ice bucket and refilled their glasses. "Once here in San Francisco, I purchased a gaming house and saloon on Portsmouth Square."

Serena had listened in awe to his tale. She remembered her stroll around the Barbary Coast. Darrel was probably there then. She thought it better not to mention that. Instead, she shook her head and said, "I did think you looked prosperous, but something like this is staggering!"

"Dame Fortune smiled on me." He shrugged. "As I think I have mentioned to you in passing, a gambler drinks the finest of champagne one day, and on the morrow he might find his pockets too empty to buy a glass of beer."

"But surely that will never happen to you now?"

"It is always possible, love." He shrugged again. "I can never resist a game with high stakes. The next time, I might not be so fortunate."

"About me . . ." Serena hesitated, clearing her throat. "I mean, do most people believe I killed Madeline?"

"I'm afraid so, Serena," he said soberly. "Certainly the law does, and it would appear that they have enough evidence to convict. I had a talk with Spencer Hurd before I left. He, at least, believes you to be innocent and stands ready to defend you if it ever becomes necessary."

"But didn't they even try to learn if someone else killed her?" she asked despairingly.

"Why should they, Serena?" He spread his hands. "They believe you guilty, so why go to all that extra effort. That is the way the law usually thinks, unfortunately. There is a warrant outstanding for your arrest."

"I can't hide from the law for the rest of my life, Darrel!" she cried. "Maybe it would be better if I went back, gave myself up, and let the Judge defend me."

"You'll hang, Serena. Do you understand me?" he said roughly. "So don't talk nonsense! Stay here with me." He reached across the table to take her hand. "I'll see that nothing happens to you. In time, maybe we'll both get tired of this place. Maybe we'll move on to New Orleans when the war is over. You'd like New Orleans, Serena. Will you stay with me?"

She sighed. "I don't seem to have much choice, do I?" She looked up quickly. "Forgive me. I didn't mean that the way it sounded, Darrel."

"I know you didn't, love. But you *will* stay with me?"

"Yes, Darrel, that goes without saying. If you want me."

"I want you, you can wager on that." He smiled broadly and tipped the champagne bottle over their glasses. "This calls for another toast."

Again they clicked glasses and drank. Darrel said, "Now tell me what has transpired with you."

By this time Serena was giddy from the unaccustomed champagne. With an effort she pulled herself together, assuming a sober face, and said, "Nothing as glamorous as what has happened to you, I'm afraid."

She launched into her story, beginning with the confrontation with Madeline Dubois and the subsequent flight from Virginia City. The telling of it took a long time, taking them through another bottle of champagne, a marvelous supper, and a glass each of Sazerac brandy. Darrel ordered oysters for them, followed by partridge under glass. Serena, her appetite spurred by the champagne, ate as though starved.

Darrel, watching her across the table as she ate and talked, marveled anew at what a beautiful woman she was. He gave silent thanks to Dame Fortune for directing him into the Opera House this evening. It only reinforced his theory that man was not at all in control of his destiny. Had some impulse not urged him into that Opera House tonight, the odds were heavily against his ever knowing that Serena was in San Francisco.

When she had finally told it all, Darrel loosed an

288

explosive breath. "Well! I don't know about glamorous, but it seems to me you've had enough excitement to do you for two lifetimes. This Chinese gent who tried to abduct you at gunpoint . . . you have no hint as to who may have sent him after you?"

"Not the slightest, Darrel."

He was frowning, moving the silverware around on the table, as though arranging troops for battle. "That is very strange, and certainly means we'll have to be on constant guard. If nothing else, it means that somebody here in San Francisco means you harm."

"I thought it might be someone sent from Virginia City, someone sent by the man in the gold mask."

Darrel looked thoughtful before shaking his head. "I don't think so, Serena. Maybe it's just a hunch, but I believe it's someone here in San Francisco."

"But why, for God's sake!"

"Now that I don't know." He stood up and held out his hand. "Let's go home now."

Serena didn't question the word home, just let him help her up. Outside the restaurant, Darrel hailed a carriage and helped her into it. The address he gave to the driver meant nothing to Serena.

She was full of wine and food, and very weary now, her thoughts hardly moving at all. Inside the carriage, Darrel kissed her gently, without passion, and she snuggled against his shoulder and dozed.

Some time later, he shook her awake and they got out of the carriage. They were on a hillside street shrouded in fog. Gas lamps at intervals along the sloping street were merely yellow blobs in the thick mist. Darrel put his arm around her, and they mounted steep steps. The chill of the fog cleared Serena's head a little, and at the top of the steps she drew back with a gasp. The house looming before them was large. "My God, it's a mansion!"

"Doesn't really belong to me." His voice held a smile. "I leased it from a very wealthy man who is traveling in Europe for a year. I knew him slightly, and he wanted someone living here who would see after things."

"You're all alone here?"

"Except for a couple of the owner's servants. Or perhaps you mean do I have a woman living with me?"

The fog blew away for a moment, and she could see the teasing smile on his face. She snapped, "No, I didn't mean that. It's none of my business who you have here!"

"That's true, it isn't. But to answer your unasked question, no, I'm sharing it with no one . . . not at the present time."

Her temper stirred. "I said I didn't mean that!"

"I know what you said, love." He took her arm. "Come on, it's chilly out here."

The inside was sheer magnificence itself. The rooms were floored with mosaic and carpeted with richly textured rugs. Every room had at least one crystal chandelier.

A beautiful chandelier hung from the ceiling in the enormous entryway. "The gent who owns this place bought that chandelier from the palace of a Venetian doge and had it brought over here and converted to gas. God only knows what it cost him," Darrel said. "He even has his own gas works, the gas supply provided by the city being not too reliable as yet."

From the entryway a sweeping staircase rose to the second floor. "There are ten bedrooms upstairs," Darrel said. "He's famed for giving grand balls, with sleep-over guests."

He took her through the rooms downstairs. Everywhere Serena saw splendor beyond her wildest imaginings. When they finally returned to the foot of the staircase, she was dizzy from what she had seen.

Grinning, he said, "Now would you care for a tour through the bedrooms upstairs, madam?"

"Let me get my breath first. This place must have cost a fortune!"

"Somewhere in the neighborhood of two and a half million, I understand."

She stared at him in wonder. "Your leasing it must have cost you dearly, even for a year."

"I told you that a gambler either lives high on the hog or starves to death. My motto is, while you've got it, use it." He shrugged negligently. "To be truthful, it didn't cost me as much as you might think, since he leased it to me not for the money, but to assure that it would be in good hands during his absence." He looked at her with questioning eyes. "It does get lonely here, by myself. Will you live with me, Serena, and be my love?"

"Are you . . . ?" Her hand went to her throat. "Are you asking me to marry you, Darrel Quick?"

"No, no. I thought we had an understanding about that. I am not a marrying man. I'm asking you to live with me."

"Won't that cause talk?"

"Gossip, you mean? Living in sin, as it were? I doubt it," he drawled. "So what if it does? I certainly will not care. I should think your experiences of these past months would have made you immune to gossip, Serena."

She was silent, her head filled with conflicting emotions.

"Of course, if you think it necessary," he said in a dry voice, "we could always practice a little hypocrisy. I could introduce you as my wife. No one would question it, since I'm not that well known here yet and have yet to open the house socially."

"That won't be necessary." Her head went back. "If I live here, it will be on your terms, no pretense necessary."

He said then, a touch impatiently, "Well?"

"Yes!" she cried, throwing her arms wide.

Darrel felt himself go almost limp with relief; he hadn't realized how tense he had been while waiting for her decision.

"Ah, Serena!" he murmured and swept her into his arms.

This kiss was totally different from the one in the carriage. Serena felt her pulse quicken, her passion leaping into life. She had forgotten how his touch could stir her.

But even as she responded to his kiss, Serena thought of Tang P'ing and the Chinese woman's fatalistic acceptance of her unpredictability . . .

She pulled back from the circle of Darrel's arms. "And that reminds me!"

Darrel looked bewildered and slightly dazed. "Reminds you? Of what? Sometimes *you* remind me of a cricket, hopping from thought to thought!"

"The two people who have been with me all along. You met them in Virginia City. Tang P'ing and her son, Shu-toe."

"What about them?"

"Can you find a place for them here?"

"I'm sure it can be managed. The two servants already here are Chinese, and with you here, two more may be needed. I'll be buying a carriage, so we'll need a driver . . ." He scowled. "But not your whole damned troupe of circus players!"

"Of course not," Serena said, laughing. "But I do have to finish up the season, only two more nights. I couldn't let Professor Trapp down."

"All right, love," he said in resignation. "Not tonight, I hope. You don't have to worry about letting him down tonight?"

"Oh, no. Tonight, what's left of it," she laughed again, "is mine to do with as I please."

"Then shall we get the upstairs tour out of the way?"

He extended his arm, Serena took it, and they started up the broad marble stairs.

Serena's mind was a riot of wicked thoughts. How her folks would have been shocked at what she was thinking, at what she was *doing*!

At the top of the stairs, she drew Darrel to a halt. "The upstairs . . . all bedrooms, am I right?"

"Right, love."

"Then why don't we continue the guided tour in just *one* bedroom for tonight?" Startled at her own daring, Serena held her breath.

He darted a look at her. "My, my, our Serena has grown up, but it's a hell of an idea." He stepped to the nearest door and opened it wide. He made a small bow. "The master bedroom, my lady, the one I've been using."

Serena went in. She stopped short just inside, her gaze raking the room. It was the largest bedroom she had ever seen, and wondrously decorated. Heavy, rich

293

draperies covered the windows. Framed pictures hung on the walls. Serena knew very little about art, but she felt certain that the paintings were by famous artists and very costly.

Darrel confirmed this. "Yes, Serena. The pictures in here are worth a small fortune. A Rembrandt, a Rubens, and a Holbein. All too lush and dark for my liking, but they say there is no accounting for tastes in paintings."

Against one wall was an enormous fireplace, with a veined marble mantel. A small fire burned in the hearth. There was an elaborate dressing table, with a mirror framed in gilt, a number of richly upholstered chairs, and a sofa.

Dominating the room was a huge bed. It was a four-poster, the posts rising at least eight feet high. A gold-tasseled fringe extended around the bottom edge of the canopy, and filmy lace curtains hung to the floor.

Into her ear Darrel said, "I think the bed was what sold me on taking the place. It cries out for revelry. Sadly, the master and mistress of the house are both ancient and stuffy, and I very much doubt they have put it to good use for a long time, if ever."

She said tartly, "But I'm sure you have."

"If you mean has anyone shared this bed with me, no," he said calmly. "If you mean have I been celibate since last I saw you, the answer to that is no, as well . . ."

"I'm sorry, darling." She kissed him quickly. "I have no right to pry."

Without another word, she crossed to the bed and began undressing.

A little baffled, Darrel stood watching her. He had

always thought he understood women better than the general run of men, but just when he thought he understood Serena Foster, she did something totally unexpected. Probably he would never have a handle on her. There was, however, a bright side to that—he would never become bored with her either.

While these thoughts raced through his mind, Serena had removed her dress, shoes, and stockings. Now she shucked her undergarments and stood proud and naked before him. She faced him, still as a graven statue, hands at her sides. Darrel's gaze moved over her—over the swift rise and fall of her full breasts, the softly rounded belly, and the breathtaking loveliness of long legs. She was all curves and hollows, her flesh glowing as if lit from within.

My God, he thought, she *is* a lovely creature! His breath was coming fast, and he was fully aroused. He began to unfasten his clothes.

Serena grinned suddenly, that elfin, puckish grin, and dived into the bed.

The bed was down-soft, and she almost sank out of sight in it. It was like resting on a cloud and was the most luxurious bed she had ever lain in. She stretched her arms and legs as far as she could and sighed contentedly.

The light dimmed as Darrel turned down the gas jet. Serena could hear the pad of his naked feet and felt the bed give under his weight.

Perversely, smothering a giggle, she rolled to the far edge of the bed. It quivered as he groped for her.

"Where the devil are you?" he grumbled. "Serena, stop playing games!"

"I'm sorry." She crawled over to him. "It was such

a temptation. A person could sink in this bed, and disappear forever! Did you realize that?"

He silenced her with his mouth, and Serena went soft and pliable in his arms.

Despite their long separation and his urgent need of her, something warned Darrel to take it slow and easy. Although his experience told him that Serena was ready, even eager, to bend to his will, he sensed a certain restraint in her, a holding back that he felt certain Serena herself was not aware of.

So, he made slow and leisurely love to her, handling her as tenderly as he would a virgin bride. It was not that difficult for him. Darrel had early learned that a man's pleasure was much heightened sexually if he succeeded in arousing his female partner to a correspondingly high pitch of desire. In moments of introspection, Darrel liked to cultivate the conceit that he was to sensual matters what a gourmet was to fine foods—savor, sample, tease but never overstimulate the taste buds.

He explored her body as though it was completely new to him, using all his skill and experience. He held the kiss for a long time, his hands moving over her body, fondling, searching out the touch-buds of her passion.

Finally, Serena tore her mouth away to gasp for air. She murmured against his neck, "I've missed you, darling. I've missed this. I didn't know how much!"

"Yes, my love. That goes for me as well."

As he continued to caress her, Serena's world took on a rosy glow of warmth, of growing need and passion. Boldly, she touched his body. Everywhere his own hands touched her, Serena felt her flesh leap in response. The feel of his slender musculature against her fingertips sent thrilling messages along her nerve-ends.

Her passion mounted until Serena had to bite her lip to keep from crying out. His lips sought her breasts, his tongue gently laving the nipples. The texture of his tongue had a rough yet exciting feel, and she felt her nipples open and grow hard.

Serena nipped at the lobe of his ear, and whispered, "Now, my darling, now! It's time!"

Still he caressed her, as though she hadn't spoken. It became a drawn-out torture for Serena. She began to urge him to her with clutching hands.

Finally he gave a soft laugh and moved above her, and then they were one. As they began the rhythm of love, Serena knew sweet rapture such as she had never before experienced.

Her ecstasy was so intense and prolonged that Serena came close to fainting. When she floated back up to complete awareness, she was lying in the crook of Darrel's arm, her head on his chest. She could feel his heart pounding like a drum against her ear.

She ran her fingers over his chest. "Your heart feels as if it's about to burst loose."

"If it does, I'll die content. Of course, it will be your fault."

"Sweet, you're sweet." She raised up to brush her lips across his. "You do know how to make a woman feel wanted and cherished. And safe from all harm."

His arms tightened around her, and he said in a rough voice, "You are safe now, Serena. I'll see to that."

"I know, darling, I know."

They lay in contented silence for a little. Serena was tired, and very sleepy, yet a question nibbled at the edge of her mind, a question that had been nagging her all evening. She knew she wouldn't be able to sleep until she got an answer.

Finally, trying to appear casual, she came out with it. "How is Rory Clendenning? Do you know what has happened to him?"

Darrel was silent for so long that Serena began to fear that he was angry with her. He wasn't asleep, so she knew that he had heard and understood her. Afraid she would make too much a point of it, Serena dared not to repeat the question.

Then she heard his chuckle. "Your preacher's son is fine, and doing well for himself. He now owns a freight line, half-owner anyway. Hauling ore down to the mills."

Serena raised her head. "But how did he manage that? The last time I spoke with him, he was working a miner and hating it."

"Whatever else he is, Rory Clendenning has a good head on him. He got the idea that Virginia City needed another freight line, and a good idea it was."

"But where did he get the money to start it?"

"From me."

"What!" Serena reared up in astonishment. "How did that happen? And why did you . . . ?"

"I had a conversation with Spencer Hurd about you shortly after I hit my big bonanza. He told me that Clendenning was having trouble managing a loan, and so . . ." She felt him shrug. "Why, I'm not sure. I was flush and feeling on top of the world, so I loaned him the ten thousand dollars he needed." The soft snort of laughter again. "Probably I was feeling some guilt, after all, about winning his horse and all his money out in the desert. Whatever the reason, it was good business. He's making the loan and interest payments regularly, so he must be doing well."

"You *are* a sweet man, Darrel Quick."

Still laughing, he pulled her down into his arms again. "About this partner of his, Serena . . ."

"Yes? What about him?"

"It's not a him, love. It's a woman, by the name of Kate Rogan, and a fetching female she is, too." A slight touch of malice had crept into his voice. "And I strongly suspect they're partners in other ways than business."

Chapter Fifteen

Rory Clendenning was humming under his breath as the long team of mules pulled the empty ore wagon up the winding road toward Virginia City. It was close to sundown, and he was Lord God tired. He knew that the mules were too, since they merely crept along unless he urged them on. It had been another long, tiring day, four times down and back with the ore wagon, yet it was only another of many such days, and Clendenning didn't mind. Every trip was that much more profit for the Clendenning-Rogan Freight Line.

He broke off humming as he realized that the song was "Sweet Betsy from Pike." He grinned to himself. He had been around Spencer Hurd so much of late that not only had he picked up the habit of humming to himself, but the Judge's song as well. Next, he would be smoking the Judge's stinking cigars!

Clendenning came out of his reverie as he realized

that the mules, with their animal cunning, had taken advantage of his inattention to stop dead in their tracks. Some of them were leaning forward with heads down, dozing in the harness.

From under the wagon seat Clendenning took the long bullwhip, curled it back over his head, then flicked it over the mules' backs. It writhed like a long, striking snake and made a sound like a pistol shot as the end popped. The mules came to life, and Clendenning yelled, "Move out, you lead-ass donkeys!"

The mules leaned into the harness, and the wagon began to move again. Clendenning recurled the whip and stowed it under the seat, smiling. Over the past year he had become quite handy with the bullwhip. He wasn't yet good enough to "flick a fly off a mule's ass without roughing hide," but he was getting there.

Two-thirds of the way up the grade now, Clendenning looked ahead. The narrow road curved sharply to the left around a bluff. It was a dangerous curve, since a driver had to go into it blind, unable to see what might be coming. On the right, the land dropped away steeply, over a hundred feet almost straight down to the bottom of the gulch. Many a loaded freight wagon coming down the road at too great a pace had been unable to negotiate the hairpin curve and ended up a mass of wreckage at the bottom.

As Clendenning neared the curve, he saw a man leaning negligently against the bank. Clendenning paid the man little heed until he suddenly straightened up and whistled shrilly.

Clendenning cursed under his breath, anticipating what was coming. He sawed on the single jerkline, and the mules came to a halt. Clendenning dipped

302

under the seat again and came up with a double-barreled shotgun loaded with buckshot. He stood up, feet braced wide apart, and waited. He knew what was being planned. Over the past month, the Clendenning-Rogan Freight Line had lost two wagons and teams, both drivers killed, in just such a manner.

He heard the pounding hooves before the first pair of mules poked their noses around the blind curve. The rest of the team followed, pulling a loaded ore wagon. By the time the team and wagon had negotiated the curve, they were already straddling the middle of the road. They kept coming, moving recklessly fast, and inching farther and farther to the left all the while. There was no longer any doubt of the driver's intent—he had been waiting around the curve for the approach of Clendenning's wagon. Now he intended to crowd Clendenning's mules and wagon off the road and into the canyon. At the very last instant the driver would try to fling himself off and roll free, both teams and wagons, and Clendenning, ending up in the ravine below.

Clendenning brought the shotgun to his shoulder, cocked both barrels, and aimed it at the driver, Although he knew he couldn't be heard over the thunder of hooves, he shouted, "Back on your side or take a full load of buckshot, you sonofabitch!" He gestured slightly with the gun, to the left. The other driver was close enough so that Clendenning could see his eyes flare wide in alarm.

Frantically, he began pulling his mules hard right. A deadly collision was barely avoided, and the other team and wagon came to a skidding stop, the left front, eight-foot-high wheel almost touching the left front wheel of Clendenning's wagon.

The driver's face was white as flour, his eyes round. He choked out, "Are you crazy, man! What were you going to do with that shotgun?"

"I was going to blow you off that seat before you could jump," Clendenning said calmly.

"Jump? What do you mean, jump? I ain't denying that I took that curve too fast, but I woulda gotten her back in hand before I hit you. I did, didn't I?"

"Sure, after you saw the shotgun. Don't bother to lie to me," Clendenning said wearily. "Lord God, it's happened twice already. Your boss is willing to lose a few mules and wagons to drive me out of business. But it's happened for the last time. All my drivers are carrying shotguns and they're on the lookout. So tell Brad Stryker that he's going to start losing drivers. After he loses a few, we'll see how easy it is for him to hire replacements. But never mind." He motioned with shotgun. "I'll tell him myself. On your way, and thank your God, if you have one, that you're lucky to be alive."

The driver, still ashen-faced and trembling, shook the jerkline, and his team began to move.

"Hi-up!" Clendenning shouted at his own team, and the wagon was rolling again.

Still seething with anger, Clendenning sat back down. Since his and Kate's freight line had started to give Brad Stryker stiff competition, Stryker had tried varied and devious means to put them out of business. When all else failed, he had resorted to forcing their wagons off the road, at first by brushing perilously close. They had eight wagons now, and Clendenning had screened the drivers carefully. They were all skilled and not easily frightened by close calls, so that tactic hadn't worked. Stryker finally became desperate enough to sacrifice his own mules and equipment, and even lost one driver of his own.

This was the first time Clendenning had been personally involved, and he had to marvel that his drivers hadn't all quit rather than risk their lives day after day. Well, it was time it came to a stop; it was long past the time he faced Brad Stryker with it. He resolved to do so before this day was done.

This decision made, his anger receded a little, but remained smoldering in the core of him.

The wagon was around the hairpin curve now, and it was mostly a straight pull into Virginia City, although uphill all the way. The mules, sensing food and water and a night's rest, needed no urging now, and pulled together without any prodding from the driver's seat.

Clendenning relaxed again, his thoughts going back, counting the blessings that the past year had brought to him.

The morning after he and Kate had struck their bargain, Clendenning had gone directly to Spencer Hurd.

The Judge had listened while Clendenning outlined his plans—his hopes and dreams. Then Hurd had sighed and said, "I applaud you, young Clendenning, for your initiative, your desire to get out of the hellhole of those mines. And I think your idea is a fine one. Virginia City is badly in need of another freight line. If Brad Stryker had his way, he'll be the only one left operating, and then he can charge whatever freighting prices he can get away with. But there is a slight problem, I'm afraid . . . financing. I would gladly loan you the money, but in spite of my sage advice to my clients as to how they should

305

handle their money, I, sadly, don't follow it myself. I, as the fellow says, don't even have that well-known pot."

"But there's a lot of money in Virginia City, and you must know many money men."

"I do, I know a great many of them, and I will be happy to put in a good word for you. But I fear that won't be enough. Unfortunately, most of the mon-eyed men on the Comstock got their money through sheer luck and have about as much business sense as geese. They will happily lose five thousand dollars in a night's poker game, but when they're approached for a business loan, they become skinflints." Hurd's glance was speculative. "How much do you calculate you will need, young Clendenning?"

"To start with four wagons and the mules, and add onto Kate's stable, I will need ten thousand at least."

The Judge nodded. "I'll talk to a few people, and you're free to use my name as a reference, but I doubt *that* will be of much value to you."

For close to a week Clendenning scoured Virginia City in an effort to find a man willing to lend him the money he needed.

Many of them laughed when he gave Spencer Hurd as a reference. One man said, "The Judge is a good lawyer, and an honorable man, but he knows nothing of business. Why, do you know that he often defends people in court without even charging them a fee?"

Time after time, Clendenning was turned away, with phrases like no collateral, risky venture, no business background. But most of the time, he was turned down because he was a relative newcomer to the West, and because he had no previous experience in the freighting business.

He was becoming discouraged, yet he still turned a deaf ear to Kate's suggestion that they use her money. He said, "No, I won't do it!"

"Why, Clendenning?" She gave him a derisive look. "You won't stoop to accepting a loan from a woman? Is that it?"

"Not entirely. If I accepted your money, what would I be bringing to our partnership? Nothing! If I can't offer *something*, we'll just forget about it.'

Then he received word that Spencer Hurd wished to see him. He hurried to the Judge's office. Hidden behind a cloud of cigar smoke, Hurd leaned forward across his desk, his face wearing a huge grin.

Sitting down, Clendenning said eagerly, "Who is it?"

Still grinning, the Judge said, "It was a stroke of luck, in more ways than one. Oh . . . here he is now!" Hurd waved a hand. "Come in, come in!"

Clendenning turned in his chair to stare at the tall man entering the room. Clendenning frowned. There was something vaguely familiar about him. He stood up as Spencer Hurd said, "Rory Clendenning, meet . . ."

"I know who he is," Clendenning broke in in a hard voice. "You're Darrel Quick, the gambler who fleeced me out in the desert." He took a step toward the man. "Lord God, I've promised myself that I'd bust your skull should we ever meet again!"

Darrel Quick moved back a little. His hand darted under his frock coat and came out holding a Colt pointed at Clendenning. He said coolly, "I am not so foolhardy as to engage in a fist fight with you, Clendenning. But if you take another step toward me, I'll blow a hole in you. Not kill you, but I'll put a bullet in your shoulder, which will lay you up for a long spell."

Spencer Hurd was around the desk. "What is this foolishness all about? Do you two already know each other?"

"We do, Judge," Darrel Quick said, his gaze holding steady on Clendenning. "We met out in the desert, and I beat him at poker. For your information, Clendenning, I did not fleece you. I always play an honest game of poker. Is it my fault you're a poor poker player, as well as a poor loser?"

Clendenning looked at the Judge. "Is this the man who's supposed to lend me the money?"

"It is."

"How come?" Clendenning stared hard at Darrel Quick. "Why would *you* loan me ten thousand dollars?"

Darrel Quick smiled slightly. "I've been trying to figure that out myself. One reason, I won quite a large sum of money in a poker game two nights ago, so I'm flush. When a gambler is flush, he tends to be generous. But I suppose the real reason is Serena . . ."

Clendenning tensed. "You know Serena?"

"I do."

"Do you know where she is, *how* she is?"

"I do not. I know no more of her whereabouts than you do. To continue, it seems she knew about our poker game, and did her damnedest to make me feel guilty about leaving you out there. Maybe she succeeded, I'm not sure. Anyway, Mr. Hurd told me of your situation, so I'm willing to make you the loan. Understand now, suh." The man's voice hardened. "It will be strictly a business proposition, a note of indebtedness from you, with whatever the go-

308

ing rate of interest is. There will be no such nonsense as my refunding the money you lost, or the price of your horse. Is that clearly understood?"

Clendenning stared at the gambler. He felt as if he was barefoot on a bed of coals, with no idea of which way to jump. He desperately wanted to accept Quick's generous offer. His pride rose up in his throat, almost choking him, but hadn't his damnable pride gotten him into enough trouble already? Certainly it had driven a wedge between him and Serena.

Looking at this man, he had to wonder how intimately Darrel Quick had known Serena. Yet, what concern was that of his? He had no hold on Serena. In that instant, and for the first time, he realized that *she* had a hold on him that would probably never be broken by time or distance.

"Well, young Clendenning?" Spencer Hurd said. "It strikes me as a fair proposition."

Clendenning sighed and made his decision. "It is a fair proposition, Judge, and I accept. Thank you, Mr. Quick."

Darrel Quick smiled now, a warm, charming smile. He holstered the Colt and held out his hand. After a moment's hesitation, Clendenning accepted it.

Quick said briskly, "If you will draw up the necessary papers, Judge, I will drop in tomorrow and we will close the deal. I leave for San Francisco the day following." He turned the smile again on Clendenning. "When next we meet, Clendenning, I sincerely hope it will be under more pleasant circumstances than our first meeting." He inclined his head. "Good day to you, suh."

He started out.

"Mr. Quick?"

"Yes?"

"If you happen to see Serena . . ."

"Yes, Clendenning?"

Clendenning motioned. "Never mind."

Darrel Quick said gravely, "Should I be so fortunate as to come across Serena Foster, I will give her word of you, you may be sure."

With the loan from Darrel Quick, the Clendenning-Rogan Freight Line had soon been in full operation and prospering. Clendenning had no difficulty in making the loan payments to Quick, and it would soon be paid in full. The only hitch was the continued harassment by Brad Stryker.

Clendenning sat up as the wagon entered the outskirts of Virginia City. He turned the team down the side street and soon pulled into the yard before the stable. The stable had been increased to twice its former size, and a large corral had been constructed behind it, all the way down to the boundary of Kate's large lot. The first move from Stryker—at least Clendenning assumed it was Stryker's doing—had been to open the corral one night and let the mules out. It had taken them several days to round all the mules up again. Since then, an armed guard patroled the corral at night.

Shotgun under his arm, Clendenning got down from the wagon as the hostler came out of the stable. "Feed them good, Ned," he said. "They've had a hard day. The other wagons make it through the day all right?"

"All safe and sound, Mr. Clendenning."

"Good." He cradled the shotgun under his arm and started toward the street.

310

Just then Kate came out onto the side porch. "Clendenning, where are you going?"

He waved at her, and called, "I'll be a little late for supper, Kate. I have some business to attend to first."

"Carrying a shotgun?"

"I'll explain when I get back."

"Well, be careful now. Just be damned sure you *get* back!"

Smiling, Clendenning strode on. Of all the blessings this past year had brought him, Kate was the best of all. She was very dear to him, and he knew that if he could ever get Serena out of his mind, he could give himself more fully to her. He had casually mentioned marriage once to Kate.

"Marriage!" She had given that hoot of laughter. "Marriage is not for me, Clendenning. I'd never be content tied to one man for life. A wife in a mining camp has a rough time of it."

"It doesn't have to be that way."

"No, Clendenning. Thanks for the offer . . . if it *was* an offer."

Since it had only been something Clendenning felt an obligation to bring up, he hadn't mentioned it again.

He stopped at Spencer Hurd's office on his way to see Brad Stryker.

Hurd sat up, almost choking on the smoke of his cigar, when he saw the shotgun. "Going hunting, are you?"

"Yes, for Brad Stryker," Clendenning said.

"He's a bastard, I know that, but killing him will only get you in dutch with the law, as much as he may deserve killing."

311

"I don't intend to kill him, not today," Clendenning sat down. "Maybe scare him a little."

"Brad Stryker doesn't scare easily, my friend." The Judge sighed. "What has he done now?"

"What he's been doing for months, trying to force my wagons off the road. Only this time it was me. One of his drivers tried to force me off into the canyon." He told Hurd what had happened.

Hurd nodded. "I don't blame you for being angry, but I really don't know what you can do about it, Clendenning."

"Well, you say the law can do nothing . . ."

"That's right. Stryker always claims it was an accident, and how can we prove otherwise? With these narrow, dangerous roads, and so much wagon traffic, there *are* accidents almost every day. You know that."

"These aren't accidents."

"I know, I know. But proving they aren't is something else again. I warned you you'd have to tangle with Brad Stryker. This is not a new tactic with him. Before you went into business, he used to be sued constantly by other freighters for destroying their wagons. Stryker always came to me to get them to settle out of court. I got so disgusted I finally refused to represent him. I've offered before, Clendenning, to institute a suit in your behalf . . ."

"A lawsuit is not the answer."

"Then what is the answer?"

"I don't know. But until I find out, I'm going to let him know that he's not going to scare me out of business, like he has the others." Clendenning got to his feet, hefting the shotgun, and started out.

Spencer Hurd called after him, "Just be careful of

that temper of yours, young Clendenning. Don't let it push you into any rash action."

"I'll do my best, but Lord God, I'm sorely tried."

Stryker's office was above his stable at the north end of town, two blocks off C Street.

Clendenning didn't go inside the building. He planted himself in the yard, feet wide apart, the shotgun pointed at the ground, his thumb on the hammers. He called loudly, "Stryker! Brad Stryker, come out here! I want a word with you!"

When a full minute had passed with no response, he said, "If you don't come out and face me, I'll put a double load of buckshot through your door!"

The door opened, and the bulky figure of Brad Stryker emerged. He stopped on the stoop and scowled at Clendenning.

"What's this all about, and who might you be, standing out there, braying like a jackass?"

"I'm Rory Clendenning."

"Oh, Clendenning." Stryker smiled tightly. "So we finally meet. What can I do for you, Mr. Clendenning?"

"I'm here to warn you. You've destroyed two of my freight wagons. Both drivers were killed . . ."

"Yes, I'm sorry about that." Stryker pulled a long face. "My sympathies, Mr. Clendenning. I've warned my drivers to be more careful. But accidents will happen."

"They were no accidents, Stryker. I know it, and you know it. I'm here to tell you that all my drivers are armed with shotguns, and they have orders to shoot if any of your ore wagons get within spitting distance, accidentally or not."

Stryker's face tightened. "Are you threatening me?"

313

"A warning, threat, call it what you like, Stryker. I'm simply telling you that I'm Lord God sick of it. And if it happens again, just one more time, I'm coming for you." He raised the shotgun until it was pointing at Stryker.

"I don't take kindly to threats, Clendenning. And it's not my habit to go armed." Stryker lifted the tails of his coat to show that he wasn't wearing a gunbelt. "As you can see."

"Then you have two choices, *Mister* Stryker," Clendenning said in a harsh voice. "Do not bother my ore wagons again. Or start carrying a weapon. Because the next time one of your drivers tries to force a wagon of mine off the road, not only will he likely be dead, but I will come looking for you. With this shotgun. I bid you good day, sir."

Clendenning turned on his heel, lowered the hammers of the shotgun, and strode away. He found that a crowd had gathered, listening avidly to the exchange. He pushed his way through them and went home to Kate.

Brad Stryker was boiling inside as he watched the arrogant young whelp walk away. One of his men was standing right behind him, wearing a gunbelt. Stryker had to forcibly restrain himself from snatching the man's pistol and shooting Clendenning in the back. But he knew it would never do, not before witnesses, and there were at least two dozen loiterers around who had heard the exchange, had heard him, Brad Stryker, humiliated in public. Few men had ever talked that way to him and lived.

Stryker turned away, pushing his man roughly out

of the way, and strode into the building and upstairs to his office.

There was a bottle in his desk. He slugged it twice, waiting for the liquor to bring his anger under control. He then settled back, pondering the problem of what to do about Rory Clendenning.

The first solution that came to him was the obvious one. He could send one of his men after Clendenning some dark night and have the cocky young whelp gunned down. But with all the witnesses to the exchange a few minutes ago, suspicion would immediately attach to him. Stryker wasn't worried about it being proven that he was behind it, but he didn't need that kind of hassle just now.

Perhaps it would be best to lay low for awhile, leave Clendenning's wagons alone. The man's competition wasn't really hurting his that much; Stryker had all the freighting business he could handle anyway. It was just that it would be better for him with less competition. Then he could hike his freighting fees sky high. Let the mine owners scream. They would *have* to use his wagons, or let their ore pile up, which they couldn't afford to do.

However, if he let some time go by, let Clendenning think he had frightened him off, perhaps with the passing of time, Clendenning would relax his guard, and people would forget about the scene outside. Then, when he had the young whelp taken care of, it would be thought just another killing. It galled Stryker to let Clendenning even *think* he had gotten away with humiliating him in such a manner, yet it would be best over the long haul.

Stryker snarled wordlessly and struck the desk a blow with his fist. If only that damned girl, Serena

Foster, was eliminated once and for all, he wouldn't have to worry about such chicken-shit stuff as a freight line. He would be rich beyond his wildest dreams!

He had discussed the situation with Spencer Hurd, bringing it up casually, so the man wouldn't suspect anything.

"Nothing can be done about Serena's estate, Stryker," Hurd had said curtly, "until she is found."

"But what if she's already dead?"

"In that event, the law states that a certain length of time must pass before the estate can be settled . . . unless proof of the legatee's death can be established. I don't happen to think she *is* dead." He gave Stryker a probing look. "I don't understand this sudden interest of yours. You're in that much of a hurry to inherit a whorehouse?"

"It's not that, Judge," Stryker said hastily. "But you've closed it down and all. It's a damned shame for a fine house like that to stand empty."

"Well, it remains that way. I'm looking after Serena's interests, and everything is going to be done legal and aboveboard. When and if she's found, dead or alive, then we'll see."

In his office, Stryker took another pull of the bottle. How he wished, oh how he wished, that he *could* produce proof that Serena Foster was dead to show to that stubborn old man! It was baffling, what had happened to her. She seemed to have disappeared off the face of the earth. The last communication he'd had from Li Po, some months back, the Chink had seemed convinced that she wasn't in San Francisco.

Meanwhile, Stryker knew that all he could do was wait and stew. He well realized that it would do no

316

good to talk to Spencer Hurd again. He was in disfavor with the Judge these days; the lawyer even refused to handle legal matters for him any more, the pigheaded old fool!

He slapped the desk and got to his feet. It might be a good idea to light a fire under Li Po. Yes, he would send him a wire right now. Maybe if he offered a large enough reward it might stir the Chink into action. It might also make him suspicious. Let him be suspicious. Stryker knew that no matter what Li Po might suspect, he would keep his trap shut. He had too much on Li Po for him to risk speaking out of turn.

Leaving the building on his way to send the wire, Stryker thought about what he should say.

Kate Rogan had kept Clendenning's supper warm for him. As he ate, he told her what had transpired with Brad Stryker and what had brought it about.

Kate contemplated him across the table. "Do you think your threat will stop him?"

"Maybe not stop him, not entirely." He shrugged. "But it might cause him to think a little. After all, it's different when somebody starts fighting back. Knowing we're all armed and willing to shoot will certainly make his drivers more cautious."

"Speaking of that, Clendenning . . . would you really have used the shotgun on that driver today?"

"Damned right, I would have," he said emphatically.

"Has it occurred to you that if you had shot him, it wouldn't have stopped his team and wagon? They would still have run into you, and you would likely be lying dead at the bottom of the canyon right now."

Clendenning thought back. "I guess I never really thought about it. I was too angry at the time."

"Well, think about it the next time! All right?" She said in a tart voice. She looked more serious than he could remember seeing her. Then she strove to make light of her concern. "Without you around, the firm of Clendenning and Rogan would no longer exist."

"Dear Kate." He stretched across the table to take her hand. "I suspect that you would survive without me."

"I probably would," she retorted. "But I'd rather not, if you don't mind."

He released her hand and drained his coffee mug. When he looked up, he found her still staring at him, a bemused smile on her face. "Now what?"

"I was just thinking of how much you have changed in eighteen months. You're a man now, and quite a man, Clendenning."

Nettled, he said, "What was I before, a boy?"

"Not exactly." Her smile was affectionate now. "But the Clendenning I found sleeping in my hay barn would not have dreamed of doing the things you are capable of nowadays."

"And I suppose you think credit is due you for that?"

"Some," she answered with an infuriating air of smugness. "I think some credit is due me, yes. At least, in certain . . . well, shall we say private matters?"

He gave a snort. "Sometimes, you can be exasperating, woman!" He pushed his chair back and got to his feet. "I'm going out on the porch for some air."

Her hoot of laughter followed him. Clendenning began to smile as he sprawled in the rocking chair. He wasn't really angry with Kate. She was right. He had changed radically over the past year or more. He was no longer the green, naive young man who'd almost died out in the desert. He felt that now he could survive anything. And Kate had had a hand in it. Especially in bed.

His smile grew. How awkward she must have thought him that first night they made love. With tenderness and affection she had taught him that there was more to making love than getting it over with as quickly as possible. If the chance ever came when he could take Serena to bed again, it would be far different than the near-rape that night by the Carson River...

Clendenning pulled his thoughts away from Serena and back to Kate.

She had been a great help to him in running the business, as well. They worked fine together. Only once had they come close to quarreling. When they had purchased the first four wagons and Clendenning had started hiring drivers, Kate had insisted on driving one of the wagons herself. About this he had been firm. It was hard, dangerous work even for a man, and he absolutely refused to let her take the risk. She hadn't spoken to him for days, but in the end she had accepted his decision as final. Now she kept the books, paid the bills, and made most of their purchases. She was very good with figures, and Clendenning soon found that he was only interfering when he butted into the business end of their...

"Clendenning!"

He awoke with a start. He had fallen into a doze, and Kate was shaking him by the shoulder.

"It's time for bed."

He sat up, yawning. "I was more tired than I thought. I guess I dropped off there for a minute."

"A minute! You've been asleep for more than an hour. Come on to bed now."

Still only half-awake, he followed her into the house and down the hall to the bedroom. Kate didn't light a lamp. By the time Clendenning had fumbled his way out of his clothes, she was already undressed and in bed. He found his way to the bed and stretched out beside her.

"Lord God, this bed feels good," he said with a sigh. "I've had a day."

"Just how tired are you, Clendenning?" she asked, with laughter in her voice.

"Probably not that tired," he said, smiling in the dark. He rolled against her. "Let's find out."

He moved his hands over the heated length of her body. He kissed her lingeringly, one hand cupping a rounded breast. Her nipple began to swell under him thumb. Clendenning continued to caress her, slowly, almost languidly. They were experienced lovers now, not driven by urgency, each body as familiar to the other as a contoured map long committed to memory. Arousal was slow and building, but nonetheless powerful and all-consuming.

Shortly, Kate gave the signal that she was ready, and he moved to take her. They joined together smoothly, their desire still building.

Kate's rich laughter sounded. "Ah, that's my sweet, sweet Clendenning! Not so tired, after all, hey?"

"Would it have mattered if I had been?"

"Not a great deal, sweet. Ah-h, that's it! That's my man, my good strong man!"

She fell silent then, abandoning herself to sensation, her hands stroking his back. Then she dug into his back with strong fingers, as she raised her head, and found his mouth with unerring aim, in the dark.

As her passion peaked, Kate rose, clinging to him, holding him until Clendenning's own ecstasy reached an almost unbearable tension and then broke over him like a warm flood.

For a long moment he lay atop her, then he rolled aside to lie beside her, broad chest heaving, heart thundering. Kate snuggled against him, touching his face with gentle fingers.

"Do you know what these past eighteen months have meant to me, Clendenning? I've never spoken of it before, I'm not a woman to spill out everything she feels. But I was well on my way to becoming a vinegar-tongued, leather-skinned old maid, until you popped into my life. You not only brought me affection, and understanding, but you gave a purpose to my life. I would have continued as the crazy hay barn lady until I was too old, or until the boom was over, and Virginia City had dried up and blown away.

Clendenning had never heard her speak with such intensity. Even her voice sounded different, slightly hoarse with emotion. He was moved by it, yet at the same time made uncomfortable. He said gruffly, "I'm not the only man in the world, Kate. Another would have come along."

"I doubt that. At least not one like you, one I could shape to fit my needs." Now her voice was normal again, with that hint of mocking laughter in it.

Clendenning was unoffended, knowing the twists

and turns of her humor well by this time. With feigned anger, he growled, "So you think you've shaped me, do you?"

Now her hoot of laughter sounded. She ran the tip of her tongue along the side of his jaw. "Well? Ain't I?"

Chapter Sixteen

Serena, attired in a new ball gown of a pale gold, almost the same shade as her hair, felt a happiness so intense that she had the fancy that people seated close to her could feel it coming off her, like a glow of heat.

The occasion was a grand dinner and ball Darrel and she were giving, their very first social affair, and it was all so dazzling that Serena existed in a daze.

Everyone invited—thirty people in all—was in attendance. The past month had been a very good one for Darrel's casino and saloon, and he had given Serena carte blanche to arrange the massive dining room in the Nob Hill mansion as she saw fit.

Serena had consulted a florist, and together they had transformed the dining room into a grotto of fairyland. All the recesses formed by the bow windows of the dining room had been turned into miniature conservatories. It had been Serena's idea to place large mirrors against the windows as a background for the plants. The reflection of the foliage in the mirrors gave the impression of many entrances to greenhouses of great depth. In one window was a little grove of orange trees and banana plants; the second was a miniature forest of tropic palms bending gracefully to the richly textured carpet; and the third was filled with lovely ferns of every sort.

In the ballroom down the hall, a string quartet played light music while the gentlemen and ladies dined. There would be dancing later, for those who were interested.

The *pièce de résistance*, as Darrel called it, was also Serena's idea. As each guest had been seated, he, or she, found before them a solid silver plate, highly polished, the silver dug from the Comstock Lode. An elegant border was engraved on each side of the plate, enclosing embossed letters. On the front was a simple inscription: "Darrel Quick, and friend, are honored by your presence on this occasion. Dec. 15, 1864. San Francisco."

And on the bottom side, planned by a haughty French chef, especially for the occasion, was the following:

Menu

Huitres

Chablis

Consommé Royal

Sherry, Isabella

Saumon glacé au four à la Chambord

Sauterne

Boudin blanc à la Richelieu

Château la Tour

Filet de Boeuf à la Providence

Champagne

Pâte de Foie Gras

Château Yquem

Timbale de Volaille Americaine au Sénateur

Clos Vougeot

Cotelettes d'Agneau sauté au pointes d'asperges

Sorbet

Becassines au Cresson

Château Margeaux

Salade à la Française

Dessert

The plates alone cost forty dollars each and were to be taken away by the guests as mementos of the occasion.

Serena had been hesitant about approaching Darrel with the idea. She had waited tensely as he studied a mock-up of the proposed plate, and a bill of what the plates and the elaborate dishes and the wine list would cost. It amounted to a small fortune.

Darrel studied the plate and the total prices in frowning silence, glancing up at her once with a quizzical look, then back to the items again. Finally he put them down, and gazed at her with elevated eyebrows. "Serena . . ."

"I know, it's too expensive," she said in a rush. "Tang P'ing has already scolded me. I don't know what I was thinking of. Forget it!"

All at once, he roared with laughter. He laughed until tears came into his eyes. Finally he gasped out, "Well, I suppose I asked for it, didn't I? I gave you a free hand, expense be damned. But I must say, when you do a thing, my love, you do it in grand style! But what the hell! Let's go for broke. If nothing else, I'll remember it for the rest of my life. And I'm sure it will be the talk of San Francisco for a long time to come."

"You're sure it's all right?" Serena was still dubious.

"I said so, didn't I?"

"But now, on second thought, it seems awfully extravagant and . . . well, splashy."

"Of course it's extravagant! It's an extravagant age, Serena. And splashy, yes. That's something expected of a gambling man. Besides . . ." He grinned. "It'll be a good advertisement, drawing people to my casino out of curiosity."

Now Serena looked down the length of the table at Darrel, resplendent in his own finery, and found him gazing at her. He winked, his face solemn.

326

The bright silverware, the splendid dishes, the bare, powdered shoulders of the ladies, the jewelry of both ladies and gentlemen—all glittered in the light from the gas jets on the walls and from the rays of the sixty-four wax candles rising from the radiant candelabra used as a centerpiece for the table.

There were a number of dignitaries of San Francisco among the guests. Serena had been surprised at their acceptance of the invitations and so benumbed by the magnificence of the event that she would have found it difficult to put a name to any face around the table. She had been certain that she would be snubbed by many, since it was known that she was living with Darrel out of wedlock, yet she had been accorded courtesy by all present, and had not noticed any sly glances, nor heard any innuendos whispered.

When she had earlier expressed her fears to Darrel, he had said, "When you have money, or even *appear* to have money, it tends to dampen gossip. Oh, you can be sure that gossip and rumor will sweep the town. It'll be delicious gossip for the ladies to exchange, but probably with very little malice. I wouldn't be at all surprised that you receive a proposition or two from some of the gents here."

In this, he was proven correct. After the guests left the dinner table, several of them went into the ballroom for dancing. Darrel claimed the first dance with Serena. He danced as well as he did everything else. Serena, having had very little practice at dancing, felt clumsy and awkward in his arms, as he swept her across the polished floor.

At the end of the dance, he stepped back with a slight bow. In a low voice, he said, "I'll leave you now to the mercy of the gallants here . . ."

"No, don't leave me, Darrel!" she said in a panic. "I'm a terrible dancer, as you can see, and I won't know what to say to them."

"They'll not notice your dancing," he said amusedly. "And they'll do the talking. Just look beautiful and nod intelligently once in awhile."

Serena danced until she was weary. She did receive two indecent proposals, though couched in gentlemanly language, and there were several attempts to fondle her. One man even pinched her on the rear. By then she was confident enough of herself to fend them all off with laughing ease.

It was long after midnight before the last guests said good night. Darrel and Serena stood at the door watching the last couple make their way down the long flight of steps to the coach waiting on the street below. Darrel put his arms around her shoulders, and Serena leaned against him with a tired but happy sigh.

"Have a good time, Serena?"

"If I were to die right now, I'd die happy."

"Let's try to postpone that for a time yet."

"Oh, Darrel. Thank you!" She straightened up, threw her arms around him, and kissed him. "I will remember this night for the rest of my life!"

Darrel had heard the expression, "stars in her eyes," and had scorned it as romantic nonsense. Now he revised his opinion. If anyone could ever be said to have stars in her eyes, it was Serena Foster right this moment. The thought that he had, in some measure, contributed toward that sparkling happiness touched Darrel deeply. To hide his emotion, he took her arm and turned her toward the stairs.

And to lighten the moment, he said, in his usual

sardonic manner, "How shocked these people here tonight would have been had they known you were an illusionist's assistant, sawed in half nightly, only a short time ago."

"Probably not as shocked as some were at my living here in sin with you ..."

"Serena," he broke in, "I wish to hear no more of this. You are *not* a farm girl back in Illinois now. I forbid you to speak of it again!"

"I'm sorry, Darrel, I won't, I promise. Besides ..." She turned that elfin grin on him. "I have found living in sin, with *you*, delightful beyond measure. Truly I have. Cross my heart!"

"That's better. And I feel complimented, madam." Smiling he dipped his head.

They started up the stairs. Halfway up, Darrel said, "I forgot to tell you, Serena. I bought two tickets to the opera next week. Adelina Patti is singing the lead. Now that you have finally made your debut, in a manner of speaking, it's time I showed you off in public."

Serena felt the chill of fear. It was not fear of danger to her person. Feeling as secure here with Darrel as though wrapped in a protective cocoon, she seldom thought nowadays that danger might still be lurking out there for her.

But to be placed in public view! She said, "Do you think it will be all right?"

"Why shouldn't it be? It was all right tonight, wasn't it? You can't stay hidden away here forever." He pressed her hand. "I'll be with you. I'll see no harm comes to you, love."

They were upstairs now, in their bedroom. In her

happiness, Serena moved away from him, spinning around twice. "Did you like the dress?"

"I liked the dress," he said gravely. "And so did everyone else, both men and women. You were the queen of the ball, my love. We'll have to buy you another for the opera, equally stunning."

They undressed together, and made slow, exquisite love in the big bed. Serena's cry of joy at the end was as much from the happiness the evening had brought her as from the rapture she felt.

Afterward, snug in Darrel's arms, she said sleepily, "Do you really think people will remember the dinner tonight?"

"Believe me, love, it'll be the talk of the town tomorrow. *You'll* be the talk of the town."

"Me?" she stirred, raising up. "I'm not sure I'll like that, being the talk of the town."

"Why not? I know you're not a vain woman, Serena, but all women, all people, have a touch of vanity about them. Now go to sleep."

He pulled her back into the warmth and closeness of his embrace, and Serena went to sleep, her doubts quieted.

Li Po muttered a curse under his breath. Crumpling up the telegram from Brad Stryker, he threw it on the floor.

Did the foolish Occidental believe that an offer of ten thousand dollars would goad him on to any greater effort to find Serena Foster?

Li Po had never stopped looking for her. Unaccustomed to being thwarted in any endeavor, he had commanded his henchmen to be on constant watch for the woman or any word of her. Any new woman they saw with yellow hair, they had orders to report to him immediately. Now almost a year had passed, and she was not to be found. Li Po was convinced that the woman had long since left San Francisco, and he doubted that she would return. Apparently the encounter with Fong Jin had frightened her, and she had fled the city. She was undoubtedly somewhere on the other side of the country now, and would not be so foolish as to return here. Nevertheless, Li Po intended to prod his men into keeping up the search, and he certainly needed no reward from Stryker to spur him on to greater effort.

He was curious, however, as to why Stryker should have such a strong interest in having the woman found, strong enough to offer ten thousand American dollars. Li Po's thin nostrils quivered. It was possible that a profit might accrue to him in this matter. He might, after all, send word to the man Stryker should he find the woman with the yellow hair. *After* he had toyed with her . . .

A hesitant knock sounded on the door. In harsh Chinese he called out, "Enter!"

It was one of his *boo how doy*. Hands tucked in his sleeves, the man in black approached, bowing.

Li Po said, curtly, "What is it? Why do you bother me?"

"It is about the woman with yellow hair, lord. It is said that the gambler, the white man by the name of Darrel Quick, has taken this woman into his house as his concubine."

Li Po sat up. "Is this a fact or rumor? How did this knowledge come to you?"

"One of the house servants in the man Quick's house told me, lord."

Li Po held up a hand for silence. Closing his eyes, he thought back to that time in the opera house in Virginia City. Serena Foster had been with a man. He tried to recall the appearance of the man. It was difficult, since all of Li Po's attention had been on the woman. Yet it seemed to him that the man had been wearing the garb of a gambler ...

He opened his eyes. "You will keep a close watch on both the man and his concubine. When you have seen both clearly enough to describe them accurately, report back to me."

"Yes, master." The man in black bowed himself out.

Three days later, the man came back with his report. Eyes closed, Li Po listened closely as his man described Darrel Quick and the woman with yellow hair. Excitement quickened Li Po's blood, and he felt a stirring in his loins. It was her, he was certain of it!

Keeping his face expressionless, he opened his eyes. "Is that all?"

"One more thing, lord. From the tongue of our informant in the house of Darrel Quick, the man and his concubine with the yellow hair are to attend the opera tomorrow evening."

"Ah!" Li Po blew out his breath. He would also be present, in his box. Adelina Patti was his favorite diva. He would be able to make positive identification of Serena Foster himself. It was unfortunate that he would not be able to fully concentrate on the opera.

"One more thing you must learn for me," he said crisply. "The seats to be occupied by this pair."

"It shall be done, lord."

"And tomorrow evening you will accompany me to the opera. Also . . ." Li Po named four more of his *boo how doy*. "Inform them that they are to accompany me." Then he motioned languidly. "That is all."

"Your wishes shall be carried out, master." Bowing his head humbly, the man in black backed out of the room.

Feeling far from languid, Li Po was on his feet the moment the door closed. He paced the room, in a high state of excitation. He could not recall when he had experienced such anticipation. Over the years, Li Po had known, again and again, just about every experience of the senses. Of late, he had become jaded.

But just the thought of the yellow-haired woman, with her fine features and China-white flesh, excited him immensely.

That was not all to the good, Li Po realized. He was not so young any more.

He strode into the other room. He was badly in need of a calming pipe of opium.

In the carriage on the way to the opera house, Darrel said, "I think we make a fine-looking pair. Don't you agree, my love?"

"You look wonderful, that's for sure." Serena took his hand and held it in her lap. He did indeed look splendid, in new evening clothes, with a high, black silk top hat. He was so handsome Serena became breathless just looking at him.

"Are you fishing for a compliment, Serena?" he

teased. "You know very well how grand, how beautiful, you are tonight."

She colored slightly, aware that she *had* been looking for a compliment. Her new silk evening gown, a soft lavender in color, dipped low at the neckline, leaving her powdered shoulders bare under the lace shawl she wore against the evening chill. The neckline was daringly low, revealing the luminous mounds of her breasts. Tang P'ing had brushed her hair until it shone like burnished gold. A dusting of rouge on her cheeks, and a touch of lip rouge to her mouth, gave high color to her face.

"Thank you, darling." She leaned across to kiss him and felt the hard bulge of the gun on his hip. She made a face. "Do you have to wear a gun, even to the opera?"

"I'm never without it, especially now that I have you to protect. I would feel undressed without my Colt."

Serena said nothing, suppressing a small chill. Her days now were so filled with excitement and happiness, that she rarely ever thought of any danger to herself. She was convinced that she was no longer in personal jeopardy, yet she supposed Darrel was right. It would be foolish to take unnecessary chances.

They were riding in a hired carriage tonight. She had given Tang P'ing and Shu-toe the evening off, so they could visit with friends in Chinatown. The carriage drew up before the opera house, and they got out. The assemblage before the opera house was a gathering of the elite of San Francisco. The gleam of the flickering gas jets was reflected in sparkling shards of light from the jewels of the ladies in their splendid gowns. The men in top hats and evening clothes smoked cigars, while the ladies gossiped.

"Shall we go on in and find our seats?" Darrel whispered. "The curtain will rise shortly." He laughed softly. "I don't smoke cigars, and I'm sure you're not interested in gossip, unless it's about yourself."

"And it probably is," she retorted. As he gave her a warning look, she added hastily, "Yes, let's go in."

Making their way through the crowd before the opera house, silence fell around them, and many glances were directed their way. In their wake, the talk started up again. Serena could not hear what was being said, but she was sure they were talking about her. She knew better than to mention it again to Darrel.

The house was already filling up as they searched out their seats. By the time the overture began, the house was filled to capacity. An expectant hush fell over the audience as the first strains of music began to swell.

Serena leaned over to whisper to Darrel, "I've never attended an opera. I hope I'll like it."

"Don't expect to understand the words," he whispered back. "It'll be in Italian. Just listen, and enjoy the music and the singing. Opera takes a little getting used to."

Li Po had entered his private box early, and he had kept his glance riveted on the seats to be occupied by Darrel Quick and his concubine. He tensed when a man and a woman took the seats. The woman had yellow hair . . . she turned her head to gaze around the house, and Li Po let his breath go. It was her! It was Serena Foster. At long last, his search was at an end!

Before the overture began, he beckoned his henchmen around him. In a terse voice he gave implicit instructions. Four of his men left the box before the opera even started, and Li Po was left with just one bodyguard. Even after the house lights were dimmed, Li Po seldom removed his glance from Serena Foster, not even when the diva came on stage and began his favorite aria.

He remained until the opera was over and Darrel Quick and the yellow-haired woman had departed. Then, accompanied by his bodyguard, Li Po left the opera house and entered his private coach, which had been parked in an alley nearby. The coach proceeded directly to the house at the intersection of Clay and Dupont, and Li Po went up to his suite.

There, he paced from room to room, impatience riding him like a spurred demon. He never once considered the opium pipe. Tonight, he did not desire the dream-state of the pipe. He wanted all his senses tingling in anticipation of the moment when Serena Foster would be carried into his suite. It could be a lengthy wait, since it was likely that she and her escort would tarry over a late supper.

Li Po paced. He could wait. He had waited this long. What was another hour, more or less?

"You were right, Darrel," Serena said. "I didn't understand it, not a single word!"

"I'll let you in on a little secret, love," he said in a conspiratorial whisper. "At least half of the people there didn't understand it, either. Not only that, but

336

they didn't appreciate the music or the singing. But attending the opera is a social occasion, a chance to show off fine clothes and jewels, a chance to see and be seen, an opportunity to exchange juicy gossip."

They were at Winn's Fountain Head again, having a late, light supper.

"But you seemed to enjoy the opera, and you didn't understand it."

"Not the words, no, but I enjoyed the music and the singing. I've seen and heard Adelina Patti before, as I think I mentioned. She's probably my favorite diva."

Serena was shaking her head. "I very much doubt I'll ever really like opera. How can I enjoy something I don't understand? Not that I didn't enjoy attending. I had a lovely time. It was really grand!"

Darrel smiled. "You would, I think, come to like it eventually. As I said before, it takes some getting used to. I've attended opera for years. The first time my father . . . the first time I went to an opera, I thought it was a deadly bore. But you're becoming a woman of taste, Serena, and you will need to be exposed to cultural events of many types, so you can improve your knowledge and widen your experience."

Serena laughed suddenly. "At least there was no shooting tonight. Remember that night in Virginia City?"

"I well remember," he said with a grin. "But it can happen here. Last year, so I've been told, some madman attended the opera with a bomb. He was going to toss it onto the stage. Fortunately, it went off before he could throw it, killing only himself."

Serena shivered. "There's such violence in the

West! Even here, in San Francisco. I don't think I'll ever get used to it."

"It's still frontier country, Serena. Violence is a way of life. The people who come and go through the city, most of them, are fresh from the mining camps, and violence and death are something they witness every day. You, of all people, should know that."

"Yes, I should, shouldn't I?"

"I'm sorry, Serena, forgive me. I shouldn't have mentioned it. Are you ready to go? It's quite late."

Outside, they found the street thick with fog. It was so dense that it was difficult to see more than a few feet. It took a little time for Darrel to hail an empty carriage.

The fog was even thicker on Nob Hill, and Serena could see only halfway up the steps when they got out of the carriage before the house. Darrel paid the driver, and she took his arm as they cautiously mounted the steps.

The gaslight outside the front door was out, and Darrel had to bend down with his key, muttering under his breath, as he tried to fit the key into the lock.

Serena heard a soft, shuffling sound and whirled around. Two men were converging on them out of the fog, one from the left, and one from the right. Both wore black and had the strange, flat hats she had seen on the men that day fighting in the alley in Chinatown. Both carried pistols.

Serena uttered a small scream. "Darrel!"

At her side, Darrel straightened, spinning about. Without hesitation, his hand dipped under his coat, and the Colt appeared almost magically in his hand. With his left hand he shoved Serena behind him. The Colt thundered, and the man on their left was knocked backward by the bullet, tumbling down the steps.

Darrel immediately whirled toward the second man, but he was too late. As Darrel was turning, the Chinese in black discharged his weapon. The bullet caught Darrel in the left side of the chest, propelling him back against the door. He slid slowly to the stoop. The Colt fell out of his hand and clattered down the steps.

For a horrified instant, Serena stared down at Darrel's still form. Belatedly, she glanced up, tensing for flight. She saw that it was useless to even try. There were two more men now. All three were advancing on her, spreading out slightly. There was no chance she could get past them and reach the steps. One of the men carried a long rope, the other a sack of some sort.

She screamed at the top of her lungs. One man seized her by the arm and spun her around, twisting her arm brutally up behind her back. The pain was blinding. Just as Serena opened her mouth to scream again, the sack was tossed over her head, and the sound of her screaming was muffled. She struggled with all her strength, and a terrible pain tore through her from the twisted arm. It felt as though the arm was being ripped from the socket.

Serena was dimly aware that the rope was being wound around her upper body. The heavy sack made it difficult to breathe. Her struggles grew steadily weaker. The last thing she remembered was being picked up and carried off into the night.

Chapter Seventeen

Serena kept drifting in and out of consciousness; peripherally aware of the fact that she was lying on something soft and that the room in which she was lying was semi-dark.

There was a sweetish, cloying odor in the air, and her body felt languorous and heavy, as if it would take more strength than she possessed to lift her arms and legs. She was totally unable to remember anything that had happened before awakening, but she felt no sense of danger or discomfort.

She lay quietly for a few moments, trying to focus her thoughts. Her body felt cool, and with a great effort she lifted her head slightly, enough to see that she was completely nude and that she was lying on a large, pillow-like bed. She had the feeling that her situation should alarm her, but the thought drifted away; dissolved by her growing sense of euphoria. She was not even concerned when she became aware that another person was in the room.

Opening her heavy-lidded eyes, Serena looked up and saw, through a haze, the figure of a man. He seemed preternaturally tall and thin, almost a giant to her drug-dazzled eyes. Then she managed to focus on his face, an Oriental face with narrow eyes and thin lips, a long, yellow face—it seemed to her as yellow as gold. Her mind made the connection, and the image of the gold Chinese mask flashed before her. She gasped and cried out. It seemed to her that the cry hung in the room for moments afterward.

"There is no need to cry out, Golden Poppy," a high, cultured voice said soothingly. "You will enjoy our little interlude, you will see. Screaming will avail you nothing. There is no one to hear or care."

For a moment her vision cleared, and she saw that the speaker was just a man, not a demon. He was dressed in a long robe of shimmering silk, shot through with threads of gold. He was no one she had ever seen before.

The strain of keeping her eyes open was immense, and Serena let her eyelids close for a moment. As she did so, she suddenly became aware of her condition; she was naked, and a strange, frightening man was standing looking down at her. What was happening? How had she come to be here?

Her eyes snapped open, and she felt panic tighten her throat. The man leaned down toward her, and she saw his incredibly long nails. His thin fingers touched her breasts lightly. Serena shuddered as she felt their cold touch on her belly and thighs. Her euphoria was fading fast, to be replaced by an icy fear and awareness. Her throat felt painfully dry.

"Please . . . who?" she managed to croak.

The thin face creased in a cold smile. "My Golden Poppy is thirsty. We will take care of that. I will soon assuage your thirst."

As the man turned away, Serena tried desperately to make her mind function. Where was she? Why was she here? There was *something* that she should remember. A gunshot. Had there been gunshots? Shadowy, menacing figures in black. It seemed to her that someone had died. *Who had died?* Her thoughts tangled, and drifted, and would not obey her will. She stared at the back of the tall Oriental. Who was this man?

Li Po was smiling evilly as he opened a teakwood cabinet in one corner and took out a metal goblet and a glass of rice wine. He filled the glass two-thirds full, then selected two vials from a rack in the cabinet. From both vials he poured a liberal amount of powders into a wine goblet. One was an ancient Chinese aphrodisiac, and the other was a strong opium derivative. It was not powerful enough to put the woman to sleep. She would still be awake enough to know what was happening to her, yet powerless to offer any resistance.

Tilting the goblet to his own lips, Li Po took a draught from it. It was just right. The strong wine would absorb any taste of the powders. Not that she was likely to notice anything out of the ordinary. In any event. Not in her condition. The incense burning in the red-shaded holders was in itself a powerful drug, enough to dull the brain until the woman's wits would not function sufficiently for her to realize much of what was happening. The powders would have a double effect—slowing her mental processes and at the same time heightening the sensuality of her body.

Returning to Serena, he knelt and gently raised her head. In a crooning voice, he said, "Drink this, Golden Poppy. It will relieve your thirst." He held the goblet to her lips.

Golden Poppy? Why did this man keep calling her that? That wasn't her name, was it? She tried to remember her name and failed. Then she felt the cold rim of the metal goblet touch her lips, and she drank greedily. Dimly she recognized the taste of rice wine. She drank until the goblet was empty.

She heard a sigh of satisfaction from the man. "Excellent, that is excellent! Now you will feel fine."

But Serena didn't feel fine. Her thoughts dimmed further, until her brain no longer had any control over her motor impulses. She felt hands on her body, gently stroking, fondling. One thought—this is wrong!—cut through the fog of her mind for an instant and then vanished in the mist that clouded her brain.

Managing to raise her head off the pillow, Serena saw that the thin Oriental was naked, his body angular and yellow against the flickering light. Slowly, he was bending over her. The thought came again, sharp as fear. This was wrong, it must not happen, but there was nothing she could do. She might as well have been paralyzed from the neck up.

Then she realized that his body was coupling with hers, and she was responding in spite of herself. Her lower body moved languidly in the motions of intercourse. It seemed to go on for a long while, but Serena dimly sensed that she had lost all track of time.

Finally, she heard a sharp grunt and several words

344

spoken in guttural Chinese, and he was still. Serena knew that he was still, that his weight was resting on her, yet she felt little beyond a core of revulsion and shame pulsating somewhere far back in her mind.

She welcomed the drugged sleep, and knew no more.

Li Po uncoiled his long length from the supine body of Golden Poppy, and stood up. His face wore one of its rare smiles. His anticipation had not been in vain. Coupling with the woman had brought him more pleasure than he had experienced in a long while. Sated for the moment, he stood staring down at the beautiful, still body of his new plaything—the tumbled hair like fine strands of gold, and the flesh like porcelain, with subtle undertones of pink.

He nodded to himself. In her present condition, she would sleep for a long time. He could safely have a pipe of opium now, and then seek repose himself.

Time lost all meaning for Serena. Later, piecing it together, she knew she had been in this place for five days and nights.

Like a person in delirium, she drifted in and out of consciousness, with a few moments of lucidity. A number of times she was given the goblet of wine to drink; each instance was followed by a fevered bout of sensuality when the tall, naked Oriental used her body—never roughly, always gently, with the consideration he would give a treasured doll. And each time, despite the burning core of abhorrence in her mind, Serena could not prevent her traitorous body from responding.

A number of times she was fed, hand fed by the

Oriental man, bits of spicy food that she usually gulped down without chewing.

There was one very clear, lucid moment when she asked, "Who are you? I don't know you!"

"I am called Li Po, Golden Poppy."

The name churned in her mind, conjuring up fear. There was some dreadful horror connected with that name. But before Serena could think of a reason for the horror, she drifted away again.

Li Po stared down at her curiously, wondering why a look of fright had flitted across her face at the mention of his name. How could she have recognized it? To the best of his knowledge, she could never have had occasion to hear his name. Certainly he had never been introduced to her. Could it be Brad Stryker's doing?

Perturbed now, Li Po pulled on his embroidered robe and went into the other room to smoke a pipe. The opium cleared his brain of all extraneous thoughts, and he concentrated on the disturbing fact of Serena Foster's recognition of his name.

It could have only come about through Stryker. Not that Li Po was particularly concerned that he could be in any personal danger. He felt as invulnerable here as he would have been housed in a fortress.

He sighed. Five days now the woman had been at his mercy, and he had used her a number of times. Li Po had to face the fact that he was growing sated. He had been confident that this time he would not become jaded so easily. Clearly, he had been mistaken.

It was time to rid himself of her. It had been his original intention to sell her to the white slave circuit, shipping her out of the country. However, he would not receive nearly as much as Brad Stryker was offering for her. So why spurn a nice profit for himself?

Li Po's instinct for profit, which rarely failed him, told him that there was much more to Stryker's attempt to locate this woman than was apparent. He had felt that for some time. Stryker's interest had to be personal, and there probably was a great deal of money involved. The Brad Stryker Li Po knew would not offer a reward of ten thousand dollars simply for the capture of a woman wanted for murder.

Li Po reached a decision. He would play Stryker's game and see what happened. First, he would send the man a wire informing him that he had found Serena Foster; then he would dispatch a couple of his minions to Virginia City with instructions to maintain a close watch on Stryker.

His mind made up, Li Po quickly wrote out the wording of the wire. In English block letters, then gave the bell rope a tug. In a short time, one of his men knocked softly on the door.

Li Po called out for him to enter. He gave the man the paper with the wording of the wire, and ordered him to send it off at once.

The man nodded, bowed, and backed out of the room.

Serena's lucid periods were more frequent now and lasted longer. Gradually, she gathered her scattered thoughts together, and began to make some sense out of what had happened to her. She recalled, vividly, Darrel being shot down and her own abduction. She still had no idea of where she was, and the cause of her unreasoning fear at the name, Li Po, still eluded her. Darrel . . . was he dead?

She found herself weeping weak tears. At that moment a man in black came quietly into the room carrying a tray with streaming rice and a cup of tea. It was the first time anyone other than Li Po had been in the room with her. Serena covered her nakedness hurriedly, as the man placed the tray on a small table. Serena dashed the tears from her eyes and waited until the man had left the room before sitting up.

She heard the bolt thrown home after him. Now that her mind was clearer, Serena discovered that she was very hungry. She could remember eating very little, and her body seemed to have lost weight. She ate all the rice in the bowl and drank the tea.

For the first time since she had been captured, Serena was aware enough to study her surroundings. Although the walls were hung with silk tapestries, and the floor covered with a thick carpet, the furnishings were few. Aside from a small teakwood cabinet against one wall, the short-legged table, and the pillow-bed, there was nothing else in the room.

Getting to her feet, Serena found her legs were weak and trembling. Leaning against the wall, she made her way around the room, searching for windows beneath the hangings, but there were none. The door was of heavy, carved teakwood, impossible to force.

How long was she going to be kept here? She already knew the purpose: at least she knew one reason. Hot shame flooded her mind as she recalled those times Li Po had taken her, and her own shameless responses . . .

Li Po! Now she made the connection. He was the

Chinese crime lord who ruled the underworld in San Francisco's Chinatown, the man who had ordered Shu-toe's tongue torn out, and the owner of the house in Virginia City where she had been whipped and raped. Could he be the same man, the one in the gold mask? Serena immediately dismissed that as not possible. This man was tall, thin, almost skinny, while the man in the mask had been broader, stronger, with a powerfully muscled figure. Yet there must be some connection between the pair, since the rape had taken place in Li Po's house.

The tea and rice had renewed her strength. She looked around the room for her clothes, but they weren't in sight. She sat down on the bed and pulled the coverlet around her.

There was one thing she was sure of. With her mind functioning clearly, she was determined to fight this Li Po, should he try to force himself on her again. He had been keeping her drugged. There could be no other explanation ...

Serena sat upright suddenly. There had been a sound, like a gunshot, muffled by many doors. There, there was another! She listened intently. Now she heard shouts, the sound of running feet, and a shriek of pain.

She heard a scrabbling sound from the other side of the door and shrank back against the wall, drawing the coverlet tightly around her. Finally the bolt was thrown back, and Li Po darted into the room. From the pocket of his embroidered robe, he took a large key and locked the heavy door.

"What is it?" Serena demanded. "What is happening?"

He ignored her, hurrying to the teakwood cabinet. He rummaged in it, muttering in Chinese.

Then he slammed the cabinet shut in frustration. His glance darted frantically around the room. "Curses on the gods! There is no weapon here!"

He seemed to be terribly agitated, and it was obvious that he was truly frightened. Serena was glad of that, of course, but what could terrify this composed, usually inscrutable Oriental? Then her heart gave a great leap of hope. There could only be one reason . . .

The door knob rattled, and rattled again, as a fist pounded on the wood. Serena darted a glance at Li Po. He was backed up against the wall, teeth bared in a grimace of fear.

Something heavy thumped against the door. It shivered, but did not give. Again and again, the door was hit, and Serena realized that someone on the other side was hurling their body at the door. The door was exceptionally strong. How could one person break it down?

Once more, the body outside battered at the door. This time, the lock gave, with a splintering sound, and the door flew open, slamming against the wall.

"Shu-toe!" Serena exclaimed.

Shu-toe didn't spare her a glance. His eyes were riveted on Li Po. Shu-toe's face was battered and bloody, his tunic torn to shreds. Serena gasped as she saw the bleeding wound in his left shoulder. He had been shot!

Now Shu-toe advanced with deadly purpose. He swayed from side to side, and as though he was about to fall, yet he kept coming.

Li Po snatched up the heavy, low table, and held it over his head by two short legs. As Shu-toe came within range, Li Po brought the table down upon him. Shu-toe ducked, taking the blow on his wounded shoulder. His mouth opened in a soundless cry of agony.

As Li Po raised the table again, Shu-toe reached up and tore it from his grasp, throwing it behind him. Then he flattened Li Po against the wall, his huge hands gripping the older man's slender throat like a vise.

Li Po, eyes bulging, hit out at Shu-toe with his hands and feet. He might as well have been beating at a brick wall. Shu-toe did not relax his grip for an instant. On his face was the same intent, chilling expression Serena had glimpsed the night he had set fire to Li Po's house in Virginia City.

Serena watched, fascinated and repelled, as Li Po's face slowly turned black. She opened her mouth to command Shu-toe to stop, but the memory of the indignities she had endured at the hands of Li Po flooded her mind, and the words died in her throat.

It was too late, anyway. Li Po was dead. Shu-toe shook him once, then stepped back, taking his hands from around the man's neck. The body of Li Po slid to the floor. Shu-toe stood over it for a long moment.

Then he gave his head a hard shake and turned to Serena. He motioned and offered her a hand up. As Serena got to her feet, clutching the coverlet around her, Shu-toe swayed, and almost fell. Serena put an arm around him, supporting his weight for a moment.

Then he took a deep breath and tried to smile at her.

"Are you all right, Shu-toe?"

He nodded and gestured that they should go.

Some strength seemed to return to him as they left the room and started down the stairs. There was a man in black lying crumpled up at the top of stairs, another halfway down, and yet another at the foot of the stairs. Later, Serena learned that there had been four men in the house besides Li Po. Shu-toe had fought his way through all four to get to her and Li Po.

In that room without windows, day or night had not existed for her, and she was surprised to discover it was daylight outside. There was a carriage parked up the street, and as Serena and Shu-toe appeared in the doorway, the carriage moved quickly up to them. Serena and Shu-toe got in. Tang P'ing was inside the carriage. She looked worriedly at her son and uttered a cry of distress at the sight of the bullet wound. Shu-toe gave her a weak, reassuring smile and leaned back against the seat, eyes closing.

Serena said, "I think he will be fine, Tang P'ing, but we must get him to a doctor as quickly as possible."

"And you Se-rena," Tang P'ing said softly, "are you all right?"

"I . . . I'm fine." She swallowed. "Now."

Tang P'ing gazed deep into her eyes, and what she saw there caused her to shake her head sorrowfully. She took Serena's hands in hers. "Am sorry, Se-rena. Took so much time to learn where you were. Then word came to us that Li Po had you captive."

"Li Po is dead, Tang P'ing. Shu-toe killed him."

Tang P'ing flashed a look at her son. She smiled. "Is good. Son now have vengeance on evil one who cut out his tongue."

"Darrel," Serena said urgently. "Is he dead? The

352

last I saw of him, he had been shot and seemed to be dead."

"Darrel Quick not dead. But very, very sick. In hospital."

"I must go to him at once. But not like this. Can we go to the house so I can put on some clothes first?" She looked past Tang P'ing at Shu-toe. "Shu-toe, can you wait that long? Then we will have you tended to at the hospital."

Opening his eyes, Shu-toe nodded. He talked rapidly on his fingers to his mother.

"Shu-toe say wound not serious," Tang P'ing said. "What call flesh wound. Much pain, but bullet go all way through, not break bone." She laughed impishly at Serena's look of astonishment, "Shu-toe wish to be doctor of medicine, some day. Doctor own people. Has studied much."

Serena could think of no immediate response to that. The thought of a doctor who couldn't speak to his patients struck her as incongruous. Yet, knowing Shu-toe, his determination and intelligence, she supposed it was more than possible.

The carriage was on their street now, laboring up the steep hill. Serena asked, "Do the police know what happened?"

"Police know, yes. When Shu-toe and Tang P'ing come to house that night, find tong man dead at bottom of steps, and your Darrel Quick very bad. Had to call police, Se-rena, to get Darrel Quick to hospital. Police come, and Darrel Quick wake up enough to tell what happened."

Serena's heart gave a lurch. "The police know my name, know I was involved?"

"Do not think police believe about you, Se-rena.

353

Not to worry. They not search for you. Tang P'ing think they believe your Darrel Quick not speak truth. Tang P'ing overhear one police say the man Quick a gambler. Believe some person lose much money to him, come kill him."

Tang P'ing's words didn't relieve Serena's fears. My name, she thought bleakly; every policeman in San Francisco must know that Serena Foster was wanted for murder in Virginia City.

Still, there was some hope. It had been over a year. In the interim they must have been given the names of many other wanted people to look out for. Anyway, it would serve no useful purpose to fret about it now. She couldn't run away; Darrel would need her.

"One thing puzzles me," she said. "You and Shu-toe came back to the house, and found Darrel lying unconscious, and the other man dead at the bottom of the steps. There were two gunshots, that many I remember. Why didn't the other servants come to investigate? They were in the house that evening, I know."

"Not know, Serena." Tang P'ing shrugged. "Nobody here. They leave, not return."

"There can be only one explanation for that. They were paid informants of Li Po."

"Maybe not paid. Could have been afraid. Many Chinese afraid of Li Po." She smiled. "Is good Li Po is no more. Chinese people have less fear now."

They stopped before the house. Shu-toe remained in the carriage, while Serena and Tang P'ing hurried upstairs. Serena dressed as quickly as she could. Fifteen minutes later, they were on their way to the hospital where Darrel lay close to death.

They helped Shu-toe inside and gave him into the

care of a doctor. Then Serena was directed to Darrel's room. In the corridor outside, she noticed two men loitering. So anxious was she to see Darrel that she scarcely noticed them. Tang P'ing remained just outside the door as Serena slipped into Darrel's room.

It was a small room, strong with the odor of disinfectant. The only light came through one tiny window. Darrel was a still figure under a blanket on a narrow bed. The single chair was occupied by a plump, middle-aged woman in gray.

At Serena's entrance, she got to her feet and met Serena halfway into the room. In a hoarse whisper, she said, "You a relative? His wife?"

Serena simply nodded.

"Good, that's good, dearie." The woman in gray smiled. "The only people in to see the poor man have been that pair of heathen Chinee."

"How is he?" Serena said in an equally low voice.

"Not the best, dearie. He's still in sorry shape. He's lucky to be alive. It'll be some time before he's up and around, you can be sure. The bullet, the doctor said, grazed his lung. I'm sure he'll be the better now for you being here." She patted Serena's hand. "I'll leave him alone with you, dearie. He wakes up from time to time. Sometimes he knows what's going on, sometimes the fever has him out of his head."

The woman in gray eased herself out, and Serena slipped quietly into the chair she had vacated. She sat very still, hands crossed in her lap. Darrel's face was gray as ashes, his breathing stertorous.

Despair swept over Serena. It was actually her fault that he was so close to death. She had been very selfish in accepting his protection, knowing very well that someone, some mysterious someone, was deter-

355

mined to see her dead. Now Darrel's life might be the price exacted for her selfishness. She closed her eyes and prayed for the first time in a long while, prayed to God that Darrel would not die.

"Love? Is that you?"

Serena started. The voice had been so soft, that at first she thought she was imagining it. Opening her eyes, she saw that Darrel's eyes were also open. He was staring at her in dawning recognition.

She leaned over to take the one hand that was out from under the blanket. "Darling! I'm so glad . . . how are you feeling?"

"Weak as a kitten at the moment." A ghost of his old sardonic smile flickered on his mouth. "But I'm alive. At least I think so, unless I'm in Heaven, and you're a ministering angel."

"No angel, Darrel." She laughed softly. "And you are alive."

"That's good. All these years, it never entered my mind I'd end up in Heaven. It would be a shock to be proven wrong now."

"Darling, thank God you *are* alive!" She squeezed his hand.

"How long have I been here, Serena?"

"Several days. Almost a week."

He frowned. "I don't remember too much. But there were some men in black. I shot one, as I recall, and then I guess I took a bullet in return. Since then, all I can remember are a few lucid moments in this damned place, and asking question and receiving no decent answers. Some damned doctor keeps telling me I'm lucky to be alive."

"Darrel, should you be talking so much?"

"Yes, dammit! You're the first person I've talked to

willing to talk back and make any sense." His voice had gained strength. "I want to know what happened to you, Serena, after I lost consciousness. Are you all right?"

She hesitated, finally saying slowly, "It's a long story, Darrel. I don't think I should tax your strength now. You concentrate on getting well."

His eyes searched hers. "But you are all right?"

"I'm fine." She forced a laugh. "Don't I look all right?"

"We-el, yes and no. You seem . . . different somehow."

"It's because you've been very ill, Darrel. When you're up and around again, you'll see I'm fine. Cross my heart!"

Again that flicker of a smile crossed his face. "I've heard you say that before, and I've found it usually means the opposite. But I'm not in much of a condition to argue right now, am I?" His head fell back on the pillow, and his eyes closed.

But in a moment, his hand turned over and closed around hers, squeezing weakly. "Serena?"

"Yes, darling?"

"I think I'm about to go under again. Be here when I wake up again. Promise?"

"I promise," she said in a soft voice.

She didn't let go of his hand right away. He was asleep again, but this time his slumber seemed easier, not so labored. When she was sure he was sound asleep, Serena disengaged her hand, leaned over, and kissed him tenderly on the cheek, then tiptoed out of the room.

As she stepped out into the corridor, Serena was

confronted by the two men she had seen loitering there earlier.

One man said, "Are you Serena Foster?"

Serena knew what was coming. As strongly as she could, she replied, "Yes, I am."

"We are from the Pinkerton Agency. We are empowered to place you under arrest and return you forthwith to Virginia City, to stand trail for murder."

A gasp came from Tang P'ing, who moved up to stand beside Serena. Serena said, "All right, gentlemen. May I have a private word with my companion first?"

The two men exchanged glances, then the one who had spoken nodded, and the pair moved off a short distance, but still kept a close watch on her.

Tang P'ing said, "I will go with you, Se-rena."

"No, Tang P'ing. I do appreciate your devotion, but no. There is absolutely nothing you can do there to help me. They might even arrest you for helping me to escape. You have much to do here. You have to look after Shu-toe. And both of you must look after Darrel, and tend him when he is home again. It will be a long time before he is up and about again."

Tang P'ing lowered her head in acquiescence, looking subdued.

"And Tang P'ing . . ." Serena hesitated, placing her hand on the woman's shoulder. "Tell Darrel . . ." She swallowed. "Tell him I'm sorry I won't be there when he wakes up. Tell him that I will think of him often and be forever grateful for the kindnesses he has shown me. Will you do that for me?"

Tang P'ing nodded. She glanced up now, eyes glinting with unshed tears.

Serena kissed her gently, then embraced her. "And thank you, and Shu-toe, for all you have done for me. Goodbye, dear Tang P'ing."

Screna turned on her heel without another word and marched over to the waiting Pinkerton detectives. In as steady a voice as she could manage, she said, "I am ready to go with you, gentlemen."

Chapter Eighteen

For the next three days, Serena was held in San Francisco. The two Pinkerton men who had arrested her took her to a downtown hotel, where she was kept locked in a room. Her meals were brought to her by one or the other of the men, and one of them stood guard outside the door at all times.

One of the Pinkertons was named Harry Simms. Serena never learned the name of the second. In fact, she never heard him speak a word during the time she was in his presence.

On the second day, she asked Harry Simms, "Why am I being kept a prisoner *here?*"

He smiled, not unpleasantly. "You'd rather spend the time in a jail cell, Miss Foster?"

"Of course not!" she snapped. "But I thought I was being taken back to Virginia City?"

"In that much of a hurry to hang, are you? I'm sorry . . ." He motioned. "I shouldn't have said that. A rotten thing to say. We've wired Virginia City for instructions, and we're waiting for a reply."

"But I thought you were the law?" Serena said in some surprise.

"Not exactly, ma'am. Pinkertons are usually hired by a private party, or by companies."

"Who hired you this time?"

"Again, I'm sorry." He shook his head. "That information is confidential."

He left Serena more puzzled than ever. For what earthly reason would some private party hire the Pinkerton Agency to take her back to Virginia City? The only companies of any substantial worth in Virginia City were the mining companies, and they certainly would have no interest in her. Could it be some relative of Madeline's? Serena vaguely remembered someone, either the Judge or Madeline herself, mentioning that Madeline had no relatives.

On the third day, they left San Francisco on a Concord stagecoach bound for Virginia City. The stage was crowded, but the Pinkerton men commandeered seats inside. Serena sat between them. She supposed she should be grateful that she wasn't placed in irons. For all the other passengers knew, they were simply three friends traveling together.

Such close and long proximity with the other passengers naturally brought about attempts at conversation to relieve the boredom. Every time someone directed a question to either Serena or her companions, Harry Simms always answered, curt, unfriendly responses, and after the first day, the trio was generally ignored.

Serena now learned what it was like to travel in these lumbering stagecoaches. True, the stages were elegant in appearance, beautifully painted, and made watertight for fording rivers. The interior seated eight passengers, four across. There was a thin padding on the slab seats, but it wasn't long before Serena felt as though she was riding on solid planking.

The stage had two drivers, spelling each other for four-hour shifts. The drivers seldom slowed the teams for anything, bouncing over ruts and rocks in the road, throwing the passengers about and against each other. On the flats the stages traveled at breakneck speed. When the stage finally pulled into a way station to change animals, the four horses were lathered with sweat like soapy foam. Except for two meals a day for the passengers, they rarely tarried at the stations for long.

One thing Serena learned dismayed her. It had been her thought that the stages laid over for the night at those way stations offering accommodations. True, some of the stations did provide rooms, but the stage they were on traveled day and night, discharging no passengers.

On the second day of this, during a brief stop, Serena complained to Harry Simms. "Dear God, are we to travel all the way to Virginia City without stopping overnight?"

"I'm afraid so, ma'am. We go straight through."

"But for God's sake, why? Surely they can't be in that much of a hurry to try me after all this time!"

"Has nothing to do with you, Miss Foster. One reason we were so long delayed in San Francisco was the difficulty of getting three seats on a stage. If we stop for a night's rest, this stage will continue on, and the odds are heavy that the next one will have no room for us. If it was only one person, he might be squeezed in somewhere, on top if nowhere else. But three, no. We might have to wait for days."He shook his head. "No, I'm sorry, ma'am. I'm afraid you'll have to suffer through it."

With a sigh Serena resigned herself. When they began to climb into the mountains, the stage at least had to go much slower. But remembering the trip up the mountain in the buckboard with Tang P'ing and Shu-toe, the stages thundering past them at reckless speeds, Serena dreaded to think of the trip down the other side of the mountain.

It never came about.

A half-day out of Placerville, there was a sudden commotion outside, and the stagecoach came to a jolting stop. Serena, who had been dozing, was jarred awake. She looked around dazedly, wondering what it was all about. She could hear nothing over the jabber of sudden conversation inside the coach.

Before anyone knew what was happening, the door was suddenly thrown open, and a masked man looked in at them. He was carrying a shotgun. Silently, he motioned everybody out.

"For God's sake, it's a holdup," Harry Simms said in disgust. "Of all the times for this to happen."

His hand started under his coat toward his holster. Then he froze as the muzzle of the shotgun centered on him. With a shrug he got out with the others.

Outside, Serena saw four men on horseback and two on the ground. All wore rough clothing, their faces masked, and carried drawn guns. The passengers and the two men from the driver's seat were relieved of their weapons, which were stacked in a pile.

The passengers and drivers were then lined up alongside the stage, but no attempt was made to search any of them for weapons.

Now one of the masked pair on the ground mounted up. It wasn't until then that Serena noticed there was an extra horse. The man still on the ground distributed the weapons taken from the drivers and passengers among his mounted cohorts.

He was a large, bulky man, this one, and something about him struck a familiar chord. Before she could explore the thought, he came to her and took her arm, not ungently, and led her to one of the empty horses. He made a gesture indicating that the horse was for her.

Two things struck Serena forcibly at the same time. First, the bandits had not spoken a single word during the whole time. Secondly, they weren't hold-up men at all—they had come for her!

Numbly, Serena allowed herself to be hoisted into the saddle. Then the big man vaulted onto his own horse, motioned with his hand, and the seven horses were sent at a gallop up the road, in the same direction the stage had been heading. Around the first curve, the leader again beckoned, and those men carrying the confiscated weapons dumped them onto the ground, in the middle of the road where they would certainly be seen when the stagecoach came along.

They continued at a hard pace down the road for almost a mile, then turned off into a small, narrow canyon, riding single file now, with Serena in the middle. Still stunned by the suddenness of her rescue, Serena found it difficult to remain in the saddle. There was no trail, and the underbrush was thick—so dense that the branches kept whipping against her face, and she had to continually fend them off. Even so, it wasn't long before her face and hands were scratched and bleeding.

After an hour's ride, they came out of the canyon into a small mountain meadow with a stream running through it. The masked men drew up by the stream and dismounted, letting their horses drink. The big man came to Serena and helped her down. It was quite cold, and there were patches of snow on the ground.

One by one the men removed their masks. Serena look from face to face. They were all Chinese.

The last to remove his mask was the big man. Serena wasn't really surprised to see Shu-toe's smiling countenance. She had already guessed his identity.

"Dear Shu-toe." She took his hand and stood on tiptoe to kiss him.

Shu-toe turned red and looked down shyly. After a moment he scowled around at the other men. All wore solemn faces. Serena was sure they were laughing inside, but dared not show it.

"Shu-toe," she said. "Darrel sent you after me, didn't he?"

Shu-toe nodded vigorously, broad face beaming.

Brad Stryker glared at the man across his desk. "I don't believe it! After all the time and trouble, not to mention the money I paid out to your agency, you let her be taken away?"

"I'm sorry, Mr. Stryker." Harry Simms shrugged. "There just wasn't a damned thing we could do. They caught us completely by surprise. They were armed and had us outnumbered, six of them, and everyone thought it was a robbery attempt. You know how often the stages along the Placerville Route are held up."

"Goddamnit it, man, why didn't you go after her?" Stryker was close to choking on his rage and frustration.

"How?" Harry Simms spread his hands. "We were a half-day's journey from the nearest stage station where we could get horses. The stagecoach horses would have been useless to us. The drivers wouldn't have let us use them, anyway. They were just happy they weren't held up, and couldn't have cared less about a woman prisoner of ours. It would have been a waste of effort to chase after them when we did get to where there were horses. They had well over a day's start on us. Hell, they could have been anywhere by that time!"

"Jesus Christ! Of all the rotten luck!" Stryker reached down for the bottle in his desk and took a drink, without offering the Pinkerton man one. He leaned across his desk. "Now you listen to me and listen good. You two gents get the hell out of Virginia City and back to San Francisco on the first stage. And if you ever breathe a word to anyone that I hired you for this job, I'll kill you myself. Is that clear?"

"We don't operate that way, Mr. Stryker," Harry Simms said with wounded dignity. "We'll leave as soon as possible, and will talk to nobody."

"Get out." Stryker motioned wearily, drained of anger now. "Just get out."

After Harry Simms left, Stryker took another drink, his mind churning.

He was right back where he had started. He knew now that he should have obeyed his first impulse. On receiving the wire informing him that Li Po had Serena Foster, Stryker's first inclination had been to send a couple of his men after her, men he could trust. They would have been instructed to start back with her for Virginia City, but see that she never reached here alive, leaving her buried in a lonely grave somewhere in the mountains.

Common sense had prevailed, or so he had thought at the time. It would never do for it to become known that he had any interest in her. It was far better, less risk for him, if she died legal and aboveboard. There was little doubt in Stryker's mind that she would hang; the evidence against her was too strong.

So, he had wired the Pinkerton office in San Francisco with instructions for two agents to go to Li Po and arrest Serena Foster. He had been astounded by a return wire stating that Li Po was dead and Serena Foster wasn't with him. But almost on the heels of that had come a second wire. The Pinkertons had learned that Serena had been living with a Darrel Quick, who was in the hospital close to death. They had staked out his room and there had caught Serena. Stryker had wired back, instructing them to return her to San Francisco as soon as possible.

Stryker had been jubilant. His elation sprang not only from her capture, but from the death of Li Po. Now he wouldn't have to pay the ten thousand he had promised and wouldn't have to worry about Li Po knowing the truth of his interest in Serena Foster. The fact that Darrel Quick, the gambler who had humiliated him in the Silver Dollar Saloon, might also soon be dead, only added to his elation.

Now it had all gone up in smoke, as if it had been

nothing but a dream, and he was no closer to being a wealthy man. The situation was even worse than it had been before. He was reasonably confident that the Pinkerton men would keep quiet about his hiring them, but there was no keeping quiet the fact that Serena Foster had been alive only days ago and on her way back to Virginia City. That bit of news would be all over town by this time.

A few days ago she had been missing for eighteen months and presumed by many to be dead. It was possible that even that old hardhead, Spencer Hurd, would have given up, pronounced her dead, and turned the Hetty Foster estate over to one Brad Stryker.

The news that Serena Foster had been alive and well a few days ago would only mean that the Judge would become even more stubborn.

Stryker contemplated the whiskey bottle. It was over half full. He tilted it up and drank. What the hell, he might as well get drunk and pass out. That would assure him of at least a *few* hours when he wouldn't have to think of the damn woman.

Spencer Hurd was of two minds about the latest news of Serena. Naturally, he was pleased that she was alive. He had been afraid that she was dead. Not only was she alive, but she had escaped the clutches of the law once more.

That was what troubled him slightly. Now people would be more than ever convinced that Serena had killed Madeline. Not that many people had ever believed in her innocence, but with all the time that had passed, a great many had virtually forgotten that

369

Serena Foster had ever existed. Now it would be in the forefront of their minds again.

Serena would eventually have to face her accusers, unless she fled to some other country. Spencer Hurd was a firm believer in law and order, of the orderly process of a trial and a jury verdict of innocence. Or conviction. That was the nub of it, naturally. Should she be placed on trial, what were her chances of an acquittal?

Hurd had long since concluded that her chances were not of the best. He considered himself an able defense attorney, probably the best in this part of the country. That, he realized wryly, was not saying a great deal, given the level of competence of most lawyers out here. The majority of them were busy chasing the dollar, handling the numerous civil cases involving mining claims and such, most of them on the side of the big companies along the Comstock. That was where the big money was, not in defending penniless criminals.

On the plus side, however, Hurd had defended clients where the evidence was just as black as that against Serena and had won acquittals. Any verdict was possible where the decision lay with a jury of her peers. Her peers! He laughed harshly, blowing smoke from his cigar. The juries in Virginia City were selected from . . .

"What's so funny, Judge?"

At the sound of the familiar voice, Spencer Hurd almost choked on cigar smoke. He batted the smoke away from his face and stared in gaping astonishment at the door, which had been left standing open as usual.

Standing there, smiling at him, was Serena.

"Great Godalmighty, girl! You came near to making an old man's heart stop!"

He was out of his chair and around the desk. Serena started toward him, and he enfolded her in a bear hug.

Voice muffled against his chest, she said, "You don't know how wonderful it is to see you again, Judge."

"The same here, my dear. Twice over." He held her away from him. "Let me look at you."

The dress she was wearing was travel-stained, the blonde hair was disheveled, and several scratches were healing on her face.

Serena smiled wanly. "I'm afraid I don't look too grand right this minute, Judge. I've covered some distance to get here."

"You look marvelous to these old eyes. Here, sit down."

He helped her to a chair. Serena sank down gratefully. Hurd stood looking down at her, shaking his head in wonderment.

Finally, he went around behind his desk, putting his cigar out in the can, and sat down. "Now, tell me what happened to you, before I burst with curiosity. Or maybe you're too weary and would like to freshen up a bit first?"

"No, I better get it over with. But there's so much to tell. I hardly know where to begin."

"You can start with telling me how you come to be here. The story's all over town, of course, about your being taken off the stage. How did that come about, and why did you come here?"

"My rescue was Darrel's and Shu-toe's doing. That's right, you don't know about Shu-toe. He's a Chinese youth. I'll get back to him later . . ."

371

"No, I don't know about Shu-toe, but I do know Darrel Quick, if he's the Darrel you mean. What does he have to do with this?"

"That's right. Darrel did tell me he met you. Darrel is in a hospital in San Francisco. He was shot trying to protect me."

"I'm sorry to hear it. Shot trying to protect you?" Hurd shook his head. "Godalmighty, Serena, protect you from what?"

"That's a long story. First, you wanted to hear about my escape."

"Yes, I'm sorry. Tell it your own way, my dear." Hurd leaned forward, listening intently.

"Well, Darrel sent Shu-toe and some Chinese friends of his to take me at gunpoint from the stage. They managed that well enough. We got away easily. Darrel had told Shu-toe to return me to San Francisco. Well . . . I simply refused to go! I've had my fill of running. I decided it was time I came back and faced my accusers, get it over with one way or another. So I sent Shu-toe and his friends back to San Francisco, and I came straight here." She paused, looking at him almost pleadingly. "Did I do the right thing, Judge, coming back here?"

Caught unawares by the question, Hurd started to speak, then checked himself. He thought for a moment, started to speak again, and once more checked himself. He saw that Serena was becoming dismayed at his silence. He raised and lowered his hands. "Serena, could we discuss that later, after I've heard your story? This has all come about so suddenly." He made what he knew was a weak attempt at a smile of reassurance. "You know how we lawyers like to procrastinate."

372

It was indeed far from reassuring, and Serena began to question her wisdom in returning.

"I'll tell you what." Hurd looked out the window. "It's dark now. Why don't we go somewhere so you can freshen up, maybe have a jolt of whiskey and something to eat? Then you'll feel better, rested enough to talk easier. Do you have a change of clothing?"

"No, I don't have a change of clothes, only what I have on. After I left Shu-toe, I rode to the first stage station and caught a stagecoach straight here. That took all the money I had." She smiled wanly. "I did leave behind a trunk of clothing at Ma Taylor's."

Hurd was nodding. "I know, she stormed in here and told me. I took them out to the house."

"The Paradise?"

He nodded again.

"What's happened to the Paradise?"

"I closed it down." He added dryly, "Took the sign down."

"It's setting there empty?"

"Empty except for Foxy. That's Foxy Parks, the gimpy barkeep and bouncer Hetty hired some years back. He's old now, nobody will hire him. I pay him a pittance to stay there and see that vandals don't steal everything in sight."

"Then can we go out there?"

Hurd hesitated. "You sure it won't bother you? I mean . . . Well, Madeline being killed there and all?"

"Why should it bother me?" She looked at him fiercely. "I didn't kill her, Judge, if that's what . . ."

He was already waving his hands. "Now, now, Serena, I didn't mean that. I've never believed that." He heaved himself to his feet. "If that's what you wish, it's fine with me. Let's slip out the back way and sort of sneak up on the house. I don't want anyone to know you're in town. Not yet. Not until I figure out the best way to handle it."

They made their way without trouble to the Paradise, meeting no one they knew. Except for the missing sign, the house looked the same. There were lights burning in two of the rooms. The Judge went up the steps, tipping the rocking chair as was his habit, and fished a key out of his pocket. He rapped on the door and called out, "Foxy! It's Spencer Hurd, don't get spooked."

Fitting the key into the door, he said, "This will make things simple. Foxy is a good cook. He can whip us up some victuals, while you freshen up and change."

Now that she was actually faced with entering the house where Madeline had been killed, Serena felt a shiver of apprehension. She scoffed at herself and followed the Judge inside. Serena didn't believe in ghosts, so why should she feel queasy about this house? It was hers after all.

A balding man of about sixty, with a sharp, pointed face and faded blue eyes, limped toward them.

"Foxy Parks, meet Serena Foster, the new mistress of the house."

"She gonna open up the Paradise again?" Foxy said in a grumbling voice.

Before the Judge could speak, Serena said, "No, Foxy, I'll just be living here . . . I hope." She held out her hand. "And I want to thank you for looking after the house while I've been away."

After a moment's hesitation, Foxy accepted her

hand. His faded eyes lit up. "A proper house is what it should be. Never did believe in it being a whorehouse . . . excuse me, ma'am. I worked here 'cause I couldn't get a job anywheres else. Not that Hetty Foster weren't a proper lady."

"I know," Serena said gravely. "Hetty was my aunt."

Now Foxy smiled, showing stained teeth. "That's right, I forgot. You're her niece. Welcome home, Miss Serena."

Hurd said, "We're starved, Foxy. Have you any beefsteak? And maybe you could whip us up some of that redeye gravy of yours?"

"Yes, siree bob, Judge! Right away!"

As he started to limp away, Hurd said, "And heat up some water for Serena, will you? She wants to freshen up."

"In a jiffy, Judge."

As Foxy limped out of hearing, Hurd said with a smile, "I think you've made a conquest, my dear."

"You say Aunt Hetty hired him as a bouncer? How could he handle that job?"

Hurd laughed. "He's tougher than he looks, tough as dried rawhide. And he used to be good with a gun, and is still better than fair with one. That's what happened to his leg. He was a gun for hire for years, but a bullet in his leg and his age put a stop to that. But he's handy with a sawed-off billiard cue, which he used to keep behind the bar. Anyone used to get too feisty in here, he'd whack 'em over the head with it . . . Serena, I put your clothes in Hetty's old room. It's back there at the end of the hall." He gestured. "The only bedroom on the ground floor."

Serena thought of asking if Madeline had been

using the room after Aunt Hetty's death, but kept still about it. She simply nodded and started in that direction.

Hurd called after her, "You'll find me in the parlor having a drink when you're finished, Serena."

Hurd watched her until she entered Hetty's old room. Then he went down the hall and into the parlor. Everything was free of dust; Foxy kept the place immaculate. The Judge poured himself a liberal portion of the good whiskey, sat down, and lit a cigar. He was concerned about how to handle the situation with Serena. He sipped and smoked, ruminating, until Serena appeared about thirty minutes later.

She was wearing a pretty pink dress, her face and hands scrubbed, her hair brushed.

Hurd came to his feet. "You're even lovelier than I remember you, Serena."

Serena hesitated on the threshold, her glance darting around the room. "Is this where it . . . happened?"

"I'm afraid so," he said somberly. "Yes, Madeline was killed in here. Does it upset you? If it does, we can go into another room."

"No. I have to get used to it." Serena set her chin and advanced determinedly into the room.

"Would you like a glass of whiskey? Or a brandy?"

"A brandy, I think, Judge." Serena sat on the sofa, smoothing her skirt.

The Judge brought the glass of brandy and sat down on the other end of the sofa. He raised his whiskey glass. "Here's to the reunion of old friends."

They drank, and Hurd leaned back, crossing his legs. "Now . . . Do you feel like going on with your story, from the beginning this time?"

376

Serena took another sip of brandy and commenced her story, beginning with the night she had been taken to Li Po's house and raped. Before her tale was finished, Foxy came in to announce supper, and they went into the dining room. Between bites, Serena told the last of it.

Spencer Hurd shook his head incredulously. "Godalmighty! Serena, why didn't you come to me and tell me about this attack on you? My God, that's dreadful!"

"Judge, I thought of it, but I finally decided that it would do no good, that I was just a victim of circumstances."

"I can't think you ever believed that. And in view of what has transpired since, that's certainly not true, is it? Someone is out to kill you, someone here in Virginia City."

"It would seem so."

"And you have no idea who?"

"Not the slightest. The only thing I do know, the man who held me in Li Po's house here wore the same gold Chinese mask as the leader of the men who killed my folks."

"Must be the same man." Hurd fell silent, thinking hard. Absent-mindedly, he fired up a cigar without asking Serena's permission.

Foxy came in and filled their mugs with fresh coffee.

Serena said, "You not only make delicious coffee, Foxy, but you're a great cook."

Foxy glowed. "Thank you, Miss Serena."

When he left, Hurd said, "The only person I can think of in Virginia City with any reason to want you dead is Brad Stryker, and that's ridiculous on the face of it."

Serena became alert. "Why ridiculous, Judge?"

"Because he has no motive, damnit! Sure, he stands to inherit Hetty's estate if you're deceased, but what does her estate consist of? Five thousand dollars, which you have already received and spent. And this house. As mean as Stryker is, he wouldn't kill your parents, and you, just to get possession of this house."

"There was that time in the Silver Dollar Saloon, when I interfered with his abusing Shu-toe."

"Still not enough reason." Hurd shook his head. "If anything, he'd go after Darrel Quick. Quick is the one who made him back down. No, it has to be someone else." Thoughtfully, Hurd tapped his cigar ash into a saucer. "These Pinkerton men . . . some private party hired them, you say? And they wouldn't tell you who?"

"I gather it was a private party. And no, they wouldn't tell me who."

"I'll fire off a telegram to San Francisco. Since I'm a lawyer, maybe I'll get a little more cooperation."

He was silent again, thinking.

Serena made an impatient sound. "What happens now, Judge? You've been avoiding answering that question all afternoon."

He looked across the table at her and sighed. "There is that question. I've been thinking about how to handle it. We can't delay too long. There is one thing in your favor, Serena. You came in voluntarily. That will have some weight with the court."

"Will I have to go to jail?" Serena asked apprehensively.

He stirred. "Godalmighty, I hope not! That I will

378

try to avoid, if at all possible. The only jail we have is a pig pen, used to house drunks, and the lowest kind of criminal. It's certainly no place for a woman."

"But how do you intend to keep me out?"

"Arrange bail, of course."

"On a murder charge?"

"It's possible. A magistrate here has broad powers. And we're fortunate in one respect. Judge Underwood, currently the present judge in Virginia City, is not the greatest judge I've ever seen, but he's a fair man. And he's a Southerner, like myself, with a great respect for the gentler sex. If I argue persuasively enough, perhaps I can get him to set bail for you."

"Perhaps? You're not all that positive, are you?" she pressed.

"Of course I'm not positive, Serena!" he said irritably. "About the courts and the law in a place like Virginia City, nothing is positive!"

Chapter Nineteen

Judge Elmo Underwood was a corpulent personage, about Spencer Hurd's age. His round face sported an enormous red nose, which he tugged at continually, and a drooping moustache. His only concession to his office was a frock coat, green with age, and a vest spotted with food stains. Apparently not one to go in for frills, he used a carpenter's hammer for a gavel, and his bench had once been a schoolteacher's desk.

The courtroom was small, stuffy, and overly warm from the heat of a roaring wood stove in one corner. There were a dozen benches behind a railing to accommodate spectators. A long table, with another bench, served both the defense and the prosecution.

At the moment there were only three people in the courtroom beside Judge Underwood—Serena, Spencer Hurd, and Jake Burns, the deputy sheriff Hurd had collected on the way to the courtroom.

The deputy's jaw had dropped when he was introduced to Serena, and he had spluttered all the way to the courtroom, demanding that Serena be placed under arrest and jailed.

"All in good time, Jake," Spencer Hurd had said. "Just consider her taken into custody now, and don't forget that she came in of her own free will and gave herself up . . ."

"To you, not the law!"

"Amounts to the same thing, Jake," Hurd said, unruffled. "I'm an officer of the court. Now just simmer down until we see what Judge Underwood has to say."

Serena looked demure and sedate in her most subdued garments. This had been the Judge's final instructions last night. "Elmo Underwood is an old-fashioned gent and has old-fashioned ideas about how a woman should look. Should you come before him looking fine and sassy, he would right away assume that you were a wanton woman."

Now Judge Underwood pulled his nose, rapped lightly with the hammer, and leaned forward. In a rumbling voice, he said, "Now just what is this all about, Judge?"

"Well, Judge, I am here with . . ." Hurd broke off, smiling slightly. "Elmo, we're going to create some confusion if we go on calling each other judge, wouldn't you say?"

Judge Underwood gave an answering grin, and a rumble of laughter. "You could be right. So what do you suggest?"

"How about Your Honor and Counselor?"

"Well now . . ." Judge Underwood tugged at his nose, a trace of a smile on his lips. "Can't see anything wrong with that. Fact is, I kinda like Your

Honor. Certainly I've been called worse things." He cleared his throat and assumed a sober countenance. "Proceed, Counselor."

"Your Honor, the young lady at my side is Serena Foster. As I am sure you are aware, there is a warrant outstanding for her arrest for murder."

"I have heard of such, yes, I have," said Judge Underwood, staring severely at Serena.

"Judge . . . Your Honor, sir," Jake Burns said angrily. "She ain't even under arrest yet!"

Judge Underwood transferred his gaze to the deputy. "Who are you, sir? And what is your purpose in my court?"

"Why, you know me, Judge!"

"Anyone appearing before this bench must identify himself for the record."

Burns sighed. "I'm Jake Burns, deputy sheriff here in Virginia."

"So noted for the record. Now what is your purpose here, Deputy Burns?"

Serena couldn't help smiling. Insofar as she could see, no one was taking a record of the proceedings. Spencer Hurd nudged her and she became sober-faced again.

Jake Burns said, "The Judge here came into the office a bit ago and announced out of the blue that this here woman is Serena Foster. The sheriff himself is off somewhere, and I'm in charge of the office. The Judge wouldn't even let me put her under arrest!"

"A mere quibble," said Spencer Hurd. "That can be taken care of in due time."

Judge Underwood said, "But if she ain't under arrest, for what reason did you roust me out for this here hearing, Counselor?"

"I wish to arrange bail for my client, Your Honor . . ."

"Now wait just a damned minute! The charge is murder!"

The hammer rapped. "Deputy. I allow no cursing in my courtroom! And with a lady present as well, Now, just suppose you apologize to the young lady."

"Lady?" Jake Burns sneered. "I say she ain't no lady . . ."

The hammer pounded this time. "Sir, you will apologize at once, or I will fine you for contempt of my court!"

Jake Burns inclined his head and said ungraciously. "I apologize for cursing, ma'am."

"That's better. Now, Counselor, what is this about bail? Ain't that a little premature, considering she ain't under arrest at this time?"

"The arrest is purely a formality, Your Honor. I wish to make sure that she does not spend any time in jail here. You know the condition of our jail, the filth, and the type of person therein."

"Would you have any objection, Counselor, if your client is placed under arrest before we consider your motion? Just to make everything legal like?"

"No objection, Your Honor." Hurd stepped aside with a flourish. "Do your duty, deputy."

Jake Burns stepped up to Serena. "I do now place you under arrest, Serena Foster, for the murder of Madeline Dubois, on the date of . . ." He floundered, looking around for help.

From the bench Judge Underwood said, "Dates ain't necessary, Deputy Burns. For the sake of saving time, this court now considers one Serena Foster under official arrest." He nodded to Hurd. "Continue, Counselor."

"I ask the court to place my client under reasonable bail, and that she be released into my custody. I will guarantee her appearance for trial at the proper time."

Jake Burns was fuming. "Judge . . . Your Honor, sir, this woman is charged with murder! Ain't no bail for a person charged with murder!"

"Well now, that's for me to decide, ain't it? It's my court. I can do as I damned well please . . . my apologies, ma'am. Got carried away there." He glowered at Hurd. "How do you intend to plead your client, Counselor?"

"That's a little premature, Your Honor. Like you say, it isn't even official yet."

"It is now, and it might make some difference about how I rule on bail."

"I intend to plead my client not guilty, of course, since she has not committed any crime."

Jake Burns snorted.

Judge Underwood bent a glare on him, but then looked back at Spencer Hurd. He gave his nose a tug. "She'll be released in your care, Counselor?"

"That is correct, Your Honor. I assume all responsibility for her."

Judge Underwood tapped his hammer. "Defendant is freed, depending on the posting of a thousand dollars bail . . ."

"Your Honor, I protest . . ."

The hammer rose and fell. "You have no say in the matter, deputy. Trial will commence December 26."

"Your Honor," Hurd said in dismay. "That gives

the defense less than a week to prepare, and part of that time will be the Christmas holidays . . ."

"That's why I set it for December 26."

". . . and there is no prosecutor."

"I'll appoint one today, Counselor. And he'll have less time than you to prepare. That should make you happy."

Although he kept a sober face, Spencer Hurd was quite content with the arrangements. Now he could only hope that Judge Underwood would appoint a reasonably scrupulous, if not too astute, attorney to represent the prosecution.

While he had been thinking this, Jake Burns had been yammering at Judge Underwood, who was now pounding with his hammer in full anger. "Mister Burns, I do not care if you are a law officer, you do not talk back to me in my court! This is the last warning. One more yap out of you and I'll fine you a hundred dollars!"

Jake burns shut up.

Hurd smiled at the wan Serena, gave her arm a squeeze, and whispered, "Wait here for a minute, while I take care of arranging bail for you with His Honor."

Serena sat down and mopped at her face. First she had been chill with apprehension, now she was sweltering in the heat from the roaring stove and weak with relief at not having to spend any time in jail.

Spencer Hurd and Judge Underwood retired to a room behind the bench. Jake Burns lingered, pacing back and forth and watching Serena malevolently.

In about ten minutes Hurd came back alone. "It's all arranged, my dear." He glanced at Jake Burns.

"You can go about your duties now, Jake. Don't worry about Serena."

"I'd better not have to worry, Judge, or it'll be on your head," the deputy said in a growling voice and stomped out.

Spencer Hurd gave Serena a hand up.

"Thank you, Judge," she said. "I'll have to admit that I was afraid I'd be jailed."

"It's Counselor now, didn't you hear Judge Underwood so proclaim?" he said with a grin.

More at ease now, Serena laughed. "You'll always be Judge to me."

They started out. Before they were halfway to the door, it opened, and Rory Clendenning burst in. He was dressed in rough work clothing and muddy boots. At the sight of Serena, his face lit up. "Serena! Lord God! I just heard you were here!"

Serena's breath caught in her throat. Seeing Rory Clendenning after all this time made her realize how much she had missed him.

She forced herself to speak calmly, "How are you, Rory?"

"I'm fine, Serena, fine," he replied, coming toward them. "But the question is, how are you?"

"In most ways, I'm all right. But up until a few minutes ago, I thought I'd have to go to jail."

Clendenning scowled fiercely at Hurd. "She shouldn't have to go to jail! It's not right!"

The lawyer batted a hand. "Now just simmer down, young Clendenning. Nobody's going to jail, Not yet, anyway. Serena's free on bail until the trial. Then we'll see."

"What do you mean we'll see?" Clendenning said

belligerently. "She's no more guilty of murder than I am!"

"I go along with you there, but the law holds a different view, and until we prove them wrong, she has to stand trial. That's why Serena came back."

"Rory, it's the way I want it," Serena said. "I don't want to spend the rest of my life being hunted as a murderess."

"I'm sorry," Clendenning said less forcibly. "Your being gone all this time and me not knowing what happened to you . . . sometimes I thought I'd never see you again. What has happened to you all the time you've been away?"

"It's a long story, Rory . . ."

"And too long to tell here," Hurd broke in. "Suppose we go out to the house and have Foxy fix us a bite to eat, and she can tell it all over again. If you can spare the time, young Clendenning."

"I'll make the time."

They left the courtroom. It had snowed during the night, and the ground had a blanket of white. The wind was strong and cold. Hurd paused in the entryway to fish out a cigar.

While Hurd stepped out of the wind to light his cigar, Clendenning said in an undertone to Serena, "I've missed you, Serena."

"Thank you for that." She placed her hand on his. "And I've missed you, Rory."

Outside, the wind was stronger, carrying flakes of snow. As they began walking toward the house, Serena noticed that several people stopped to stare at her; others stopped to whisper and point. She walked with her head held high.

Clendenning also noticed. He clenched his fists. "I should knock a few heads together."

"Have to expect Serena to attract some notice, young Clendenning," Hurd said. "It'll grow worse, I'm afraid, between now and the trial. But after that's behind her, it'll soon die down."

"I can bear it, Rory. Don't worry about me. If stares and whispers are all I have to contend with, I'll survive," Serena said, remembering Darrel's advice in San Francisco. The thought of Darrel gave her a wrench. Shu-toe had told her that he was much improved and was soon to be moved home. In a way, she regretted not being there to tend him, but if Shu-toe and Tang P'ing gave him as much devotion and care as they had her for so long, he would be fine.

To get her thoughts away from Darrel, she said, "I understand you're doing very well for yourself, Rory."

"My freighting business is doing quite well, yes," he said somewhat gruffly.

Hurd laughed. "He's doing *very* well, Serena. Young Clendenning has a good business head, and he's the first freighter tough enough to fight back at Brad Stryker and get away with it."

Serena recalled Darrel telling her that Rory Clendenning had a partner, a woman. Darrel had hinted that their relationship was more than business, and she was strongly tempted to ask Rory about the woman who was his partner. She stopped herself in time. It would be a petty thing to do, and his relationship with the woman was none of her business. She'd known men intimately since she had last seen Rory, so she had no right to be critical of him. Of course, she didn't know for sure that he was sharing the woman's bed, but the fact that he had said "*my*

389

freighting business" meant that he hadn't wanted her to know. In one way, it was also cheering, since it meant that Rory cared enough for her to be wary of her jealousy.

It was close to noon when they reached the house and Serena told Foxy to prepare them something to eat.

They went into the sitting room. Spencer Hurd headed directly for the sideboard. "I'm in need of a little liquid sustenance after that farcical court appearance. How about you two?"

Clendenning said, "Yes, I'll share a glass of whiskey with you, Judge."

"I'll have a glass of wine, if there is any."

"A bottle of good sherry, Serena."

Hurd prepared their drinks. He sat on the sofa with Serena, and Clendenning pulled up a chair facing them.

After a sip of wine, Serena said, "Why did you say 'farcical', Judge?"

"For our side, it wasn't farcical, of course, but Godalmighty!" Hurd sighed. "Judge Underwood *is* a farce. Do you know that he got all his law out of books? He never went a day to law school, nor any other school to my knowledge."

Serena sat up in alarm. "But you said he was a fair man!"

"Oh, he's fair, right enough. But he doesn't know the law, damnit! He runs his courtroom like he's ringmaster in a circus. I'm sorry, my dear. I don't mean to alarm you." He leaned over to pat Serena's hand. "For us, it's probably all to the good, although I must warn you that it could turn against us. But it just gets my dander up to see a judge with no law training to be on the bench!"

Clendenning said, "Then how come he got the position, Judge?"

Hurd shrugged. "Simple. Nobody else wanted it. It doesn't pay all that well. No lawyer with a degree would accept an appointment such as his. Why should they, when they can make ten times the money working for the mining companies?"

Clendenning lost interest in the discussion, turning to Serena. "You promised to tell me what has transpired during the time you've been away."

Serena finished her wine and told her story again. He interrupted a couple of times, once to question her more closely about the man in the gold mask. And when she got to point in her story of meeting Darrel Quick again in San Francisco, he began to frown, and Serena told him very little of Darrel. She sensed it would certainly be a mistake to tell him she had been living in Darrel's house when Li Po's men abducted her, so she said that it had happened while they were getting out of a carriage before her lodgings. She darted a quick glance at Hurd, and saw that he was grinning behind a screen of cigar smoke. She hid her mouth behind her hand and stuck out her tongue at him.

Hurd started to laugh, quickly covering it up under the pretense of having a coughing fit from the cigar.

When Serena had finished her twice-told tale, Clendenning shook his head. "Lord God, you've had an ordeal, haven't you, Serena?"

"It wasn't *all* bad. I certainly enjoyed my tour with Professor Trapp."

"Surely you don't intend living here alone?" He waved a hand around.

"Why not?" she said spiritedly. "It's my house."

"But someone is trying to kill you, Serena! He killed your folks, and tried with you. He must still be here, in Virginia City, and it hardly seems likely he'll give up. If I could just get my hands on him!" His hands curled in his lap.

"I won't be alone. Foxy will be here . . ."

"He's an old man, Serena."

"The Judge says he served Aunt Hetty well as a bouncer. He'll watch out for me. That reminds me, Judge." She looked over at Hurd. "I bought a derringer before I left Virginia City, Darrel Quick taught me how to use it. But I left it back in San Francisco. Would you buy a new one for me?"

"Glad to, my dear."

"A derringer!" Clendenning snorted. "What good will that do you? You must not stay here, Serena. It's isolated. Anyone could break in any time."

"What would you have me do? Live in a boarding house again? That was where I was abducted the first time. I suppose I'd be safe from harm in jail. Would you prefer I tell the Judge to forget about bail and house me in jail until after the trial?"

"Of course not! You're not being fair, Serena. I was only thinking of your welfare."

"Then think of something constructive!" All of a sudden she was quite furious with him. "If you have a reasonable alternative to my staying here, let's hear it!"

"All right, the pair of you. That's enough now," Hurd said sharply. "Just settle down. Serena's right, young Clendenning. What alternative does she have

392

but to stay here? Foxy is a better man than you think. We could hire an extra man, a bodyguard. But who will pay his salary? I am hard put to pay Foxy's pittance, and Serena has no money . . ."

"I'll take care of it," Clendenning interrupted. "Better yet, I'll send one of my own men here to stand guard. He's been guarding the corral at night, but I don't think we . . . I'll be having trouble from Brad Stryker for awhile."

Serena was not only grateful, but ashamed. Now she realized that she had flared up at Rory through *her* jealousy. She said contritely, "I not only appreciate your offer, Rory, but I accept and apologize for my sharp tongue."

Clendenning smiled, relaxing. "Then I'll send him over tonight."

Foxy limped in to announce that their meal was ready, and they went into the dining room. During the meal, as though by mutual consent, their conversation took a more pleasant turn. Serena questioned Clendenning about his business. He waxed enthusiastic as he told of his success. "One thing I haven't mentioned, and I should," he said without looking at her. "I have a partner, Serena. Kate Rogan. Without her it would never have happened. She already owned the stable, which we enlarged, and enough land to build a large corral for the mules."

"I know. Darrel told me about her."

"Darrel Quick, yes. I owe him a debt of gratitude also. Without the loan he made me, the business would never have gotten off the ground." He added somewhat defensively, "Kate's a fine woman, Serena. I think you'd like her."

Serena hesitated, then said quickly, "I'm sure I would, Rory."

Hurd, anticipating another buildup of tension between them, stepped in. "Tell us more about this traveling circus of illusion, Serena. It sounds fascinating."

Welcoming the change of subject, Serena regaled them with amusing anecdotes of her circus tour. She explained how Professor Trapp's illusions worked, and Hurd was soon roaring with laughter. Even Clendenning was smiling.

When they were finished eating, Hurd took out a cigar and pushed back his chair. "I have to get back to my office and get to work preparing your defense, my dear. I don't have a great deal of time. By the way, I sent a wire to the Pinkerton Agency in San Francisco today, wording it pretty strongly. Maybe it'll get some results, maybe not."

Clendenning also got up. "I have to leave, too, Serena. I've lost the whole morning. At least I can get in a couple of trips down the canyon this afternoon. I'll send my man over this evening."

Serena saw them to the door. She said, "It's only a few days until Christmas. I'd like to have a small celebration. Could you come to Christmas dinner, Judge? Or do you have family to spend Christmas with?"

"No family, my dear. And I'd be most happy to come."

"Wonderful! And you, Rory? And your . . . your partner, too, of course."

Clendenning looked deeply into her eyes. "I will come. And I'll ask Kate." He took her small hand in

394

both of his. "Serena, I'm glad you're safe and sound. My apologies if I sounded kind of prickly."

"It's all right, Rory. And thank you." She stood on tiptoe and kissed him quickly on the cheek.

Clendenning colored and darted a glance at Hurd, who was pointedly looking away while lighting his cigar.

Serena stood in the doorway and watched the two men walk out to the street and turn left toward town. It was snowing again, and she watched until the falling snow hid them from her sight. Seeing Rory Clendenning had aroused conflicting emotions within her. She realized that time and distance had not dimmed the strong attraction he had for her. And she was woman enough now to sense that he felt the same attraction. Was it too late for them? Rory had a woman now. Serena knew from the way he tiptoed around talking about Kate Rogan that they were lovers. However, their affair must have been going on for some time, and they were not yet man and wife.

Serena knew that Darrel Quick was very dear to her, but however charming and attractive he might be, she did not love him. Rory had captured her heart, and she was going to make a determined effort to have him for her own.

This wasn't the time for such thoughts. She was still under suspicion of murder, and until she could come to him without the possibility of standing convicted as a murderess, Serena wouldn't feel free to do anything about her feelings.

Turning back into the house, Serena decided to explore it. There were many rooms in the house she had yet to see. In fact, she had not been upstairs at all. One by one, she went through the bedrooms. Although decorated with some taste, there was no doubt that the purpose of all the rooms was for entertaining men. The beds were spacious, soft, and covered with bright quilts. Each room was done in different colors—pink, yellow, red, et cetera. Once, Serena knew, she would have been shocked. Now she was merely amused.

Finally she found herself back downstairs in the small room used for an office, first by Aunt Hetty, then by Madeline Dubois. A memory of something Madeline had said came to her. That night she and the Judge had dined here, Madeline had said, "Your aunt had a small strongbox, Serena, with her private papers. It's locked and I've never opened it. But I do have a key. When you have the time, I think you should open it. I don't know if there's anything of value in it, but I would think it likely, since Hetty treated it like a treasured possession. She even had her initials burned in the lid."

Serena began looking for it. It was nowhere in the office. Gnawing her lip thoughtfully, she went in search of Foxy. She found him in the kitchen. A fire was glowing in the iron range. He was in a straight chair tipped back against the wall, dozing.

"Foxy?"

He started, the chair crashing down. "Yes, Miss Serena?"

"I understand that Aunt Hetty had a strongbox, with her initials burned in the lid. Do you know about it?"

"I saw it once or twice, yes, ma'am. Hetty was always careful with that box. Kidding her once, I said that she must have the crown jewels in it. She just gave one of her snorts."

396

"Do you know where it might be?"

"No'm. Want me to help you look?"

"No, never mind. I'll look."

An hour later, after carefully searching every room in the house, she gave up, baffled. The strongbox was not to be found.

It was possible that the Judge had it in his possession, but in that event he surely would have mentioned it. She made a mental note to ask him.

Brad Stryker was caught on the horns of a dilemma again.

His reaction to Serena Foster's unexpected reappearance was mixed. It was good news that she had been placed under arrest, yet it could be bad news that she was out on bail, free as a bird. Spencer Hurd was an ornery old coot, but with that silver tongue of his, he could talk a virgin out of her drawers!

But Stryker was worried more about Judge Elmo Underwood. The man must be getting senile! He had to be to let a suspected killer roam free on bail. Stryker chewed over it, occasionally striking his boot with the quirt he had taken to carrying with him almost everywhere. If Serena Foster went nosing around, would she be able to find anything to incriminate him—either at the Paradise or elsewhere?

Stryker believed he had covered his tracks well, and he was certain that she had no hint that he had led the crew on that foray when they had killed the Fosters. The man he'd had with him had long since been sent packing from Virginia City, their pockets bulging with money, so that he had no fears on that score. And with Li Po dead, Stryker could see no way that he could be connected with the assault on the Foster woman in the house that night. He was equally certain she hadn't recognized him. If she had, she would have sent Darrel Quick gunning for him before she fled from Virginia City.

Yet it continued to nag at him. Free, she might possibly sniff out *something*. He knew she was staying at the Paradise. Was it worth the risk to kill her? It should be easy enough to accomplish.

Stryker decided to wait a few days, until the trial started, and see how that went. If it seemed she was going to be convicted, there was nothing to worry about. Earlier, he had been convinced that she would be. But now, with that damned Underwood acting up, it was no longer a sure thing.

Stryker grinned suddenly, an evil grimace. There was one thing he could do—pack the jury with some friends and tell them how to vote, or it would be their asses!

Yes, that would help swing it the right way. Still grinning, he took a swig from the bottle in his desk.

"You're going to get yours yet, Serena Foster," he said. Absently, he struck his boot repeatedly with the quirt, making a swishing sound in the empty office. "One way or another, I'll see to that!"

Serena had just finished a lonely supper when there was a knock on the front door.

As she got up from the table, Foxy came limping through, carrying a gun. He motioned to her. "You just stay there, Miss Serena. The Judge told me not to let anybody in until I had checked them out first."

Serena waited. In a moment she heard the door open and then a familiar voice.

She hurried into the entryway. "Rory! I didn't expect to see you again today!"

He shifted his feet nervously, looking embarrassed. "My man was delayed, and can't come over here for a couple of hours. I thought I'd keep you company until then. If you don't mind?"

"I don't mind at all. I'm delighted. I was feeling lonely."

She looked at him more closely. He had shaved and changed into a new suit. It looked so new that Serena sensed this was the first time he had worn it. His boots were polished, and his black hair was still damp from being wetted down. Snow dusted his shoulders.

"I see it's still snowing out."

He nodded. "Coming down pretty hard now. It's going to slow us down some. That road down the canyon can become slick as glass when covered with snow, and in freezing weather."

She reached out for his hand. "Come into the sitting room for a brandy, Rory. It'll warm you up."

Serena was both amused and touched by his coming here. She suspected that the man he was to send over to guard her had been delayed on Rory's orders. Her heart began to beat faster as she realized what that meant.

Foxy went ahead of them into the parlor and stoked up the iron stove in the corner, then left them alone. Serena seated Clendenning on the sofa and fetched two brandies. She sat down close to him. They took sips of the brandy.

Serena sighed contentedly. "This is nice, and cozy. Do you know that this is the first time we've really

399

been alone since that night out in the desert?" She looked into his blue eyes.

He squirmed, reddening. "I want to apologize for my behavior that night. If I hadn't been so pigheaded, I would have apologized while you were still here."

"There's no need for that, Rory." She put her hand on his. "Really there isn't."

"Serena . . . this Darrel Quick. What is he to you?"

She stiffened. "That's a little presumptuous, isn't it, Rory?"

"I know. It's none of my business. But the thing is . . ." He swallowed, then blurted, "I love you, Serena!"

Stunned by his sudden declaration, Serena didn't speak for a moment. She remembered her thoughts that afternoon. She should be alive with happiness, but it didn't seem quite right somehow.

Finally, she said inanely, "This is a little sudden, isn't it?"

"Not with me, it isn't. I knew I loved you after you were gone from here, and I began to miss you. After it was too late."

It was on the tip of her tongue to inquire as to where Kate Rogan figured in it, but her woman's instinct sounded a warning.

Clendenning continued, "I know this is sort of a surprise, Serena, but I had to tell you. I guess I'd better go now." He started to his feet.

"Sit down, Rory, for God's sake!" she said irritably. "You've hardly touched your brandy. What kind of a man are you, to say you love a person, then rush off?"

He fumbled for words. "I thought maybe I'd embarrassed you."

"I see you still have a great deal to learn about women." Her smile was slow. "Any woman would be flattered by a man declaring his love, unless it was some man they detested."

"Well . . ." He sat down with a thump. He laughed. "That's something, at least. You don't detest me."

"Of course, I don't detest you," she said crossly. "But this is hardly the time to talk of love, with me about to go on trial."

"That's of no importance." He waved a hand.

"You can say that. You're not the one being tried," she retorted. "What if I'm found guilty? What then?"

"You won't be. You *can't* be."

"You can't be that sure." She shook her head. "Even the Judge isn't that sure, and he's had experience in such things."

"Serena . . ." He leaned toward her. "Someone here in Virginia City killed your folks, then tried to kill you. Then killed this Madeline. It has to be the same person."

"There may not be any connection at all. We have no proof that there is."

"I'm going to find proof. If nobody else cares enough to look for this man, I'll devote my time to it."

"How can you, Rory? How about your business? You can't neglect that." She hesitated, then said quickly, "What will your partner think?"

"She'll have nothing to say about it," he said. "I'm my own man now, Serena. Besides, the freighting business slows down in winter. Often, the canyon road down to the Carson River is impassable for days at a time."

The mention of Kate Rogan had placed a constraint on them. Clendenning sat in glum silence, gulping at his brandy. Then he looked down at the glass, as though amazed that it was empty.

"Would you care for another brandy, Rory?"

"No, I'd better go now." He stood up. "I'll send the guard over."

Serena also stood up. They locked glances for a moment, and Serena felt the pull of his gaze like a magnet. She made up her mind suddenly. Placing a hand on his arm, she said softly, "Don't go, Rory. Stay."

"Stay?" He blinked confusedly.

"You said you loved me. I love you, too. There! See, I've said it!"

He took a step, and she was in his arms, his mouth hungry on hers. She returned the kiss with fervor and an equal hunger.

Her body was on fire, but she forced herself to step back. "Not here, my darling. Come."

She led him back to the bedroom down the hall. Dimly, she knew that Foxy was somewhere in the house. But he was probably dozing in the kitchen. Anyway, she didn't care! The only thing she cared about at the moment was this man she loved with all of her heart.

In the bedroom, in the dark, they undressed in clumsy haste, and Serena guided him to the bed.

This time was far different from the night out in the desert. Clendenning was tender and knowing, no longer a fumbling, inexperienced youth.

In her mind Serena said, Thank you for that, Kate Rogan; I shall always be grateful.

She gasped aloud, arching to his mouth as he kissed her breast. His hands, which had before been soft, were now rough with calluses, but this had the effect of arousing her more than ever. The ridged calluses had the feel of a kitten's tongue caressing her. Also, his hands now possessed an incredible strength, and Serena sensed that he was using great restraint so as not to hurt her.

She found his mouth and drew him down to her, her own hands playing over the smooth muscles of his strong back. She leaped with passion now. Taking her mouth from his, she whispered, "Now, darling Rory! I want you now!"

Serena took him to her, and they were one, spinning in a maelstrom of pleasure. His restraint was still evident, as he timed his thrusts to her own rhythm.

Soon, their pace quickened, and as their ecstasy peaked, Serena clung to him fiercely, crying out, and Clendenning moaned deep in his throat, his kiss rough and urgent now.

Even when their passion had receded, Serena would not let him go for a long while. She gripped him with all her waning strength, holding him to her, wishing they could remain like this forever, so close that their heartbeats sounded as one.

Finally, she relaxed with a gusty sigh and allowed him to move away from her.

Lying on his side, Clendenning caressed her moist hair. "Dear, sweet Serena, this is what I have longed for all this time, to hold you in my arms again, in mutual love, not like that night by the Carson River."

Slowly her scattered thoughts collected, and Serena turned to practical matters. "Rory . . ."

"Yes, sweetheart?"

"There is a problem, you know. Your partner, Kate Rogan."

Clendenning didn't think to question how she knew about Kate. He sighed. "I know."

"You'll have to tell her. It wouldn't be fair to her, otherwise."

"I know, I know. I'll tell her. But I'll have to pick the right time for it." His voice was a bit testy. "About Christmas dinner . . . do you still want her?"

Serena thought a moment. "Did you ask her yet?"

"Yes, this afternoon. She said she'd be glad to come."

"Then of course, I want her here. It would be rude of me to take back my invitation now. Besides . . ." Her voice was impish. "I'd like to meet her. Who knows, I might like her, and I am grateful to her."

Clendenning made a sound of astonishment. "Grateful to Kate? Lord God! For what?"

"See if you can figure it out." Her laughter was rich and full.

Chapter Twenty

Spencer Hurd had no knowledge of the strongbox. "Hetty never mentioned it to me, Serena. But then, as well as I knew her, she was still secretive about many things. I suppose, if the strongbox had anything of value, she thought it would be opened on her death, and the contents go to your folks."

"But it isn't in the house, Judge! I've looked into every nook and cranny. Do you suppose a thief killed Madeline, someone she caught stealing the strongbox? Maybe it contained valuable jewels or a large sum of money."

"I doubt either to be the case, my dear. Hetty was not one to adorn herself with jewelry, and she did once tell me that she kept little money on the premises. She said if a girl would lie on her back for money, she'd also steal if the opportunity presented itself."

"Then what happened to it, Judge?"

Hurd shrugged. "I have no idea, and I doubt it figures in Madeline's death. One of the girls could have taken it out of spite, or in the hope it did contain valuables. They weren't overjoyed about me closing down the Paradise."

Shortly, Serena left Hurd's office. It was the day before Christmas, and she had gone there to borrow money for Christmas shopping. Hurd had loaned her what she needed without question, but Serena left his office burning with shame. Before the trial was over, she was going to be deeply in his debt. And he hadn't once mentioned his fee.

Rory Clendenning had tentatively asked if she needed money, but Serena absolutely refused to accept money from him. The connection between living in what had once been a whorehouse and taking money from a lover was too close for comfort.

She spent a couple of hours browsing through the stores along C Street, buying gifts—a box of the Judge's favorite cigars, a watch chain for Rory, a new shirt for Foxy, and a small locket for Kate Rogan. She hesitated over this last present, but finally decided she couldn't very well give the others gifts and ignore Kate Rogan.

When she got back to the house, she found a surprise waiting for her. Foxy had chopped down a small pine tree and set it up in the parlor.

She clapped her hands in delight. "Why, Foxy! How nice!"

Foxy glowed. "Afraid we ain't got anything to decorate it with. Hetty never held much with celebrating Christmas."

"I think I know just the thing."

Serena hurried upstairs and rummaged through the dresser drawers in all the bedrooms. Soon, she came back downstairs with her arms laden with ribbons she had found left in the rooms upstairs, ribbons of all the colors of the rainbow. "We'll drape the tree with these!"

Foxy eyed them dubiously. "Ain't that the ribbons them girls wore in their hair? Don't seem fitting somehow."

"Christmas is a time of good cheer and fellowship." She was already decking the pine branches with the ribbons. "And forgiveness."

"So I've heard," Foxy said in a grumbling voice. But he limped over to help her.

Soon the small tree was gaily decorated with colorful bows. Serena stood back to survey it. "It's not too bad. It would be better if the room had a fireplace, instead of that iron monster." She gestured to the stove squatting in one corner. "Then we could hang stockings on the mantel."

"Don't go in much for fireplaces out here. They put these houses up in too much of a hurry."

"We need something else . . ." She cocked her head, studying the tree. "I know! We don't have a star, but if we can put a candle on top of the tree, that would serve."

Foxy fetched a red candle and a small holder. With some difficulty, they managed to tie it onto the top of the tree.

"Now, that looks like Christmas! Here, Foxy." Serena delved into her purse and gave Foxy some money. "Buy us a goose and all the trimmings. We want a good dinner tomorrow."

As Foxy left with the money, Serena stood looking

at the little tree, her face sad. She was thinking of her parents. It was at times like this that she missed and mourned them the most, but perhaps it was just as well that they weren't here to witness the coming trial and its attendant notoriety. She sighed and turned away.

When Serena got up late on Christmas morning, it was snowing heavily outside, and for once the wind was not blowing. A white Christmas!

Shivering in the cold, she got dressed quickly and went down into the warmth of the kitchen, determined to forget all her problems for this one day and enjoy it.

Foxy had been up for hours, cooking the Christmas dinner. There were two pumpkin pies cooling on the table.

"Pumpkin pies! Where did you get pumpkin, Foxy?"

"They grow 'em down in the Carson Valley."

From the oven of the range, the tempting aroma of the roasting goose filled and warmed the air. Serena sniffed in delight and poured herself a cup of hot coffee. Foxy started to cook her breakfast.

"I can do that, Foxy. You have enough to do."

"Today you do nothing, Miss Serena. I'll do the work. When you've had your breakfast, you get out'n my kitchen and stay out," he said, feigning a growl. "You'd only be in the way."

As she ate her breakfast, Serena's thoughts winged back to the farm in Illinois. Before the war, before times became hard for the Fosters, they always had a nice Christmas, with food enough for a half-dozen

408

people and gifts to exchange. She felt tears burn her eyes and determinedly blinked them away.

She went into the parlor, wrapped the gifts she had bought, and put them under the tree. Dinner time was set for two o'clock. She busied herself tidying the house, even though it really didn't need it. Finally, she toted hot water to her bedroom, took a leisurely bath, and then put on her prettiest dress.

Spencer Hurd was the first to arrive. Serena stood framed in the doorway while he stomped the mud from his boots and shook the snow off his coat. He was carrying a large, gift-wrapped package. Smiling, he started toward her, then detoured to start the chair to rocking.

"I think I'm getting superstitious about that damned chair!"

"An unbeliever like you, Judge? A man with a logical mind, superstitious?" she said mockingly.

He shook a finger at her. "Never flaunt the gods, young lady, in trying times, believe in them or not. Here, this is for you," he said gruffly, handing her the large package. "Merry Christmas."

"Oh, Judge! Thank you." She swallowed the lump in her throat and hugged the package to her. "You shouldn't have."

"How do you know I shouldn't have? Might be a bundle of law books, for all you know."

"I know it isn't. I'd love to open it right this minute."

"Well, go ahead. No law says you can't."

"No," she said resolutely. "We won't open the presents until Rory and . . ." She broke off.

"Kate Rogan, Serena. That's the woman's name." Hurd came in, closing the door against the cold.

"Anyway, we'll open presents when they get here."
She linked arms with him. "Come on into the sitting
room and see what I've got."

Spencer Hurd stopped short just inside the parlor
and stared. "A Christmas tree! Godalmighty . . .
wait." He went over and inspected the decorations,
then swung around, braying with laughter. "Ribbons
from the girls' hair, am I right?"

Serena let her own laughter go. "Right!"

Hurd choked off his laughter with an effort. "My
dear, you are priceless! Hetty would have adored
you."

"Foxy mixed a bowl of egg nog." She motioned to
the small table near the tree. "Or would you prefer
whiskey?"

"Whiskey, my dear." He made a face. "Egg nog is
for sissies."

The Judge had scarcely started on his drink when
Clendenning and Kate Rogan arrived, carrying packages. Serena was surprised to discover that Kate Rogan was several years older than Rory, but she was a
good-looking woman, with lovely, long red hair. She
wore a dress of green, in the current fashion, and Serena had a strong feeling that she had bought it just
for this occasion.

Clendenning was clearly uncomfortable as he introduced them. They shook hands warily, taking each
other's measure.

"I've heard about you, Serena, and your troubles.
I'm happy to finally meet you. Clendenning has mentioned you numerous times. Has he told you about
me, the crazy hay barn lady?" She looked sidelong at
Clendenning, a glint of amusement in her eyes.

"The hay barn lady?" Serena said, puzzled.

"Sure, that's what they call me in Virginia City. Ain't that right, Clendenning?"

"Now, Kate, you know that isn't true." Clendenning ran a finger under his collar. "It's what she calls herself, Serena. She's highly respected in town. Nobody thinks her crazy."

"How about you, Judge Hurd? For instance, how many times have you seen me in a dress?" Kate spun around once. "Clendenning here, this is the first time for him."

"Well now," Hurd drawled. "All I can say is, Kate, if you're crazy, you're the prettiest crazy lady in Virginia City. And I'll drink a toast to that!"

Kate's face crinkled, as though squeezing back tears. "Ah-h, you're a sweet man, Judge." She ran to him and kissed him full on the mouth.

That broke the tension in the room, and Hurd helped even further by briskly serving egg nog to everyone. They sipped and talked easily after that. Despite herself, Serena found that she liked Kate Rogan. Kate had a sudden, dry wit that had Serena laughing helplessly. Seeing that the two women were getting on fine, Clendenning seemed to relax.

Shortly before it was time for Foxy to announce dinner, Serena said, "Let's open our presents!"

There was a chorus of agreement, and Hurd said, "You're the hostess, Serena. Distribute them. Play Santa for us."

Serena passed around the presents. Then she opened her own. She opened Kate's first—a lovely, blue, crocheted shawl. She hesitated about which to open next, wanting to leave Clendenning's until last, but she had the feeling that wouldn't be too diplo-

411

matic, so she opened his next. She drew in her breath. It was a delicate cameo broach. She smiled her thanks. She watched as the others opened their gifts. Although she wouldn't have admitted it, she was very curious as to what Rory had given Kate.

Kate's present from Clendenning was a fine silver and enamel bracelet, which Kate fastened upon her wrist with apparent delight. It was lovely, to be sure, but privately, Serena thought it not as nice as the cameo. She felt a certain satisfaction in this conclusion.

Finally, Serena unwrapped the Judge's large package. She exclaimed with delight. It was a long, fur-trimmed cloak. She held it up for all to see.

"I thought maybe you could use it," Hurd said, his voice hushed by embarrassment. "You've been running around freezing to death. Gets a mite colder here than it does in San Francisco."

Serena draped the cloak around her shoulders and went over to hug him fiercely. "You're a dear man, Spencer Hurd, and if you weren't such an old roué, I'd marry you!"

"Old?" He raised his eyebrows. "Now I take exception to that."

They all laughed and had another round of drinks before Foxy came in to announce dinner.

The dinner was a huge success. The goose was golden brown, oozing juices and the savory aroma of dressing. The biscuits Foxy had baked were light as snowflakes, and the vegetables he had somehow managed to obtain were cooked just right. The pumpkin pie, topped with whipped cream, that followed was roundly praised.

Spencer Hurd leaned back with a sigh. "Best meal I've ever tasted, including the pie."

Clendenning and Kate murmured their assent.

Serena said, "Since it's Christmas, Judge, you may smoke one of your cigars without asking permission. So long as it's one from the box I gave you."

"I will do that." He got a cigar from the box and lit it.

It wasn't long before Clendenning and Kate took their leave.

As they were about to go, Clendenning said, "Rafe will be a little late, Serena. I told him to have Christmas with his family first."

"It's all right, Clendenning," Hurd said. "I'll stick around until he gets here."

In the sitting room, Hurd put on a sober face. "I hate to inject a serious note into the festivities, but tomorrow it starts, Serena. The selection of the jury. That's going to be our first, maybe our worst, hurdle."

"Why should that be a problem, Judge?"

"Because of the way juries are picked here, and because of the caliber of the juror usually selected." He spoke in what Serena was coming to think of as his "lecturing" voice. "Respectable men who have a business to take care of, working men—men of that quality can't spare the time to serve on juries. What happens is the presiding judge sends a deputy sheriff out into the courtroom among the spectators asking for volunteers. If he can't get enough that way, he goes out into the streets until he rounds up about two dozen men. Naturally, they're idlers, drunkards, or even worse. Then these twenty-odd names are dropped into a hat, the names are drawn out one at a time until there are twelve men in the jury box." Bitterness tinged his voice. "As you can see, twelve good men and true. A jury of your *peers*, Serena . . ."

Clendenning and Kate had little to say on the way home. But Clendenning was upset, and once they were inside the house, he said, "You made a spectacle out of yourself before the Judge and Serena with that "crazy hay barn lady' show you put on. Why did you act like that, Kate?"

She spun on him, green eyes blazing. "Why? *You* can ask why? You've been in her bed, haven't you, Clendenning?"

Taken aback, Clendenning searched for words. "I . . . how did you know?"

"I'm a woman, Clendenning. All I needed was to see the pair of you together. So don't bother to lie to me!"

"I'm not going to lie to you, Kate." Clendenning tried to collect his shattered dignity. "I should have told you, I know. But I didn't know how, without hurting you."

"Hurt me? You think tonight didn't?" The green eyes had the shine of tears. Her fists were clenched. Now she opened one and hurled something against the wall with all her strength. Clendenning saw that it was the locket Serena had given her.

The outburst seemed to calm her. Her features had smoothed out as she faced him again. "I know we had no hold on each other; we've talked about that. It's just that this was so sudden and something of a shock.

I knew it would happen sooner or later." She gave a bitter laugh. "It's just that I suppose I hoped it would be later. You've never loved me, not as a man should love a woman. And you've never lied and said that you did. I respect that, Clendenning."

"What do we do now?"

"I'll tell you one thing I will not do, Clendenning! I will *not* share you with another woman."

"You want me to move out?"

"Move out?" Kate considered for a moment. "Yes, I think that would be best. Certainly, you'll not be sharing my bed again. And if you're in this house, it might happen. I've found that I'm a weaker woman, in some ways, than I thought."

"I'll move into a boarding house tonight." He added wretchedly, "And I want you to know that I'm . . ."

"No!" She held up a hand. "Don't tell me you're sorry. Of all things, that I don't want to hear from you."

He stared at her helplessly. "All right, Kate, I won't." He hesitated. "What about the business?"

"What about it?"

"I mean . . . well, do we continue as partners?"

"Why not? I fail to see what one thing has to do with the other. We sure as hell couldn't swing it alone at this stage, either of us."

Clendenning nodded. He stood a moment, feeling awkward, trying to think of something more to say. He finally added lamely, "Good night then, Kate. I'll see you tomorrow."

He made it halfway to the door before she said, "Clendenning?"

415

"Yes, Kate?"

"We had some good times, didn't we?"

"We did, Kate," he said gravely. "I will remember them for the rest of my life."

"Thank you for that," she said softly.

He was almost to the door when she said, "Clendenning?"

"Yes?"

"I like your Serena. It hurts me like hell to say this, but I really do like her."

When Serena and Spencer Hurd entered Judge Underwood's courtroom the next morning at nine o'clock, they found it was crowded. Every available seat behind the railing was taken. Heads turned at their entrance, and whispers rustled through the room like a gust of wind.

There was one difference from the time Serena had been there before—along one wall twelve, straight-back chairs had been placed, two rows of six. Jake Burns sat in one. He scowled as his glance encountered hers.

Hurd escorted Serena to the long table. There was another man already seated there, a tall, middle-aged man, with a long face, melancholy brown eyes, and a balding head.

Hurd said, "Well, Robie, are you prosecuting?"

"So Elmo Underwood tells me, Judge," the man said gloomily.

"This is Robie Garth, Serena. This is the defendant, Robie. Serena Foster."

The man got to his feet and bowed awkwardly.

"How do, Miss Foster. I can't very well say it's a pleasure to meet you, can I? Not under the circumstances."

Serena smiled. "How do you do, Mr. Garth."

After they had sat down, with Hurd between Serena and Garth, the Judge whispered in her ear, "Judge Underwood didn't make a bad choice. Robie Garth is a competent attorney and has had experience in criminal cases. He's an honest man, and not likely to try any dirty tactics . . ."

He broke off as the hammer rapped, and they turned to see Judge Underwood settling down behind the school desk. "This here court is now in session. Now I'll have no fussing or talking among you men out there in the spectator's section. That happens, I'll have Deputy Burns throw you out. I hope that's all clear to everyone. Deputy Burns . . ."

Jake Burns rose from his chair. "Yes, Your Honor?"

"I reckon we're ready to start. Why don't you pick us out a jury?"

"Yes, Your Honor."

Jake Burns went through the audience, talking to one man after another, writing names on slips of paper, which he dropped into his hat.

Hurd twisted around to watch. In a low voice, he said, "I'm a little surprised by one thing. Usually the spectators at a trial are a bunch of galoots with no other way to spend their time, as I think I told you. This seems to be quite a respectable bunch. Many of them I see should be at work or tending to business."

"I guess a woman on trial for her life attracts a little more attention, Judge. More than, say, a horse thief," Serena said wryly.

417

Hurd still looked troubled. "There is that, of course, but still . . ."

Within a remarkably short time Jake Burns returned to the desk. "Twenty-four names, Your Honor."

"Should be enough." Judge Underwood looked at the table. "You still aim to plead your client not guilty, Counselor?"

Hurd stood. "I do, Your Honor."

Judge Underwood nodded. "So be it. Now I aim to be fair about this, so I'll let you and the prosecutor . . . I reckon you two are acquainted?"

"We are, Your Honor," Hurd and Garth said in unison.

"Fine and dandy. Now, I'm going to let you two take turns drawing names from Deputy Burns' hat. As each name is drawn and the man seated in the jury box, you'll each take turns with your questions. Now, I don't want this trial to drag on all winter, so I'm going to limit you to six questions and to six challenges each. We've got twenty-four names here, so we'll make up a jury even if both of you use up your challenges. All right with you, Prosecutor?"

Robie Garth said, "Fine with me, Your Honor."

"Counselor?"

Hurd rose, hesitated, then sighed and said, "The defense agrees, Your Honor."

Sitting down, he leaned over to Serena to whisper, "The old coot knows we're legally entitled to more leeway with the prospective jurors. But should I register a protest, it would only get his back up."

The prosecution got the first draw. When the prospective juror, Lester Tompkins, was seated and sworn in, Garth asked his questions without moving from his chair. The questioning was perfunctory; Garth's main concern seemed to be if the juror would be as willing to find a woman guilty of murder and sentence her to hang as he would a man. Lester Tompkins said that he certainly would, and Garth accepted him. Hurd had been scribbling his questions on a tablet.

When his turn came, he got to his feet, and said, "Mr. Tompkins, do you know the defendant, Serena Foster?"

"Not personally, no, sir."

"But you have heard stories about the murder of Madeline Dubois and the defendant's alleged guilt?"

"Sure have." Tompkins' leathery face cracked in a smile. "Guess everybody in Virginia has heard."

"But you wouldn't allow that to affect your verdict? In other words, Mr. Tompkins, would you let anything you have heard outside this courtroom have any bearing on your deciding the guilt or innocence of the defendant?"

"No, sir." Lester Tompkins looked virtuous. "I'd go only on the, uh, things I hear in this courtroom."

"On the evidence, you mean?"

Tompkins nodded vigorously. "That's what I mean, yes, sir!"

"And because the defendant is the legal owner of a place called the Paradise, once a bawdy house, although she had never operated it as such . . . would that affect your verdict in any way?"

Snickers raced through the courtroom, and the hammer pounded as Judge Underwood glared furiously. The room quieted.

The man in the juror's chair had been smiling. Now he sobered and sat up straight as Hurd said, "Would you answer the question, sir?"

"Nope, I'd wipe that clean out of my mind."

"Mr. Tompkins, have you ever sat in judgment on female defendant before?"

Before the prospective juror could answer, Robie Garth was on his feet. "Your Honor, I believe Mr. Hurd's arithmetic is faulty. The limit is six questions, and defense counsel has now asked *seven* questions."

Judge Underwood smiled. "Got you there, Counselor. Afraid you just ran out of questions."

Hurd opened his mouth to protest, then shrugged and sat down. "Defense accepts this juror."

The questioning of the remaining prospective jurors followed much the same pattern, except Spencer Hurd changed one question. He asked each man if he was married. Then he used all six of his challenges to dismiss married men.

The panel of twelve men was picked and sworn in just short of noon. Hurd leaned back, humming slightly under his breath, his glance roaming over the twelve men. In a low voice he said, "Not too bad, considering. Better than I expected, in fact. At least these are all reasonably respectable men. How logical and fair-minded they might be is something else again."

"Judge, why did you dismiss all the married men?"

"Simple, my dear. A man's wife has a great deal to say about how he votes while on a jury. To the females of this town, you're still a scarlet woman, no matter how unfair that opinion may be. Do you think they would be happy should their spouses vote such a woman innocent? At least the single men will be free of *that* influence."

The hammer sounded. "Close to the noon hour. I'm mighty pleased that you gents picked a jury so speedily. We will adjourn court until two o'clock. At that time, you gents may make your opening speech to the jury, if you have one in mind."

Hurd stood, gathering up his papers. The twelve jurors filed past the table, carefully averting their eyes from Serena.

"Why won't they look at me, Judge? Does that mean they already consider me guilty?"

"I hardly think that follows, Serena." His smile wasn't convincing. "At least I hope not. Why not give them the benefit of the doubt and believe they view you as a beautiful woman and are embarrassed at having to sit in judgment on you?"

Serena didn't believe it for an instant, and she was convinced that Spencer Hurd didn't either. A coldness spread through her, a draining away of hope.

As the knock sounded on his office door, Brad Stryker hastily stowed the bottle in his desk drawer and called out, "Come in!"

The door opened and closed, and Stryker grinned when he recognized his visitor. "Well, Lester! How did it go?"

"Smooth as silk, Brad." Lester Tompkins smiled broadly. "There're eight of the men you wanted on the jury. I was the first man picked."

"Eight, huh? Not bad." Stryker thought for a moment. Absently, he picked up the quirt from his desk and trailed it caressingly across the palm of his other hand. "No, not bad at all. With the eight of you, a good majority, you should be able to lean on any of the other four who might balk. Not that I think that'll happen. We all know she's guilty, right?"

"Right, Brad."

Stryker took the bottle out of his desk and held it out. "Have a snort, Lester."

"Don't mind if I do." Tompkins tilted the bottle up, drank deeply, wiped the bottle mouth on his sleeve, and handed it back.

"Now we understand how important this is, don't we, Lester?" Stryker swished the quirt against the desk. "We all know that this woman, innocent looking though she might be, is guilty as sin. And just because she *is* a woman, that is no reason she shouldn't hang."

"Oh, we all understand that, Brad."

"My only interest in this is to see justice done. If this woman doesn't hang, people will think we have no law and order here at all. We have to show the country that a woman can't get away with murder here. A woman has to pay for her crimes the same as a man. I was afraid that if it was left up to some soft-hearted gents on that jury they'd let her off."

Tompkins was nodding. "We all understand, Brad, and we'll see to it that justice is done. We need more men like you here in Virginia, with a concern for justice."

After the man had left, Stryker leaned back in his chair, smiling contentedly. It was going to work out just fine.

He closed his eyes, recalling that night in Li Po's

house, and Serena Foster naked and at his mercy. He struck the palm of his hand with the quirt, harder than had been his intention. It stung like fire, and he cursed aloud.

Chapter Twenty-one

The prosecution made the first speech to the jury. Robie Garth talked for a half hour; a long, rambling speech, outlining the case he hoped to prove against Serena. Every few minutes he warned the jurors not to let the fact that the defendant was a woman have any bearing on their verdict.

At the last he whirled about and pointed at Serena with a dramatic flourish. "The woman there, Serena Foster, is guilty as charged, guilty of murder most foul, and the prosecution intends to prove it beyond a shadow of a doubt, gentlemen of the jury!"

As Garth started back to the table, there was a round of applause from the spectators.

Judge Underwood hammered on the desk, glowering. "Any more such clapping and I will have this court cleared!"

Hurd strode to a position before the twelve jurors. In a dry voice, he said, "I can readily understand why the audience responded with applause. The prosecutor gave a great dramatic performance, well worthy of the stage. But this is not a theater, gentlemen of the jury. It is a court of law, and we are here on a serious matter, to find the defendant guilty or innocent. I am sorry that I cannot provide you with entertainment as did Mr. Garth. I have only a few words for you, gentlemen of the jury. My opponent has made extravagant claims as to the preponderance of the evidence pointing to the guilt of the defendant. In truth, the proof he has to present is all purely circumstantial, and the defense will make this abundantly clear as the trial proceeds. All I ask is that you gentlemen keep open minds, and decide the guilt or innocence of the defendant after the evidence is all in, and *only* then. I thank you for your kind attention."

As Hurd resumed his seat, Judge Underwood cleared his throat. "You may call your first witness, Prosecutor."

The prosecution's first witness was Jake Burns. After Burns was sworn in, Garth led him through the usual questions—name, age, profession, et cetera. "Now will you tell us, please, Deputy Burns, what transpired on the day in question. Just tell it in your own words."

Jake Burns crossed his legs, aimed a baleful glance in Serena's direction, and told how one of the girls from the Paradise, called Maudie, came running into the sheriff's office around noon, screaming and in a state of shock. It took him some time to get any kind of sense out of her. When he finally pieced together what had happened, he hurried out to the Paradise and found Madeline Dubois dead, on the sofa, with a .38 derringer, one bullet discharged, on the floor.

Madeline had been shot between the eyes at close range.

At this point Garth interrupted. "One moment, Deputy." He crossed to a small table before Judge Underwood's desk on which rested several items. He returned with a derringer. "I show you this derringer, Deputy. Is this the weapon you found?"

"It is. It has a tag on it, you see. A tag I placed there at the time, with my initials on it."

"This, then, is the murder weapon?"

Jake Burns was nodding.

Hurd got up before the deputy could speak. "This calls for speculation from the witness, Your Honor. Since Deputy Burns was not present when the murder was committed, he is not qualified to answer the question."

Garth bent a glare on Hurd, seemingly about to explode. He got his exasperation under control with a visible effort and turned again to the witness. "We will pass that question for the moment. Now, Deputy, in your opinion how long had the deceased been dead?"

"Well, now that's hard to answer. Madeline . . . the victim was cold and stiff long since. I'd judge ten, twelve hours at the outside."

Jake Burns was staring directly at Serena, and she felt a shiver pass down her spine at the picture his words conjured up.

"And you arrived around noon?"

"Shortly before noon, yes, sir."

"In your judgment then, Madeline Dubois had been dead at least ten hours when you examined her?"

"About that, give or take."

"That would mean then that she was killed around midnight, at about the time she was heard quarreling with the defendant, or not long thereafter?"

Hurd arose to object. Garth, as though anticipating his objection, was looking back over his shoulder. Hurd changed his mind and sat back down with a shake of his head.

"At around that time, yes, sir," Jake Burns said.

"That's all the questions I have of this witness, Your Honor."

Hurd rose to say, "No questions of the witness at this time, Your Honor. But I reserve the right to call him back for cross-examination later."

Judge Underwood said, "Call your next witness, Prosecutor."

The second witness for the prosecution was Bob Jenkins, the gunsmith. Garth questioned him closely about how long he had been a gunsmith, making it abundantly clear that he was well qualified in his field.

Then Garth crossed to the small table, picked up the derringer again, and returned to the witness.

"I show you this derringer, Mr. Jenkins, and ask you to identify it as the murder weapon . . ."

"I object, Your Honor!" Hurd was on his feet. "We do not know that the derringer in the prosecutor's hand is the actual murder weapon!"

Garth gaped at him. "Now come on, Judge. This derringer, fired once, was found by the victim's body Deputy Burns has so testified."

"That still does not prove that this derringer is the murder weapon. Unfortunately, we as yet have no means of establishing that particular bullet was fired from a particular gun."

"All right, gents." The hammer rapped. "That's enough of that. Any murder trial I have presided over, Counselor, the weapon found at the scene of the crime has always been considered the murder weapon. Afraid I'm going to have to overrule your objection."

Hurd sat down, satisfied. At least his objection would lodge some doubt, however small, in the minds of the jurors.

Garth turned back to the witness. "Would you take this derringer and see if you can identify it, Mr. Jenkins?"

Jenkins accepted the derringer and identified it as the derringer he had sold to Serena Foster and Darrel Quick last year.

"How can you be positive this is the same derringer, Mr. Jenkins?"

"It has a serial number. See?" He pointed out the number on the gun. "And I have this to jog my memory . . ." Jenkins dug into his pocket for a slip of paper. "A receipt of sale for this here derringer, same serial number, made out to Serena Foster, that woman sitting right there!"

Dramatically, the witness pointed a finger at Serena. Hurd started to object, then changed his mind.

Garth said, "There is no doubt in your mind then, that this derringer is the same as that purchased by the defendant?"

"None whatsoever. Nope."

Garth took the receipt from Jenkins. "The prosecution will mark this as an item of evidence. No more questions. Your witness, Mr. Hurd."

Hurd stood. "Mr. Jenkins, is there, to the best of your knowledge, any method whereby the bullet that

429

killed Madeline Dubois may be identified as coming from the particular weapon . . ."

"Object, Your Honor! The question calls for a conclusion from the witness, not testimony as to fact."

"A conclusion I should think the witness is eminently qualified to make, since he is a gunsmith." Hurd added dryly, "For over twenty years, as the prosecutor had the witness testify to."

"Seems we've already covered this ground, Counselor," Judge Underwood said sourly. "But ask your question. The witness may state his opinion."

Hurd said, "Will you answer the question, Mr. Jenkins?"

"Never heard of any such a way. But the bullet that killed the woman came from this derringer, seems to me."

"The jury is not interested in how it 'seems' to you, Mr. Jenkins. Is there any means of establishing definitely that the bullet that killed Madeline Dubois was fired by this particular weapon? Just answer yes or no, Mr. Jenkins."

"No," Jenkins said sullenly.

"Thank you, Mr. Jenkins. That will be all."

Hurd sat down. Now Robie Garth started a parade of witnesses, all the girls who had been working at the Paradise at the time Madeline was killed. Hurd knew they were all going to be hostile to him, since his closing down the Paradise had forced them out of their happy home.

As soon as Garth had identified each girl, carefully skirting the area of their profession, he asked them to relate what they had heard of the quarrel that night between Serena and Madeline.

When Garth asked the first girl this question, and

she launched into her story, Hurd stood, opening his mouth to protest that it was hearsay testimony, and then changed his mind. Even if he won his point, which was doubtful, it would only make the jurors angry because he had deprived them of hearing all the juicy details.

Judge Underwood arched an eyebrow at him. "Yes, Counselor?"

"Nothing, Your Honor. I beg the court's pardon."

When the prosecutor was finished, Hurd asked each girl the same three questions.

"Ma'am, did you hear a shot, an altercation of any kind, following this quarrel you *overheard*?"

All replied in the negative.

"Then, to the best of your knowledge, Madeline Dubois was alive and well after the defendant departed the premises?"

Some replied readily enough that Madeline was alive, to the best of their knowledge. Others were more reluctant, and the admission had to be wrung from them.

The hostility became almost palpable when Hurd asked his third question. "Ma'am, what is your profession?"

Robie Garth jumped up. "I must protest, Your Honor! I fail to see what the witness' profession has to do with this case!"

"It goes to the heart of the creditability of the witness, Your Honor," Hurd said smoothly.

Over Garth's strenuous and continued objections, Judge Underwood allowed the question to be asked and answered.

The replies Hurd received were varied, and would have been humorous under different circumstances.

Some said they were entertainers, others said dance-hall girls, and two admitted candidly that they were whores. In view of their hostility, Hurd allowed all the answers to stand as given.

The next witness for the prosecution was Foxy Parks. Foxy had told Hurd that he had been summoned to testify, and had been quite willing to refuse to appear. Hurd had instructed him to go ahead and testify, telling the exact truth as he knew it.

Robie Garth now had a hostile, uncooperative witness on his hands. As he listened to Garth's examination of the witness, Hurd couldn't decide if this was good or bad for their side.

". . . You were working that night, cleaning up the barroom around midnight, is that not right, Mr. Parks?"

"Just like I did every night, that's right."

"And you overheard the bitter quarrel between Madeline Dubois and the accused, heard the accused threaten the life of the deceased?"

"Nope."

"What . . . ?" Garth stopped to stare. "Let's clarify for the jury . . . the barroom in the Paradise is downstairs, only a short distance from where the quarrel took place, and has no door, only a beaded curtain. Is that not correct?"

"Yup, you're right there."

"Yet you heard nothing?"

"Didn't say that. I didn't hear all them things you said. I'm not like some, all ears when it comes to other people's business. I do my work and close my ears."

"You have heard all the other witnesses testify as to what they heard?"

"Sure did."

"Yet *you* heard nothing?"

Foxy said patiently, "Let's put it this way, Mister lawyer. I heard right enough, but I didn't listen. Figured it was none of my business."

Garth said angrily, "Your Honor, I wish to remind the witness that he is under oath to tell the truth here! Do you know what perjury is, Mr. Parks?"

"Sure. I'm not stupid. It means you lie on the witness stand."

"And it also means that you can go to jail if you do lie!"

Unruffled, Foxy said, "Yup, I know that too."

"Then will you tell the jury the substance of what you heard of the quarrel between Madeline Dubois and the accused?"

"Heard nothing."

Hurd hid a grin behind his splayed fingers as Robie Garth glared at the man in the witness chair in frustration. Serena whispered in Hurd's ear, "Bless Foxy. I could kiss him!"

"Just remember, he's just claiming he didn't listen," Hurd whispered back. "He's in no way contradicting the testimony of the other witnesses."

Garth was turning away from the witness. Hurd got up and strolled over.

"Mr. Parks, you are presently keeping house for Serena Foster, in a manner of speaking. Is that right?"

"That's right, Judge."

"You have come to know her well during this time?"

Foxy smiled over at Serena. "I sure have."

"What opinion have you formed of her character, Mr. Parks?"

Garth was on his feet. "Objection, Your Honor! The witness' opinion of the defendant's character is not germane to these proceedings!"

Hurd faced around. He said genially, "Well now, Mr. Garth, it seems to me we have listened to an almost endless parade of witnesses testifying to the *character* of the defendant. And may I remind the prosecutor that Mr. Parks is *his* witness? I have the right to cross-examine him as to . . ."

The hammer tapped. "I agree with Counselor, Prosecutor." Judge Underwood grinned. "You opened the door here, Prosecutor. Like they say, never does much good to lock the barn door after the horses are out. You may continue, Counselor."

Hurd said, "Well, Mr. Parks?"

"Miss Serena is a fine woman. One of the finest women I have ever known. She is a lady all the way."

"From the impression you have formed of her, is it your belief that she is capable of murder?"

Foxy snorted. "Wouldn't hurt a fly; not Miss Serena."

Robie Garth was up, shouting.

Hurd waited patiently, smiling, as the prosecutor made his objections. Judge Underwood ruled in his favor, but Hurd was satisfied, content that the jury had heard the question and answer.

"Mr. Parks, you have testified here that you heard words spoken in anger between the deceased and the defendant, but did not listen. Very commendable, of course. Did you hear anything else that night?"

Foxy seemed to hesitate, and when he did answer, it was guardedly. "Like what, Judge?"

Something tickled at Hurd's mind. Years of questioning witnesses had given him a sort of sixth sense about when something more than the words lurked behind a witness' response. He shoved the problem into the back of his mind for a moment. "Like a gun shot?"

"Nope, didn't hear nothing like that."

"You worked until how late . . . wait, did you hear Serena Foster leave the house?"

"Heard the door slam after her."

"Now, how late did you work that night?"

"Must have been a half hour or so after she left afore I got done cleaning. One o'clock, more or less."

Hurd nodded. He paced for a moment, pondering. Then he faced the witness again. "The sound of a derringer being fired is not terribly loud. The ladies have testified that they heard no such shot. But they had retired. They might not have heard it upstairs. Is that a reasonable assumption?"

"Yup."

"But you, Mr. Parks, working on the ground floor, not very far from the sitting room, would have heard it?"

"I would purely think so. May be old, but I ain't deaf yet."

"Now think carefully . . . did you hear anything else that night?"

Foxy looked around the courtroom, shifting uneasily in the chair. Finally, he said, "Yup."

Hurd leaned forward, anticipating the importance of what was to come. "What did you hear?"

"Heard voices. From the sitting room."

"Voices? How many?"

"Two."

"Male or female?"

"Both."

"In other words, one man and one woman?"

"Yup."

"Did you recognize either?"

"Yup. Recognized Miss Madeline's."

"But not the voice of the man?"

"Nope."

"Did you overhear what was said?"

"Nope. Like I said, I never . . ."

". . . listen to other people's conversations. We know, Mr. Parks." Keeping a straight face, Hurd paced for a moment, thinking furiously. He was peripherally aware of the waiting silence in the courtroom, as though no one dared take a breath. He faced the witness chair again. "Mr. Parks, this male voice . . . had you heard it before?"

"Once or twice."

"The owner of this voice . . . you never saw him? Have no idea who he was?"

"Nope. 'Twasn't my business to know."

"Mr. Parks, for the benefit of the jury, let us construct a picture of the sitting room in the house once called the Paradise. There is a side door to the outside, is there not?"

"You know there is, Judge."

"Then Madeline could have slipped anyone, a man for instance, through that door, without using the front entrance, without any person in the house being aware of it?"

"She sure could."

"Prior to the night in question had she, to your knowledge, admitted men through that side door?"

"Yup."

"The same man?"

"The same man and . . . others."

The courtroom erupted with noise. Judge Underwood pounded with the hammer and thundered threats until quiet resumed.

Hurd paced. "In essence, you're telling us, Mr. Parks, that Madeline Dubois had lovers, several lovers?"

"At least three that I know of. It started after Miss Hetty died."

"Did you ever see any of them to recognize?"

"Never did."

"Why have you not come forward with this information before this, Mr. Parks?"

"Nobody ever asked me. 'Sides, didn't figure it was any of my business."

Hurd was silent for a moment, thinking of some way he could get the next question in before Garth could object. "It is possible, is it not, that this man, or perhaps one of Madeline's other lovers, could have been admitted by the deceased, and this visitor, this *man* killed her, perhaps in a jealous rage?"

"Seems quite likely to me."

Robie Garth was on his feet, shouting. "Not admissible! Mere speculation on the part of the witness! I object mostly strongly, Your Honor!"

Hurd turned away, closing his ears to the prosecutor's argument, knowing the objection would be upheld. But, again, it didn't matter. The jurors had heard Foxy's answer.

He felt drained as he sat down. Serena gripped his hand in her excitement. "That's great, isn't it, Judge? It proves that someone else could have killed her. Her lover!"

437

"It's a plus for our side, yes, my dear. About the first one. But don't get your hopes up too much." He passed a weary hand down across his face, wishing he could fire up a cigar. "We still have a long way to go. And this lover, if such he was . . . we're still in the dark as to who he is."

"But it casts some doubt on my guilt, doesn't it?"

"Oh, yes, for men of logical minds. But who can tell how logical those twelve good men are?"

As he had surmised, Judge Underwood ruled in favor of the prosecutor, and now Robie Garth was attacking Foxy's story with the most ferocity he had exhibited so far.

Garth hammered at the witness for almost an hour, but he gained little advantage from it. Foxy remained as steady as a rock, and Garth was unable to shake his story in the slightest.

Finally Garth turned away in defeat, mopping his sweating brow with a large red bandanna.

The hammer rapped. "It is near onto five. This here court is adjourned until nine o'clock sharp tomorrow morning."

The spectators began to leave, the courtroom emptying quickly. Foxy drifted over to the table, his sharp face wearing an anxious frown. He waited until Robie Garth had left, then said, "Did I do all right, Judge?"

Serena leaned forward. "You were great, Foxy! Thank you very, very much!"

Hurd said, "You did fine, Foxy. But I want to ask you one question . . . why didn't you come to me with this information about these lovers of Madeline's *before* the trial?"

Foxy's face took on a puzzled look. "I didn't think

438

it was important, Judge. You kept saying that Miss Serena would get off. Besides, it was none of my . . ."

". . . none of your business, I know." Hurd felt his temper rise, but he checked himself. There was no use to castigate this man. Strange though it might be, Foxy had his own personal code of ethics, which was a hell of a lot more than could be said for most people. "You did fine on the witness stand, Foxy. Thank you."

Foxy glowed. He said, "I'll hurry home and start supper then, Miss Serena."

As he started off, Serena turned to Hurd. "Why the long face, Judge? You said this was a plus for our side."

"It was, my dear, but it's far from over. And . . ." He hesitated, then said gloomily, "I received some bad news today. I wasn't sure I should tell you, but I don't want your hopes *too* high. I received a telegram from the Pinkerton office in San Francisco. They absolutely refuse to divulge the name of the man in Virginia City who hired them to bring you back. We've reached a dead end there, and I had great hopes . . ."

Chapter Twenty-two

The next morning Robie Garth tried to repair any possible damage Foxy's testimony had done to his case. One by one, he put all the Paradise girls back on the stand and asked them if they had either heard or seen any man admitted through the side door by Madeline Dubois. Each one stoutly maintained that she had not.

In his brief cross-examination, Hurd had two questions: "Is it not true that you usually retired after the Paradise closed for the night?" "And is it not also true that, exhausted from the evening's activities, you immediately went to sleep and slept soundly?"

In most instances, he received a surly, reluctant yes to both questions.

Now Garth did something that both surprised and amused Hurd. He placed several men on the witness stand, all men who had patronized the Paradise while it had been a brothel under the supervision of Madeline Dubois. Of each, he asked one question: "Did you, sir, during the times of your patronage of the Paradise, see or hear a man being admitted by the side door, or did you see such a man lurking about?"

Some of the witnesses were red-faced with embarrassment, reluctant to answer; others were rooster-proud of their patronage of the Paradise. All answered the question in the negative. All the while Hurd was wondering how Garth had gotten these men to come forward to testify. The truth finally dawned on him. In the beginning Garth had been lackadaisical about the case, but now he was all fired up, determined to use every possible means to convict Serena.

Hurd declined to cross-examine any of the witnesses; it would serve no useful purpose, only embarrass them further. It might even anger some of the jurors, since Hurd was sure that most, if not all, of them had visited the Paradise at one time or another.

When the last of the men left the witness chair, Robie Garth said, "That completes the case for the proscution, Your Honor."

"Counselor, are you ready to proceed?"

"The defense is ready, Your Honor. I would like to recall one of the prosecution's witnesses for a few questions. Deputy Burns. I earlier reserved the right to call him back to the stand, you may remember."

Jake Burns, both hostile and puzzled, was returned to the stand.

"Mr. Burns, who took charge of the body of the deceased after your investigation was completed?"

"Why, old Doc Kenwick. He always handled the corpses in a killing. You know we ain't got a coroner here."

Hurd frowned. "That would be Dr. Jonas Kenwick?"

"That's the one, old Doc Kenwick."

Hurd sighed inwardly, cursing himself. He should have been better prepared for this. "And Dr. Kenwick died some months back, did he not?"

"That he did."

"Do you know, Deputy, of your own knowledge, the extent of his examination of the victim?"

"Told me she died of a bullet between the eyes." Burns grinned. "Which I already knew my ownself."

"Did his examination extend beyond that?"

Burns scowled. "I don't follow you."

"Did he examine the rest of her body?"

"Not that I know of. No reason he should have, and Doc never put himself out more than was necessary."

"He didn't file any kind of report with the sheriff's office?"

"Not that I know about. Doc was never much of a one for paper work."

Hurd paced, thinking. "Did *you* examine the victim more than just to ascertain that she was killed by a bullet?"

"I'm afraid I don't follow you, Judge."

"Well to phrase this as delicately as possible, did you by chance remove her clothing and examine her body?"

A gasp of shock raced through the courtroom, and Jake Burns looked horrified. "Take clothes off'n a dead woman? I wouldn't dream of doing such a thing!"

Garth jumped up, objecting, and Judge Underwood leaned forward with a frown. "Does seem you're skirting bad taste there, Counselor. Just what are you getting at?"

Hurd ran a hand over his hair distractedly. "Your Honor, if I may be allowed one more question of this witness, I will drop this whole line of questioning."

Judge Underwood looked dubious. "Well . . . all right, go ahead. But be careful, Counselor." He tapped the hammer. "Objection overruled."

"Mr. Burns, did you observe any scars or marks on the deceased that might have come from a beating, or a whipping?"

"Not on her face and hands," Burns said promptly. "And I didn't look anywheres else. Wouldn't have dreamed of lifting her skirts."

Hurd sighed and waved his hand, dismissing the witness. Back at the table, Serena whispered urgently. "What were you getting at, Judge?"

"It occurred to me . . . too late, unfortunately. But I thought that if Madeline's lover was this galoot in the gold Chinese mask, he might have used a whip on her, like he did on you, my dear."

"But why would he do that, even if it was the same man?"

"Serena, it should be obvious to you that this man is a sadist. You think you're the only woman he might have used a whip on in an . . . uh, situation like yours?"

Judge Underwood was speaking loudly and sarcastically, "If I may have your attention, Counselor?"

"I'm sorry, Your Honor. I was conferring with my client."

"Next time get permission from the bench for that. Now, call your next witness. Let's move along here."

Hurd stood. "I call Chu Chin to the stand."

The courtroom buzzed, a sound that turned into a swelling murmur of displeasure as Hurd went down the aisle between the benches and opened the door to let in two Chinese—Chu Chin and a middle-aged man.

The noise from the spectators increased in volume. The hammer pounded. "Order and quiet! If I don't have quiet and order in my courtroom, you gents will be sorry!" Gradually, the crowd quieted, and Judge Underwood scowled up at Hurd, who now stood before his desk with Chu Chin on one side and the Chinese male on the other. "Now just what is this, Counselor?"

"The woman, Chu Chin, is my next witness, Your Honor. Unfortunately, her English is not of the best, so I thought, with the court's indulgence, that it would facilitate matters if we used an interpreter. Mr. Ho, the owner of a Chinese laundry here in Virginia City, was happy to volunteer his services in that capacity . . ."

"Objection! Objection!"

"To what are you objecting, Prosecutor?" Judge Underwood demanded.

"Why . . . why, to this . . ." Garth spluttered, face reddening. "This woman is a Chink, Your Honor! Chinks can't even vote, so how can she testify in court?"

Hurd said dryly, "You've paraded a number of ladies on and off the witness stand, Mr. Garth. They cannot vote either."

"It's not the same thing. This woman is not a citizen of the United States!"

"What does that have to do with the woman testifying?" Judge Underwood seem honestly puzzled.

"I'll tell you what it has to do, Your Honor. Chinks, they're not even people!"

Judge Underwood rocked back and forth, then slammed the hammer down on his desk so hard splinters flew. "Now that will goddamned well be enough of *that,* Mister Prosecutor!" He waved the hammer. "Swear the witness in."

Confusion resulted when Jake Burns presented the Bible to Chu Chin and instructed her to place her right hand on it and swear to Almighty God to tell the truth and nothing but the truth. There was a rapid exchange of Chinese between Mr. Ho and Chu Chin. Finally Mr. Ho turned to Judge Underwood with an apologetic shrug and spoke in impeccable English, "I am sorry. Chu Chin does not understand the oath-taking process . . ."

"You see, Your Honor!" Robie Garth jumped up again. "Pagan, pagan pure and simple! Doesn't even recognize our Christian god!"

This time Judge Underwood didn't employ the hammer. He leaned forward and said in an icy voice, "Mr. Garth, I have warned you for the last time. One more such outburst from you and I will slap such a fine on you that it will send you to the poorhouse for the rest of your life!"

Good for you, Elmo, Hurd thought gleefully. The old boy has more sand and tolerance than I gave him credit for.

With a look of dismay on his face, Robie Garth dropped down into his seat.

Judge Underwood said, "Mr. Ho, ask the witness if she agrees to tell nothing but the truth on the stand, never mind the swearing in business."

Mr. Ho spoke rapidly to Chu Chin, who bobbed her head. "Chu Chin promises to tell the truth, sir."

"Good! She may take the stand then. You may question the witness, Counselor."

Hurd started questioning Chu Chin, beginning with the moment early on that long ago morning when she had found Madeline Dubois dead. It was a slow process, Mr. Ho repeating the questions in Chinese, then translating the answers into English.

Hurd led Chu Chin through the discovery of the body and then to the shack of Tang P'ing.

"Why did you go there, Chu Chin?"

Mr. Ho said, "Chu Chin say she knew that Tang P'ing was a friend of Miss Foster. Having overheard the women quarreling, Chu Chin was fearful of Miss Foster's welfare and thought Tang P'ing should know."

Chu Chin then told of Tang P'ing sending her son for Serena, Serena's arrival at the shack, and her shock on learning of the murder.

"What, if anything, did the . . . what did Serena Foster say when she learned the news?"

Before the question could be translated to the witness, the prosecutor was on his feet. "I object, Your Honor. Anything this . . . this woman might have heard the accused say is hearsay evidence, and as such is inadmissible."

Hurd was ready for him. "Your Honor, I have sat here in this courtroom and listened to the prosecution present witness after witness testifying as to what they *heard* Madeline Dubois and the defendant say on the night of the murder. I allowed Mr. Garth all the leeway possible and never objected once. Now I think the defense should be accorded the same privilege."

Judge Underwood chuckled. "Looks like you've done it again, Prosecutor. Trying to lock the barn door after it's too late." The hammer rapped. "Objection overruled. Counselor, proceed with your questioning."

Garth sat down with a thump, and Hurd permitted himself a grin of triumph in the prosecutor's direction.

He turned back to the witness chair. "First, Chu Chin, what was Miss Foster's reaction to the news of Madeline's death?"

"Chu Chin say she was stunned, in a state of shock. Miss Foster denied that she committed murder."

"Yet she fled Virginia City. Can you explain that?"

"Tang P'ing told her she would hang if she remained here. Tang P'ing said everyone would believe she killed the sporting house woman. Tang P'ing convinced Miss Foster to go. Miss Foster did not wish to leave Virginia City, but she finally agreed."

"In essence then, she left against . . . well, against her better judgment?"

"Chu Chin say yes."

Hurd rubbed his chin in thought. "Going back a little, Chu Chin . . . the night of the murder, you overheard the quarrel between Madeline Dubois and Serena Foster, did you not?"

"Chu Chin say yes."

"Did you see Serena Foster leave?"

Mr. Ho said, "Chu Chin say she was in the back of the hall and saw Miss Foster go."

"Fine. Now this is very important, Chu Chin, so think very carefully. Did you see Madeline Dubois *alive* after Serena Foster left?"

Mr. Ho said, "Chu Chin say she was finished with

her work for the night. She left the house immediately after Serena Foster. In so doing, she passed by the open sitting room door and saw the sporting house woman alive, sitting on the sofa."

Hurd thought hard, started to turn the witness over to Garth, then said, "One last question . . . as you left the house, did you see a man outside the house, anywhere about?"

"Chu Chin say she did not."

"Did you *ever* see a man slip into the house late, by the side door?"

"Chu Chin say she always leave the house earlier than Mr. Foxy. She have to come back to the house early in the morning. She say she never saw a man slip in, any time."

Hurd concealed his disappointment, and said, "Thank you, Chu Chin. You may cross-examine, Mr. Garth."

As Hurd sank down at the table, Serena whispered, "A plus for our side, Judge?"

"I think so, my dear." Hurd leaned back, feeling exhausted. "Godalmighty, I hope so! We can use all the pluses we can get."

Watching Robie Garth cross-examine Chu Chin, Hurd almost felt sorry for the man. He must be very frustrated. The language barrier was simply too much for an effective cross-examination. Every time he attacked Chu Chin on a crucial point, his momentum was lost by the time it took for Mr. Ho to repeat the question, then frame the answer in English.

Once, Garth lost his temper and stormed at Mr. Ho, accusing him of making up false answers to Chu Chin's responses. Mr. Ho smiled and smiled, remaining unruffled, and Judge Underwood remonstrated with the prosecutor.

Finally, Robie Garth threw up his hands in disgust and stalked back to the table.

As Chu Chin, escorted by Mr. Ho, passed by the table on her way out of the courtroom, Serena smiled at her gratefully. If she hadn't been on public view, Serena would have leaped up and embraced the woman.

The rest of Hurd's case consisted of character witnesses, and their number was meager. He had sent a wire to Darrel Quick in San Francisco. In a return wire, Darrel Quick had told him that he was much improved, but still was unable to travel.

In desperation Hurd placed Ma Taylor on the stand. The big woman was hostile, but Hurd did manage to win some points. He forced her to admit that Serena Foster had seemed a proper lady, and that her first impression had been favorable. She admitted that she had even grown fond of the girl, but all that changed when she learned from the newspaper article that Serena owned the Paradise, that house of sin!

"But to your knowledge, Mrs. Taylor, she never operated it, did she?"

Ma Taylor sniffed. "How would I know? It was then when I realized how sneaky she was!"

"Did she not swear to you that she had refused to have anything to do with the Paradise?"

"She must have, she killed that woman, didn't she?"

"Your Honor, I ask that the answer be disregarded by the jury as not being responsive."

"So ordered, Counselor."

"Mrs. Taylor, if the accused did operate the Paradise, why did she not live there, instead of residing in your boarding house?"

Ma Taylor groped for an answer. Finally, she said triumphantly, "Because she thought she'd hide it from decent folks!"

Hurd turned away, dismissing the witness. Robie Garth, with a smug grin, waived cross-examination, and Hurd wondered if he hadn't made a grave error in putting the woman on the stand at all. He concluded that it had done some good, hopefully more good than harm.

His last witness was Rory Clendenning. Clendenning had eagerly volunteered to testify, but Hurd was dubious, and he still wasn't sure it was wise. But he was down to grasping at straws, and young Clendenning was a straw.

Hurd made much of Clendenning being a preacher's son, come west to make his fortune. He established that Clendenning had arrived in Virginia City without money, had gone to work in the mines, and now was half-owner of a thriving freight business.

Then he had Clendenning tell of his being saved from death in the desert by the Foster family, and the subsequent chain of events, including the murder of Serena's parents. He was frequently interrupted by objections from the prosecutor, but Judge Underwood ruled in favor of the defense in most instances.

Finally Hurd said, "Now, Mr. Clendenning, would you give the jury your impression of the character of the defendant?"

"Your Honor, I must object again!"

Hurd said wearily, "Your Honor, Mr. Clendenning

451

is a character witness, and as such is entitled to testify as to the character of the defendant as he sees it."

"You may proceed, Counselor. Objection overruled."

"Mr. Clendenning?"

Clendenning leaned forward, his face lighting up, blue eyes warm and glowing. "Serena Foster is a fine woman, sir. She tended me out in the desert, and since that time I have never seen her behave like anything but the proper lady she is."

Serena, listening, gaze clinging to his face, felt her heart ache with love for him. It took all the force of her will to keep tears from welling into her eyes.

"May I ask you this, Mr. Clendenning . . . in your considered opinion, is Serena Foster capable of murder?"

"Absolutely not! She's incapable of harming a living soul!" Clendenning leaned forward. His hands were locked together in his lap. "I swore to Almighty God to tell the truth here. Now, as God is my witness, I would willingly, gladly, stake my life on this . . . Serena Foster could never bring herself to kill another person, no matter what the provocation!"

Bravo, young Clendenning, Hurd thought; bravo! Deciding to leave well enough alone, he turned the witness over to Garth and resumed his seat.

The first intimation he had that all was not well was when he noted the smirk on the prosecutor's face as Garth approached the witness. Tightening inside, Hurd leaned forward.

Garth took up a wide-footed stance, hands laced together behind his back, rocking slightly to and fro.

"I applaud your fervor in springing to the defense
452

of the accused, Mr. Clendenning. However, I wonder if there isn't more here than is apparent."

Clendenning eyed him warily. "I don't get your meaning, sir."

"You will, Mr. Clendenning, you will." Suddenly, Garth's voice thundered out. "Are you not this woman's lover, sir?"

Stunned, Serena tried to make herself small, shivering with shame. The room spun around her, and she feared that she would faint. Dear God, this was too much!

Clendenning had half-started from his chair. "What . . . ? How dare you!"

Garth turned, leveling a finger at Serena. "Do you deny, under oath, that you have been cohabiting with the accused?"

"How dare you?" Clendenning said again, in the grip of a great rage. "You are a scoundrel, sir, dirtying a lady's name in public!"

Garth pounced. "Ah, then it is true!"

Clendenning got all the way to his feet and advanced on the prosecutor, fists clenched.

Garth backed up, bleating, "Your Honor! Your Honor!"

The hammer pounded. "What's the meaning of this, young man? This is a court of law!"

Clendenning turned a dazed look on him. "Sir?"

"This is a court of law, not a saloon for brawling," Judge Underwood motioned with the hammer. "Now, resume your seat."

Hurd had watched in dismay, desperately wanting to object, but he knew it would be useless. He had opened the door for this. Now he got to his feet and was making calming motions with his hands behind Garth's back.

Clendenning saw the gesture and nodded. He returned to the witness chair.

The courtroom was in an uproar, and Judge Underwood was hammering for order. Under cover of the noise, Serena gripped Hurd's arm, and whispered, "Can't you do something, Judge?"

"There is nothing I can do, Serena. It's all up to young Clendenning now."

When order was restored, Garth said silkily, "Well, Mr. Clendenning?"

Lie, Clendenning, Hurd said to himself prayerfully; lie your head off.

He knew it was a futile hope, and Clendenning immediately proved him right.

Garth said, "Mr. Clendenning, you have not answered the question. Are you cohabiting with the accused?"

"No, sir, I have not answered the question," Clendenning said steadily. "And I have no intention of doing so."

"Your Honor, would you please instruct the witness to answer the question?"

"Young man, you must answer Prosecutor's question."

"I'm sorry, Your Honor." Clendenning swiveled his head to look at Judge Underwood. "I refuse to answer."

Judge Underwood's face flushed red. "Young man, if you refuse to answer, I have the power to fine you!"

Clendenning shrugged.

The hammer crashed down. "The witness is fined fifty dollars!"

Grinning, Garth said, "Now will you respond to my question, Mr. Clendenning?"

"No, sir, I will not."

Again the hammer slammed down. "The witness is fined one hundred dollars!"

Strutting with triumph now, Garth paced back and forth. "Since the prosecution has no desire to bankrupt you, sir, I will not repeat the question." He faced the jury. "I am sure that the answer is clear in the minds of the jurors, very clear." He wheeled back to the witness. "Mr. Clendenning, perhaps you will answer this . . . you have stated in this courtroom that you do not believe the accused capable of murder. Would it be a fair assumption that your . . . uh, relationship with Serena Foster clouds your judgment?"

"Relationship?" Clendenning was guarded. "By that, do you mean the fact that I know her well, that she is my friend?"

Garth shrugged. "If you wish to phrase it in those terms, yes."

"If she was a complete stranger to me, of course I could not make a judgment of her character. But the fact that I happen to know her well does not mean that it colors my judgment." In a firm voice, he added, "Nothing you, sir, or anyone, can say will change my mind. Serena Foster is totally incapable of murder!"

"Have you, Mr. Clendenning, ever known anyone, close friend or otherwise, who was a murderer? Or a murderess?"

"Of course not!"

"Then you are hardly an expert in judging an individual's homicidal tendencies, are you, Mr. Clendenning?" Garth turned aside, waving his hand in a contemptuous gesture. "No more questions of this witness, Your Honor."

Judge Underwood took out his pocket watch and scowled at it. "Since the hour is late, court is adjourned until two o'clock tomorrow afternoon." His glance went to the table. "In case you two gents are wondering, this here court has other business to attend to in the morning." The hammer rapped.

As the courtroom began to empty, Hurd said dully, "I knew in my bones that I shouldn't have put him, on the stand. It was the worst mistake of my life!"

Serena said timidly, "Judge . . ."

His head swiveled around, and he spoke to her in anger for the first time since she had known him. "And you, Serena Foster! I'm not sitting in judgment on your private life, but Godalmighty, why didn't you tell me Clendenning had been intimate with you?"

"I didn't think it was anybody's business but ours!" she snapped.

"When you're on trial for murder, girl, never keep *anything* from your attorney. I should have guessed, I suppose, but I've been busy trying to save you from hanging. If I had known about this, I would never in a hundred years have put him on the stand."

"I'm sorry, Judge. I should have told you, I see that now," she said in a small voice. "But I can't understand how anyone found out."

"Any one of a hundred people could have sniffed it out. You're the center of attention in this town right now. People watch your every move. Naturally, whoever found out, trotted right to Robie Garth with it."

"Do you suppose it was Kate Rogan? She knows about us."

"I don't know," Hurd said tiredly, the anger gone now. "What difference does it make? The damage is done. In the minds of that jury right now, you're capable of just about anything."

"Maybe if I testify in my own behalf, Judge?" she said hopefully. "You said in the beginning that it would depend on how the trial went."

He studied her thoughtfully. "I just don't know, Serena. It probably couldn't make matters any worse. Think you could stand up under Garth's grilling? He's all het up now, got the bit in his teeth. He's probably itching to get at you."

Serena set her chin. "I can stand up . . ."

"Judge?"

They looked up. The courtroom had emptied, except for Rory Clendenning, who stood across the table from them, looking miserable. "I messed things up, didn't I?"

"Let's put it this way, young Clendenning. You sure as hell didn't help," Hurd growled. "Why couldn't you have lied?"

Clendenning looked astonished. "It never once occurred to me. Lord God!" He was plunged into gloom. "I should have. I'd sworn to myself that I'd do anything to help Serena, and I couldn't even tell a lie."

"Well . . ." Hurd heaved a sigh. "A man's what he is. I don't suppose you can change just like that." He dug into his pocket for a cigar, lit it, inhaled, and leaned back with a sigh of pleasure.

"Rory, dear." Serena stretched across the table to take Clendenning's hand. "Don't worry about it. I wouldn't have wanted you to lie. And I'm proud of you."

"I see little reason for you to be proud of me," Clendenning said glumly. "Not after what just happened."

"All right, stop feeling sorry for yourself," Hurd said sharply. He dredged up a grin. "Like old Elmo is fond of saying, the horse is out now. And we're not finished yet." He waved his cigar. "By nature a lawyer is always optimistic. If he ain't, he's finished. Now let's get the hell out of here and have a snort. I sure by God could use one!"

Brad Stryker had quietly left the courtroom following the testimony of the Chink bitch. It was his first visit to the courtroom. He hadn't wanted to make himself conspicuous by appearing at the trial. But word had gotten to him that the former Chinese cleaning woman at the Paradise was going to testify, and Stryker was curious as to what she had to say. He had sent one of his men to the courtroom early that morning to find and hold a seat for him in the back row. Then he had mingled with the other loiterers outside, those unfortunates unable to get seats, and watched until Spencer Hurd had come out to escort the Chinese pair inside. Then Stryker had slipped inside to take the seat occupied all morning by his employee and listened to Chu Chin's testimony in mounting fury.

Walking up the street after leaving the courtroom, Stryker drummed the quirt against his thigh. Was he always going to have trouble with Chinks? In his opinion, they were all vermin and should be eliminated wholesale. If he only had this Chu Chin alone somewhere, he would see to it that she never raised her slanty eyes again in the presence of white people. Come to think of it, she wasn't a bad-looking female, for a Chink.

Stryker forced his thoughts in another direction. Since this had all happened, he had been careful what women he had seen. As much satisfaction as he received from tying a young Chinese beauty down and whipping her into near unconsciousness, before throwing himself on her in lust, he had refrained. The situation was too touchy to take any unnecessary chances.

Stryker was concerned about something else. Lester Tompkins had reported faithfully to him every day after court adjourned, repeating almost verbatim the testimony given in the courtroom. Stryker was worried about Foxy Parks. Did the gimpy old bastard know more than he was telling? It would seem that Foxy would have told everything he knew on the witness stand. Yet an old man's memory was tricky. Stryker knew that oftentimes something popped back into their minds that they had completely forgotten. What if that happened with Foxy Parks? What if, during Stryker's secret trips to visit Madeline, he had been briefly seen by Foxy, and Foxy eventually remembered? Stryker had never spoken directly to the man, so there was not much chance Foxy could identify him by voice alone.

But the risk was there, however small. Striding along, he worried at it, like a dog gnawing a bone.

There was no moon this week. The nights were dark, and it would be easy to sneak up to the Paradise, isolated as it was. Although he had seldom used it, Stryker still had a key to the side door, the door into the sitting room. Two nights ago, unable to sleep, he had been compulsively driven to scout the Paradise and had noted the presence of a guard who came out of the house once an hour to circle the premises. As far as Stryker could ascertain, there was only the one man, and it shouldn't be too difficult to sneak up on him in the dark, and put him out of commission.

He walked on down C Street, his mind a battleground of conflicting thoughts. It worried him that, more and more of late, he had trouble making a firm decision about anything. At one time, he could make up his mind to a course of action and act on it at once, never doubting the end result.

Stryker was heading toward his office and the stables, where he spent much of his time these days, even sleeping there. He had been to his hotel room rarely since the trial of Serena Foster began.

"Rory, I'm scared," Serena said.

Clendenning tightened his arm around her shoulders. "What are you frightened about, darling?"

"The Judge might put me on the witness stand tomorrow." She raised her head from the cradle of his shoulder to look into his face. It was after ten, and they were in bed in the downstairs bedroom, with a lamp burning, the wick turned low. "He said that if I did take the stand Mr. Garth would hammer at me. I told him I could stand up to it, but now I don't know. If I fall apart under Garth's cross-examination,

460

the jury is sure to find me guilty . . . not that they probably won't anyway."

"I don't think you should be alarmed about Garth, Serena. You have more spirit than any woman I know. All you have to do is tell the truth. Just like I did." His mouth had a bitter twist. "Only in your case, it will be the right thing to do. Me, I didn't have the guts, or the good sense to lie."

"Rory, stop scourging yourself. I respect you much more for *not* lying. You . . . well, I'm ashamed of myself, to tell the truth. For just a minute, I felt shame, our love being publicly exposed like that. Then I knew I was wrong. I felt pride, and I *am* proud of you." She kissed him tenderly, then looked off, frowning. "I'm still puzzled as to who found out about us."

"It could have been anybody."

"That's what the Judge said, but I wonder. Do you suppose it could have been Kate?"

"Kate? But why?"

"She loves you, Rory. Oh, I know, you told me she didn't, that she *said* she didn't. But I could tell. She might have told Mr. Garth out of jealousy."

Clendenning was shaking his head. "Not Kate. She's not like that."

"Jealousy is a monster, and can make us do strange things, Rory. But let's not talk about that any more. You're here, and for the moment I'm safe and warm in your arms. Love me, darling!"

He raised up to kiss her, his mouth tender and warm and sweet. Mouth still locked to hers, his hands roved over her body under the sheet. They had been together every night now since the day after Christmas, and he had become familiar with her body. He knew the places to stroke, to kiss, to arouse her.

For a time Serena lay passive, eyes closed, enjoying the closeness and warmth, and the slow building of her passion.

She cupped his face between her hands and murmured, "I love you with all my heart, Rory Clendenning."

"Yes, yes," he said almost harshly. "I love you too, Serena."

Further conversation was cut off as Serena's passion took command of her. She moaned, her body writhing. She clutched his head to hers, breathing nonsense words into his ear. She let her hands drift down, fluttering with the gentleness of a butterfly's wings, down across his back. She locked her hands together in the small of his back and urged him to her.

They joined, and Serena was swept up in a tide of love and pleasure. Clendenning prolonged it, his thrustings slow and measured, until Serena was nearly mindless with ecstasy.

They climaxed as one, and for Serena the feeling was so intense as to be almost painful. She bit down on her lips to keep from crying out.

As they lay together in drowsy aftermath, Clendenning said, "I want you to marry me, Serena. I want you for my wife."

"I want that, too, Rory. But this is not the time to talk of that. Not until we know what the future holds. Not until after the trial."

"No!" he said sharply. "I want us to get married now, before the trial is over. I want everyone in Virginia City to know what I think of you, to fully realize how much I treasure you."

462

"It's sweet of you, darling, but no. I love you, and I want to marry you, eventually. But don't you see? If we get married now, and even if I do go free, I'll always wonder, in a tiny part of my mind, if you weren't just being gallant."

His face took on a wounded look.

"Now, don't look hurt," she scolded. "Think about it, you'll see I'm right. Go to sleep. You told me you had to get to work early tomorrow, with the weather turning so nice." She kissed him on the lips. "So turn out the lamp, and let's go to sleep."

Brad Stryker stood in a small grove of trees about fifty yards south of the Paradise. He was in black clothing and had a pistol stuck in his belt. In his hand he carried the gold Chinese mask.

From where Stryker stood he could see the front and one side of the house. There were two lights burning—one in the kitchen, and one in the bedroom in the back, the room where he had often gone with Madeline. How many times had he lashed her thighs until the blood streamed down her legs? And never a whimper from her. That had always surprised him a little. Most women cried and begged for him to stop. But not Madeline. She had always let him have his way, her eyes bright, lips open and moist, and always welcomed him in the heat of passion when he was ready.

In a moment the light in the bedroom went out. Stryker tensed as he saw the front door open and the bulk of the guard emerge. Stryker had watched enough times to know the man always followed the same routine—once all the way around the house and back inside.

Stryker waited until the man turned the corner, then donned the gold mask and raced, bent over, toward the house. Once there, he sidled down to the corner, flattening himself against the wall, and waited. When he heard the heavy footsteps of the guard approaching, Stryker raised the pistol by the barrel and held his breath.

Unsuspecting, humming softly, the guard rounded the corner. Stryker sprang at him, bringing the pistol butt down. It connected solidly. The guard grunted sharply, his knees buckling, and he sprawled unconscious on the ground.

Stryker scurried down the house to the side door of the sitting room. Holding the pistol in one hand, he fumbled the key out of his pocket with the other. In the dark it took him three tries to fit the key into the lock.

He turned it, pushing the door open, and slipped inside. It was dark as a cave in the parlor, even with the door open behind him. Stryker stood very still, trying to remember where the door was located. And where was Foxy? It just now occurred to Stryker that he had no idea whether Foxy slept upstairs or on the ground floor. In fact, he wasn't even sure the gimp slept in the house at all.

He muttered a curse and started across the room, placing one foot carefully before the other. He felt a sense of satisfaction when his hand closed over the doorknob. Easing it open, he stuck his head out. His glance went down the hall to Madeline's old bedroom. The light in there was still out, he noted. He smiled to himself. Maybe after he had taken care of the gimp, he would drop in to visit Miss Foster. Finish it all off in one night. He wished he had thought to bring the quirt with him . . .

He thrust the thought from his mind, for now, and looked the other way. A faint spill of light came from the direction of the kitchen. Stryker started down the hall, walking quietly.

At the open kitchen doorway, he peered in cautiously. Foxy Parks was asleep in a chair tipped back against the wall, mouth open and snoring.

Pistol in hand, Stryker started toward him. He was not that good a shot; he had to get closer. Halfway across the room, a board creaked loudly under his feet. He froze.

Foxy's eyes flew open, and the chair hit the floor with a thump. His eyes flared wide in recognition of danger, and he reached for the pistol lying on the chopping block beside him.

Stryker brought his gun up fast and fired. Foxy fell from the chair onto the floor.

The sound of the gunshot brought Clendenning wide awake. He sat up in bed. "Lord God, what was that?"

He was already out of bed and scrambling into his trousers. On the bed behind him, Serena was sitting up. "Rory, what is it? What's wrong?"

Without answering her, he hurried to the door, barefoot, wearing only his trousers. There was no weapon in the room. Why hadn't he thought to bring along the shotgun? Without hesitation he threw the door open. Behind him, Serena lit the lamp, and Clendenning stood framed in the glow of light.

Looking down the hall, he saw a man in dark clothing, wearing some kind of a mask, running toward him. The masked figure skidded to a halt, raised a hand holding a pistol, and snapped off a shot. The bullet thunked into the door jamb beside Clendenning.

Then the masked man ducked into the sitting room. Without thought of personal danger, Clendenning started at a dead run down the hall. Behind him, Serena called out. He ran on.

Clendenning plunged into the sitting room, remembering at the last moment to duck to one side. No bullet came at him. Across the room he saw the side door standing wide. As he reached it, he glimpsed a figure running toward the grove of trees at the edge of the clearing.

Clendenning jumped down to the ground and started after the fleeing man. The cold, rock-strewn ground hurt his bare feet, and after a few steps he slowed. It was not only useless to pursue the man, barefoot and wearing only his trousers, but foolhardy without a weapon of any kind.

He stood a moment, listening. He heard the faint sounds of a body crashing through the underbrush. Then the sounds faded and were gone. Discouraged, Clendenning turned back toward the house. He stopped as he heard a sound like a groan alongside the house. He followed the sound and almost stumbled over the prone figure of the guard. The man was stirring.

Clendenning dropped to one knee. "Carl, are you all right?"

"I . . . I think so. Is that you, Mr. Clendenning?"

"Yes." Clendenning helped the man to sit up. "Can you tell me what happened?"

"A man jumped out at me in the dark, clobbered me over the head . . . ouch!" Carl was feeling the back of his head. "That hurts like hell. A bump the size of an egg."

"I don't suppose you have any idea who it was?"

"No way I could. It was dark, and it all happened too fast."

Clendenning shivered. The wind splashed at his bare chest and shoulders like a dousing of ice water. "Let's get you inside where it's warm."

He helped Carl up and supported him down the side of the house and into the sitting room. Clendenning closed the door. Carl moved away from him.

"I can make it fine now. Still rocky, but I'm coming around."

In the hall Clendenning heard Serena's voice coming from the kitchen. The two men headed that way.

Foxy was stretched out on the floor, but he was conscious. Serena was in the process of tearing his shirt away from his right shoulder. There was a bloody bullet wound high on the shoulder.

Serena turned up a tearful face. "He needs a doctor, Rory."

"In a minute." Clendenning dropped to his knee. "Can you tell us what happened, Foxy?"

"I was dozing here, in the chair. I heard a sound and woke up. There was this booger halfway across the room. He snapped off one shot. Lousy shot, he was." Foxy twisted his head to look at the wound.

"I don't suppose you recognized him?"

"Naw. He was wearing some kind of a mask."

Clendenning and Serena exchanged glances. Clendenning said, "A gold Chinese mask?"

"Don't know about that. All I know is that he had his face hidden." Foxy closed his eyes.

"Foxy, I'll go for a doctor in a moment, but I don't think you have much to worry about. It's only a flesh wound. Dig the bullet out, and you'll be as right as rain." Clendenning got to his feet, hauling Serena up with him. "You know what this means, don't you, Serena? This intruder, the man in the mask, not only killed your folks, but Madeline as well. The side door was locked, but he came in that way, so he had to have a key, a key Madeline must have given him."

"But why . . . ?" Serena pushed her fingers through her hair. "I can see why he might have come here to kill me, but why Foxy?"

Clendenning hesitated for a moment, staring down at Foxy, who had slumped into unconsciousness. He said slowly, "I think it has to do with Foxy's testimony. This man is afraid Foxy might eventually identify him as Madeline's lover." He motioned. "I have to throw on some clothes and find a doctor for Foxy. Carl . . ." He turned. The guard was swabbing his head with a wet towel. "Are you all right enough to watch things here while I go for a doctor? He can take care of your head, too. I doubt very much this man will venture back tonight, but just in case . . ."

"Sure, I'll be all right, Mr. Clendenning. And don't worry." Carl closed his hand around the butt of his holstered pistol. "He won't slip up on me so easily the next time."

"Fine." Clendenning leaned down to kiss Serena. "I won't be gone long, darling. Have you got a key to lock that side door?"

"Yes, there's a key. The only one, I *thought*."

"Then lock it," Clendenning said grimly. "And stay here in the kitchen with Carl until I get back."

In the midmorning, wrapped in the fur-trimmed cloak the Judge had given her, Serena went downtown to do some shopping. Since court didn't reconvene until that afternoon, she had the morning free. Foxy was resting in one of the bedrooms upstairs, and the doctor had said he would be fine after a few days in bed. But there was little food in the house. Clendenning, having neglected his business during the trial, had taken the ore wagon down the canyon this morning.

"I have to take advantage of this brief spell of good weather," he had told her. "Now, you stay in the house, Serena. I don't think he will risk anything in the daytime, but stay inside with the doors locked. Don't take any chances."

By the middle of the morning, Serena felt she couldn't remain inside any longer. She had to get out. Surely she would be safe from harm in daylight, and amid the throngs of people along C Street.

The weather was nice. The snow from the Christmas storm had melted, except for the shady spots. The long icicles melting from the eaves of the shops and the chill bite of the wind were the only reminders of winter.

Serena strolled along C Street, looking in the shop windows, enjoying the brief respite from the trial's tension, the feeling of freedom, however short it might be.

Serena tried to push thoughts of the trial and her

possible conviction out of her mind, yet it remained in one small corner, a constant, nagging reminder.

Several blocks farther, she noticed a crowd of people on the wooden sidewalk in front of her, blocking her way. Serena's first thought was to cross over to the other side of the street. Then curiosity got the better of her, and she squirmed her way through until she could see what was attracting all the attention. Some of the men were grinning in obvious enjoyment.

Finally she got close enough to see. Her first reaction was anger and revulsion. A Chinese male was on his knees on the sidewalk. Over him towered a large, bulky man, his back to Serena. The big man had a quirt in his hand, and he was flailing away at the Chinese with the quirt, whipping at his head and shoulders. The Chinese was vainly trying to protect his face with his hands, and bloody welts were appearing on the backs of his hands.

Serena started to move in closer, to register a protest. Then she froze, her attention captured by the way the man with the quirt hunched his broad shoulders as he brought the quirt down. There was something hauntingly familiar about him. What was it?

Now he turned slightly, until he was sideways to Serena, his face still hidden. The quirt rose and fell, rose and fell again, whistling viciously as it slashed the air.

Serena went cold with dread. She knew, knew beyond any doubt. The big man was the one who had whipped her in Li Po's house!

Abruptly, he stopped lashing at the man on the sidewalk, leaned down to whisper something, and then stepped back. He turned, looking around, his

470

face red from exertion. He seemed surprised that he had an audience. His glance seemed to linger on Serena, and she cowered back, afraid that he would recognize her. He turned then and strode up the street, strutting, striking his thigh with the quirt.

Before he had turned his back, Serena recognized him, and terror struck at her, as cold and frightening as though one of the long icicles on the overhead eaves had been driven into her heart.

The man with the quirt was Brad Stryker.

Chapter Twenty-three

Stryker had slept very little the night before. Following the raid on the Paradise and his narrow escape, he had made his way to his freight office via the back streets, pausing frequently to see if he was being followed. At the office he had sat up for the rest of the night, finishing off almost a full bottle of whiskey.

He had not expected to find Clendenning in the Paradise, and the sight of the tall, broad-shouldered man looming in the bedroom doorway had shaken him to the roots. Snapping off one shot at him, and knowing he had missed, Stryker had fled, grateful that he had gotten away unscathed.

But at least—until this morning—he had been sure that he had snuffed out the gimp. After polishing off the bottle, he had dozed in his desk chair, awakening when the first wain drivers began showing up for work before sunrise.

Then, the gold mask wrapped in a burlap bag, he

had slipped away to his hotel room for the first time in days. The room was musty, and a film of dust lay over everything. Ignoring the room's condition, he quickly stowed the mask in the locked chest; he was leery of leaving it around the stables, even in his office, for fear that someone might stumble onto it.

He fetched a pan of hot water, removed his clothes, and washed himself, then shaved the night's stubble of beard from his face. He put on a fresh suit, as the clothes he had worn last night were torn and filthy from his flight through the underbrush. From the chest he took a quirt from the growing collection he kept there, shoved the chest under the bed, and left the room, locking the door after him. The hotel management had orders to enter his room under no circumstances. When the dust got too thick, Stryker let a cleaning woman come in, but he remained there the whole time, watching her.

Outside the hotel, suddenly realizing that he was hungry, Stryker went into the first restaurant he came to and consumed a huge breakfast of steak and eggs.

Finished, he sat for a few minutes, elbows on the table, picking his teeth with a match. Two men were eating at the next table. Idly he listened to their conversation. The food he had just eaten suddenly turned into a sour ball in his belly.

Foxy Parks was not dead. The word was out all over town about the intruder in the Paradise who had shot Foxy. Foxy's wound was superficial, and he would recover just fine.

Such was Stryker's fury that a red curtain seemed to descend before his eyes. He plunged from the restaurant without even paying for his breakfast. Outside, he strode along, pushing people out of his way, blind to everything but the rage consuming him. He swished the quirt against his thigh, ignoring the bite of pain.

None of the faces he passed registered on his consciousness, then suddenly a face jumped out at him. Leaning against a building stood a man he recognized. The Chink named Ho! Who said one Chink looked the same as another, Stryker thought with savage glee. This one he would recognize anywhere.

Without even breaking stride, Stryker swung to his right, seized the smaller man by the shoulder, and forced him to his knees on the sidewalk. The face of Mr. Ho showed a brief flash of fear, then went blank. Viciously Stryker brought the quirt down across that round, sallow face. A zigag streak of blood appeared. Mr. Ho raised his hands to cover his face. Stryker continued to lash at him, across the head and shoulders, and the backs of the protecting hands.

He kept on until his arm ached with weariness. Then, his anger spent, he stopped. He leaned down to hiss, "That'll teach you, you Chink bastard, to stand up before white men and tell lies."

Stryker turned about, and felt astonishment at the crowd gathered around. He had not been aware of anyone watching. His glance moved in bold challenge around the circle of faces. Many of them were grinning. Those who had looked disapproving dropped their eyes as his stare swept over them and turned away. His gaze paused briefly on a few familiar faces.

Then Brad Stryker walked on down the street, his step arrogant, triumpant, the quirt swishing against his leg, gently now.

The crowd dispersed once Stryker started off, and Serena also started to move away. Then she hesitated, turned back, and approached Mr. Ho, who was still on his knees, his hands over his face.

"Mr. Ho," she said gently. "It's all over."

He blinked up at her. "Miss Foster."

She helped him to his feet. "Should I get a doctor for you?"

"No, no doctor." He smiled painfully. "American doctors are reluctant to help my people. If you would help me into my place of business, please."

For the first time Serena noticed that they were standing before a Chinese laundry. Mr. Ho leaning on her, they made their way toward the door. A tiny Chinese woman darted out. She gave a cry of distress when she saw Mr. Ho's face.

Mr. Ho tried to stand erect, tried to smile at Serena. "I will be all right now, Miss Foster. My wife will tend me. I thank you for your kindness."

"Mr. Ho, I am terribly sorry about this. That awful man!" She hardened her voice. "I promise you this . . . he will pay for this dreadful thing!"

"It is all right. My people are accustomed to it. We have learned to survive. Again, my appreciation for your solicitude."

Using his wife for support, Mr. Ho went into the laundry.

Serena stood for a moment, torn by indecision. What now? She knew instinctively that it would do no good to turn to the law. What could she tell them? That she had a feeling that Brad Stryker had killed her parents and Madeline Dubois, and tried to kill her? She could visualize herself trying to convince Jake Burns, for instance. He would laugh at her.

476

Should she go to Spencer Hurd then? But what could he do? She had no proof to offer, and certainly the Judge was no match for Stryker physically.

There was only one person left—Rory Clendenning. Serena realized that she had been seeking some other way for two reasons. First, in his righteous wrath, Rory might kill Stryker outright, and if he did that, Serena would be no better off than she was now. Second, if Rory faced down Stryker he might be killed. Or if the reverse happened and he killed Stryker, he might well face a murder charge himself.

For a mad moment, Serena considered confronting Stryker personally with her knowledge of his guilt. Common sense prevailed. To do such a thing would be foolhardy in the extreme.

Already she was hurrying up C Street toward the location of the Clendenning-Rogan Freight Line. As she turned down the side street and saw the small, neat house of Kate Rogan, Serena's step slowed, remembering. Rory wouldn't be here; he was taking a load of ore down the canyon this morning.

There was the house of Kate Rogan, the house Serena had never entered, the house where Rory had shared a bed with another woman for over a year. If she walked up to that house now and knocked for admittance, the red-haired Kate would be the one to admit her. Or turn her away without listening.

With a toss of her head, Serena marched up the walk and knocked on the door. She had to knock loud and long before the door opened. Kate Rogan, attired in a man's shirt and trousers, looked at Serena with raised eyebrows.

"It's so seldom anyone comes to the front door I

wasn't sure I heard a knock . . ." She broke off, stepping back. "I'm sorry, come in, Serena."

Serena said, "I wanted to see Rory."

"Clendenning took a wagon down the hill early this morning. Serena . . ." Kate peered at her closely. "You look upset as the devil. What is it? Come on back to the kitchen. I was just about to have a cup of coffee. Join me and tell me what's troubling you."

In the spotless kitchen, warm from the range, they sat across from each other at the table, sipping coffee, while Serena told of recognizing Stryker as the killer they'd been seeking.

"Brad Stryker! We should have known. He's always been rotten to core but this . . . !" Kate struck the table with her hand. "You still don't know what's behind it?"

Serena shook her head. "That's still the mystery."

"And you have nothing to go to the law with, right? Well, Clendenning will handle Mr. Brad Stryker." She smiled. "Clendenning has become quite a man. As I'm sure you know . . . oh, I'm sorry, honey." She reached across to pat Serena's hand. "I didn't mean anything snide by that."

"I know," Serena murmured. And she did know. Watching Kate, her chin propped on one hand in frowning thought, Serena was ashamed of her suspicions of this warm, kind woman. She was sure now that Kate hadn't gone to Garth with the tale of her and Rory being lovers. Serena knew that this woman had never harbored a vicious thought in her life.

Kate slapped the table again with her hand. "The best way to handle this is for me to saddle up and ride down the canyon. Clendenning should be empty and on his way back by this time. He can take the horse, and I'll drive the wagon back."

"I'll go with you."

"No, Serena. It's better you stay right here. You're safer here, out of Brad Stryker's way, and I can make much better time alone. It's nearly noon. There's a pot of stew rewarming from my last night's supper. You have something to eat . . ."

"Noon! I just remembered, Kate. I have to be in court this afternoon. I'd better go see Judge Hurd . . ."

"No, you stay right here, honey!" Kate said sharply. "I'll send Ned, our hostler, to see the Judge. He can tell him something's come up and you will be delayed. Ned's the only man around. All the others are driving today."

Kate got to her feet, hesitated, then came around the table. "Serena, I want you to know something . . . if Clendenning had to find another woman, I'd rather it be you than anyone I know. I wish the pair of you nothing but the best."

Impulsively, Serena stood up and hugged the other woman. She whispered, "Thank you, Kate. You're a nice person."

"Sure, I am, honey," Kate said in a choked voice. "Maybe after this is all over, we can be friends, huh? The crazy hay barn lady and you?" She laughed suddenly, a rich, full laugh.

Serena said, "I'd like that, Kate."

"Me too, honey. Hell, yes. Be back soon." With a wave Kate was gone, out the side door. In a few minutes Serena heard hoofbeats and looked out the kitchen window in time to see Kate riding away on a big chestnut horse at full gallop.

Serena returned to the table and finished her

479

coffee. The smell of the simmering stew made her realize that she was hungry. She filled a bowl, found a loaf of fresh-baked bread, poured another mug of coffee, and sat down to eat.

Her mood was more cheerful than it had been since the trial began. It was quite possible that all the mystery would be cleared up before the day's end, Brad Stryker in jail, and she would be a free woman again.

Serena's thoughts moved ahead, and she daydreamed of a rosy future as Rory's wife. She sat at the table, in a state of euphoria, long after she had finished eating.

Abruptly, she was startled by the sound of horses and a wagon outside. Could Kate be back with the ore wagon this quickly? Serena hurried to the window. To her surprise, a huge ore wagon was drawn up beside the house, blocking her view of anything else.

Then she heard footsteps on the porch. Heavy, a man's footsteps. It must be Rory!

Serena ran toward the door. Just before she reached it, the door opened, and Brad Stryker stepped into the room.

Frozen in a moment of terror, she stared at his evilly grinning face. Stryker sneered. "Recognized me, didn't you, bitch? I saw that look on your face. Now I'm going to finish off the job I started a long time ago."

Serena's paralysis broke then. With a scream, she whirled and started to run from the room. Stryker was on her in two giant steps and caught her shoulder in a crushing grip. He jerked her against him, laughing. "Go ahead and scream. Nobody around to hear you. I watched and waited until everybody left."

Deftly, he twisted her arms behind her back and

lashed them together. All the while Serena, made almost senseless by her terror, was kicking, thrashing, screaming—all wasted effort. Now Stryker wrapped a huge handkerchief around her mouth and tied it behind her head.

"Can't have the bitch screaming along the streets. She might attract undue attention."

What chilled Serena the most was the manner in which he talked now, as though she couldn't hear, as though he was discussing her with a third person.

Stryker picked her up like he would a log of wood, one arm around her chest, and lugged her outside. Handling her as easily as he would a doll, Stryker climbed up atop the high wagon wheel, hoisted her over the sideboard, and let her fall.

It was a long drop, and Serena hit with enough force to drive the breath from her lungs. To make it even worse, the wagon bed was strewn with a number of small rocks, which bit sharply into her flesh. The pain was excruciating, and for a few minutes she knew nothing. When she was next aware, the ore wagon was in motion.

Stryker drove along the side streets toward his stable, head down, hat tipped over his eyes, as though dozing on the wagon seat. At the stable, he drove the wagon right inside, then hopped down and closed the double doors. The stable was empty. He had given the stablehands the afternoon off. Now he could do what he pleased with Serena Foster and nobody would be the wiser. After dark, he would dispose of her body at his leisure.

He lowered the towering tailgate. Serena twisted around to glare at him, her eyes murderous with hate.

481

Stryker laughed, reached in to clamp a hand around her ankle, and dragged her out. Catching her again under his arm, he carried her to an empty mule stall, and dropped her face down. He took the thonged quirt from his belt loop. Serena tried desperately to turn over.

Stryker hooked a boot under her side and flipped her over onto her back. He gloated down at her, stroking his left palm gently with the quirt.

"Remember the night at Li Po's, Serena?" The hate in her eyes turned to fear. "Ah, I see that you do." Stryker laughed again, a grating sound. "Well, that night was nothing compared to what's in store for you now. I should have killed you then. You have caused me a peck of trouble, Serena Foster. Before I'm through with you this time, you'll be begging me to kill you!"

He stooped to seize the hem of her dress and drew it, and her petticoats, up above her waist. He stared hotly at her smooth, white thighs, exposed and vulnerable above her stockings. Serena tried to fling herself over onto her back. Almost casually, Stryker placed his booted foot on one thigh, pinning her to the ground.

A moan of pain came from Serena, filtering through the gag, and she closed her eyes.

Stryker stood staring down at her, prolonging the delicious moment, the quirt swishing against his palm. Then he drew his arm back, and brought the quirt whistling down . . .

Rory Clendenning pulled the lathered chestnut to a stop at the side street leading to Kate's house. Kate had told him that Serena was there. Clendenning yearned to see her, to reassure her, but on second thought he decided it would be best if he faced Brad Stryker first and got it over with. He had no weapon with him. Kate had wanted him to take along the shotgun.

Clendenning had refused. "You may need it, Kate. And I have no intention of using a gun on Mr. Stryker. I want at him with my bare hands!"

He kneed the chestnut into a canter, riding on down C Street. He could make better time using the side streets, but he wanted to check Stryker's hotel room out first, just to make sure he wasn't there. Impatiently he weaved the chestnut in and out of the heavy traffic until he was abreast of Stryker's hotel. There, he dismounted, tied the chestnut to the hitching rail, and hurried into the hotel and up to the second floor. He had made it a point long since to learn Brad Stryker's room number.

At the door he knocked hard, calling out, "Stryker! Are you in there? Open up!"

There was no sound from inside. He tried the doorknob. As expected, it was locked. He hesitated for a moment. Something nudged at his mind, a hunch that he should search the room.

Clendenning backed up a couple of feet, raised his right foot and slammed it hard against the door just below the knob. It took him three tries before the door splintered, flying open. Clendenning charged in. The small, dusty room was empty.

Again he hesitated, about to leave, but the hunch was stronger than ever. Quickly he began a search of the room. His heartbeat quickened when he discovered a locked chest under the high bed. It didn't take him to long to break open the chest.

Clendenning drew in his breath sharply at the contents of chest. First, there was a collection of a half-dozen whips and quirts, but most important of all was a wooden strongbox. He picked it up and examined it closely. He saw the initials H.F. burned into the lid, and Clendenning knew this was the one Serena had been looking for. It was also locked. He pondered for a moment. It belonged to Serena, it was her private property, yet the circumstances demanded that he open it. There was no key, and he had to use the blade of his pocket knife to pry it open. The blade broke in half as he pried, but the remaining stub was strong enough to snap the lid.

In the strongbox were two objects. One was a legal-looking document containing several pages. Clendenning gave it only a cursory glance before unfolding the other item. It was a letter, a single sheet of paper, addressed to Hiram Foster. Clendenning scanned it quickly.

Also in the chest was a burlap bag. Clendenning ran his hand inside the sack. He pulled out a gold Chinese mask. Heart pounding, he stared at it. There was no doubt. He had seen it clearly only once, but this was the mask worn by the leader of the band that had slaughtered the elder Fosters!

The two documents, plus the Chinese mask, were enough to hang Brad Stryker!

He replaced the mask in the sack, tucked both the sack and the strongbox under his arm, and hurried back outside. He mounted the chestnut and made it to Stryker's building as quickly as he could. There was a strangely deserted look about the place.

Clendenning went into the office section first. No doors were locked, and Stryker wasn't in his office. Clendenning went back outside and stood on the steps looking around. Where could the man be in the middle of a business day?

His glance lit on the double doors of the stable. Strange that they should be closed in the daytime. He bounded down the steps and to the stable doors. He pulled them open, and stood blinking at the sudden change from bright sunlight to dimness. There was an ore wagon parked in the lane between the mule stalls. Clendenning thought it an odd place for an ore wagon.

Then he heard a noise from a stall down the line; it sounded like a muffled scream. Puzzled, he started that way, calling out, "Stryker? Brad Stryker, are you in here?"

Before he could reach the stall, a man emerged. It was Brad Stryker. There was a short quirt in his hand. He turned, his eyes widening at the sight of Clendenning. He tossed the quirt back over his shoulder into the stall.

"Well, if it ain't Mister Clendenning!" His full lips peeled back in a snarl. "What are you doing here? If you don't have any business with me, get the hell out!"

"Oh, I have business here," Clendenning said softly. From the burlap bag he pulled the Chinese mask and tossed it onto the ground. It landed face up and seemed to leer obscenely. "I believe that belongs to you, Stryker."

Stryker went pale, his gaze fastened on the mask.

"And this . . ." Clendenning held out the strongbox. "This doesn't belong to you, but . . ."

485

"You've been sneaking about in my room!" Stryker bellowed, and made a lunge for the strongbox.

Clendenning stepped nimbly aside. "I have indeed, and the things I found there are enough to hang you for murder . . ."

His head swung around as he heard a moan from the stall Stryker had backed out of a moment ago. Clendenning stepped quickly to the stall opening. Serena lay on her back on a pile of straw, her hands behind her, a handkerchief over her mouth, skirts pushed up around her waist. "Serena, what are you . . . ?"

Then he noticed the streaks of blood on her thighs. His gaze jumped to the quirt where Stryker had tossed it. The thongs were stained with red.

As he realized what had been happening, Clendenning's rage was almost too much. He took a step toward Serena.

There was a whistling sound, then pain raced down his back like a streak of fire. He whirled about, dropping the strongbox. Stryker stood a few feet away, grinning savagely. He had snatched a bullwhip from where a number of them hung on the wall on pegs.

"Now I'm going to cut you to bloody ribbons, Clendenning," Stryker said. "You'll never tell what you know!"

A cold, killing fury gripped Clendenning, and he said through gritted teeth, "You'll have to kill me, Stryker, or I'll kill you for what you've done to Serena!"

Stryker drew his arm back, and the whip snapped at Clendenning like a striking snake. Clendenning ducked, but not before the whip had cut into his flesh again, this time alongside the neck.

Before Stryker could draw the bullwhip back again, Clendenning darted past him to the line of pegs and jerked down a bullwhip for himself. The heavy butt of the whip gripped in his hand, he danced back, avoiding yet another slash of Stryker's whip. With a sideways motion, he sent his whip curling through the air. It struck Stryker in the side, drawing a yowl of pain.

"So it's going to be that way, is it?" Stryker said. There was a loose set to his grinning mouth, and his eyes had a glazed look. "I was handling these things when you were still wearing baby dresses, kid. Killed a man once with one. Now I'm going to kill you!"

Without warning, the bullwhip snaked out and slashed Clendenning's trousers open at the thigh. During the next few minutes, Clendenning discovered that Stryker's threat was no idle boast. He was better with a bullwhip than it seemed possible for any man to be. While Clendenning had to draw the whip back and over his shoulder before he could snap it forward, Stryker could pull it toward him only halfway, then flick it out again with deadly accuracy. This put Clendenning at a distinct disadvantage.

The battle raged back and forth, around the ore wagon parked in the aisle. All the while Clendenning was being slowly forced back toward the far end of the stable, where there was no door. He was already cut and bleeding in a dozen places. One slash was over his eyes, and blood streamed down, obscuring his vision. In contrast, Stryker had only been cut twice.

Clendenning fought on grimly. Abruptly, his back was up against a wall. He risked a glance behind him and saw a ladder leading up into the loft above where hay was stored. He was cornered, and there was no longer any room to maneuver. He knew that if he tried to run past Stryker, the man would cut his legs out from under him, then kill him.

As a last, desperate resort, Clendenning felt with one foot behind him for the bottom rung of the ladder, and began to mount the ladder backward. If he could only make it to the loft, he could at least prevent Stryker from climbing up after him.

"Ha, now you've had it, kid!" Stryker trumpeted. To prove it, he snapped the whip, and agony burst in Clendenning's leg. Ignoring it, he took two quick steps up the ladder. Now he was over halfway up.

Again the whip lashed out. This time it curled around his ankle and snagged momentarily. Stryker tugged at it, cursing. Clendenning hooked his left arm over a ladder rung and quickly brought the bullwhip up and out. Off-balance, his aim was faulty. Instead of striking the other man in the chest, as had been his intention, the whip curled around Stryker's neck, once, twice, like a reptile strangling its prey.

Gagging, Stryker dropped his own whip and clawed at the one around his neck. He tried to turn in an attempt to uncoil the whip. Unfortunately, he turned in the wrong direction, drawing the whip even tighter. High up the ladder, Clendenning couldn't snap the whip loose. When he tried, he only succeeded in tightening it more. Then Stryker fell backwards and his neck snapped, with a sound like a tree limb breaking, and he slumped to the ground.

Clendenning leaped down to kneel beside him. He touched the man's head, and it lolled loosely on his shoulders. He was dead, of a broken neck. A phrase jumped into Clendenning's mind: ". . . hang by the neck until dead."

Clendenning came to his feet at a strangled sound. Serena was coming toward him, staring down at Stryker. Clendenning untied the handkerchief from around her mouth, then began on her bound hands.

Serena had to swallow a couple of times before finding her voice. "Is he . . . ?"

"Yes, Serena, he's dead."

She said in despair, "Now we'll never prove that he was the murderer!"

"Yes, we will, darling. Come."

He led her up front and showed her the mask on the ground. "I found that in Stryker's room." Serena shuddered, and clutched at his arm. Clendenning continued, "And that's not all." He picked up the strongbox from where he'd dropped it.

Serena exclaimed, "It's Aunt Hetty's strongbox!"

"Yes, also found in Stryker's room. But here's what's important." He opened it and showed her the legal document. "A land deed. And this." He gave her the letter.

Serena read:

"Dear Brother Hiram:
I was keeping this as a surprise. Not even Spence knows about this. I know you would be shocked to the depths of your soul about inheriting a hoorhouse. But I am sure this will help you recover fast enough. Eli Stryker told me it would be worth something some day. The only person who knows I own this land is Brad, Eli's son. The only reason he knows is because I used it as security for a loan from Eli. I wish you to know,

489

Brother, that I still love you, in spite of your Puritan nature. Try to have kind thoughts about your strayed sister.
Love, Hetty."

Serena looked up at Clendenning, who nodded at the question in her eyes. "Yes, Stryker killed your folks, and was determined to kill you. Then *he* would inherit the land, which probably is rich with ore."

"I can understand that. But why Madeline?"

"I can only guess, but I think it's an accurate guess. Madeline had told you of the strongbox and you were going to open it?" Serena nodded. "She must have told Stryker about that. He couldn't have that happen, of course. So he killed her to get the strongbox and to shut her mouth. I'm sure he would have managed to have it found, after you were dead and buried."

Serena took a shuddering breath. "It's all over, isn't it, Rory?"

"Yes, Serena." Then he added, "Almost."

In the small office Serena was penning a letter:

"Dear Tang P'ing:
It's finally over, and I'm cleared at last! It's been three days now since Rory found all the damning evidence in Brad Stryker's hotel room. Finally, just yesterday morning, Judge Underwood delivered his verdict. It's official now. Brad Stryker killed my father and mother, and Madeline. I am free, free! It feels so wonderful, I cannot tell you!

"I hope you and Shu-toe are well. Spencer
490

Hurd has been looking into the land deed Aunt Hetty left me. The land itself is on Sun Mountain, and the Judge says several mining companies are clamoring to buy it. The Judge advises me to lease the land, with a royalty agreement. He says I'll end up a wealthy woman! Can you imagine!

"If that happens, Tang P'ing, I wish to do something..."

Serena halted, pen poised over the paper. Her thoughts were on the morning three days ago when she had offered to fetch a doctor for Mr. Ho, and he had told her that most doctors would not treat his people.

She put the pen to paper again:

"If I come into a fortune, I wish to pay Shu-toe's way through medical school. I know it will be difficult for him, but I believe he is intelligent enough, and will make a fine doctor. I make this offer not through any feeling of gratitude for all the things you and your son have done for me, although I feel that too, but because I think Shu-toe *should* become a doctor, as is his desire. His people need him.

"Tell Darrel that I..."

Serena hesitated again. Maybe it would be better if she didn't pass any message on to Darrel...

Her head came up as she heard voices in the hall and the booming laughter of Spencer Hurd. Serena put down pen and paper and hurried out into the hall.

Hurd, Rory Clendenning, and Judge Underwood

were coming toward her, followed by a grinning Foxy, just out of his sick bed that morning. Serena was faintly surprised to see all three of her visitors dressed in their best. It was only the middle of the afternoon, and she would have expected Rory to be driving the ore wagon.

Smiling in greeting, she went to meet them. "Well, gentlemen! This is a pleasant surprise!"

After an exchange of greetings, Spencer Hurd handed her a telegram. "This just came for you, Serena."

Serena opened the telegram and read it quickly: "Congratulations on your victory, love. It seems we will never see New Orleans together. I am leaving for that city soon. May Dame Fortune always smile on you and the preacher's son, Serena. Darrel."

Hurd said, "I wired him that you were cleared, Serena."

Serena, blinking back a sudden rush of tears, looked up. She smiled mistily at Clendenning and kissed him. She said brightly, "Well, may I offer you gentlemen a drink?"

"Not now, Serena," Clendenning said. "Afterward."

Serena looked at him in bewilderment. "After what?"

"After Judge Underwood marries us. That's why he's here."

"Marry . . . ?" Serena gasper, temper stirring. "Without me even being consulted? Rory Clendenning, you haven't even proposed to me!"

"Oh, yes, I have," he said firmly. "And you said you would marry me when it was all over, when you were no longer charged with murder. Well, it's all over, and we're getting married. Right now!"

492

For a long moment Serena struggled with her temper. Then suddenly she was laughing helplessly. "I did say that, didn't I? Then what are we waiting for? Gentlemen . . ."

She made a sweeping gesture, and they all trooped into the parlor.

Judge Underwood looked around the room, ran a finger under his collar, and harumphed.

"What are you looking for, Your Honor? Your hammer?" Hurd said gravely. "You won't be needing that today. Everything you need is here . . . the bride and groom. The groom has just bought the ring, and Foxy and I will serve as witnesses."

Judge Underwood said gruffly, "I ain't performed many weddings."

"Seems to me one wedding is the same as another, Your Honor."

Spencer Hurd arranged Serena and Clendenning side by side before Judge Underwood. Then he and Foxy stood on either side of the bride and groom, bracketing them. Hurd took out a cigar, eyed it longingly, then returned it to his pocket. He fixed his gaze on Judge Underwood. "We're ready when you are, Your Honor. Fire away."

"If we were in my court, Counselor, I'd fine you for contempt," Judge Underwood growled, his face red. He coughed. "Will the bride and groom please join hands?"

Serena and Clendenning clasped hands. Glowing now, her love opening like a flower, Serena stood on tiptoe and planted a kiss on Clendenning's cheek.

"Dearly beloved," Judge Underwood began. "we are gathered here to join this man and this woman in holy matrimony . . ."

Love's Daring Dream

by

Patricia Matthews

(The following pages are excerpts edited from the first chapter of this new novel scheduled for publication in May 1978.)

In the year 1852 Ireland was in the black grip of the Great Potato Famine. Half the population existed on the edge of starvation.

And so it was for the Donnevan family.

In the bedroom of the poorly furnished two-room cottage, Maggie Donnevan crouched upon the far end of the rough bed, her knees drawn up close to her body and her head bent forward. Through the thick waterfall of brown hair, she watched as Kathleen, her sister, placed her meager belongings in the tattered remnant of an old apron and tied the corners to form a bundle. It was a pitifully small bundle, to contain all the worldly possessions of a girl of eighteen. The salt sting of tears burned Maggie's eyes as she stared at it. It wasn't right! It wasn't fair!

She raised her gaze to her sister's face. Framed by black hair, it was a beautiful face, even with the planes and hollows caused by near-starvation. The body beneath was beautiful, too—too slender now—but with full breasts and flaring hips. Maggie bit down on her lip to keep from crying out, and put her head down upon her knees, feeling the firm push of her own budding breasts against her legs, and feeling the shame deep inside her; the fear that she was going to be beautiful too. Men would desire her, too. Kathleen's fate might be hers as well. Maggie pushed away the thought and swallowed her tears, trying to keep her voice steady.

"Kathleen, must you? Must you do it? We can get along. Things will get better. I know they will!"

Kathleen smiled sadly, a smile that did not reach her gray eyes. She moved to the bed and sat down next to Maggie. She stretched out a hand and began to smooth the younger girl's hair. "You've heard little Kevin crying in the night from the pangs of hunger in his belly. You've looked into Mum's eyes, when the men come home hungry, and there is no food to give them. What I am doing is for the best. There will be one less mouth to feed, and I will be able to bring you things, money and food. Lord Ramage has promised me this."

Maggie stared into Kathleen's eyes. Kathleen was resigned. She had made up her mind. She was going to suffer that man to ...

Maggie's mind could not complete the thought. And all because Kathleen was pleasant to look at; an object to be bought and paid for; to be used for a man's pleasure for a time, and then probably cast aside. Even at sixteen, Maggie understood this much.

Maggie threw herself into her sister's lap and gave in to the tears clogging her throat. "Why are you doing it, Kathleen? Why, why?"

Kathleen leaned over and kissed the top of Maggie's head. "I've explained that as best I can. Because it will keep us from starving, dear. So that we, the Donnevan family, can *live* a while longer."

There was only one window in the thatched hut that the Donnevan family called home. Through it, Maggie could see the coach drawn up outside; it was very large and black. It made her think of a funeral coach she had glimpsed once when a member of the gentry had died. Maggie could hear the horses snorting and stamping as though impatient to get away. The black coach stood out in sharp contrast to the green rolling Irish countryside stretching away into blue mist.

Her mother and father stood across the room, away from the window, their faces turned aside. Her mother's face was grooved with lines of sorrow as she clutched six-year-old Kevin close to her skirts with one hand. Her father's face might as well have been carved from gray stone for all the expression he showed. His eyes were bleak and unseeing.

Maggie watched despairingly as Kathleen walked quietly past her parents' backs; she paused for a moment as if waiting for a word, any word, and, when none was forthcoming, turned and walked out of the low cottage door. As the door closed behind her sister, Maggie made a vow to herself—Kathleen's fate would *never* happen to her.

Kevin set up a dreadful howling and tried to tug away from his mother's skirts, but Nora Donnevan pulled him back and bent to him, attempting to hush his cries. John Donnevan turned away and rummaged in the almost-bare cupboard for the half-filled poteen jar. Both of them seemed oblivious to the fact that their oldest daughter was leaving their home to become the mistress of the man who owned their land and their very existence.

Maggie stared at them, brown eyes flashing with a growing fury. "How can you?" she shouted, her voice cutting through the smoky room with shocking sharpness. "How could you let her go!"

She ran to her father and yanked at his sleeve. Without changing expression, he shoved her roughly away.

"You will not mention her name again in this house," he said harshly. "She is going into a life of sin. A strumpet, that's what she's become. She is no longer a daughter of mine." He set the poteen jar upon the broken wooden table with a thump and dropped down onto the low wooden stool next to it.

Tears streaming down her face, Maggie walked stiff-legged up to the table and faced him.

"She's doing it for us. For me and Kevin and Patrick and Dan, and mother and you. Yes, *you*, too. So we won't starve. She's doing it for us. How can you talk about her like that?"

He glared at her. "Shut your mouth, girl! I am the man here, and I expect my children to show me proper respect!" He took a swallow of the poteen and slammed the jar back down onto the table. "That's what comes of letting a girl-child run too free," he muttered. He glanced accusingly at his wife. "I've told you and told you, Nora, to control this girl. Now look at what you've wrought, a mouthy wench who talks back to her own pa. If you can't control her, I'll be forced to take my belt to her!"

Maggie looked to her mother for support, but the older woman lowered her eyes and withdrew, as surely as if she had left the room. Only her twisting hands, fiercely pulling at the worn material of her apron, give away her inner feelings.

Maggie knew and feared her father's anger, but she had an anger of her own now, and had gone too far to stop. In her short span of years she had never been so angry. In that moment she hated her father. He was a stupid, arrogant man, who considered women little better than cattle, and treated them as such. Maggie had long since realized this. Now it had to come out!

"You revile Kathleen, and call her names, yet where did the money come from to buy that which you are drinking? Where did the money come from that made the porridge with which you filled your belly this morning? From Kathleen, whom you call a strumpet!"

Nora Donnevan raised her thin hands as if to ward off the spill of bitter words coming from her daughter, but Maggie, ignoring the look of pain on her mother's face, could not stop.

"You are too proud a man, you say, to have a daughter who lives in a state of sin, and yet you aren't too proud to accept the food and drink bought with money from this same daughter, all the while pretending you don't know from where it comes! A fine, proud man you are, a . . ."

Maggie's words died in mid-sentence, as her father, with a bellow of pure rage, pushed the wooden table from him with a mighty shove that sent it crashing halfway across the room, and lurched erect. Kevin wailed with fright.

Maggie felt her throat tighten with fear. Her father would strike her now, as he had so many times before, and his hand was heavy, particularly when affected by the drink, but she had said what she must.

She watched him as he stood there, weaving slightly, his face flaming. She refused to shrink back as he took one step toward her; and then an amazing and frightening thing happened.

John Donnevan's expression changed. It was as if he had forgotten what he intended to do; as if he was looking inward to something only he could see. Then, an expression of horror and pain twisted his mouth into a grimace. Clutching his chest with both hands, he fell forward to the floor like a stunned ox, his big body hitting the floor with a dull, thudding sound.

Nora Donnevan sank to her knees by his side. Maggie could do naught but stand and stare, frozen motionless by the shock of the moment. She only stirred when her mother looked up at her, all expression wiped from her face, her eyes like clear, blue glass.

"He's dead," she said in a flat voice. "Himself is dead." A spark glowed in her eyes suddenly. "The guilt will always be on your head, Margaret Donnevan, you being the death of your own father!"

Maggie opened her mouth to deny her responsibility, then stopped herself as she saw her mother lower her head. The woman rocked back and forth, making a keening sound of grief. Tears fell like slow rain on her dead husband . . .

*   *   *

The horror of her father's death shocks young Maggie to the very core of her soul, but it is only the first of a series of harsh blows she must face as she struggles to save her family, and her sanity. Fate has charted a wildly adventurous life for our heroine . . . an ordinary woman would never survive the crushing tragedies and humiliations Maggie will experience, but too few women could ever know the ecstasies of romance and passion that also come to visit her.

Maggie Donnevan inherited poverty and grief, but earns a legacy of love . . .

—PATRICIA MATTHEWS—

A former poet, secretary, and housewife—for a time, simultaneously—and a native Californian, Pat Matthews now lives in Los Angeles and devotes her full time to writing novels of historical romance. She is married to Clayton Matthews, also a professional writer. Prior to writing the runaway bestsellers, *Love's Avenging Heart* and *Love's Wildest Promise*, Patricia had written a variety of juveniles, gothic novels, short stories, and poems. She notes that Edgar Allan Poe and Alexander Dumas have been most influential in her reading and writing, and she plans to widen her horizons by doing even more reading and traveling.

Pinnacle Books wants to publish the type of books you enjoy. For this reason would you please fill out this questionnaire so that we can learn more about your reading tastes.

1. Are you _____ female _____ male?

2. What is your age?

_____ Under 15?
_____ 15 - 24?
_____ 25 - 34?
_____ 35 - 44?
_____ 45 - 54?
_____ 55 or over?

3. What is your level of education?

_____ Currently — Jr. High _____
_____ High School
_____ or College
_____ Some high school
_____ High school graduate
_____ Some college
_____ College graduate

4. Where did you buy this book?

_____ Bookstore
_____ Drugstore
_____ Chain
        variety store
_____ Supermarket
_____ Department store
_____ Discount store
_____ Newsstand
_____ Bus or
        train station
_____ Airport
_____ Other _____

(continued on next page)

5. What types of books do you like best?

_____ Hardcover bestsellers when available in paperback
_____ Historical romance
_____ Gothics
_____ Occult
_____ Mystery and suspense
_____ Science fiction
_____ Cookbooks
_____ Self-help and "How-to" books
_____ Biography and autobiography
_____ Nonfiction
_____ Westerns
_____ War
_____ Action/adventure
_____ Other_____

6. Why did you buy this book?

_____

(Please give title)

(You may check more than one answer)

_____ Recognized the title   _____ Saw author
_____ Author's reputation   on TV, or
_____ Friend's   heard him/
        recommendation   her on radio
_____ The book's cover   _____ Subject
_____ Newspaper   matter
        or magazine ad   _____ Price
_____ Radio commercial   _____ Other_____
_____ TV commercial   _____
_____ Free preview booklet

Name _____

Address _____

City_____State_____Zip_____

Please return questionnaire to:

Pinnacle Books, Inc., Dept. LKB
One Century Plaza
2029 Century Park East
Los Angeles California 90067